# CÉSAR BIROTTEAU

## A novel by Honoré de Balzac

*Translated from the French
by Frances Frenaye*

With an introduction by
Edward D. Sullivan

*César Birotteau,* one of the best-loved novels
in Balzac's great *Human Comedy,* is the story
of the perfumer's Birotteau's ill-fated rise to
affluence, his bankruptcy, and his slow, steep
climb to rehabilitation. César, an honest, hard-
working, kind, somewhat pompous man, is led
on by a real-estate prospect and by a new formula for hair oil (which will, he thinks, put
Macassar Oil out of business!) into overextend-
ing himself. At a great ball he celebrates his
looked-for success, but shortly thereafter his
notary Roguin absconds, his prospects fail, and
he finds himself at the mercy of his creditors.
He seeks help from the unscrupulous banker
Nucingen and the speculator Du Tillet, and from
the evil old usurer Gobseck, but they all betray
him, and he is forced at length into bankruptcy.
Balzac pictures César as "a martyr of commercial probity." Painfully, with the aid of his faithful wife Constance and his daughter Césarine,
the perfumer earns enough to pay back every
penny of debt. The effort costs him his life, but
he has attained a moral superiority over his
exploiters.

This novel perhaps more than any other in
the *Human Comedy* is distinguished for its live-
liness and humor, for the color with which it
depicts Parisian commercial life and the characters who inhabit this world, and for its great
sympathy and warmth. In *César Birotteau* Balzac
aspired to write "the hitherto untold epic of the
middle class," an epic as viable today, in this
new translation made especially for the Juniper
Press series, as in 1837, when it first appeared.

# CÉSAR BIROTTEAU

# CÉSAR BIROTTEAU

by

## HONORÉ DE BALZAC

JUNIPER PRESS

NEW YORK

*Translated by Frances Frenaye*

COPYRIGHT 1955 BY JUNIPER PRESS

The Juniper Press
41-15 44th Street
Long Island City 4, New York, N.Y.

Drawings by Luben Balabanov
*Library of Congress Catalogue Card No. 55-7791*
Manufactured in the United States of America
Edwards Brothers, Inc. Ann Arbor, Michigan

# INTRODUCTION

As the self-styled secretary and historian of his period, Balzac has brilliantly recorded for posterity the peculiar flavor and atmosphere of the first half of the nineteenth century. He was, of course, far more than a mere observer or historian of manners; he was above all a great creator, and, although he had a boundless enthusiasm and affection for the sights, sounds, smells, people, and events of his time, he was constantly looking beyond them. Like all great novelists, he knew that his task was not merely to show things as they are but also to discover what they conceal. "It is with fiction as with religion," wrote Herman Melville, "it should present another world and yet one to which we feel the tie." The world of Balzac, the world he created and called the Human Comedy, is in fact a complete world, a world apart, and yet one to which we of the twentieth century can feel the tie even as closely as Balzac's contemporaries did.

Precisely because the world of Balzac is a creation and not a mere description does it survive: it continues to exist in its own right, and, self-contained, outlives both its creator Balzac and the nineteenth-century events which he purports to record. The Human Comedy, which Balzac carried for years in his head, comprising some two thousand characters moving through nearly a hundred novels, was far more real to him than the Paris he lived and worked in. Obsessed by his own creation, he would cut short discussions about contemporary events with an impatient : "That's all very well, but let's get back to reality: Who is going to marry Eugénie Grandet?"

Early in his career Balzac began to search for a method of organizing into a single unit, into a vast novelistic structure, the whole of his literary production. The device he hit upon was a simple one, but one that required sustained genius and power to an extraordinary degree, namely the systematic reappearance of characters from novel to novel. Although César Birotteau is the major figure in the novel that bears his name, he is surrounded by characters who are not simply minor, to be quickly forgotten, but people of equal stature whose lives are completely projected in other novels. The most immediate consequence of all this for the reader of Balzac is that every character, however insignificant his role in a given novel, has a complete biography, a life of his own. Andoche Finot, for example, whose part in César Birotteau's life was limited to writing advertising copy and acting as publicity man for César's new hair-oil, went on to a fascinating career in journalism that is traced in *La Rabouilleuse, Les Illusions perdues, Splendeurs et Misères des Courtisanes,* and other novels. Similarly, Rastignac, whose debut in Parisian society was so entangled with the tragic end of old Goriot, is a major figure in the Balzacian world, appearing in over a dozen works.

The reader who has not yet made the acquaintance of Balzac can enter the Human Comedy at any point, since each novel can stand by itself; but as he goes on to a second and a third, he will be fascinated by the intricate weaving of the tapestry as people and objects gradually take on a familiar air and the very passers-by turn out to be old friends. Each new work of Balzac that one reads builds on the base already established and finds its authenticity, not in its fidelity to nineteenth-century life and manners (of which most of us know only what we read in Balzac anyway), but rather in the congruity with which it takes its place in the constantly expanding universe of Balzac's own Human Comedy.

To meet Balzac at his best, then, we need to follow his people through a number of novels. Unfortunately, the American reader who sought Balzac in translation at his bookstore could find, until now, only a very few scattered volumes. One of the great virtues of this present series, aside from providing fresh and living translations, is to offer ten novels of Balzac carefully chosen to represent all the important aspects of the Human Comedy; each of them is a remarkable individual novel in its own right, and taken together, the ten give a comprehensive vision of the world of Balzac. This is a world swept by the violent winds of passion, the movement in the novels being generated by the intensity of the individual drives. *César Birotteau,* as Balzac says, "aspires to be the hitherto untold epic of the middle class," and it is the inordinate social ambition of a Parisian perfumer that leads him to that thoroughly middle class tragedy of bankruptcy. This same aspect of Parisian life forms the background for *Les Petits Bourgeois*, while other more tempestuous and more diversified aspects of Paris are revealed in *Splendeurs et Misères des Courtisanes*. The latter novel and *Les Illusions perdus* lie at the very center of the Human Comedy, and in these two vast works live and move Balzac's major figures and a host of minor ones, who radiate from this center to fulfill their destinies in a dozen different volumes. *Les Chouans*, a novel of military life, deals mainly with the passion of love set against the backdrop of a royalist uprising during the French Revolution. Descendants of some of its characters play important rôles in *Béatrix*, which begins, like *Les Chouans*, in Brittany and explores other kinds of passion which motivate three women : the calculating Béatrix de Rochefide, the maternal and tender Mlle des Touches, and the intellectual Camille Maupin, who seems to have been modeled on both George Sand and Mme de Staël. *La Rabouilleuse*, set in the provinces, describes in a beautifully complicated plot the passions unleashed by the struggle for an inheritance; and *Une Ténébreuse Affaire*, concerned with similar plottings of a political nature during the Napoleonic period, provides an extraordinary portrait of a political opportunist in Malin de Gondreville. *Le Lys dans la Vallée*, whose Mme de Mortsauf is an angelic character not unlike Eugénie Grandet, dramatizes the classical subject of love versus duty, and through its characters has innumerable rapports with the Parisian scene which is the center of the Balzacian world.

  *La Recherche de l'Absolu* is in a different category, belonging to the section called Philosophical Studies, and is not connected to the other works by the reappearance of characters. It stands, however, as the novel in which Balzac's essential subject and plan are revealed most clearly : to trace the devastating effects of an overwhelming passion. In this case Balthazar Claës neglects his family and dissipates a fortune in his single-minded search for the Absolute, the absolute unity of matter. All of Balzac's people are in quest of some Absolute, hence their intensity, their ruthlessness, their energy, and the terrible effects of their passion on those who are near them. "Neither his fellows, nor his gods, nor his passions will leave a man alone," wrote Conrad, defining the subject of the novel; Balzac's people are obsessed by this three-fold preoccupation: they are egoists driven by their own passions, immersed in the thick texture of society and the conflicting thrusts of their fellows, searching obscurely through it all for some kind of Absolute, like Balthazar Claës, even if most often they only succeed in making an Absolute of their own dominant passion.

*Princeton University*                    EDWARD D. SULLIVAN

# PART I

## César at the Height of His Career

# I

ON WINTER NIGHTS THERE IS ONLY A MOMENT'S RESPITE
from noise on the Rue Saint-Honoré; the carts of vegetable
dealers on their way to market follow almost immediately
in the wake of carriages returning from the theater or a ball.
In the midst of this pause which occurs in the vast Parisian
symphony of sound around one o'clock in the morning, the
wife of Monsieur César Birotteau, a perfumer near the Place
Vendôme, awakened with a start from a terrifying dream. Madame Birotteau had just seen a double image of herself, one
clad in rags, with a dry, wrinkled hand turning the knob on the
door of her own shop, and the other seated in her place behind
the counter—in other words, both asking and dispensing
charity at the same time and in the same voice. She reached
out for her husband, but her hand met only the cold sheet.
This frightened her so greatly that her neck stiffened and
she could not move it, the walls of her throat stuck together,
her voice failed, and she was rooted in a sitting position,
staring wide-eyed into the darkness, her hair on end, strange
sounds ringing in her ears, her heart contracted but still
beating, and her body icy cold but cover d with perspiration,
in an alcove whose double door was wide open.

Fear is a half-sickening sensation, which exerts such pressure upon the human machine that its faculties are either
taxed to their full limit or else thrown into complete dis-
organization. Physiologists have long been baffled by this
phenomenon, for it upsets all their systems and assumptions.
It acts like a stroke of lightning within the body, and takes
as many bizarre and unpredictable forms as any electrical
occurrence. This comparison will seem quite obvious, on

the day when scientists recognize the important role played by electricity in the human thought process.

So it was that Madame Birotteau suffered pangs which might be called dazzling, caused by a discharge of the will expanded or contracted by some unknown mechanism. Within a space of time very short according to our human measurements but immensely prolonged in terms of the impressions it contained, the poor woman acquired the monstrous power of calling up more thoughts than she would ordinarily have conceived in a whole day. Her poignant monologue can be summarized in the following potpourri of absurd and contradictory phrases:

" There is no reason why Birotteau should have got out of bed. Of course he ate so much veal that it may have made him sick, but if he'd been taken ill he'd have wakened me. In all the nineteen years we've slept in this bed and in this house together, the poor lamb has never stirred without letting me know. The only times he sleeps out are when he's on guard duty. Let me see, was he here when I went to bed last night? How stupid of me! Of course he was!"

She looked over at the other side of the bed and saw her husband's nightcap, which was still impressed with the almost conical shape of his head.

" Then he must be dead! Has he killed himself, and if so, why? In these last two years, since they made him deputy to the Mayor, he's been different, somehow. What a ridiculous idea to put him in a public position! His business must be going well; he gave me a shawl, didn't he? Or is it going badly? If so, I'd surely know it. But how can one ever know how much a man has in his purse, or a woman either, for that matter? And it's just as well. But didn't we take in five thousand francs in the shop today? Besides, a deputy can't very well kill himself, he's too familiar with the law. Where, oh where, can he be?"

She was still unable to turn her neck or reach out her hand to pull a bell-rope, which would have brought a cook, three shop clerks, and a delivery boy to her aid. And because, although she was half awake, she was still under the sway of her nightmare, she forgot that her daughter was sleeping peacefully in an adjoining room, whose entrance was just at the foot of her bed. At last she cried: " Birotteau!" or at least thought she did, but there was no answer because the cry had issued not from her lips but only from her mind.

" Has he a mistress? No, he's too stupid for that, and besides he loves me too much. Didn't he tell Madame Roguin that he'd never been unfaithful to me, even in his imagination? Why, he's virtue personified; if ever a man deserved to go straight to heaven, he's the one. I often wonder what he can say to his confessor. Being the kind of Royalist he is, without knowing why, he doesn't even dare make a display of religion; he goes off to Mass as secretively as if he were going to a bawdy-house. God is quite enough to terrify him; he doesn't need to be threatened by the pains of hell. How could he ever have a mistress? Why, he hangs onto my apron-strings until I'm bored to death with him. He loves me better than his own eyes, in fact he'd gladly give up his sight for me. For nineteen years he's never raised his voice to me. He loves me far more than his daughter. . . . Why, of course, Césarine is there! Césarine. . . . Césarine! . . . Birotteau's never had a thought that he didn't confide to me. He was quite right, when he first came to the Petit-Matelot, to say that only with time should I come to know him. And now he's not here. . . . It's unbelievable!"

She managed to turn her head and look fearfully across the room, whose nocturnal appearance would have defied verbal description and seemed meant for the brush of a genre painter. Words could not have conveyed the terror of the zigzag shadows, the curtains billowing in the wind, the flickering glow cast by a bedside light against folds of red calico and reflected in a curtain-hook whose glittering center was for all the world like a thief's eye, a gown which looked like a figure on its knees—in short all those fantastic shapes which now worked upon an imagination open to foreboding. For a moment Madame Birotteau fancied she saw a gleam of light in the next room which must be fire; then a red scarf looked to her like a pool of blood left after a struggle between her husband and a thief, which had also overturned the furniture. When she thought of the amount of money in the cash-box a healthy terror overcame the paralyzing effect of her nightmare and she jumped out of bed, in her nightgown, to rescue her husband from the onslaught of an imagined intruder.

" Birotteau! Birotteau!" she cried, this time quite audibly.

She found him in the middle of the next room, with a ruler in his hand, measuring empty air, and so incompletely covered by his brown and green dotted cotton dressing-gown that although he was too absorbed to take notice, his legs were red with cold. When he turned around and said: " Well, Constance, what is it?" he was so lost in calculations that his ingenuously astounded air made his wife burst into laughter.

" You really do look funny," she said. " Why did you leave me alone without any warning? I didn't know what was wrong and almost died of fright. What are you doing in this draft? You'll catch a terrible cold. Do you hear me, Birotteau?"

" Yes, my pet, here I am," he said, coming back into the bedroom.

" Come, warm yourself and tell me what in the world has got into you," said Madame Birotteau, shaking down the ashes and rekindling the fire. " I'm frozen. It was silly of me to get up in only my nightgown. But I thought you were being murdered."

The perfumer put his candlestick up on the mantelpiece, wrapped his dressing-gown about him and mechanically fetched a flannel petticoat for his wife.

" Put this on, dear," he said. ". . . Twenty-two by eighteen," he added, going on with what he had been figuring,

" and we shall have a most magnificent drawing-room."

" Birotteau, are you crazy? Are you dreaming out loud?"

" No, my dear, I'm working out some figures."

" Surely you could have waited until daylight to do something so silly," said his wife, fastening her petticoat around her in order to go look in at her daughter in the next room. " Césarine's asleep and can't hear us," she added a moment later. " Tell me all about it. What's the matter?"

" We'll be able to give the ball."

" A ball? We should give a ball? Upon my word, dear heart, you're dreaming."

" I'm not dreaming at all, my beauty. One must always live up to the requirements of one's position. The government has brought me into prominence, and I belong to the government. Hence it is up to us to study the government's aims and seek to forward them. The Duke de Richelieu has just put an end to the occupation of France, and according to Monsieur de La Billardière, every official of the city of Paris should organize, within his own sphere, some sort of celebration. Our patriotism must put that of those damned intriguing Liberals in the shade. Don't you suppose that I love my country? I want to show my Liberal enemies that loyalty to the King means loyalty to France!"

" My poor Birotteau, and do you think you have so many enemies?"

" Of course we have enemies, my dear. Half of our neighbors are among them. They go around saying: ' Birotteau is lucky. Birotteau was nothing at all and now he's deputy to the Mayor. Everything seems to come his way.' And they have another surprise coming to them. You are the first person to know that yesterday the King signed the papers making me a knight of the Legion of Honor!"

" Oh!" exclaimed Madame Birotteau with emotion. " Then we must really give the ball? What have you done to deserve the cross?"

" Yesterday, when Monsieur de La Billardière told me the

news, I asked myself the same question. But later on I came
to appreciate the government's reasons. First, I am a Royalist
and I was wounded at Saint-Roch in the month of Vendémiaire. Surely it means something to have borne arms on
the right side then. Furthermore, according to my acquaintances in the trade I have been a fair referee in various commercial law cases. Finally, I am deputy to the Mayor, and
the King had made up his mind to give crosses to four city
officials. When it came to making a choice among the
various deputies, the prefect put me at the head of the list.
Besides, I think the King may remember my name. Thanks
to old Ragon, I supply him with the only powder he can
bear to use, and we still possess the formula for the mixture
used by that dear, innocent victim, the late Queen. Then
the Mayor stood up for me. What could I do? If the King
gives me the cross without my soliciting it, it would be
disrespectful of me to refuse. I didn't try for the position
of deputy to the Mayor, either. Anyhow, since the wind is
in our sails, as your Uncle Pillerault says when he is especially jolly, I have decided to make our style of living
match our good fortune. I must be ready to rise to whatever
station God calls me, even that of sub-prefect if such is my
fate. It's a mistake, my dear, to believe that after twenty
years of selling toiletries a man has acquitted himself of his
debt to his country. If the State calls for our aid, it is our
bounden duty to give it, just as we pay taxes on our income,
the number of doors and windows in our house, and so on.
Do you want to stay behind your counter forever? God
willing, you've been there quite long enough. This ball will
be our own private celebration, and will mark the end of
your servitude. I shall burn the sign that says ' The Queen
of Roses,' do away with ' César Birotteau, Perfumer, Successor to Ragon,' and put in its place ' Perfumery ' in big
gilt letters. I'll install the office, the cash-box and a private
cabinet for you on the mezzanine floor, and turn the dining-
room and kitchen into a storehouse. Then I'll rent the

second floor of the next house, open a door through the wall and turn the staircase around so as to have the same level throughout. After that we'll have a truly noble apartment! Yes, I'll do your room over too, add a dressing-room to it and fix up something pretty for Césarine. The new shop girl, the chief clerk and your personal maid (yes, you're to have a personal maid!) will be lodged on the third floor. The fourth floor will be the kitchen and quarters for the cook and house-boy. On the fifth floor we'll store our china jars and crystal bottles, and in the attic we'll put our workers, so that passers-by won't see them in the process of filling, corking and labeling the receptacles. That was all very well when we were on the Rue Saint-Denis, but it won't do for the Rue Saint-Honoré, where our shop must be as luxurious as a drawing-room. After all, mustard and vinegar makers hold commands in the National Guard and are favorites at the Château. Why shouldn't we follow their example, enlarge our business and at the same time break into high society?'"

" Birotteau, do you know what I'm thinking? That you're going out of your way to look for trouble. Do you remember what I said to you when there was a possibility of your becoming Mayor? ' Think first of your own peace and quiet! You're just about as suited to the role of a public figure as my arm is to being a vane of a windmill. Greatness would be your undoing.' You didn't listen to me, and now we're undone. A political career costs more money than we possess. Would you burn a sign that cost you six hundred francs and give up the Queen of Roses, to which you owe so much glory? Leave ambition to others. If you stick your hand into the fire you're pretty sure to singe it, and politics now is a fiery furnace. Haven't we a hundred thousand francs tucked away and invested outside our own business? If you want to increase your fortune, do what you did in 1793. Government bonds are at seventy-two francs; buy some of them and you'll have a ten-thousand-franc income, without doing any harm to your perfumery. We can marry off our daughter, sell the shop and retire to the country. For fifteen years we talked about buying Les Trésorières, that attractive bit of property near Chinon, with its brooks, meadows, woods, vineyards and farms, which brings in a thousand francs a year, and now you want to be somebody in the government! Remember, after all, we are cosmetic makers. Sixteen years ago, before you invented Sultana Cream and Pink Lotion, if anyone had come to you and said : ' Soon you will have enough money to buy Les Trésorières,' you'd have been sick with joy. There was a time when you talked of nothing else, and yet now that it is within your grasp you want to throw away the money we sweated so hard to earn. I say ' we ' because for years I've sat, like a dog in his kennel, behind the counter. Wouldn't it be better to be able to visit your daughter when she is the wife of a notary in Paris and to live eight months of the year at Chinon, than to let your money slip through your fingers ? If we wait for government bonds to go up, we can give Césarine eight thousand francs a year, keep two thousand a year for ourselves, and with the profit from the sale of the business we can buy Les Trésorières. There in the country, considering what our furniture is worth, we can live like princes, whereas here, unless we have a million francs, we can't cut any swath at all."

" There, my dear, is where I was waiting to trip you up," said César Birotteau. " I'm not such a fool (although you seem to think so) as not to take everything into consideration. Just listen. Alexandre Crottat would be the ideal son-in-law, and he'll eventually take over Roguin's practice. But do you think for a moment that he'd be satisfied with a hundred-thousand-franc dowry ? (That is, supposing we give all our liquid assets to our daughter, as I propose that we shall do, for I'd be happy to live on dry bread the rest of my life in order to see her happy, to see her, as you say, married to a notary.) Well, I can tell you this, a hundred thousand francs aren't enough to buy Roguin's practice. And 'little Alex,' as we like to call him, has like everyone else an exaggerated idea of our fortune. If that stingy farmer father of his doesn't sell another hundred thousand francs' worth of land, his son will never be a notary at all, because Roguin's practice is worth four or five hundred thousand francs, half of which has to be in cash in advance. Césarine needs two hundred thousand francs for a dowry, and I want us to retire with an annual income of fifteen thousand. So there! If I were to tell you that such a possibility is in sight, wouldn't it cut the ground from under your feet?"

" Well, of course, if you have come upon a gold mine. . . ."

" Exactly, my dear!" He put his arm around his wife and patted her, with joy written all over his face. " I didn't mean to tell you about this piece of business until it was certain, but it may be settled tomorrow. Here it is. Roguin has proposed an investment so safe that he's bringing Ragon, your Uncle Pillerault and two of his other clients into it. We are going to buy some land near the Madeleine, for a price which Roguin calculates is only a quarter as much as it will be worth three years from now, when the leases have expired and we are free to develop it. There are six partners, but I'm putting up three hundred thousand francs in order to have a three-eighths interest. If any of us needs more money, Roguin can secure it for him by taking a mortgage on his share. In order to control the situation, I have arranged to be nominal owner of half the property, which will be held in common by Pillerault, Ragon and myself. Roguin's part will be held in the name of a certain Monsieur Charles Claparon, my co-owner, who like myself will issue counter-deeds to his associates. The property will be secure through options until we control all the land. Roguin will decide which purchases will have to be carried out, for he's not sure we can dispense with registration of the deeds and put that expense upon the people to whom we later sell lots. It's too long a story to go into in detail, but that's the gist

of it. Once we have paid for the land, all we have to do
is twiddle our thumbs and wait for three years to pass. By
that time Césarine will be twenty, and we can sell our perfumery and begin to live in style."

"And where are you going to get the three hundred
thousand francs?" his wife asked him.

"My dear, you know nothing about business. I'll use
the hundred thousand Roguin has in his keeping. Then I'll
borrow forty thousand on our factory buildings on the
Faubourg du Temple and add twenty thousand in cash,
making sixty thousand. After that I'll need a hundred and
forty thousand more, for which I shall give notes to Monsieur Charles Claparon, who happens to be a banker and
will let me have the sum total of the notes, minus the interest
deducted in advance. So there is the money, and as they
say, a debt cannot be collected before it is due. And by that
time, we'll have pocketed our profit. In case we haven't,
Roguin will lend me money at five per cent, in exchange
for a mortgage on my share of the land. And as a matter
of fact, I may not have to borrow any money at all, because
I've discovered an oil that will cause hair to grow! Comagene
Oil! It comes from hazelnuts, and Livingston has installed
a hydraulic press with which to squeeze it out. Inside a
year, as I see it, I shall make at least a hundred thousand
francs. I'm thinking about an advertisement which will run:
'Throw away your wigs!' Yes, I've spent many a wakeful
night mulling these things over, but you never noticed.
For the past three months the success of that damnable
Macassar Oil has kept me from sleeping. I'm dead set on
putting Macassar out of business!"

"So you've been hatching all these wonderful plans in
your head, without so much as a by-your-leave to me!
I just dreamed that I was a beggar at my own door, and now
I can see that it was a warning. Soon we'll have nothing left
but our eyes to weep with. No, César, you'll do these things
only over my dead body. There's some catch to the whole

business, and the trouble is you're too honest to see through it. Why would anyone offer you millions for nothing? You're to hand over everything you have and a lot that you haven't, and if your new oil doesn't work out or you can't borrow money or the land doesn't increase in value the way you hope, then how are you to pay your debts? With nut-shells, is that it? A few minutes ago, you said in order to rise on the social ladder you wanted to take your name out of trade and burn the sign advertising the Queen of Roses. And now you propose to blaze your name on a whole new series of billboards for a hair tonic."

"No, you don't understand. I'll set up a branch in the vicinity of Rue des Lombards and put the Ragons' young nephew, Anselme Popinot, in charge. They seem to me to be in a bad way and they'll be grateful to me for giving him a chance to make his fortune."

"Those people are all after your money."

"What people? Do you mean your Uncle Pillerault, who considers us his particular pets and dines with us every Sunday? Or Ragon, our predecessor in the perfumery business, who has forty years of square dealing behind him and plays cards with us of an evening? Or Roguin, a man forty-seven years old, who's been notary here in Paris for the last quarter of a century? His position alone would guarantee his ethics, if it weren't that honest men are to be found in every rank of society. Yes, all these good associates will stand by me. So why do you accuse me of hatching a plot without your knowledge? There's something I must tell you to your face after all these years: you've always been suspicious. As soon as we had a few francs in our cash-box, you thought every customer had come to steal them. And now I have to get down on my knees and beg you to be rich! It's not like a girl born and brought up in Paris to be totally lacking in ambition. If it weren't for your fears, I'd be the happiest man in the world. If I'd listened to you I'd never have made either my Sultana Cream or my Pink

Lotion. The shop provides us with a living but these two discoveries, along with our own brand of soap, are the sources of the hundred and sixty thousand francs we have today. Without my inventive genius—because in the field of perfumery I have just that—we'd be petty shopkeepers, trying to make both ends meet. I'd never have been chosen to run for the office of referee in the commercial court or have served in these legal cases. And obviously I'd never have become deputy to the Mayor. Do you know what I'd be? Just a shopkeeper like old Ragon—no offense intended, since we owe the beginnings of our fortune to a shop. After selling toiletries for forty years, we should, like him, enjoy an annual income of three thousand francs, and since the cost of living has doubled since the time of his retirement that would be a tight squeeze. (Yes, those old Ragons worry me more every day. I shall have word of them from Popinot tomorrow.) . . . As I was saying, you're such a worrier, always wondering whether what you have today will still be there tomorrow, that if I'd followed your advice, I'd have no credit, no Legion of Honor and no political prospects such as are now opening up before me. Yes, you can shake your head all you like; if this piece of business goes through I may be a deputy to Parliament. It's no accident that my name is Caesar; just look at the success I've had so far! It's incredible, when you come down to it: everyone in the outside world thinks I'm a very able fellow, but here at home the person whom I sweat blood to please takes me for an idiot!"

These phrases, shot out like so many bullets, with eloquent pauses in between, in true recriminatory manner, nevertheless expressed so long-lasting and deep a devotion that Madame Birotteau was touched. But, like any other woman, she took advantage of the love she inspired in her husband to get the better of him.

" If you love me, Birotteau," she said, " let me be happy my own way. Neither of us has had any education, and we know nothing of the bowing-and-scraping ways of the world. How can you expect us to make a success in public life? Les Trésorières is the place for me; I've always loved animals and birds, and I ask nothing better than to spend my life looking after a barnyard. Let's sell our business, arrange a marriage for Césarine and say good-by to all the rest, including that Imogene or whatever you call it. We can spend the winters in our son-in-law's house in Paris, and none of the ups-and-downs of politics or business can affect us. Why do you want to step on others in order to get ahead? Can't we be happy with the money we have? When you become a millionaire, will you have an appetite for two dinners instead of one and require a second wife? Look at Uncle Pillerault, for instance. He's content with his modest lot and spends his life in good works. He doesn't need new furniture. I speak of furniture, because I'm sure you've already ordered some. I saw Braschon on his way here and he wasn't coming to buy toiletries, I know that."

"Yes, my beauty, I've already ordered new things. The remodeling is to start tomorrow, and an architect recommended by Monsieur de La Billardière is to supervise it."

"Merciful God, preserve us!" his wife exclaimed.

"You're unreasonable, my pet. At thirty-seven years of age and pretty as you are, surely you can't want to bury yourself at Chinon. I'm only thirty-nine myself, and if fortune hands me something on a silver platter I'm not going to refuse it. If I'm careful, I can carve out a place of honor for myself in respectable Paris society, so that people will speak of the Birotteaus the way they speak of the Kellers, the Jules Desmarets, the Roguins, the Cochins, the Guillaumes, the Lebas', the Nucingens, the Saillards, the Popinots, and the Matifats, all families that have made their mark in one part of the city or another. Come, come! If this business weren't as solid as gold ingots . . ."

"Solid you call it!"

"Certainly I do. For two months, without drawing attention to myself, I've been gathering information from architects, contractors and various municipal offices about the fine points of building. Monsieur Grindot, the young architect who's going to work on our apartment, is in despair because he hasn't the money to come in on our investment."

" Of course, since it involves building, he wants to push you into squandering more money."

" Now you don't think that men like Pillerault, Charles Claparon and Roguin are fools, do you ? I say that it's just as sure a thing as Sultana Cream."

" But why does Roguin need to gamble, if he is established in his practice and has made his fortune ? I see him go by sometimes looking as care-laden as a member of the cabinet and with an evasive expression that I don't care for at all. He's trying to hide some worry. In the course of the last five years he's acquired the face of an old roué. How can you be certain that once he has your money in his pocket he won't make off with it ? It's been done before. And although he's been our friend for the last fifteen years I wouldn't swear by him. He has a foul smell and doesn't sleep with his wife; I suppose he has kept mistresses and they've brought him to ruin. Otherwise I see no reason for his being so down at the mouth. While I'm getting dressed I have only to look through the shutters to see him coming home early in the morning. And where's he coming from ? No- body knows. But it looks to me as though he is keeping up two establishments. Is that the kind of life for a notary to lead, I ask you ? If he makes fifty thousand francs a year and spends sixty, then inside twenty years his fortune is gone and he's naked as the day God made him. Because he's accustomed to cutting a fine figure he is bound to turn to robbing his friends, all on the theory that charity begins at home. For another thing, he's intimate with that little wretch of a du Tillet, who used to be our clerk, and I don't see anything good in that. If he can't see through du Tillet, then he's blind, and if he knows him for what he's worth,

why is he so attached to him? Of course you may say that
his wife has a weakness for du Tillet. Well, I shouldn't
expect much of a man who has no regard for his wife's
honor. . . . And then I come back to the point : why should
the present owners of this land sell it for a fraction of its
value? If you were to meet a child that didn't know the
worth of a twenty-franc piece, wouldn't you tell him? It
looks to me as if your investment were the next thing to
robbery, if you don't mind my saying so."

" Good Lord, what strange creatures you women are,
always mixing things up! If Roguin weren't in it, you'd
say: ' César, you're doing something without Roguin, so it
can't be any good.' And yet now that he's there as a guarantee
you say . . ."

" No, that's this Monsieur Claparon."

" But a notary can't lend his name to a venture of this
kind."

" If it's illegal, then why does he do it? You're always so
intent upon the letter of the law!"

" Let me go on. Roguin's in it, and you say it won't do.
Is that reasonable, I ask you? Then you say: ' He's doing
something that's illegal.' And I tell you that, if necessary,
he'll let his name appear. Then you say: ' He's rich.' Isn't
that true of me as well? Would Ragon and Pillerault ever
come to me and say: ' Why are you in this, when you're
rolling in money?' "

" Businessmen aren't in the same category as notaries,"
Madame Birotteau objected.

" Well, my conscience is clear," César went on. " People
who sell, sell because they have to. We're not robbing
them any more than if we bought government bonds from
them at a price of seventy-five francs. We're buying the land
at today's market price, and three years from now the price
will be different, just as in the case of bonds. Look here,
Constance-Barbe-Joséphine Pillerault, you'll never catch
César Birotteau doing anything that isn't perfectly honest,

or in harmony with his own conscience and the law. Why should a man established in business for eighteen years be suspected in his own house of dishonesty?"

"Calm yourself, César! A woman who's lived with you as long as I have can't help knowing you through and through. And, of course, you are the master. You've made your own fortune; it belongs to you and you are free to spend it as you like. Even if we become as poor as church mice, neither your daughter nor I can utter a word of blame. But listen to this. When you put your Sultana Cream and Pink Lotion on the market, you were risking no more than five or six thousand francs. Now you're gambling everything you have, and you're not the only one in the game; you have associates who may be shrewder than you. Go ahead and give your ball and remodel the apartment. That is silly but it isn't ruinous. But when it comes to this land purchase, I am dead set against it. You are a perfumer, and you should stick to your trade instead of going into real estate. We women are guided by our instincts. At any rate, I've warned you; now go ahead and do as you like. You've been a referee in the commercial court and made a success of your career, so I shall follow you as my lord and master. But until I see our fortune solidly established and Césarine happily married, I shall tremble. God grant that my dream may not be prophetic!"

Birotteau was actually irritated by his wife's submissiveness, and he had recourse to an innocent ruse which he had employed upon other occasions.

"Look here, Constance, I haven't given my word, but it amounts to the same thing."

"There's no more to say, César, let's drop the subject. Go to bed now, my dear, for we've no more wood to put on the fire. Besides, we can talk better in bed, if you want to. Oh, what an ugly dream! It's no joke to see one's own self! How terrible! But Césarine and I shall make novenas for the success of your new enterprise."

" God's help can't do any harm," said Birotteau gravely.
" And this nut oil won't hurt either. Just as in the case of
Sultana Cream, I discovered it quite by accident. The first
I came on while I was reading a book, this time I was looking
at a print of Hero and Leander. A woman pouring oil over
her lover's head, do you think that's very nice ? The safest
ventures are those based on vanity and love of show. Such
instincts are always with us."

" Alas, I can see that for myself ! "

" At a certain age a man will do anything to get back his
hair. Hairdressers tell me that they sell great quantities
not only of Macassar but also of various dyes which are
reputed to have reviving powers. Since the war ended, men
have been after the women more than ever, and women
don't like a bald head, do they, dear ? So politics, you might
say, is in back of the current demand for hair tonic. A formula beneficial to the health of the hair is sure to sell like
hot cakes, especially as the Academy of Science will doubtless approve it. Perhaps my kind friend, Monsieur Vauquelin,
will help me again. I'll go consult him tomorrow and take
him a certain engraving which I know he admires. Someone turned it up for me in Germany, after a two-year search.
And Chiffreville, Vauquelin's assistant, told me that his chief
was working just now on the analysis of human hair. So
that if my discoveries fit in with his, the oil will be in demand
by both sexes. I tell you, there's a fortune in it. It's all
I can do to sleep. Fortunately young Popinot has a very
fine head of hair. And if our new salesgirl has hair down
to the ground and is willing, with no offense to God or man,
to say that my oil has something to do with it, then there
will be as many bald pates at my door as there are beggars
in the world.

" And now, my dear, what about the ball ? I'm not a
malicious man, but I'd like a chance to meet that little
du Tillet, who is all puffed up over his success and avoids
me at the Stock Exchange because I know something which

isn't to his credit.  Perhaps I was too lenient with him,
when you come down to it.  Isn't it strange, my dear, that
we should always be punished for our good deeds, at least
here on earth?  I acted like a father to him; you don't know
the half of what I did."

"It gives me gooseflesh just to hear his name!  If you'd
known his intentions you'd never have hushed up that theft
of three thousand francs.  I guessed at how you handled it.
But you might have done better to pack him off to the
reformatory."

"What were his intentions, then?"

"Never mind.  If you were in the mood to listen to me
this evening, Birotteau, I'd give you a piece of good advice,
and that would be to leave du Tillet alone."

"Wouldn't it look odd if I kept out of my house a clerk
whom I set up in business for himself with a twenty-
thousand-franc guarantee?  We may as well be good all the
way through.  And perhaps du Tillet has mended his ways."

"On account of the ball this whole house will be topsy-
turvy."

"What do you mean, topsy-turvy?  Everything will be
in perfect order.  Have you forgotten what I just told you
about the staircase and my plan to rent the second floor
of the next house from Cayron, the umbrella-maker?  We're
to go tomorrow to see the owner, Monsieur Molineux. . . . Yes,
tomorrow I have as many things to attend to as a cabinet
minister. . . ."

"You're driving me distracted with all your plans," said
Constance.  "I can't think straight any longer.  Moreover,
my dear Birotteau, I am ready to go to sleep."

"Good day to you then," said her husband.  "I say good
day because it's nearly morning!  Ah, the dear creature's
asleep already!  Little woman, you're going to be rich, or
my name isn't César!"

And a few minutes later they were snoring peacefully,
side by side.

# II

A GLANCE AT THE PREVIOUS LIFE OF THIS COUPLE CAN only reinforce the impression made by the arguments each one of them used in the course of this friendly quarrel. We shall note the shopkeeping practices of the time and explain how César Birotteau came to be both a perfumer and a deputy to the Mayor, a former officer of the National Guard and a knight of the Legion of Honor. By illumining the depths of his character and the origins of his strength, we shall see how the vicissitudes which a strong man overcomes with ease may be the undoing of a weak one. For events are not absolutes, and the course they take depends largely on the individual. Misfortune is a stepping stone for the man of genius, a cleansing bath for the good Christian, a treasure of experience for anyone who has his wits about him, and only for the weakling a disaster.

A peasant from near Chinon, Jacques Birotteau by name, married the chambermaid of a lady who employed him to look after her vineyards. They had three boys, but the wife died during the third childbirth and her husband soon after. The lady had been attached to her maid and she brought up François, the eldest of Birotteau's sons, alongside her own and eventually sent him to study for the priesthood. During the Revolution, he was forced into hiding to escape the guillotine. As this story begins, he was vicar of the cathedral of Tours and had left this town only once in his life, in order to visit his brother César. The turmoil of Paris so frightened the good priest that he did not dare leave his room. He called cabs "chopped-off-carriages" and marveled at everything he saw. After a week's stay he returned to Tours, swearing that he would never go to the capital again.

Jean Birotteau, the peasant's second son, was taken into the militia and early in the revolutionary wars won the rank of captain. . . . At the battle of Trébia, when Macdonald called for volunteers to storm a battery, Captain Birotteau advanced at the head of his company and was killed. Evidently fate raised up enemies to the Birotteaus wherever they might be.

The youngest son, then, is the hero of the scene which we have described above. When César was fourteen years old and had mastered the three R's, he went with twenty francs in his pocket to seek his fortune in Paris. A recommendation from an apothecary of Tours got him a place in the shop of Monsieur and Madame Ragon. At this time his wardrobe consisted of a pair of hobnailed boots, short blue trousers and stockings, a flowered vest, a peasant jacket, three heavy cotton shirts and a stout stick. His hair was cut like that of a choirboy, but he had the strong back of a peasant; if he was subject to fits of indolence—a trait peculiar to his native province—he made up for it by his ambition, and although he had little natural wit or education he was instinctively honest and had inherited the fine feelings of his mother, who had commonly been known to possess a " heart of gold." César's employer let him sleep on a mattress in the attic, where the cook had her quarters, and he was given his food and a salary of six francs a month. The other young fellows in the shop, who taught him how to tie up parcels, run errands and sweep the floor of the shop and the pavement outside, ribbed him mercilessly, in accordance with the tradition that teasing is the basis of an apprentice's instruction. Monsieur and Madame Ragon spoke to him as if he were a dog, and no one took any notice of his fatigue, although at night his back and feet ached unbearably. This application of the maxim " Everyman for himself and the devil take the hindmost " made César feel that life in Paris was very hard indeed. Many a night he wept for his beloved Touraine, where the peasant works his land at the pace he chooses and the mason lays as few or as many stones in the course of the day as his strength allows. Finally, however, he dropped off to sleep without any thought of running away, for he knew that there was work to be done the next morning and he was as faithful as any watchdog to the concept of duty. If ever he did voice a complaint, the young chief clerk said with a jovial air:

" Life isn't so rosy at the Queen of Roses, is that it? And quails don't fall roasted from the trees; you have to catch them with your own hands and find a sauce in which to cook them."

The cook, a stout woman from Picardy, took the best of everything for herself and never spoke to the boy except to complain of the fact that Monsieur and Madame Ragon were too watchful for her to be able to rob them. After he had been there a month, one Sunday when she was obliged to stay home, she finally started a conversation. In her Sunday clothes Ursula seemed positively beautiful to poor César, and but for a stroke of good luck he might have foundered then and there upon the first reef of his career. For like any unprotected youth, he was ready to fall in love with the first woman who smiled at him. Ursula took him under her wing, and an affair resulted which made the boy more than ever the butt of his companions' jokes. The good luck was that two years later the cook went off with a young deserter, heir to a bit of land in her own part of the country, who was hiding out in Paris and eventually was persuaded to marry her.

In the course of these two years Ursula fed César well, showed him the seamy side of Paris and gave him a jealous horror of the houses of ill repute to which she was apparently not a stranger. By 1792, his feet were hardened to the pavement, his back to heavy boxes and his spirit to what he called the "fakes and frauds" of the big city. When Ursula left him he was quick to recover from the shock, for she had lived up to none of his ideals of the tender emotions. Because she was crude and lascivious, deceitful

and thieving, selfish and addicted to drink, she offended his
fundamental innocence and held out no hope for the future.
At times the poor boy was appalled at the thought that his
ingenuous heart had led him into an entanglement with the
wrong woman and one of whom he would never be free.
By the time he had recovered his independence he was a
full-grown young man, sixteen years old. Ursula and his
sharp-tongued companion in the shop had developed his
business sense, although it was still hidden under an appearance of simplicity. He observed the customers who came
into the place, took advantage of every slack moment to ask
questions about the various products of the firm and soon
came to know their prices and to be in position to impart
what he had learned to apprentices younger than himself.
By this time the Ragons were so used to having him around
that he was practically indispensable.

When the terrible requisitions of Year II of the Revolution
had stripped the shop bare, César Birotteau, now second
clerk, took advantage of the situation to obtain a salary of
fifty francs a month and with tremendous pride and joy won
himself a seat at the Ragons' dining table. He had six hundred
francs in savings and was lodged in a room where there was
a place to keep the wardrobe he had gradually been acquiring.
On his day off (which according to Revolutionary usage was
every tenth day) he dressed and acted in the somewhat
rough manner demanded by the times, thus in spite of his
peasant origin and natural humility seeming as good as the
next man and surmounting social barriers which in an earlier
period would have blocked his way. Toward the end of this
year his honesty won him the position of cashier. The impressive Citizeness Ragon mended his linen and both she
and her husband treated him with easy familiarity.

In the month of Vendémiaire 1794 César exchanged the
two thousand gold francs of his savings for six thousand
francs of promissory notes issued by the revolutionary government, then, just before the devaluation, he bought thirty-franc

bonds with them and had reason to congratulate himself upon his acumen. All through this period he followed the ups-and-downs of public affairs and government securities with secret trepidation. When things looked darkest, Monsieur Ragon, who had been Marie-Antoinette's official perfumer, confided to César the attachment he still felt for the late sovereigns, and these confidences left a deep impression upon him. Their after-hours conversations, when the shop was closed, the cash-box locked and the street quiet outside, excited César's naturally Royalist inclinations to the point of fanaticism. His imagination was stimulated first by the recital of the virtues of the King and Queen and then by the account of their guillotining only a few steps from the shop door. A government that could shed innocent blood without a pang offended his sensibilities and aroused his hate. His acute business sense showed him the damage done to free trade by price ceilings and indeed by political strife in general. Besides, as a perfumer, he could not fail to be against the pseudo-Roman revolutionary style of short hair and the suppression of powder. Only absolute power, he concluded, could create the stable conditions favorable to the circulation of money, and for this reason the monarchy won his devotion. When Monsieur Ragon saw that he was thoroughly convinced he made him his chief clerk and initiated him into the innermost secrets of the Queen of Roses, some of whose customers were in reality Bourbon emissaries, who used the shop as headquarters for correspondence between Paris and the west. César was inspired by youthful enthusiasm and by his new acquaintance with the Georges, the La Billardières, the Montaurans, the Bauvans, the Longuys, the Mandas, the Berniers, the du Quénics, the Fontaines and others to throw himself into the conspiracy of the Royalists and terrorists against the expiring National Convention, on the Thirteenth of Vendémiaire, 1795.

César had the honor of fighting against Napoleon on the steps of Saint-Roch; indeed, he was wounded at the very beginning of the melee. Everyone knows what happened. Barras' chief aide won notoriety, but Birotteau was saved by the fact that he was totally unknown. Some of his friends carried him to the Queen of Roses and he was hidden and nursed in Madame Ragon's attic. This display of valor was only a flash in the pan, for during the month of his convalescence he had plenty of time to reflect upon the incongruity of an alliance between politics and perfumery. Although he remained a Royalist, this allegiance became subordinate to the commercial interests which occupied the major part of his thoughts.

After the overthrow of the Directory on the Eighteenth of Brumaire, 1799, Monsieur Ragon and his wife, despairing of the royal cause, decided to give up the perfumery and live like ordinary citizens, no longer bothering with politics. In order to get their money out of the business, they had to find a purchaser more honest than he was ambitious and possessed of common sense rather than acuteness. So it was that Ragon proposed selling out to his chief clerk, Birotteau. This young man, who at twenty years of age had an income of a thousand francs from government bonds, was hesitant at first. If he could raise his income to fifteen hundred francs and if the First Consul were to consolidate the public debt by installing himself in the Tuileries Palace, Birotteau meant to retire to Chinon. Why should he exchange his honorable independence for the risks of a business career? Already he had made more money than he had ever expected to have, by taking the kind of chances to which one only exposes oneself when young. He dreamed of marrying a girl from his own part of the country with a fortune the equal of his and settling down at Les Trésorières, a piece of property he had longed to own ever since he had attained the age of reason. Here he meant to cultivate the land so as to increase its value, raise his income to three thousand francs a year and live in beatific obscurity. He was about to refuse the Ragons' offer when the event of falling in love suddenly stimulated his ambition and caused him to alter his plans.

After Ursula betrayed him, César had become a very circumspect young man, as much because he feared the hazards of love in the big city as on account of the staggering amount of work he had to do. When passion has nothing upon which to feed it is soon transformed into necessity, and it is natural that a middle-class man should set his heart upon marriage, since this is his only means of conquering and making sure of a woman. This was César Birotteau's condition. In the Queen of Roses shop everything lay upon his shoulders and he had no time for amusement. Under such circumstances one's needs become all the more urgent, and so it was that a meeting with a young girl who would never have interested him had he been a libertine, made a tremendous impression upon him. One fine June day, as he was crossing the Pont Marie to the Ile Saint-Louis, he saw a girl standing in a doorway on the corner of the Quai d'Anjou. Constance Pillerault was the head salesgirl at a drygoods store known as the Petit-Matelot, the first of many of its kind to be set up in Paris, all of them characterized by painted signs, floating streamers, window displays of shawls suspended in air, ties stacked like houses of cards and endless other attractions, such as price-tags, fancy wrappings and show-cards, the optical effect of which was to transform the store-fronts into commercial poems. The low prices of all the Petit-Matelot's wares made it unprecedentedly successful, even in a spot remote from both trade and fashion. This head salesgirl was as famous for her good looks as was, later, the " Lemonade-Girl " of the Café des Mille Colonnes and other fair creatures who have caused more noses, old and young, to be glued against shop-windows than there are paving-stones in the whole city of Paris.

César Birotteau, whose Queen of Roses, between the Rue Saint-Roch and the Rue de la Sourdière, dealt in nothing but toiletries, had never so much as suspected the existence of the Petit-Matelot, for the various small businesses of the city are generally unknown to one another. Now he was so smitten with Constance's beauty that he rushed in and proceeded to buy material for half a dozen shirts, calling for roll after roll to be shown him and haggling over the price for all the world like an English old maid hunting bargains. Constance soon saw signs of a kind any woman recognizes which indicated that he was interested in her rather than in the goods she was supposed to be selling him. He gave her his name and address, but she was indifferent to his obvious admiration. He had not had to make much of an effort to win the good graces of his first and only mistress, Ursula, and as a result he was still painfully naive. Now emotion made him clumsier than ever and he could hardly get out a word. At the same time, he was in too much of a daze to notice the indifference that came over the salesgirl's face once she had smilingly made her sale.

For a whole week he went every evening to mount guard outside the Petit-Matelot, begging for a look from Constance as if he were a dog begging for a bone. He paid no attention to the teasing of the clerks and girls, stepped humbly aside to let customers pass and watched the way the shop was run. After a few days he entered its heavenly portals for the second time, ostensibly to buy some handkerchiefs but in reality to voice a wonderful idea.

" Mademoiselle, if you need any toilet goods, I'd be glad to supply you with them," he suggested.

Every day of the week Constance Pillerault received dazzling propositions, in which there was no question of marriage, and because her heart was as pure as her face was fair, six months were spent in negotiations before she consented to listen to César's declaration of love, and even then she would give no definite answer. After all, with so many suitors, prosperous wine merchants and tavern-keepers among them, she could not commit herself in a hurry. César finally enlisted the aid of her uncle, Monsieur Claude-Joseph Pillerault, a hardware dealer on the Quai de la Ferraille, whose existence he had ferreted out with all the resourcefulness and guile that distinguish a true lover. The pace of this story compels us to pass over in silence the joys of innocent young love in a Parisian setting and all the details of a clerk's courtship: the gifts of rare, fresh fruit out of season, the dinners at Vénua's before the theater and the Sunday carriage outings. Although César was not particularly handsome, his appearance was anything but unlovable. The months he had spent shut up in a shop had lightened his ruddy, peasant complexion. His thick black hair, powerful Norman body and honest, forthright air all spoke in his favor. Pillerault, who was not only Constance's uncle but her guardian as well, investigated the young man's background and gave his approval. And under a linden tree at Sceaux, in the merry month of May 1800, Constance-Barbe-Joséphine consented to marry César Birotteau, who fainted away at the good news.

"My dear, you are acquiring an excellent husband," Monsieur Pillerault told her. "He has a warm heart and a keen sense of honor; he's straightforward and good all the way through, in fact I call him a prince among men."

Constance cheerfully gave up the brilliant future of which, like any self-respecting salesgirl, she had been wont to dream, and took it upon herself to become a good wife and mother, according to the religious ideas of the society in which she moved. And this program was much better suited to her temperament than the vanities which engage the imaginations of so many young women of Paris. Constance had a limited intelligence and all the characteristics of the lower middle class. She did her work thoroughly, though she displayed a changeable temper which often caused her to refuse something she wanted and then grow angry when her refusal was taken literally; her tireless concern was divided between the cash-box and the kitchen, between business matters and the invisible mending of her household linen. She was

affectionate in a scolding manner and could cope with only
the simplest ideas, the small change of the mind; she reason-
ed everything out, made close calculations, was prudent to
the point of being timorous and always had an eye on the
future. Her candid, somewhat cold beauty, her freshness
and something appealing in her expression prevented Birotteau from perceiving her faults, and as a matter of fact she
made up for them by her delicate, feminine probity, natural
orderliness, unflagging energy and selling ability. At this
time Constance was eighteen years old and had eleven
thousand francs. With love firing his ambition, César bought
the Queen of Roses and moved it to a handsome house near
the Place Vendôme. Finding himself at twenty-one years
of age married to a beautiful and devoted girl and with a
business of his own which he had three-quarters paid for,
he had every reason to see the future as very rosy and did
indeed so see it, all the more so when he looked back over
the distance he had covered since his humble start. Roguin,
the Ragons' notary, who drew up the marriage contract,
wisely advised him not to use his wife's dowry to make the
final payment on the business.

" Keep some funds on hand for another investment, my
boy," he told him.

Birotteau looked on the notary with admiration, fell into
the habit of consulting him often and made him his friend.
Like Ragon and Pillerault he had so much confidence in the
legal profession that he entrusted all his affairs to Roguin
without hesitation. With Constance's eleven thousand francs
to fall back on he would not have exchanged his lot even
for that of Napoleon, then First Consul and plainly destined
for greater things to come. At the beginning the Birotteaus
had only one servant, a cook, and they lived out their perpetual honeymoon in a comfortably furnished apartment over
their shop. Constance shone particularly behind the shop
counter. Her good looks had a great deal to do with the
flourishing sales, for the beautiful Madame Birotteau's name

was on the lips of all the notables of the Empire. Even if César was accused of being a Royalist, everyone paid tribute to his personal honesty, and in spite of his neighbors' envy of his success they had to admit that he deserved it. The wound he had received on the steps of Saint-Roch gave him a reputation for courage and also for a knowledge of political secrets, although actually he was not at all courageous and had no notion of politics. On this basis the people of his district named him a captain of the National Guard, from which rank he was later dismissed by Napoleon, who according to Birotteau had it in for him on account of the episode of Saint-Roch.

Here, then, is the story of the Birotteaus, who were happy in their domestic life and had no worries outside of business.

During the first year of their marriage César taught his wife how to sell toiletries, an occupation to which she took like a fish to water. But at the end of twelve months his inventory failed to satisfy him. At this rate, he thought, it would take him twenty years to acquire the modest sum of a hundred thousand francs which he had set himself as a goal. It was then that he decided to increase his earnings by manufacturing toiletries as well as selling them. Against his wife's advice he leased a plot of land with a shed on the Faubourg du Temple and put up a big sign with the name " Birotteau." Then he hired a man from Grasse on a share-the-profits basis and began to make soap and eau de cologne. This arrangement lasted only six months and led to a loss which he had to pay out of his own pocket. He was more than ever determined to succeed, if only to justify himself in his wife's eyes, although he later confessed to her that this first failure had made his head reel and that if it were not for his religious convictions he would have thrown himself into the Seine.

As he was strolling along the boulevards one evening on his way home to dinner, profoundly discouraged by the miscarriage of various other experiments (the Parisian stroller is

just as often a melancholy man as he is a lazy one), his eye
was caught by a yellowed second-hand book among a pile
lying on a stall, with the title of Abdeker, or the Art of Pre-
serving Beauty. He picked up this supposedly Arabian
volume, which was in reality a novel written by a physician
of the previous century. Leaning against a tree to leaf
through it, he came upon a page relating to toiletries, where
the writer explained the difference between dermis and
epidermis and pointed out that certain toilet preparations
sometimes produce an effect contrary to that which is expected, by toning up a type of skin that needs to be relaxed
and vice versa. Birotteau saw a fortune in this book and
hastened to buy it. But because he lacked confidence in his
own powers he went to a celebrated chemist by the name of
Vauquelin and ingenuously asked him for a formula for a
double cosmetic, that is, one which would produce different
effects upon different types of skin. True scholars, those
who never win in their lifetime the fame to which they are
entitled, are often kindly disposed toward the simple-
hearted. So it was that Vauquelin took him under his protection, gave him the formula for a hand lotion and allowed
him to patent it under the name of Sultana Cream. Then,
in order to make a complete job of it, Birotteau used some
of the same ingredients in a skin tonic, called Pink Lotion.
He proceeded to imitate some of the practices of the Petit-
Matelot and was the first perfumer to employ posters and
other advertising methods which are perhaps unjustly con-
demned as marks of charlatanism.

Sultana Cream and Pink Lotion were introduced into the
worlds of elegance and business by great colored placards,
which were headed by the phrase " Approved by the Institute." This phrase, here employed for the first time, had
a magic effect. Not only France but all the other countries
of the continent as well were plastered with red, yellow and
blue signs, and the sovereign of the Queen of Roses manufactured and supplied at a moderate price as much of his

products as the market could absorb. At a time when the East was talked of constantly and men and women asked nothing better than to be sultans or sultanas, the name Sultana Cream would just as easily have occurred to a simpleton as to a man of intelligence. But the public judges everything by its practical success and was ready, therefore, to consider César Birotteau a superior fellow, especially after he had written the text of a prospectus whose very ridiculousness made it effective. The French laugh only at people and things that are in the public eye, and no one is in the public eye for long unless he is successful. Although Birotteau would never have been so subtle as to play up his own stupidity, he was credited with having turned it to his purpose. A copy of this brochure has been found, after a long search, in the offices of Popinot & Co., druggists, on the Rue des Lombards. It belongs to what serious historians would call the category of "documentary evidence," and here, then, is its text:

*Cesar Birotteau's*

## DOUBLE-PURPOSE SULTANA CREAM
### AND
## PINK LOTION

Miraculous Discoveries
approved by the Institute

\*

For some time there has been a demand on the part of both sexes for a hand cream and face lotion possessed of qualities more efficacious than those of eau de cologne. After a prolonged study of the skin, which both ladies and gentlemen aspire to keep in a soft and supple condition, Monsieur Birotteau, a perfumer known here and abroad, has discovered formulas productive of truly miraculous results and without such damaging incidental effects as the premature wrinkles caused by harmful drugs. His discovery is based on the fact that persons of different temperament have different complexions and require different care. Thus, the white cream is suited to persons of the so-called sanguine type and the pink lotion to lymphatics.

*Sultana Cream* derives its name from its original discovery by an Arab doctor for use in the harem. The present formula has been approved by the Institute, upon presentation by the learned chemist, Vauquelin. This precious, delicately perfumed cream eliminates freckles, whitens the epidermis and checks the perspiration of the hands.

As for the *Pink Lotion*, which is a variation of the same formula, it does away with the pimples which interfere so often with a lady's intentions of going to a ball and refreshes the skin by opening or closing the pores according to the needs of the individual. So successful is the lotion that many ladies gratefully refer to it as " Beauty's Best Friend."

Eau de cologne is an ordinary perfume, while *Sultana Cream* and *Pink Lotion* are actively effective preparations which work from the inside out as well as from the outside in. Their balmy smell stimulates both heart and mind, and simple as they are, they offer ladies a new source of charm and gentlemen a new possibility of fascination.

Daily use of the lotion soothes the skin after shaving, heals chapped lips and gradually tones up the skin. A good complexion is indicative of good health and a balance of the natural humors. Hence, users may hope to be delivered from the curse of sick headaches. *Pink Lotion* may be applied by women to any part of the body; it is preventive of skin diseases and neutralizes perspiration without clogging the pores, while at the same time it softens the skin.

Sent prepaid by Monsieur César Birotteau, successor to Ragon, perfumer to Queen Marie-Antoinette, at the Queen of Roses, Rue Saint-Honoré, near the Place Vendôme, Paris.

The cream, three francs the jar; the lotion six francs the bottle.

In order to guard against imitations, the jar is wrapped in a paper bearing the signature " Birotteau," and the bottle cannot be opened without breaking a seal which bears the same name.

Actually, the success of Birotteau's venture was due in large part to his wife, who advised him to offer a thirty per cent discount to perfumers both at home and abroad, if they would handle his two products in wholesale quantities. In strict truth, Birotteau's cosmetics were better than others of their kind, and the distinction between temperaments appealed to a great many ignorant people. Every one of the five hundred perfumers of France, lured by the large percentage of profit, bought more than three hundred gross a year, and although the gain on each order was small, it added up to a considerable sum. César was soon in a position to become outright owner of the plot of land on the Faubourg du Temple, where he built a handsome factory. At the same time he redecorated the shop on the Rue Saint-Honoré and gave his wife so many small pleasures that she forgot her concern for the future.

In 1810 Madame Birotteau had a notion that rents were about to rise, and she persuaded her husband to lease additional space in the building of which they then occupied only the ground floor and the mezzanine and to transfer their living quarters to the second floor. A happy event which took place at this time induced her to shut her eyes to the extravagances of her husband. He had just been elected referee in the commercial court, a tribute to his integrity and good reputation, which classed him among the outstanding merchants of the city. In order to increase his knowledge, he got up at five o'clock every morning to read law books and treatises on business litigation. His good will, rectitude and natural feeling for justice, all contributed to his ability to deal with the cases brought before him and caused him to become one of the most highly esteemed among the referees. Even his defects only served to augment his good name. Because he was conscious of his own inferiority he gladly subordinated his opinions to those of his colleagues. They were duly flattered, and some of them attributed his attentiveness to deep thinking and sought his silent approbation, while others were so captivated by his gentle modesty that they praised him to the skies. As for the disputants, they appreciated his kindliness and conciliatory spirit, and he was often chosen to sit upon cases where common sense enabled him to give a judgment worthy of Solomon. During the time that he was in office he learned to speak a jargon made up of axioms, commonplaces and bits of elementary wisdom, all decked out in well-turned phrases which impressed the casual listener as extremely eloquent. In this way he appealed to the great majority of ordinary people, who are fated to work hard all their lives and necessarily hold views of a simple and down-to-earth kind. He spent so much time in court that eventually his wife convinced him that he must give up this costly honor.

By 1813, thanks to their understanding and the amount of ground they had covered together, the couple had embarked upon a period of prosperity, which seemed as if it would have no end. Their circle of friends was made up of Monsieur and Madame Ragon, their predecessors at the perfumery; Uncle Pillerault; Roguin the notary; the Matifats, wholesale druggists of the Rue des Lombards, who supplied them with chemical ingredients; Joseph Lebas, the draper, successor to the Guillaumes of the Chat-qui-pelote, and one of the leading merchants of the Rue Saint-Denis; Judge Popinot, Madame Ragon's brother; Chiffreville of Protez & Chiffreville; Monsieur and Madame Cochin, partners of Matifat; Abbé Loraux, confessor of most of the devout souls named above, and a few others. In spite of Birotteau's Royalist sympathies he enjoyed the public favor and passed for a very rich man although he possessed only a hundred thousand francs outside of his business. The orderly way in which he conducted his affairs, his punctiliousness, his habit of shunning debt, of never asking for delivery before payment, but of obliging other people with credit, all these things built up his good name.

He had made a lot of money, to be sure, but a good bit

of it had gone into expanding the business and his household expenses alone came to nearly twenty thousand francs a year. Then the education of Césarine, his only child, whom he and his wife adored so much that they could not be parted from her, was an expensive proposition. Neither one of them counted the pennies when it came to satisfying her desires. Imagine the good peasant's joy when he heard her play a sonata of Steibelt on the piano or sing some drawing-room ballad, when he saw her write perfect French and make exquisite sepia drawings, or listened while she read aloud the two Racines and explained their beauties! How happy he was to live again in this flower, still attached to the maternal stem, this angel whose budding graces he had followed and admired from the instant she was born, this matchless child, who was so gently bred that she would never have dreamed of looking down on her father or teasing him for his lack of formal education! For although César had learned his three R's before he came to Paris, he had been too busy since to acquire any knowledge that did not bear upon the business of perfumery. Because he mingled exclusively with people who cared nothing for science or letters and were absorbed in the special requirements of their trade, he had developed into a practical man and embraced the language, opinions and errors of the typical middle-class Parisian, who admires Molière, Voltaire and Rousseau and buys their books without reading them, who maintains that *closet* is derived from *clothes*, because that is where the women keep them. Yes, to the middle-class man, Potier, Talma, Mademoiselle Mars and actors like that were multi-millionaires, Talma ate raw meat and Mademoiselle Mars fricasseed pearls, in imitation of an Egyptian rival. The Emperor had special leather pockets in his vests, from which he extracted fistfuls of tobacco and galloped on horseback up the stairs of the orangery at Versailles. Writers and artists died miserably in the hospital because of their originality, and since they were all atheists, it was ill-advised to invite them to a decent house. On this score Joseph Lebas had a harrowing tale to tell of his sister-in-law Augustine's marriage to Sommervieux the painter. Ah, and astronomers, of course, lived on a diet of spiders! These high spots in the middle-class man's appreciation of etymology, drama, politics, literature and science give some idea of his limited intelligence. A poet walking along the Rue des Lombards may be transported by its scents to farthest Asia; the smell of cuscus in a cheap restaurant may call up exotic dancing girls before him. The bright scarlet of cochineal dye may remind him of a Brahman poem, with the religious beliefs and caste system it carries with it; if he happens to see a piece of raw ivory, in his mind's eye he climbs upon an elephant's back and under a muslin canopy he makes love there, for all the world like the king of Lahore. But the petty businessman knows nothing of the origin of the products with which he works. Birotteau, for instance, had not the foggiest notions of either natural history or chemistry. Although he recognized Vauquelin as a great man, he considered him an exception. In general, his mind was of the same caliber as that of the retired grocer who said in the course of a discussion of the transportation of tea: " Tea is transported either by caravan or by Le Havre." For in Birotteau's mind, aloes and opium were natives to the Rue des Lombards, and so-called Constantinople rose-water was, like eau de cologne, a product of Paris. All these names of faraway places were frauds perpetrated on the snobs who disdained anything from their own country. Thus an English merchant advertised his wares as " Made in France," just as his French counterpart claimed they were " Made in England."

Despite all this, César Birotteau was not really stupid. His natural honesty and kindliness threw a favorable light upon all his actions and more than made up for his ignorance. And his continued success gave him an air of assurance, which in Paris is not only the symbol but also the equivalent of power. After standing in awe of her husband for the first three years of their marriage, Constance fell into a state of chronic apprehension. She was the wiser and more foresighted of the two; she stood for doubt, timidity and opposition, while Birotteau embodied audacity, ambition and a happy confidence in his own fate. And yet, appearances to the contrary, he was essentially fearful, while she was endowed with both patience and courage. So it was that a hesitant, uneducated, uninspired, characterless, altogether mediocre man, with no apparent chance of winning so much as a toe-hold in the world's most treacherous marketplace, succeeded, on account of his good conduct, ideals of justice, his truly Christian charity and the devotion he bore to the only woman in his life, in passing for a pillar of strength and resolution. The world judged him by his success, and aside from Pillerault and Popinot, no one was in position to know his frailty. The twenty or thirty members of his circle of friends all said the same stupid things and mouthed the same commonplaces, while looking upon themselves as superior people. Their wives were interested chiefly in fine clothes and good food and had no conversation beyond derogatory remarks about their spouses. Only Madame Birotteau had the sense to speak of hers respectfully. In spite of his inner weaknesses, she recognized the fact that he had made their fortune and that she had him to thank for her share of the esteem in which they were both held. Of course, in the strictest privacy, she wondered what sort of a place the world could be if all its supposedly superior men resembled her husband. Meanwhile, the respect she showed him added to that which he already enjoyed, all the more so because most Frenchwomen are given to belittling their husbands and complaining about them.

The first days of 1814, that year so fatal to the Empire, were marked in the Birotteau household by two events which would have seemed of slight importance to another couple, but deeply impressed these two simple people whose life

had been marked by few strong emotions of any kind. They
had taken on as their chief clerk a young man twenty-two
years old whose name was Ferdinand du Tillet. This fellow,
reputed to be a business genius, had formerly been employed
by another perfumer, who had refused to give him any
share of his profits. For some time he had been doing
everything he could to get into the Queen of Roses, having
acquainted himself with the personalities and inner workings
of the house. Birotteau finally did take him in, at a salary
of a thousand francs, and with the intention of making him
his successor. He played such an important part in the
family's life that we must say something about him.

Originally he had had no other name than Ferdinand,
and at the time when Napoleon was desperately drafting
soldiers, this anonymity had seemed to him convenient. And
yet, obviously, thanks to the wanton act of a man and woman,
he had been born. According to the records, in 1793 a poor
girl from Le Tillet, a small village near Les Andelys, had
crept into the priest's garden to give birth to a child; having
tapped on the shutters, she had gone and thrown herself in
the river. The priest took in the child, gave him the name
of the saint whose feast day it was and brought him up in
his own house. Unfortunately this good man died in 1804,
not leaving enough money to provide for the rest of Ferdinand's education. The boy was set adrift in Paris, where
he became an adventurer, an existence which might have
led him either to fortune or to the gallows, to the bar, the
army, business or domesticity. Relying solely on his wits,
he became a traveling salesman, and having traversed France,
learned the ways of the world and resolved to make his
way at any price whatsoever, he ended up as a perfumer's
clerk in Paris. In 1813 he decided to acquire a legal identity.
He petitioned the court at Les Andelys to transfer the data
from his baptismal certificate to the civil registers and at
the same time to bestow upon him the name du Tillet,
because of the fact that he had been abandoned and found

in this locality. Alone in the world and accountable to no
one, he looked upon society as a stepmother: his only ideal
was self-interest and he considered no means unworthy of its
pursuit. He had dangerous abilities, overweening ambition
and some of the worst faults rightly or wrongly attributed
to his native province of Normandy. A glib way of talking
concealed his essentially quarrelsome nature. He was always
spoiling for a legal battle, and while he would grant no
rights to anyone else he was very zealous in protecting his
own, relying on his stubborn will and the passage of time to
wear down his adversary. His qualities were those of the
artful valets of classical comedy: he was extremely resourceful, always just one step ahead of the law and possessed
of an itch to take whatever he could lay his hands on. His
aim was to practice on his own behalf the theft which
Louis XV's Minister of Finance, the Abbé Terray, said he
practiced for the sake of the State. He was passionately
energetic and bolder than any soldier in asking for a favor,
good or bad, which would serve his own selfish ends. He
looked down upon his fellow-men, deeming every one to have
his price, had no scruples as to the means of obtaining what
he wanted and considered money and success as incentives
more powerful than morality. With such ruthless ideas, he
seemed fated to get ahead. Suspended as he was between the
hangman's noose and the estate of millionaire, he was necessarily quick in his decisions and vindictive to the $n$th
degree, but his feelings were as completely dissembled as
those of a Cromwell intent upon guillotining honor. His
purposefulness was concealed under a mocking air, but even
as a clerk he set no limits to his aspirations and looked
hatefully at society as if to say: "I'll thumb my nose at
you yet!" He had resolved not to marry before he was forty
years old, and he stuck to his resolution. He was a slender,
handsome young man, with manners adaptable to any company. His thin weasel face was pleasing at first sight, but
upon closer examination revealed the strange expressions

which etch themselves upon the surface when a man is not at ease with his conscience. There was a sharpness to his soft-skinned, ruddy Norman complexion and although his flecked, somewhat silvery eyes had an habitual evasive expression, he could focus them with terrifying intensity upon an intended victim. His voice was muted like that of a man who has been talking for a long time, and while his thin lips gave him an air of refinement, his pointed nose and slightly bulging forehead betrayed some discrepancy in his origins. The blackness of his hair, which looked as though it were dyed, also betokened his mixed blood. He had, or so it seemed, inherited the quick wits of a dissipated nobleman and the servility of a seduced peasant girl, and he further showed the effects of an unfinished education and of the orphaned state in which he had been brought up. Birotteau was astonished to learn that his new clerk dressed himself fashionably after office hours and stayed out late at parties given by prominent bankers and lawyers. According to his ideas, a clerk ought to devote even his spare time to the interests of the firm, and he reproached this one gently for the fineness of his linen and for the format and engraving of his calling cards, which seemed more suitable for a man of the world than for an apprentice in a business office.

As a matter of fact, Ferdinand aimed at playing the role of Tartuffe in the house of Orgon. He had sized up his employer's weaknesses as Constance had, but much more quickly, and attempted to flatter and seduce her. But although he was careful of what he said, he unwittingly revealed enough of his attitude toward life to terrify the good Madame Birotteau, who shared her husband's ideals and would never have lifted a finger against her neighbor. And Ferdinand, on his part, came to understand that in spite of her restraint she despised him. On the basis of some unanswered love letters which he had sent her, he assumed a familiar manner, as if there were some secret understanding between them. Without giving her husband the real reason,

Constance pressed him to dismiss the fellow from his service, and César agreed. On Saturday, three days before he meant to give du Tillet notice, he found in the process of drawing up his monthly accounts that three thousand francs were missing. His consternation was great, not so much at the loss of the money, as at the suspicion that devolved upon his three clerks, workers, delivery boy and private cook. Who could be to blame? Madame Birotteau never left her post behind the counter, and the cash-box was in charge of Popinot, Monsieur Ragon's nineteen-year-old nephew, who lived in the house and was the soul of honor. The figures which failed to match the cash in hand were this boy's, and indicated that the money had been removed after the accounts had been balanced. The Birotteaus decided to say nothing, but to keep watch over everyone. The next day, which was Sunday, it was their turn to entertain the circle of their friends. In the course of a card game, Roguin, the notary, put out some old gold twenty-franc pieces which Madame Birotteau remembered having received a few days before from a young bride, Madame d'Espard.

" You must have robbed an alms-box," Birotteau said with a laugh.

Roguin said that he had won the gold pieces from du Tillet, at the house of a banker, and the clerk unblushingly corroborated this story. Birotteau turned purple, but said no more until the end of the evening, when the guests had left and Ferdinand was about to go to bed. At this point he took the young man into the shop under the pretext of talking business.

" Du Tillet," he began, " three thousand francs are missing from my cash-box, and although I do not wish to throw suspicion upon anyone, the coincidence of the gold pieces is too striking to be passed over in silence. We shan't go to bed before we get to the bottom of the mistake, for of course a mistake it may be. Or else you helped yourself to an advance on your salary."

Du Tillet promptly admitted that he had taken the gold. When Birotteau opened his books he saw at once that the amount had not been debited on the clerk's account.

" I was in a hurry, and meant to tell Popinot to make a note of it," said Ferdinand.

" I see," Birotteau answered.

He insisted that the two of them stay up and go over the accounts, although he knew that the operation was pointless. At a certain point he slipped three thousand-franc notes into the drawer of the cash-box, then pretended to be over-powered by drowsiness. Not long after, Ferdinand woke him up and declared with great joy that he had found the error. And the next day Birotteau scolded his wife and Popinot for their carelessness.

Two weeks later, Ferdinand left the perfumery with the announced intention of entering a broker's office and in his new position he talked about Madame Birotteau in such a way as to make it appear that jealousy was at the bottom of his previous dismissal. A few months later, he came to the perfumer to ask him to guarantee a loan of twenty thousand francs with which he proposed to embark upon an enterprise that would make his fortune. Reading in Birotteau's face a certain astonishment at this piece of sheer effrontery, du Tillet scowled heavily and asked if César had lost confidence in him. Matifat and two other business acquaintances, who were present at the scene, noticed the perfumer's conscious effort to restrain his temper. Perhaps, he thought, du Tillet had gone back to being an honest man. He might have robbed the cash-box only in order to satisfy a capricious mistress or pay a gambling debt, and to shame him now, in front of other people, might induce him not to repent but to commit other crimes. And so, in order to give the fellow a chance, Birotteau signed his note and declared himself happy to repay him for his faithful service. Blood mounted to his cheeks as he told this kindly lie, and du Tillet not only was unable to look him in the face but probably conceived at this very moment the kind of enduring hatred that the angels of darkness bear against the angels of light.

However, upon this and other occasions, du Tillet successfully walked the tightrope of financial speculation and put on a show of wealth before it was actually in his hands. He acquired a gig and joined the circle of those who mix business and pleasure and conduct their most important dealings in the lounge of the Opéra. Thanks to Madame Roguin, whom he had met while he was in Birotteau's employ, he gained entrance to the company of bankers and financiers and embarked upon a period of genuine affluence, with the Nucingens, the Keller brothers and others of their sort for his friends. No one knew the source of the large sums of money which he manipulated, but his wealth was generally attributed to honest ability and intelligence.

Meanwhile the Bourbon Restoration had boosted Birotteau's stock and in the whirlwind of political events he quite forgot his misadventure with Ferdinand du Tillet. The wound he had received at Saint-Roch and his devotion to the Royalist cause, although he had not actively served it in the intervening years, stood him in good stead, and he was granted favors for the very reason that he did not solicit them. Only for a brief time in 1815, during the famous Hundred Days, did he become unpopular among the Liberals of his section of the city, for businessmen who had previously all been desirous of maintaining the law and order propitious to their affairs then began to embrace varying political opinions. Napoleon stripped him of his rank in the National Guard, but he rewon it, after the second Restoration, with Royalist acclaim and when there was a shake-up in the municipal government, the prefect wished to make him Mayor of his district. Because of his wife's counsels of moderation, Birotteau accepted no more than a deputy's post and recommended for the honor he was so modestly refusing Flamet de La Billardière, with whom he had become acquainted in the days when the Queen of Roses was a meeting-place for Royalist conspirators. For this he won the new Mayor's lasting friendship. He and his wife were invited to every reception given by the Mayor, and Madame Birotteau found herself involved in the charitable enterprises of ladies of high degree. Naturally enough, when there was a question of conferring decorations on certain city officials, La Billardière spoke up for César Birotteau, on the grounds of his old wound and his established reputation. So it was that the Minister of the Interior, who was anxious to wipe out the memory of Napoleon and to win artists, scientists and businessmen over to the monarchy, listed Birotteau for the Legion of Honor. This new distinction, added to the renown he already enjoyed in his district, was quite enough to widen the scope of his ideas and ambitions, especially inasmuch as everything to which he had so far put his hand had succeeded. The Mayor's announcement of the forthcoming decoration was what finally decided him to embark upon the projects which he had just outlined to his wife, with the aim of raising himself above the station of perfumer and entering high society.

César was now forty years old. The work he did in the factory had given him a few premature wrinkles and touched with silver his luxuriant hair, which bore a shiny circle all around the crown from the pressure of his hat. His forehead, where the hair grew in such a way as to come down in five distinct points, bore witness to the essential simplicity of his character. There was nothing fearsome about his bushy eyebrows, for the clear look in his blue eyes matched the honesty of his forehead. His uneven nose and wide nostrils lent him a simple, gaping air. He had full lips and a large chin, and the square cut of his ruddy face, together with the distribution of the wrinkles, gave it the mingled craftiness and innocence of a peasant's. The thickness of his limbs, the size of his feet and the powerful build of his body also revealed him as a country boy who had come to Paris. His

big, hairy hands, the huge joints of his wrinkled fingers and
his wide, square fingernails alone would have borne witness
to his rustic origin. He habitually wore the benevolent smile
of a merchant welcoming a customer into his shop, only
in his case the smile was not put on for commercial purposes
but reflected his inner gentleness and contentment. His
caution was limited to business hours and his craftiness
dropped from him as soon as he left the Stock Exchange
or closed his account books. A certain amount of suspicion
seemed to him, like printed bill forms, to be essential to
the mechanics of selling. There was a comical assurance
written all over him, a mixture of fatuousness and geniality,
which set him apart from the ordinary middle-class Parisian.
Without this touch of confidence and self-esteem he would
have been altogether too impressive, whereas in fact, he won
his way to the hearts of his fellow-men by the slight ridiculousness there was about him. While talking he usually kept his
hands crossed behind his back, and when he fancied he had
said something witty or complimentary he rose up twice in
succession on his toes and then fell heavily back on his heels
by way of underlining. At the most heated point of a discussion he would suddenly turn around and then wheel
back again with equal suddenness upon his adversary. He
never interrupted, and this courtesy often worked against
him, for his interlocutors monopolized the conversation and
he could not get a word in edgewise. His long business
experience had endowed him with certain habits that might
have been termed fixations. If a note he held fell due and
was not paid, he sent it to a collector, and unless capital,
interest and cost were promptly settled, he gave his lawyer
instructions to pursue the debtor all the way into bankruptcy.
When this point was reached, however, he would drop the
suit, absent himself from subsequent creditors' meetings
and hold on to his note. This system, and his implacable
contempt for failures, came to him straight from Monsieur
Ragon. His predecessor had come to the conclusion that

because of the amount of time wasted in lawsuits, it was better to accept a settlement out of court, no matter how modest, than to resort to wasteful legal proceedings. " If the fellow is essentially honest and gets on his feet again, he'll surely pay you back," Monsieur Ragon always said. " If he's truly penniless and miserable, what's the use of making him still more unhappy? And if he's just a cheat, you'll never get anything out of him. Your reputation for severity will discourage your debtors from trying to come to terms with you, and if they pay anyone, they will pay you and pay you in full."

César was always on the dot for his appointments, and punctually ten minutes after he had come he went away, with the result that the people with whom he had business relations were as meticulous as he was. He had adopted a style of dress which went both with his character and his physiognomy. For nothing in the world would he have given up his white muslin ties, whose ends, embroidered by his wife or daughter, hung down under his chin. He also wore blue trousers, ·black silk stockings and shoes whose bows were constantly coming untied. His white piqué vest was buttoned all the way down over his somewhat protruding stomach, while his overly capacious olive-green coat and wide-brimmed hat gave him something of a Quaker air. When he put on formal dress for one of his Sunday evening receptions, he wore silk knee-breeches, shoes with gold buckles and his customary vest, which on such occasions was open at the top so as to display his shirt ruffle. His maroon-colored suit had long tails and until 1819 he had two watch chains, although he only wore them together on special occasions.

Such then was the worthy César Birotteau. The fate that presided over his birth had denied him any superior judgment of life and politics, and there was little chance of his raising himself above the intellectual level of his class. His opinions had all been handed on to him ready-made, and he applied them quite uncritically. He was unenlightened but good, far from spiritual but deeply religious and possessed of a pure heart, in which burned a single beacon light. For his desire to better himself and whatever education he had managed to scrape together were alike inspired by the affection he bore his wife and daughter.

As for Madame Birotteau, who was then thirty-seven years old, she looked so much like the Venus de Milo that when the Duke de Rivière sent this statue to Paris all her acquaintances were struck by the resemblance. Within the space of a few months grief was to tinge her dazzling white skin with yellow and darken the bluish circles around her sparkling green eyes, till she took on the look of an aging Madonna. But there was always the same gentle, direct look in her saddened eyes, and she maintained both her good looks and her dignified bearing. At César's famous ball, her beauty made its spectacular final appearance.

Every life has its crowning point, a period in which there is a balance of forces and effort produces the maximum results. This noon of life is common not only among human beings, but among nations, ideas, businesses and institutions of every kind, which like noble races and dynasties all have their rise and fall. Whence comes the invariability with which this rule of growth and decline applies to every living thing here below? For death itself, in time of plague, has its variations of speed, its alternate moments of respite and recrudescence. Our globe itself may be no more than a rocket slightly longer-lived than the rest. The study of history, so rich in examples of grandeur and decay, should teach man to stop when he is at the apex of his powers, but great conquerors, actors, writers and beautiful women are all heedless of its warning. And César Birotteau, who had reason to consider his fortune made, mistook this moment of suspension as time for a new setting-forth. He did not know, nor have princes and principalities told us, the reason for these reversals, of which history transmits so many examples both royal and commercial. Perhaps we need new pyramids to remind us of an axiom appropriate to nations and individuals alike: *When the result obtained is no longer proportionate to the effort expended, then the process of disintegration has already begun.* But such monuments do exist, in all the ancient stones and traditions that speak to us of the past and immortalize Fate's unalterable capriciousness. For with one hand Fate sweeps away our dreams and proves that the greatest events can be accounted for by a whim: Troy and Napoleon are, when you come down to it, only poems. And this story aspires to be the hitherto untold epic of the middle class, whose vicissitudes have long been considered beneath any notice despite their obvious pervasiveness. We have here the drama not of a single man, but of a whole multitude of sorrows.

# III

Cᴇ́sᴀʀ ᴡᴇɴᴛ ᴛᴏ sʟᴇᴇᴘ ᴡɪᴛʜ ᴛʜᴇ ꜰᴇᴀʀ ᴛʜᴀᴛ ᴛʜᴇ ɴᴇxᴛ ᴅᴀʏ his wife would raise more and more cogent objections to his project, and so he resolved to get up early and settle everything. Soon after dawn he slipped out of bed, leaving his wife asleep, dressed and went down to the shop, where he arrived just as his boy, Raguet, was opening the shutters. While he waited for his clerks, Birotteau observed how the boy carried out the work which he had once done himself. In spite of the cold, the weather was fine.

" Popinot," he said, when this young man appeared, " call Monsieur Célestin to come down and watch the shop, put on your hat and come with me. We're going to have a talk in the Tuileries gardens."

Popinot was the exact opposite of du Tillet, and indeed it seemed as if he had been sent to Birotteau through the offices of some sort of an undersecretary to Divine Providence. He plays such an important role in our story that we must stop here to describe him.

Madame Ragon was born a Popinot, and the younger of her two brothers was an assistant judge in one of the district courts of the Seine. The older brother had gone into the wool business and lost all his money in it before he died, leaving his already motherless only son to the care of the childless judge. Madame Ragon had given her nephew a job in the perfumery, hoping that he might eventually be Birotteau's successor. Anselme Popinot was short and had a club foot (a defect which he shared with Lord Byron, Sir Walter Scott and Monsieur de Talleyrand, whose names I mention to reassure anyone who may feel discouraged by

such an infirmity).  He had the pink, freckled skin common
among persons with red hair, but his lofty forehead, agate-
colored eyes, shapely mouth, modest grace and the shyness
inspired by his handicap aroused a feeling of protectiveness
in all those who knew him.  Popinot, or young Popinot,
as he was called, came from a devout family whose virtues
were intelligent and whose lives were modest and marked
by an abundance of good deeds.  He had been brought up
by his uncle, the judge, and possessed all the best qualities
of youth; he was well-behaved and affectionate, shy but
ardent, meek as a lamb but a hard worker, sober, faithful,
and in short endowed with all the merits of an early
Christian.

Now, at the mention of a talk in the Tuileries gardens,
Popinot's first thought was of his future in the business and
of Césarine, the "queen of roses" in person, with whom
he had fallen in love the day he entered the shop, two months
before du Tillet.  On his way upstairs to call Célestin, the
chief clerk, he had to stop halfway in order to quiet his
wildly beating heart.  A few minutes later he and his employer were walking silently away.  Anselme was just twenty-
one years old, the age at which Birotteau had married, and
for this reason the young man could see nothing in the way
of his marrying Césarine.  It was true that her beauty and
her father's wealth were considerable obstacles; but love
feeds upon hope, and the further it is from realization the
more fervently it is believed in, so that the distance between
Anselme and his beloved only increased his ardor.  Happy
youth, who, in an age where everything was being leveled
and everyone wore the same hat, could imagine there was
such a distance between a perfumer's daughter and the
descendant of an old Parisian family!  In spite of all his
doubts he was fortunate, for he dined every day with Césarine.  To his conduct of the shop's business he brought a
tireless zeal which overcame everything disagreeable, and
because all that he did was for Césarine's sake, he was never

weary. In a youth of his age, love cannot but express itself in devotion. "He'll make his way and turn into a real businessman," César said to Madame Ragon, praising her nephew's work in the factory, his rapid grasp of technicalities and the energy he displayed when there was a shipment to get out and he went around with his sleeves rolled up, nailing down more boxes than all the other workers put together.

Where Césarine was concerned, the avowed feelings and intentions of Alexandre Crottat, Roguin's chief clerk and son of a wealthy Brie landowner, stood in the orphaned Popinot's way. And yet these were not the greatest difficulties with which he had to cope. Popinot had bottled up within him a sorrowful fact which seemed to make the gulf between him and his beloved unbridgeable. The Ragons' fortune, on which he could have counted, was in jeopardy; indeed he was contributing (with grateful joy) to their support. Even so, he had confidence in his success, having read a lurking tenderness in the apparent disdainful looks Césarine cast him. Now he walked along beside his employer, silent and inwardly trembling, in a state of mind natural under the circumstances to any very young man.

"Popinot," said Birotteau, "is your aunt in good health?"

"Yes, sir."

"For some time now she has seemed to me preoccupied. Is anything wrong? Don't be mysterious with me, my boy, for I am practically a member of the family; after all, I've known your uncle for twenty-five years. I came to him straight from the country, with hobnail boots on my feet. Although the place I came from was called Les Trésorières, my only fortune was a twenty-franc gold piece given me by my godmother, the Marquise d'Uxelles, a cousin of the Duke and Duchess de Lenoncourt, who are among our customers today. I have never ceased to pray for her and her family and I make gifts of all our products to Madame de Mortsauf, her niece, in Touraine. One member of the

family or another is always sending me customers, for
instance Monsieur de Vandenesse, who orders twelve hundred francs' worth of our stuff a year. Now gratitude comes
more often from the head than from the heart, but let me
tell you that my affection for you has no ulterior motive
behind it."

" Sir, if you allow me to say so, your hobnail boots have
carried you far !"

" Hobnail boots alone wouldn't have done it, my boy.
It took honesty and good behavior. And then I have never
loved any other woman but my wife. And love is a wonderful
' carrier,' to borrow a term I heard Monsieur de Villèle use
yesterday in court."

" Oh, love! . . ." exclaimed Popinot. " Sir, is it possible . . ."

" Look, here comes old man Roguin across the Place
Louis XV at eight o'clock in the morning !" Birotteau interrupted, forgetting young Popinot, and the hair oil which
he had intended to be the subject of their conversation.

Mindful of his wife's suspicions, he veered away from the
Tuileries and went to meet the notary. Anselme followed
his employer at a distance, puzzled by his sudden interest
in something so unimportant, but encouraged by what had
just been said about hobnail boots, a twenty-franc gold piece
and love.

Roguin was a big, rough-faced fellow with a high forehead,
and black hair ; his boldness when young had raised him from
the estate of a clerk to that of a notary. At this moment
of his life, however, a keen eye could detect the strain and
weariness brought on by the pursuit of pleasure. When a
man stoops to the gutter, he is fairly certain of getting mud
on him, and so it was that Roguin's ruddy complexion and
the pattern of the wrinkles on his face had something vulgar
about them. His skin did not have the healthy transparency
indicative of moderate habits, its blemishes betrayed the
revolt of his body against the life he subjected it to. His nose

was turned up and twisted in such a way as to stimulate its natural secretions and produce an affliction which a certain queen of France believed common to the whole masculine sex, simply because she had never got close enough to any man except her royal husband to know better. In order to conceal this condition, Roguin resorted to frequent pinches of snuff, succeeding only in producing exactly the opposite effect to that which he intended.

Is there not a large measure of hypocrisy in the literary mode of describing men in what may be deceptive terms of outward appearance and failing to reveal the role which disease plays in their life story? The relation of cause and effect between physical ailments and the moral ravages which follow upon them has too long been neglected by painters of the social scene. Madame Birotteau had put her finger on the secret trouble of the Roguin household.

Beginning on her wedding night, the notary's bride, only daughter of a wealthy banker, had conceived a violent dislike for her husband and wished to demand an immediate divorce. Roguin was so unwilling to part with her five-hundred-thousand-franc dowry (not to mention the additional riches she could hope to inherit) that he persuaded her to maintain their marriage, promising her complete freedom and accepting all the consequences of such an arrangement. Finding herself mistress of the situation, she soon treated him as a courtesan might treat an elderly lover. This was too much for Roguin to endure, and like many Parisian husbands, he set up another life for himself outside. For a time he was content with a series of little women who did not ask too much of him, but for the last three years he had been in the grip of one of those implacable passions which are apt to take hold of a man between fifty and sixty years old. The woman concerned was a truly magnificent creature, known in the world of prostitution (from which she came and in which she was eventually and notoriously to die) as *la belle Hollandaise*. One of Roguin's clients had brought her to

Paris from Bruges, and when in 1815 political events forced his sudden departure he left her to his notary. Roguin had bought and elaborately furnished a house for her on the Champs-Élysées and gradually let himself be inveigled into one expense after another.

The somber expression of Roguin's face, which he banished at the sight of his client Birotteau, was due to a mysterious complex of events involving the newly made fortune of Ferdinand du Tillet. The focus of du Tillet's ambitions had shifted when, at the first Sunday gathering at Birotteau's house, he had observed the state of affairs between the Roguins. Originally he aspired not to seduce Constance but to obtain the hand of Césarine as a reward for restraining his supposed passion for her mother, but he gave up this plan without the slightest reluctance when he discovered that Birotteau was not as wealthy as he had supposed. He proceeded to dig into the private life of Roguin, win his trust and make the acquaintance of his mistress. He soon learned the actual status of her relationship with Roguin and the fact that she was threatening to leave him if he curtailed her extravagance. *La belle Hollandaise* was the sort of woman who does not care in the least where money comes from; she would just as soon have taken it from a man who had murdered his own father. She had no thought for the morrow; the impending afternoon was her idea of the future and the first of the next month represented eternity, even when she had bills to pay. Du Tillet was delighted to have a hold over Roguin and he began by bringing *la belle Hollandaise*'s demands down from fifty to thirty thousand francs a year, a service which the aging lover did not soon forget.

One evening, after a supper accompanied by copious wine, Roguin spoke freely of his financial condition. His real estate holdings being all tied up in mortgages, he had dipped into his clients' deposits and taken from them more than he could possibly repay. When the rest of what he held in

trust was gone, he was prepared to put a bullet through
his brain in order to win, if not exoneration, at least sympathy.
In his drunkenness du Tillet had an intuitive flash of how
to make a fortune; he reassured Roguin and cemented their
friendship by making him fire his gun into the air. " A man
of your ability shouldn't do things halfway," he commented,
and he went on to advise him to invest an additional large
sum of money either on the Stock Exchange or in one of the
thousand and one speculative ventures so common in those
days. In case he was successful the two of them would set
up a bank and make an income off their depositors' money.
And if he failed, then Roguin would do better to flee abroad
than to kill himself, and he could be sure that his devoted
du Tillet would be faithful to him to the last penny. This
proposition was like a rope thrown out to a drowning man,
and Roguin did not realize that the rope was being drawn
around his neck.

Now that he knew Roguin's secret, du Tillet proceeded
to use it to gain power not only over him, but over his wife
and mistress as well. After he had informed Madame Roguin
of the disaster, of which she had no inkling before, she was
quick to accept his good offices. At this point the young man
felt sure enough of his future to have few regrets over leaving
Birotteau's employ. He persuaded *la belle Hollandaise* to
gamble with a certain sum in order to stave off the necessity
of a return to prostitution. As for Madame Roguin, she
did not hesitate to entrust what capital she could put together
to a man in whom her husband had such confidence. And
indeed the notary himself had already given du Tillet a
hundred thousand francs. Soon du Tillet was able, through
his concern for the wife's financial interests, to work his
way into her heart and to inspire her with a violent passion.
His three associates naturally proposed giving him a share
of their gains, but this was not enough to suit him and while
investing their money on the Stock Exchange he was so bold
as to reach an understanding with a competitor who made

up his supposed losses, for he gambled both on his clients'
behalf and on his own. As soon as he had fifty thousand
francs in hand he was certain of making a fortune. With
the keen insight he had into the national situation, he played
a bearish game during the battle of France and a bullish one
from the very beginning of the Bourbon restoration. Two
months after Louis XVIII's accession to the throne, Madame
Roguin had two hundred thousand francs and du Tillet
three hundred thousand. The notary, who looked upon this
young man as no less than an angel, had put his affairs in
good order.

Only *la belle Hollandaise* continued to throw away her
money; she had fallen into the hands of a bloodsucker
called Maxime de Trailles, formerly a page to Napoleon.
One of the things that du Tillet had nosed out was this girl's
real name, Sarah Gobseck. He was struck by the identity
of this name with that of a money-lender, well known to the
prodigal sons of the day, and paid him a visit in order to
find out how much credit he would extend to a relative.
The old man was flinty-hearted where his great-niece was
concerned but took an interest in du Tillet, who claimed
to be her banker and to have available money. In fact, the
usurer and the Norman got on very well and entered at once
into dealings together, for Gobseck needed an alert young
man to keep an eye on a small business operation abroad.

An auditor attached to the Council of State, who had
been taken unprepared by the return of the Bourbons,
wanted to reinstate himself by going to Germany and buying
up titles to the debts contracted by the royal family during
the period of exile, and since his purpose was wholly political, he offered the financial profit to anyone who would
furnish him with the necessary funds. Gobseck was willing
to advance the money only bit by bit and after on-the-spot
examination by his representative of every credit. He and
his kind are influenced by guarantees and not by personal
feelings; when a man is not useful to them they turn to him

a cold shoulder and they are accommodating only when it is to their interest to be so. Now, through Palma, a banker of the Faubourg Poissonnière, du Tillet knew something of the importance of the firm of Werbrust & Gigonnet, discount brokers to the business houses of the Rue Saint-Denis and the Rue Saint-Martin. He offered a cash guarantee, giving them an interest in the project on the condition that the money he deposited be invested in the firm's business. Thus he acquired some backing. Then he went with the auditor, Monsieur Clément Chardin des Lupeaulx, on a trip to Germany which lasted through the Hundred Days and brought him back at the start of the second Restoration, with increased prospects of making a fortune even if the fortune was not yet in his pocket. He had involved himself in the private projects of some of the cleverest financiers of Paris and won the friendship of the auditor whom he had been sent to watch over, which gave him knowledge of the inside workings of the whole political machine. Du Tillet was quick to grasp the essentials of any state of affairs and his trip to Germany was a liberal education.

Upon his return to Paris he found Madame Roguin still faithful to him and her notary husband no less eagerly awaiting his arrival, because *la belle Hollandaise* had ruined him again. Du Tillet questioned her, and failing to find an expenditure large enough to account for the sums that had disappeared, came upon the secret of her passion for Maxime de Trailles, who was then at the beginning of a career of gambling and vice which was to make him into one of those corrupt hangers-on indispensable to any self-respecting government. At this point du Tillet understood old Gobseck's indifference toward his great-niece Sarah. And in his capacity of banker (for he had officially set himself up as such) he advised Roguin to recoup his losses by persuading some of his most prosperous clients to enter into a piece of business which would give him the use of their money. After various operations profitable only to du Tillet and Madame Roguin, the notary felt the noose of bankruptcy tightening around his neck and found himself at the mercy of his supposed best friend.

It was at this point that du Tillet thought up the affair of the land near the Madeleine. Of course the hundred thousand francs which Birotteau had deposited with Roguin until he could decide how to invest them were handed over to du Tillet, who was intent upon ruining his former employer and had advised Roguin to victimize not strangers but rather his closest friends. "A friend will always remain within certain limits, even when he is angry," was the way he put it. Few people today know how little the value was in those times of land around the Madeleine. But a certain premium was required in order to persuade the owners to sell. Du Tillet wanted to be able to reap the profits without suffering the loss entailed in a long-term speculation, or in other words to kill the business, take over the corpse and revive it at his convenience. On such occasions, the Gobsecks, Palmas, Werbrusts and Gigonnets were all ready to lend one another a hand, but du Tillet was not intimate enough with them to enlist their aid and moreover he wanted to conceal his game and get the gain out of it without discredit. For this reason, he had to have one of those creatures known in business parlance as a front or dummy and he proceeded to trespass upon the divine rights by creating such a man. Out of a penniless former traveling salesman, without any abilities other than those of talking at great length about nothing, of playing a role without giving away what lay behind it, of keeping a secret and risking dishonor for pay, he created Claparon, the head of a fictitious banking establishment. Charles Claparon was to be thrown to the wolves if du Tillet's plans missed fire, and he knew it. But because he was pacing the boulevards with only two francs in his pocket, the meeting with his old Stock Exchange acquaintance, du Tillet, seemed to him a stroke of luck and he was more than willing to sell his future in exchange for a possible small profit. On the basis of an old friendship, gratitude for future favors and a chance to tie the loose ends of a wasted life together, Claparon was willing to say yes to anything. And once he had sold his honor, he saw that du Tillet was cautious in his use of it and acquired a doglike devotion to him. An ugly dog he was, but a faithful one. In the present affair, as we have seen, Claparon was to represent half the buyers and Birotteau the other. The notes which Claparon was to receive from Birotteau would be called in, nominally by one of du Tillet's usurer friends, and having lost the money held by Roguin, the perfumer would be forced into bankruptcy. The receivers would do what du Tillet told them, and since he would hold under other names the lots of both the perfumer and his creditor, he would arrange for the land to be sold at auction and buy it up for half the price. Roguin had subscribed to this plan in the hope of obtaining a good part of the profits, but naturally du Tillet meant to keep the lion's share for himself. Because Roguin was in no position to bring suit against his sinister mentor, he had later to be content with the bones the latter threw to him in his Swiss exile, where he at least found pretty girls at bargain rates.

Circumstances, and not the invention of a tragic author, were responsible for du Tillet's vile scheme. Hate unaccompanied by a desire for vengeance is like seed falling on stony ground. Whereas the revenge which du Tillet had vowed to wreak upon Birotteau was the result of an impulse so natural that to deny it we should have to ignore the struggle between the angels of darkness and the angels of light. Du Tillet could not very well murder the man who had caught him at a petty theft, but he could abase him and drag him down to the point where he could never bear witness against him. For a long time this impulse had been sprouting at the bottom of his heart without coming to fruition. In Paris, even the most vindictive cannot make deep-laid plans; life is too hurried and interrupted. But if its perpetual motion does not allow for premeditation, it does nevertheless serve the hidden purposes of a man clever enough to grasp an opportunity when he sees it. When Roguin confided in du Tillet, the latter saw a chance to destroy his enemy, César, and in this case his vision served him well. Meanwhile, although Roguin was about to break off with the woman he had idolized for so long, he was savoring the dregs of the cup and spending all his nights on the Champs-Élysées, whence he returned early in the morning. Madame Birotteau had guessed right on this score. And when a man has made up his mind to play the role which du Tillet had assigned to Roguin, he is bound to acquire an actor's talent, the eyes of a lynx and a clair-voyant's penetration. So it was, now, that Roguin caught sight of Birotteau long before the latter saw him, and he advanced with outstretched hand.

" I've just come from drawing up a will for a man in the public eye who has no more than a week to live," he said with a wholly natural air, " but I've been treated like a country doctor. They called for me in a cab, but they've sent me home on foot."

These words dispelled a cloud of distrust which the lawyer had seen darken the perfumer's brow. He did not mention the real estate deal, for he was lying in wait to deliver the final blow.

" Wills one day and marriage contracts another," said Birotteau. " There's life for you! and incidentally, when are we to be married to la Madeleine ? What do you say, old man ?"

With which he tapped the notary's stomach, for when two men are together, no matter how conventional their daily life may be, they feel they must talk in a ribald vein.

" It's now or never," the notary replied with a diplomatic air. " We're afraid the thing's getting talked about. Two of my wealthiest clients have already asked to be let in on it.

It's gotten to be a question of take it or leave it. I'll draw up the papers this noon and give you until one o'clock to sign. That's all. I'm on the way now to read the draft that young Crottat was supposed to draw up for me last night."

"Well, as far as I'm concerned, the deal is closed; you have my word for it," said Birotteau, running after the notary and tapping his hand. "Take the hundred thousand francs of my daughter's dowry."

"Very well," said Roguin as he walked away.

During the few seconds that it took Birotteau to rejoin Popinot, a flash of heat swept through his abdomen, his diaphragm contracted and his ears rang.

"What's wrong, sir?" the clerk asked, seeing him so pale.

"My boy, I've just spoken the single word necessary to close a big piece of business. And under such circumstances, no man can control his emotions. As a matter of fact, you're not out of it, yourself. And I brought you here, where no one can overhear us, for a serious talk. Your aunt is hard up and uneasy. Tell me how she lost her money."

"Sir, my aunt and uncle invested their money with Monsieur de Nucingen, and they were forced to accept stock in the Wortschin mines, which as yet pays no dividends. At their age it's not easy to live on nothing but hope."

"And what do they live on, then?"

"They give me the pleasure of accepting my wages."

"Good boy, Anselme," said Birotteau, with a tear in the corner of one eye. "You deserve the esteem in which I hold you. And you're going to be rewarded for the diligence with which you have attended to my business."

In saying these words the perfumer increased his stature in his own eyes as well as in those of his clerk, for he infused them with an ingenuous middle-class fervor which expressed his illusory self-assurance.

"What?" exclaimed Popinot. "Have you guessed that I am in love with. . .?"

" In love with whom?"

" With Mademoiselle Césarine."

" My boy, you are very bold," said Birotteau. " Keep your secret to yourself, and I promise to forget it. Although I can't exactly blame you. If I were in your shoes . . . What the devil? I'd feel the same way. She's such a beauty!"

" Oh, sir!" said the clerk, his shirt damp with perspiration.

" My boy, it's not a matter that can be settled in a day. Césarine is her own mistress, and then her mother has plans for her. . . . Dry your tears, take hold of yourself and let's not mention the subject again. Of course I shouldn't be ashamed to have you for a son-in-law; after all, you're the nephew of Judge Popinot and of the Ragons, and you have as much right to make your way in the world as the next man. Only there are a lot of *ifs* and *buts* to be overcome. How did you manage to introduce this subject into a business conversation? Come, sit down on this bench and let the lover give way to the faithful employee. Popinot, are you a man of courage? Are you brave enough to battle against something stronger than yourself, to fight at close quarters? . . ."

" Yes, sir."

" To carry on a long and dangerous struggle?"

" Yes, what is it all about?"

" It's about killing off Macassar Oil!" said Birotteau, drawing himself up like one of Plutarch's heros. " Let us not deceive ourselves: the enemy is strongly encamped and formidable in every way. Macassar Oil has been promoted with great skill. The idea is a clever one and the square bottle is highly original. I'm thinking of putting out our product in bottles of a triangular shape, in very thin glass, with a wicker cover, so as to give them a pleasingly mysterious air."

" That would make the bottling expensive," said Popinot. " Don't you think we should spend as little money as possible in order to give a heavy discount to the dealers?"

" That's sound reasoning, my boy. Macassar Oil is going

to defend itself, and in spite of its specious composition, it has a most attractive name. It is marked as a foreign import, while we shall be unfashionably native-born. Popinot, do you really feel strong enough to squeeze out Macassar? The place to strike the first blow is in the export field. It seems that Macassar is really the name of a place in the Indies and it makes more sense to send a French-made product to the Indians than one of their own. So there you can enlist some adventurous salesmen. Then we must fight it out in other foreign countries and finally in our own. And don't forget that Macassar Oil has been well publicized. There is no use denying the fact that it's in the public eye."

" I'll kill it off for you!" said Popinot, with a gleam in his own.

"And how do you propose to do it?" asked Birotteau. " You have all the ardor of a very young man. Wait till you hear all I have to say."

Popinot stood at attention like a soldier before a marshal reviewing his troops.

" Popinot, I've invented an oil that stimulates the growth of hair and revives its color. I'm convinced it will be as successful as my cream and my lotion, but I don't intend to exploit it myself because I'm retiring from business. And that, my boy, is where you come in. You shall be the one to launch my Comagene Oil! (The name comes from *coma*, the Latin word for ' hair,' so I have been told by Monsieur Alibert, the King's physician. Racine introduced a ' King of Comagene ' into his tragedy, *Bérénice*, as the queen's lover. She was celebrated for her beautiful hair, and it was doubtless to flatter her that he gave this name to his kingdom. How clever these great geniuses are! They work out even the least detail.)"

Popinot kept a straight face as he listened to his farfetched parenthetical explanation, which was given for his particular benefit, inasmuch as he was a well-educated young man.

"Anselme, I've picked you to set up a superior drug establishment on the Rue des Lombards. I'll be your silent partner and give you the money with which to make a start. And after Comagene Oil, we'll turn our hand to an essence of vanilla and a distillation of mint. We shall revolutionize the drug business, the two of us, by selling concentrated products instead of diluted ones. Now, my ambitious friend, are you happy?"

Anselme was so moved that he could not reply, but his tear-filled eyes gave eloquent testimony to his feelings. He took this offer to be inspired by fatherly generosity and to convey the message: "Make yourself rich and renowned in order to deserve Césarine!"

"Sir," he managed to say at last, "I *will* succeed, you have my word for it."

"Good boy!" said Birotteau. "That's just the spirit I had when I was your age, and I'd have given the same answer. You'll be a rich man even if you don't win my daughter! Come now, what's the matter?"

"Leave me the hope that one success will go with the other!"

"I can't prevent you from hoping," said Birotteau, stirred by the tone of the young man's voice.

"Well, sir, can I start today to look for a suitable location?"

"Yes, my boy. Tomorrow we'll shut ourselves up together in the factory. And before looking on the Rue des Lombards, you must go by Livingston's to see if my hydraulic press is in working order. Meanwhile, at dinner-time this evening we'll consult the illustrious Monsieur Vauquelin, who has been working just lately on the composition of human hair, its texture and the source of its coloring matter. That's the whole thing in a nut-shell, Popinot. I'll let you in on my secret, and all you'll have to do is to exploit it intelligently. Before going to Livingston's, drop in on Pieri Bénard. Let me tell you, Monsieur

Vauquelin's disinterestedness is one of the great sorrows of my life. I can't persuade him to accept a penny. Fortunately I heard from Chiffreville that he wants an engraving of Raphael's Sistine Madonna, by a certain Muller, and after two years of correspondence with Germany, Bénard has turned up a fine example on rice-paper, at a price of fifteen hundred francs. Our benefactor must find it in his front hall when he takes us to the door this evening, for meanwhile it must be framed, and that's another errand for you. In this way he will have a remembrance of my wife and myself. As for our gratitude, he has that already, since for the last sixteen years we've prayed for him every day. He is always fresh in our memory, but scientists are notoriously absent-minded; they forget their wives, friends and even their debtors. Whereas we less learned souls can console ourselves at being warmhearted. Those gentlemen of the Institute are all brains, and you'll never see a one of them in church. Monsieur Vauquelin divides his time between his books and his laboratory, but I like to imagine that he thinks about God while he analyzes His creations. . . . Anyhow, here is our agreement: I shall put up the money and entrust you with my secret; then we shall halve the eventual profits without the need of any legal paper. When success comes our way we shall have no trouble settling our accounts. Run along now, my boy. I have business to attend to. And look here, Popinot, three weeks from now I'm giving a great ball. Get yourself a proper new suit and come as a budding young businessman. . . ."

Popinot was so touched by this last kindness that he seized César's big hand and kissed it. The intimacy of the advice encouraged his deepest aspirations, and a young man in love is capable of moving mountains.

"Poor boy!" Birotteau said to himself, watching Popinot run through the Tuileries. "If only Césarine loved him! But with his limp and that copper-colored hair, I don't believe she could. . . . Young girls are quite unpredictable.

And then her mother wants to see her marry into the legal
profession. Alexandre Crottat will make her a rich woman,
and money makes almost anything bearable, while the lack
of it corrodes even the greatest happiness. Well, I've long
since resolved to let my daughter do what she likes, no
matter how crazy it may be."

# IV

BIROTTEAU'S NEXT-DOOR NEIGHBOR WAS A LITTLE UMBRELLA-maker called Cayron, from the southern province of Langue-doc, who could not seem to make a go of his business and had more than once been helped by Birotteau. He asked nothing better than to confine himself to his small shop and turn over his two second-floor rooms to the perfumer, thereby lowering the amount of rent he had to pay.

"Good morning, neighbor," said Birotteau as he walked in upon him. "My wife has consented to the enlargement of our premises. If you like, we can go at eleven o'clock to Monsieur Molineux."

"My dear Monsieur Birotteau," said the umbrella-maker, "I've not asked you for anything in return, but you know that money means everything to a man in business."

"What the devil!" said Birotteau. "I'm not rolling in wealth to that degree. And I don't know yet whether the architect will find the plan feasible. I'm waiting to see him now. He told me the first thing was to see whether our floors are on the same level. Then Monsieur Molineux must agree to the knocking down of the wall, that is if we really have the wall in common. After that, I must turn my staircase around so that one can walk straight through from one house to the other. It's an expensive proposition, and I can't afford to go bankrupt over it."

"Oh, Monsieur Birotteau, the day when *you* go bankrupt, the sun will fall from the sky."

Birotteau swayed back and forth on his heels, stroking his chin, while the umbrella-maker added:

"All I ask is that you take over some of these notes. . . ."

And he handed him a bundle of sixteen papers, adding up to five thousand francs.

" Short-term loans, eh ?" said the perfumer. " Two and three months . . ."

" I'll pay you six per cent," said the umbrella-maker humbly.

" Do you take me for a usurer ?" Birotteau asked with a note of reproach in his voice.

" I went to du Tillet, who used to be your clerk, and he wouldn't touch them with a ten-foot pole. Perhaps he was trying to see how much he could get out of me."

" I don't know any of these signatures," objected the perfumer.

" Oh, we have funny names in my trade. They're all pedlars."

" Well, I can't take care of them all, but I'll see to the ones that are first to fall due."

" Don't force me to go to bloodsuckers for a four-month loan of a thousand francs, which will eat up all my earnings ! Surely, sir, you can take them all. I have so little to do with banks that I enjoy no credit. That's the trouble with us little fellows."

" All right, then, I'll take them. Célestin will do the figuring. Meanwhile you must be ready by eleven. . . . Here comes Monsieur Grindot, my architect," he added, catching sight of the young man with whom he had made an appointment at Monsieur de La Billardière's house the previous day. " Unlike most men of talent, you take the pains to be punctual," Birotteau went on, addressing the architect, with all his best airs and graces. " And if punctuality is the courtesy of kings, as our own sovereign, who is a wit as well as a statesman, has put it, I may add that it is the fortune of businessmen. Yes, time is money, especially for an artist. And architecture, so I am told, is the sum of all the arts together. Let's not go through the shop. . . ." And he pointed to the false courtyard gate in front of his house.

Monsieur Grindot had won the *grand prix* in architecture four years before, and he had just come back from spending three of them at the government's expense in Rome. In Italy, he had dreamed of art, but now that he was back in Paris he dreamed of making a fortune. Only a government has sufficient funds to enable an architect to make his reputation, and a young prize-winner cannot but hope to follow in the footsteps of a Percier or a Fontaine. Grindot, originally a Liberal, was now a Royalist looking for government patronage, causing his fellows to call him an intriguer. Birotteau, deputy to the Mayor, and future owner of land around the Madeleine, which would eventually be developed into a handsome business or residential section, was a man whom it was to his advantage to cultivate. And so Grindot set aside the hope of immediate gains for the prospect of greater things to come, and listened patiently to the repetitious plans and projects of one of a class of men whom every artist despises and derides, nodding his head in approval of the perfumer's somewhat vague ideas. When Birotteau had finished his explanation, the young architect tried to cast it into more definite form.

" You have three windows on the street and one which is to all practical purposes lost because it is blocked by the landing of the stair. You can add to these four the two which are on the same level in the house next door, by turning the staircase around in such a way as to be able to walk from one apartment straight into the other, on the street side."

" That is it exactly," said the astonished perfumer.

" In order to carry out your plan you must light the new stairs from above and arrange a concierge's lodge underneath the socle."

" The socle ?"

" Yes, the part which will support . . ."

" I understand."

" As for your apartment, just leave me a free hand to

rearrange and decorate it. I want to be dignified. . . ."

" ' Dignified!' That's it exactly!"

" How much time can you allow for these alterations ?"

" Three weeks."

" And how much are you prepared to pay the workmen ?"

" That will depend on the total cost."

" An architect can estimate the cost of a new house to a penny," the young man told him, " but I must warn you that remodeling and repairs don't lend themselves to such accurate calculations. Perhaps a week from now I can give you an approximate idea. Meanwhile you can have perfect confidence in me. You shall have a most attractive stairway, lighted from above, with a pretty little entrance hall giving onto the street, and under the socle . . . ."

" You're always talking about the socle . . . ."

" Don't worry; I shall find room for a concierge's lodge. And the layout of your apartment will be planned with loving care. Yes, sir, it's art I care about, not money! Besides that, I need to get myself before the public, and I figure the best way to do it is to get the most out of our jobbers and work for dazzling effects at the smallest possible expense."

" Well, young fellow," said Birotteau with a protective air, " with ideas like those you're bound to succeed."

" You can deal directly with the masons, carpenters, painters and locksmiths of your choice," Grindot continued, " and I'll limit myself to checking up on their work. My fee is two thousand francs, and I can assure you you're getting your money's worth. Call your workers together for tomorrow and leave me in charge."

" Can't you give me some vague notion of the cost ?" Birotteau asked him.

" Ten to twelve thousand francs," Grindot replied. " That's not counting the furniture, which I'm sure you will want to replace. And give me the address of the man from whom you buy wallpaper. I must match my colors with his."

"I am served by Monsieur Braschon on the Rue Saint-Antoine," said Birotteau with a ducal air.

The architect jotted down the address in one of those little notebooks that are usually the gift of a pretty woman.

"Very well, sir," said Birotteau. "I shall give you free rein. Only you must wait until I have arranged to take over the two rooms next door and obtained permission to knock down the partition."

"Leave word for me this evening," said the architect. "I must sit up all night over my drawing-board. Not that I wouldn't rather work for a businessman than for the King of Prussia. Meanwhile, I might as well measure the doors and windows . . ."

"Of course, it's understood that everything will be ready by the day I have set you."

"It will have to be ready, that's all there is to it," the architect assented. "The men may have to work all night and we shall employ special procedures for drying the paint, but it shall be done. Just remember not to let the contractors cheat you. Insist on their quoting you a price and then get them to put it in writing."

"Paris is the only city in the world where one can wave a magic wand in just this way," said Birotteau, making a gesture Oriental enough to have come straight out of the Thousand and One Nights. "Sir, you must do me the honor of coming to my ball. I see that artists are not unanimous in their scorn of the businessman and I can promise you the acquaintance of some persons of note. There will be Monsieur Vauquelin of the Institute, Monsieur de La Billardière, Count de Fontaine, Count de Granville of the royal court, Judge Popinot of the district court, two referees from the commercial court, Monsieur Lebas, the draper, and Monsieur Camusot, along with his father-in-law, Monsieur Cardot, and perhaps even the Duke de Lenoncourt, First Gentleman of the King's Bedchamber . . . You see, I am gathering a few friends together to celebrate the end of the occupation and my being awarded the Legion of Honor." (Here Grindot made a peculiar motion of his hand.) "If I am worthy of this royal decoration, I suppose it is because I have sat on the commercial court and fought for the Bourbons on the steps of Saint-Roch, where I was wounded by Napoleon. . . ."

At this point, Constance emerged from her daughter's room, where she had just put on a morning dress, and her first glance cut short her husband's high-flown verbiage and caused him to couch his achievements in more modest terms.

"Well, my dear," he said to her, "here is Monsieur *de* Grindot, a young man of both distinction and talent, whom Monsieur de La Billardière recommended as architect for this little remodeling job of ours."

The perfumer hid his face from his wife's view and as he pronounced the word "little" he held his forefinger up to his lips and shot the architect a significant look, which the latter was quick to understand.

"With your kind permission, my dear, he's just about to take a few measurements," Birotteau concluded, slipping out onto the street.

"Is it going to be an expensive job?" Constance asked the architect.

"Oh no, only six thousand francs, roughly speaking."

"Roughly speaking!" exclaimed Madame Birotteau. "Please, don't start work without drawing up a definite contract. I know how things go in the building trades. Before you know it, six thousand francs have become twenty. We can't afford to be extravagant. I beg you, sir, although of course my husband is master of the house and free to do as he pleases, to give him time to think it over."

"Madame, your husband has asked me to complete the job in three weeks, and if there is any delay you will have had all your expense for nothing."

"There are expenses and expenses," Constance remarked.

"Well, just look at it from my point of view. Do you

think it's any fun for an architect who wants to erect public monuments to stoop to a job of redecoration? I'm doing it only on account of Monsieur de La Billardière, and if my figures frighten you . . ." And he made a motion of withdrawal.

"Very well," said Constance, retreating into her room, where she fell upon Césarine's shoulder. "Your father's intent upon ruining himself," she told her. "He's hired an architect with a mustache and beard, who talks of nothing but monuments. Before we know it, he'll have torn down the house and built a second Louvre on its place. César is always quick to get into trouble. He told me about this mad idea last night and today it's already in the process of execution."

"Come, come, Mother; let Father have his own way. He's always been lucky so far," said Césarine, kissing her mother and then sitting down at the piano in order to show the architect that a perfumer's daughter is no stranger to the fine arts.

When the architect came into the room, he stopped short in surprise at her beauty. Césarine, in her morning disarray, was as fresh and pink as only an eighteen-year-old girl can be, slender, blonde, blue-eyed and possessed of a resilience, very rare in Parisian women, which gave life to her delicate skin and shaded with a painter's favorite color the network of blue veins quivering under its surface. Although Césarine had grown up in the damp air of a Parisian shop, where there was seldom a ray of sun, her temperate habits had given her all the advantages enjoyed by the Trasteverine girls of Rome. Her thick hair, which grew on her head in the same way as her father's, was lifted up so as to display her graceful neck and then trained to fall in the kind of curls cultivated by every shop-girl whose wish to attract notice inspires her to follow English styles. But Césarine's beauty was not that of an English lady or a French duchess; it was that of a Rubens portrait. She had her father's turned-up nose, spiritualized by the refinement of its modeling, the essentially French nose immortalized by Largillière. The vitality of her skin, like that of a strong material, had something essentially virginal about it. She had her mother's high forehead, brightened by the absence of worry, and her liquid blue eyes were filled with tender grace. Although happiness deprived her of the pensive air which most painters consider indispensable, the vague physical melancholy natural to a young girl who has never been away from her mother to some extent idealized her features. In spite of the delicate lines of her figure, she was powerfully built. Her feet spoke of her father's peasant origin and her red hands betrayed a middle-class life. Sooner or later she was bound to put on weight. From her observation of various fashionable ladies she had acquired a taste for good clothes and a way of handling her body and head which made her seem almost worldly and quite turned the heads of all the young men who worked in her father's shop. Popinot, as we have seen, had sworn that he would have no other wife. Only this blonde girl, so sensitive that it seemed as if a single look would pierce her and a single harsh word cause her to cry, could give him any feeling of masculine superiority. So great was her charm that she inspired men with love before they had time to find out whether she had enough solid qualities to make it lasting. But then, what advantage was there in the possession of what the Parisians call " wit " to a girl born of a class where happiness is founded on virtue and common sense. Spiritually, Césarine was a copy of her mother, improved by the superfluities of education. She loved music, made charcoal drawings of Raphael's Madonna alla Sedia and read the works of Racine, Fénelon, Bernardin de Saint-Pierre and Mesdames Cottin and Riccoboni. She never appeared with her mother in the shop except for a few moments before dinner, or to replace her on rare occasions. Her father and mother, like all self-made parents, sought to raise her above them; they spoiled her in such a way as to make it almost certain that she would be an ungrateful child. But fortunately Césarine had all the middle-class virtues and did not take advantage of the situation.

Madame Birotteau followed the architect restlessly around, watching him with something like terror and pointing out to her daughter the esoteric movements of his rod and tape-measure. The rod had something of the magic of a conjurer's wand about it, and she only wished that the rooms were smaller and the walls less high. But of course she did not dare question him about the object of his incantations.

" Don't worry, Madame," he said, as if guessing her thoughts, " I shan't take anything away."

Césarine could not help laughing.

" Sir," said Constance prayerfully, without catching on to the joke, " above all things be saving, and we shall show you how grateful we can be. . . ."

Meanwhile, before going to see Monsieur Molineux, the owner of the house next door, César went to fetch from Roguin the paper Alexandre Crottat had drawn up, the signing of which would make legal the transfer of the lease. On his way out, Birotteau caught a glimpse of du Tillet standing near a window of Roguin's office. Although the fellow's affair with the notary's wife made his presence there fairly natural, for a moment Birotteau lost his self-confidence and began to wonder. Du Tillet had an animated air, as if he were engaged in discussion. Could that mean that he was involved in the real-estate deal ? Some such suspicion flitted through Birotteau's mind, but when he looked again, he saw Madame Roguin as well, and this dispelled it. " What if Constance were right?" he asked himself. " No . . . why should I listen to a woman's silly ideas ? Anyhow, I'll speak to my uncle about it later this morning." For it was only a short distance from the Cour Batave, where he was to see Monsieur Molineux, to the Rue des Bourdonnais. A more watchful man, one who had come across crooked dealing in the course of his career, would have been saved, but Birotteau's antecedents and beginnings, and above all his inability to reason inductively and connect cause with effect, conspired to destroy him. He found the umbrella-maker all dressed up and waiting for him and was about to start out in his company to call on his landlord, when Virginie, his cook, seized him by the arm.

" Sir," she said, " Madame doesn't want you to go . . ."

" Come, come," grumbled Birotteau, " more silly female ideas!"

" . . . before you drink your coffee."

" Of course!" Birotteau exclaimed. And he added, turning to Cayron, " Neighbor, I have so much on my mind that I completely forget about my stomach. Go on ahead, will you, and I'll meet you at Monsieur Molineux's door, that is, unless you want to save time by beginning to tell him the purpose of our visit."

Monsieur Molineux was a grotesque little man, as native to Paris as certain lichens are to Iceland. And this comparison is the more accurate inasmuch as he belonged to a hybrid species, a mixed animal-and-vegetable kingdom to which a satirist like Mercier might attribute those crypto-grams that flower and die on, in or under the scaling walls of the unhealthy houses where they by preference grow. At first sight, this mushroom-like individual, with a tubular blue cap for a crown, greenish trousers for a stem and gnarled slippered feet, like roots growing above ground, had a flat, whitish and not particularly poisonous air. This queer creature was the picture of a stockholder, an absolute believer in the printed word, whose final opinion on any subject was: " I saw it in the paper!" An average man, devoted to law and order, yet constantly in revolt against the powers that be, submissive over all large things and ferocious over small, as hard-shelled as a process-server where his rights were concerned, yet capable of feeding birds and stray cats, and stopping in the middle of writing out a receipt for rent to chirp at a canary, as mistrustful as a jailer, yet apt to sink his money in a piece of bad business and then try to make up for its loss by avarice of the lowest degree. This essential evil of this hybrid was apparent only through use; its venom came out only when it was steeped in some commercial enterprise, where Molineux's interests were in conflict with those of his fellow-men.

Like all Parisians, Molineux had an urge to dominate others; he aspired to the power which every one of us, even a janitor, can exercise over at least one victim, a wife, child, tenant, clerk, dog or monkey, upon whom he can avenge the slights he has received from some higher sphere. This tedious little old man had neither wife, child, nephew nor niece and he could not tyrannize his charwoman for the simple reason that she gave him a wide berth and did no more than she was paid to do. For lack of any other scapegoat, then, he had assiduously studied the laws related to rent; he knew all the subtleties of Parisian regulations concerned with abutting and adjoining, easements, taxes, sidewalk-sweeping, hangings for Corpus Christi Day, rain-water pipes, encroachments on the public right of way, health menaces, etc. All his brains and energy revolved around keeping his landlord's establishment on a war footing, and what had started as an amusement turned into a mania. It was his pleasure to protect the citizenry against violations of the law, but since such cases were rare, his passion revolved mainly about his own tenants. A tenant was to him an enemy, an inferior, a subject and serf. He claimed a right to his tenant's respect and regarded him as ill-mannered if he failed to greet him in the hall. He wrote out his rent receipts by hand and handed them out at noon of the day on which rents were due. If a tenant's payment was late he received a prompt summons, followed by seizure with costs and all the machinery of the law was automatically set into motion. Molineux never granted the slightest delay; there was a callus in his heart where the word " rent " was inscribed.

" I'll lend you money if you need it," he said to a tenant whom he believed to be in a solid financial position, " but, first of all, pay me my rent. The slightest delay leads to a loss of interest for which the law allows us no indemnity."

After a thorough study of all the possible aberrations of his tenants, who like successive dynasties, constantly threatened to overthrow the institutions of their predecessors, he had set up a charter which he religiously observed. He made no repairs and insisted that everything was in perfect order. The chimneys did not smoke, the stairs and ceilings were clean, the floors did not creak, the paint was fresh, no lock was more than three years old, the windowpanes were all in place and he never noticed any cracks in the tiles until a tenant was moving out. When he showed a place to a new tenant, he was always flanked by a painter and a locksmith, who could vouch for everything's good condition. The lessee was, of course, free to make any improvements he might desire, but if he really carried them out, then Molineux plotted day and night how to evict him so as to have a newly decorated apartment at his disposal. No violation of leases was beyond him. Because he was contentious by nature, he started out by writing his tenants agreeable letters, but behind his epistolary style was the soul of a Shylock lurking under his dully polite manner. He always started by collecting six months' rent in advance, to be credited to the final months of the lease's duration. Then there came a whole series of conditions. He had to see if the tenant installed furniture of sufficient value to guarantee the rent. And he promptly reported every new tenant to the police, for he did not want to cope with the slightest irregularity. Once a lease was drawn up, he studied it for a whole week, fearful, as he said, of the lawyer's et ceteras.

Outside his function as a landlord, Molineux seemed to be a kindly enough person. He played boston, without complaining of his partner's lack of support, laughed at the same things that others of his class found laughable, and talked of the same matters of interest: the villainy of bakers who gave short weight of bread; the corruption of the police; the heroism of the seventeen left-wing deputies to Parliament. He read *Father Meslier's Common Sense*, went to Mass simply because he could not choose between deism and Christianity, but did not partake of the sacraments, and protested against the excessive claims of the clergy. On this score, as an indefatigable letter-writer, he addressed letters to the papers, which were never honored with publication or even so much as a reply. And finally, like any solid citizen, he burned a Yule log in his fireplace, pulled the Magi out of an Epiphany cake, played April Fool tricks, strolled on the boulevards in good weather, watched the skating and when there were firework displays went early to the Place Louis XV with a piece of bread in his pocket, in order to have a " front-row seat."

The Cour Batave, where the old man lived, was the result of one of those strange building projects which are no sooner undertaken than they become inexplicable altogether. This cloistral limestone construction, with its inside passageways and arcades and a fountain at the far end, a thirsty fountain, which opened its lion's mouth to ask for water rather than to give it, was probably intended to endow the Saint-Denis section with a Palais-Royal of its own. The place was unhealthily low, and dwarfed by tall buildings on all four sides. It came alive only during the day, because it was the central point of the dark passageways which join the Saint-Martin section to the central markets by means of the famous Rue Quincampoix. At night no spot in all of Paris was more deserted; the catacombs of commerce, one might have called it. The place contained several industrial sewers, very few Batavians and a large number of grocers. The few portions of the building which were made into apartments had no outlook except over the courtyard, and for this reason the rents were very low. Monsieur Molineux lived in one corner, on the sixth floor, chiefly for the benefit

of his health, because the air was not good enough to breathe
short of seventy feet above ground. From his windows,
in the gutters outside which (against police regulations) he
grew flowers, he had an enchanting view of the windmills
of Montmartre. His apartment was composed of four
rooms, not including the precious English toilet on the
floor above, to which, legitimately, he alone had the keys,
since he had set it up. Upon entering the apartment one
could see the man's avarice at a glance. In the hall there
were only six wicker chairs, a porcelain stove and four
engravings, obviously bought at auctions, upon the bottle-
green walls; in the dining-room two sideboards, two bird-
cages, a table covered with oilcloth, a barometer, a French
window opening onto his hanging gardens and some mahogany chairs stuffed with horse-hair. The drawing-room
had old green silk curtains and a sofa which combined
white-painted wood and Utrecht velvet, while the bedroom
was furnished in the style of Louis XV, with pieces worn
out by long use, on which a woman in a white dress could
not have sat down without getting very dirty. On the mantelpiece stood a clock with two columns, one on either side
of a dial which served as a pedestal for Pallas Athena
brandishing a spear, while the floor was littered with dishes
full of scraps for cats, over which the careless passer-by
was likely to trip. Above a rosewood dresser hung a pastel
portrait of Molineux in his youth. Then some books, tables
littered with ugly green folders, a family of stuffed canaries,
and a bed which would have been too hard for even a
Carmelite nun.

César Birotteau was delighted by the good manners of
Molineux, who was wearing a gray flannel dressing-gown,
and was intent upon a bowl of milk which he was heating
on one kerosene burner and the pot of coffee which was
boiling on another. In order not to disturb him, the
umbrella-maker had run to open the door when Birotteau
rang. Molineux had great reverence for the mayors of Paris

and their deputies, whom he lumped under the title of
" city officials." So now, when Birotteau entered the room,
he remained standing and doffed his cap until the great man
had sat down.

" Ah, sir, if I had known that I was to have a city official
in any house of mine, I should have made of a point of
coming to see you, even if I am your landlord . . . or about
to be. . . ."

· Birotteau made a gesture indicating that he should put
his cap back on his head, but the other protested:

" I shan't cover my head until you cover yours. And I
pray you don't catch cold; this room is a bit chilly, because
I can't afford to . . . God bless you, sir !"

For Birotteau sneezed while he was looking for his papers,
which he proceeded to present with a remark, intended to
hasten their approval, to the effect that he had had them
drawn up by Roguin, the notary.

" I don't for a minute dispute the ability of Monsieur
Roguin, since I know the reputation he enjoys in his profession. But I have my own little ways, my peculiarities,
if you like, and I prefer to handle my own affairs. My
lawyer. . . ."

" But this is such a simple matter," said Birotteau, who
was accustomed to dealing in direct and businesslike terms.

" Simple, do you call it ?" Molineux exclaimed. " Where
leases are concerned, nothing is simple. You're not a landlord, sir, and for that you may be thankful. If you knew the
ingratitude of tenants and the precautions with which we
must hedge ourselves. . . ."

And he proceeded for the next quarter of an hour to tell
how Monsieur Gendrin, an artist, had eluded the watchfulness
of his concierge on the Rue Saint-Honoré. Monsieur Gendrin
had commited infamies worthy of a Marat; he had made
obscene drawings which would have led to his arrest, had
it not been for the well-known corruption of the police.
The immoral fellow brought women home with him at

night and cluttered up the stairway with them so that decent people couldn't get by. Of course, such behavior was hardly surprising in a man who made caricatures attacking the government. But what really lay back of all these misdeeds was the fact that he wouldn't pay up his rent on the fifteenth of the month. Landlord and tenant were about to go to court, for in spite of his failure to pay, the latter claimed a right to occupy the premises. Molineux had even received anonymous letters, threatening to kill him one night in the meanderings of the Cour Batave.

"It came to the point," he concluded, "where I went to the prefect of police (to whom by the way I suggested some modifications of the existing law), and he authorized me to carry two pistols for my protection."

And the old man went to fetch and display them.

"Here they are, sir!" he said proudly.

"But you have nothing like that to fear on my score," said Birotteau, giving Cayron a smile which mirrored his compassion for their interlocutor. Unfortunately, Molineux caught this expression on his face and found it unworthy of a city official. In any other man, he would have forgiven it, but in Birotteau it was unforgivable.

"Of course, sir," he said, "a deputy to the Mayor, an honorable businessman like yourself, would not stoop to anything so mean and low. But you are asking the owner of your house, Count de Granville, to consent to your tearing down a partition and putting it up again at the expiration of your lease. And rents are very low. They're bound to go up, I say. The Place Vendôme is increasing in value, and there's going to be building on the Rue de Castiglione!"

"Come now," said the astonished Birotteau. "What will you have? I know business well enough to realize that all your objections can be overriden by money. How much is it to be?"

"No more than what is right, sir. How much longer does your lease run?"

"Seven years," Birotteau told him.

"Seven years from now, who knows what may be the value of that second floor?" Molineux insisted. "There is no telling what someone will pay for a couple of furnished rooms in your part of town. Perhaps as much as two hundred francs a month. I'll have to make out a new lease. I must ask fifteen hundred francs a year, if I am to deduct anything from the rent paid by our friend here, Monsieur Cayron." He shot the umbrella-maker an unpleasant look and continued: "The place is yours on a seven-year lease. Of course the alterations are at your expense, and you must bring me evidence of Count de Granville's relinquishment of rights and formal approval. You will be fully responsible for everything connected with the alterations and pay me five hundred francs in advance for the eventual rebuilding of the wall between the two apartments. Since we can't know who'll still be alive seven years from now, I don't want to face the necessity of trying to collect from a total stranger."

"Your terms seem fair enough to me," Birotteau assented.

"Then you must pay me an advance of seven hundred and fifty francs here and now, which will be applied against the last six months of your rent. That will be noted in the lease. Oh, I'm willing to accept some small notes for this guarantee, marked 'value received in rent' and payable at any date you choose to specify. I handle my business with dispatch, you know. Then we shall make it a condition that you wall up the door giving onto my staircase and give up all rights to its use. But never fear, I shan't ask you to restore that to its original condition. That will be covered by the five hundred francs allowed for rebuilding the wall. You will always find me perfectly fair and square."

"We ordinary businessmen aren't anywhere near so punctilious," Birotteau observed. "We'd never get anywhere if we went in for so many formalities."

"Oh, business is quite a different matter, especially perfumery, where everything is so easygoing," the old man said with a sharp smile. " But where renting is concerned. . . . For instance, I have a tenant on the Rue Montorgueil . . ."

" Come now," said Birotteau, " I don't want to delay your breakfast. Here are the papers. Correct them as you will, for I agree to everything you have said. Let us come to a verbal agreement today and sign them tomorrow, for that is when my architect must start working."

" There's the last installment of Monsieur Cayron's rent, which he shouldn't have to pay. We'll add that to the notes for the seven-hundred-and-fifty-franc advance, so that the lease can run from one first of January to another. That way, things will be more regular."

" Very well."

" Then you must pay the concierge a penny for every pound of goods that enters the house."

" Come, come," said Birotteau. " You're depriving me of an entrance on the stairs. It hardly seems right . . ."

" Sir, you are a tenant," said Molineux peremptorily, getting up on his high horse. " That means you must pay a tax for doors and windows and shoulder your share of the upkeep. If everything is perfectly clear between us, there'll be no trouble. You're enlarging your quarters considerably, and I presume it means that your business prospers."

" Yes," said Birotteau, " but that's not the reason. I'm gathering a few friends together to celebrate the liberation and also my Legion of Honor cross . . ."

" Ah!" said Molineux. " An honor which you have richly deserved."

" Well," said Birotteau, " perhaps so, since I sat on the commercial court and fought for the Bourbons on the steps of Saint-Roch, on the Thirteenth of Vendémiaire, with a wound from Napoleon to show for it. My claim . . ."

" Your claim is just as valid as that of the soldiers of our brave army. The ribbon is red because it is dipped in blood."

These words, taken from the radical *Constitutionnel*, practically compelled Birotteau to ask the little old man to his party, and the latter outdid himself in expressions of gratitude and felt almost ready to forgive the disdain of which he had been the object a few minutes before. He escorted his new tenant out onto the landing and overwhelmed him with attentions. When Birotteau and Cayron were in the middle of the Cour Batave, the perfumer said mockingly to his companion:

" I didn't know such people existed," restraining himself from inserting the adjective " stupid."

" Ah well, sir, not everyone can aspire to your talents," Cayron answered, and because comparing himself with Molineux was bound to be flattering, Birotteau smiled agreeably at the umbrella-maker's reply and took leave of him with regal politeness.

" Here I am near the markets," he said to himself; " I might as well see about the nuts for my oil."

After an hour of search, Birotteau was directed to the familiar Rue des Lombards, center for nuts used in confectionery, where his friends the Matifats told him that dried nuts could be obtained only from a certain Madame Angélique Madou on the Rue Perrin-Casselin, who specialized in filberts from Provence and white Alpine almonds.

The Rue Perrin-Casselin is a narrow winding street in the labyrinth enclosed by the river on one side and the Rue Saint-Denis, the Rue de la Ferronnerie and the Rue de la Monnaie on the others. These entrails of the city swarm with goods of the most heterogeneous kinds, alternately odoriferous and dainty: herrings and muslins, honeys and silks, butter and delicate tulle, the staples of an infinite number of small businesses, of which the city takes no more notice than does a man of what may be brewing in his pancreas. The leech of this district was a certain Bidault, known as Gigonnet, a money-lender who lived on the Rue Grenétat. On one street, former stables served as storage spaces for tons of oil, on another were lofts stacked high with thousands of pairs of cotton stockings. In other words, here were the warehouses of all the goods sold on the retail market.

Madame Madou, a former fishwife who had got into the dried-fruit and nut business because of an affair with the late owner of her present shop, which had long been a subject of local gossip, was possessed of a rather masculine but provocative beauty which was now beginning to be engulfed in fat. She occupied the ground floor of a run-down yellow house, held together by iron cross-bars at each floor. Her late lover had got rid of all his competitors and secured a monopoly of the business, and in spite of a few gaps in her education she was able to carry on the work without any particular effort, going from one to another of her storehouses and successfully battling the insects that threatened to invade them. Because she was unable either to read or write, she had no counters or cash-books and responded to letters by shaking her fist, as if they were personal insults. For the rest, she was a good-natured woman, with ruddy cheeks and a scarf tied over her bonnet, and her deep, loud voice won the respect of the draymen who brought her wares, whose arrival she usually celebrated by offering them a glass of white wine. She had no trouble with the farmers who sent her their produce, because she paid them in cold cash and went to see them during the good weather. Birotteau found her now among a large number of bags filled with nuts of various descriptions.

"Good morning, my dear lady," he began breezily.

"Your *dear* lady, did you say?" she retorted. "Do you know me so well? Have we kept an all-night watch together?"

"I am a manufacturer of perfumery and deputy to the Mayor of this district as well. And as both a customer and a public official, I have the right to demand a more courteous reply."

"When I'm ready to get married, I'll say so," she said sharply. "But for the present I'm not hanging about the city hall and have no favors to ask there. As for my business, it is good enough to allow me to speak to my customers as I choose. If they don't like me, they can get themselves properly cheated somewhere else."

"There's what it is to have a monopoly!" Birotteau said to himself.

"Poly, did you say?" she said, more mildly. "That's my godson's name. Has he got himself into mischief? Did you come to me on his account?"

"No, I came as an ordinary customer."

"Then how did you happen to mention my godson, when I've never seen you before?"

"If you always carry on like this, you must sell your nuts very cheaply," said Birotteau, thereupon proceeding to tell her his name and occupation.

"Oh, are you the famous Birotteau who has such a beautiful wife? And what quantity of hazelnuts would you be wanting?"

"Six thousand pounds."

"That's my entire stock," she said in tones like those of a hoarse flute. "You don't do things halfway, do you? You must be a very busy man. This is big business, and your name will be inscribed in the heart of the woman I love most in all the world."

"That is?"

"Your dear Madame Madou."

"And what is your price, then?"

"For you, my good man, twenty-five francs a hundred pounds, that is if you take the whole lot of them."

"Twenty-five francs? That means fifteen hundred altogether. And I may buy hundreds of thousands a year."

"Look at the quality of these," she said, plunging her red arms into a bag of filberts. "Hand-picked by barefoot boys! Grocers sell them at a franc a pound and a quarter of that weight is made up of rotten ones. Do you expect me to lose money just to please you? You're a good fellow, but I'm not yet that daffy. If you're really taking such a large quantity, we might make it twenty francs instead of twenty-five. Of course, I can't refuse a deputy to the Mayor! That would bring bad luck to all the bridal couples! Just put your hand in there and get the feel of the nuts for yourself. Fifty of them to a pound. And they're whole; there are no worms in them!"

" Then send me eight thousand pounds, and I'll owe you two thousand francs, payable within the next ninety days. Deliver them to my factory on the Rue du Faubourg du Temple, early tomorrow morning."

" I'll be as prompt as a bride at the altar. Good day to you, sir, and I harbor no bad feelings. But if you don't mind," (she followed him out into the courtyard), " I'd rather take notes payable in forty days. I'm making you a very good price, and I need the cash. Old man Gigonnet may be tenderhearted, but he devours us the way a spider devours a fly."

" Fifty days, then. But we'll weigh the nuts in batches of a hundred pounds, so as to have no short weight. Otherwise, our agreement is off."

" The clever dog!" exclaimed Madame Madou. " No one can put anything over on him. Those creatures on the Rue des Lombards put him wise to that. They're a band of wolves, out to eat up the poor sheep."

The sheep in question was five feet tall and three feet around the waist and looked like a lamppost wrapped in a beltless, sack-like striped cotton gown.

Birotteau walked down the Rue Saint-Honoré with his mind on his campaign against Macassar Oil, the shape of the bottles, the texture of the cork, the wording of the labels and the colors of the posters. And they say business has no poetry in it! Newton himself did not cogitate any more over his famous laws than Birotteau over his Comagene Essence, for he thought of it as an essence or an oil, interchangeably. All sorts of plans swam through his mind, and he mistook this movement in a vacuum for an evidence of talent. Because he was lost in his thoughts he went by the Rue des Bourdonnais and had to retrace his steps in order to pay the projected visit to his uncle.

# V

CLAUDE-JOSEPH PILLERAULT, FORMERLY A HARDWARE DEALER
at the sign of the Golden Bell, had a character that was all
of a piece; his morals, feelings, thoughts and speech were
in perfect harmony. As Madame Birotteau's only living
relative, he had concentrated all his affection upon her and
her daughter. The good man had lost his wife, son and an
adopted child, the son of his cook, and as a result had embraced a sort of Christian stoicism, which lit up his last days
with a brightness at once cold and warm, like that of a
winter sunset. His narrow head and wrinkled face, of
yellowish-brown color, made him look like a somewhat
vulgarized version of Father Time, for business habits had
detracted from the dignity which a painter, sculptor or
clock-maker would have required in a model. He was of
medium height, heavy-set rather than stout, cut out for
hard work and a ripe old age, since he was endowed with a
powerful frame and an even temper, not impervious to
feeling but unruffled, at least on the surface. Although his
immobile expression and calm manner made him appear
undemonstrative, he was sensitive, without exaggeration,
deep down inside. His eyes, with their dark-flecked green
pupils, were bright and clear. His forehead, furrowed and
yellowed by age, was narrow and covered by a mass of
clipped silvery gray hair, and his thin lips bespoke caution
rather than avarice. The integrity of his life, his devotion
to duty and genuine modesty formed something like a halo
around his head and gave him a spiritually healthy air.
For sixty years he had led a sober and laborious life, one
not unlike that of César Birotteau, except that it had not
been crowned by the same success. He was a clerk until

he was thirty years old, and then all his savings went into his business, instead of into the bonds which César had been able to afford at the same age. He had gone through the period of price ceilings, and his goods had been requisitioned. His prudence and reserve, his foresightedness and studious reflection had always been evident in the way he did business. Most of his agreements were verbal ones, and they were invariably respected. Observant, as are most men with meditative inclinations, he let other people do the talking and sized them up from what they revealed of themselves. Very often he turned down what looked like a profitable bit of business and let his competitors take it away from him, with the result that they were very sorry to have done so and admitted that he had a better nose than they for anything the least bit shady. He preferred small but sure profits to ventures which involved a lot of money. He dealt in chimney-pieces, andirons, grills, iron and cast-iron cauldrons, hoes and other farm tools, which did not bring in large profits, considering the effort required to move them around and store them. Many a box had he packed and nailed up, and many a van unloaded. No man had a fortune more nobly and honorably earned than his. He had never overcharged or run after business, and in his last days he could be seen smoking his pipe just outside the door and watching his employees carry on the work. In 1814, when he retired, his savings came to seventy thousand francs, which he invested in government bonds which yielded five thousand francs a year. Besides this, he was owed forty thousand francs, payable without interest in five years, by the clerk to whom he had sold his shop. For the thirty years in which he had run his own business he had had a turnover of a hundred thousand francs a year and net earnings of seven thousand, with half of this sum going into his living expenses. This then, was Pillerault's financial situation. His neighbors did not envy his moderate fortune; they praised his wisdom without understanding it.

At the Café David, on the corner of the Rue Saint-Honoré and the Rue de la Monnaie, a number of retired shopkeepers met for an evening cup of coffee. There, Pillerault's friends had joked a good bit about his adoption of his cook's son, but always within the limits of the respect with which he inspired them, a respect completely unsought on his part, since he was content with the approval of his own conscience. When the unfortunate young man finally died, over two hundred persons walked in his funeral procession. At this time Pillerault attained heroic stature. His grief, contained as a strong man could be expected to contain it, won the sympathy of his neighbors, who called him a " good fellow " in the largest and most ennobling sense of the words. Even after he had retired from business, his long-standing sober habits would not allow him to be idle, and he enlivened his old age with left-wing political convictions. Pillerault belonged to that section of the working class which as a result of the Revolution had been absorbed by the class above it, and his only fault was the obstinacy with which he insisted on consolidating his newly acquired rights. At present, he thought that his economic and political position was threatened by the Jesuits, whose secret power the Liberals were always denouncing, and by the ideas which his favorite paper, the *Constitutionnel*, attributed to Monsieur, the King's elder brother. Pillerault behaved in logical accord with his ideas. His political views were not narrow and did not speak ill of his adversaries, although he was afraid of the influences at work in the royal court and esteemed the republican virtues. He thought that Manuel could not possibly be guilty of excesses, that General Foy was a great man and Courier a good one, that Casimir Périer had no ambitions and Lafayette was a political prophet. In short, he had a large stock of generous illusions.

The tenor of Pillerault's life was even and calm; he frequented his niece, Judge Popinot, the Ragons, the Matifats and Joseph Lebas. Fifteen hundred francs a year were quite sufficient to cover his needs and he spent the rest of his income on good works: presents to his great-niece, Césarine, and four times a year a dinner at Roland's on the Rue du Hasard, followed by a theater party for his friends. In other words, he was the kind of old bachelor upon whom married women can rely for the gratification of their fancies: a picnic in the country or an evening at the opera. For Pillerault took delight in giving pleasure to others, and found his happiness in theirs.

Even after he had sold his shop, he was unwilling to move away from the section of the city to which he was accustomed, and he rented a fifth-floor apartment, consisting of a drawing-room, bedroom and hall, in an old house on the Rue des Bourdonnais. Just as Molineux's strange furnishings betrayed the quirks of a man, so did those of Pillerault reflect his essential simplicity. The entrance hall, with its well-scrubbed, red-tiled floor, had only one window with red-trimmed percale curtains, some mahogany chairs upholstered with sheepskin, and on the olive-green papered walls pictures of the signing of the American Declaration of Independence, Napoleon Bonaparte as First Consul and the Battle of Austerlitz. The drawing-room looked as if a decorator had had a hand in its arrangement, as the old man's only concession to social usage. Here there were a rug and some new pieces: a sideboard topped by a vase of flowers under glass, a round table with a tablecloth and a service of liqueur glasses, a painted screen in front of the fireplace and bronze mantelpiece accessories. The bedroom was as simple as that of a monk or an old soldier, two types of men who appreciate life's essential values. The most striking thing, in view of the fact that Pillerault was such a staunch and stoical republican, was the presence of a crucifix and holy-water basin above the bed. An old charwoman came to take care of the house, but so great was Pillerault's respect for women that he would not let her polish his shoes but gave them out to a boy.

The old man always dressed in the same way, in a dark blue tail-coated suit with a waistcoat of Rouen cotton, a white tie and high shoes, except on holidays, when he wore a coat with metal buttons. He followed the same schedule of getting up, breakfasting, going out, dining and spending the evening every day, and this regularity was the secret of his good health and long life. Among his nephew, the Ragons, the Abbé Loraux and himself there were no political arguments, for they were too good friends to try to proselytize one another. Like Birotteau and the Ragons, Pillerault had great confidence in Roguin, for he thought any accredited notary must be a model of fair dealing. In the business of the land near the Madeleine, he had made a thorough investigation, which justified the assurance with which César had answered his wife's objections.

Now the perfumer walked up the seventy-eight steps leading to the little brown door of his uncle's apartment, thinking in what good form the old man must be to climb them every day. He found Madame Vaillant brushing a coat and trousers on the landing, while their owner, in a quilted gray dressing-gown, sat over his lunch beside the fire, reading the *Constitutionnel*.

" Uncle," César greeted him, " the business is done and all that's left is to sign the papers. If you have any regrets or misgivings, it's not too late to withdraw."

" Why should I withdraw? It's a good proposition, but one that will take time to mature, as is very proper. My fifty thousand francs are in the bank, for only yesterday I received the last five thousand from the sale of the shop. And the Ragons are putting up everything they have."

" Then what will they live off?"

" Don't worry; they'll live, all right."

" I know what you mean by that, Uncle," said Birotteau, pressing the old man's hands with emotion.

" How do things stand now?" Pillerault asked brusquely.

" My share will be three-eighths, and you and the Ragons

one eighth each. I'll give you credit on my books until
there's a decision about the registration of the deeds."

" Good. You must be very rich, my boy, to put up three
hundred thousand francs. I hope you're not taking too much
out of your business. But that's up to you. If you run short,
I can always sell some bonds. But if you take money from
me, you're taking it from your daughter."

" Uncle, you say the most wonderful things in the most
simple way! Those words go straight to my heart."

" General Foy's words went to mine as I was reading
the paper a few minutes ago. Anyhow, things are settled.
The land can't fly away and half of it is ours. We may have
to wait as long as six years, but we'll have a dribble of income
in the meantime. There are contractors that pay rent. We
run only one risk, and that seems impossible. . . . Roguin isn't
going to run away with our money."

" My wife said he might, just yesterday evening. She
was worried."

" Why should he?" Pillerault said, laughing.

" She says he has a runny nose, and like every man that's
at odds with his wife, he chases after. . . ."

Pillerault smiled incredulously, tore a piece of paper out
of a notebook, wrote down a figure and then signed it.

" Here's a draft for a hundred thousand francs, on behalf
of Ragon and myself. Those poor people have sold their
last fifteen shares in the Wortschin mines to that wretch
of a du Tillet. It's painful to see such good folks in trouble.
Such a well-bred, dignified couple, the cream of the middle
class. Their brother, Judge Popinot, doesn't know a thing
about it. They hide everything from him in order not to be
the objects of his charity. People that worked for thirty
years, just the way I did."

" Here's hoping I'm successful with my Comagene Oil!"
Birotteau exclaimed. " Then I'll be twice as happy. Good-
by, Uncle, and be sure to come to dinner on Sunday with
the Ragons, Roguin and Monsieur Claparon. We'll be

signing the papers day after tomorrow, because tomorrow's
Friday and I shouldn't like to start . . ."

" Don't tell me you're superstitious!"

" Uncle, no one can persuade me that the day when men
put the Son of God to death is a lucky one. Isn't the twenty-
first of January a legal holiday?"

" Very well, then, I'll see you on Sunday," said Pillerault,
abruptly closing the conversation.

" If it weren't for his politics, I think there'd be no better
man on earth than my uncle," Birotteau reflected on the
stairs. " Why does he bother about politics, anyhow? He'd
be just as well off without. Well, no one can be perfect. . . ."

" Is it three o'clock already?" he said aloud, as he stepped
into his own house.

" Sir, are you accepting these notes?" asked Célestin,
showing him the papers left by the umbrella-maker.

" Yes, at six per cent, without a commission. . . . My dear,
will you kindly lay out my clothes? I'm going to pay a call
on Monsieur Vauquelin, you know the reason. And don't
forget a white tie."

He gave a few orders to his clerks, and because Popinot
was not among them judged that he too was making himself
ready. In his room he found the Sistine Madonna, framed
according to his orders.

" Pretty, isn't it?" he said to his daughter.

" You must say ' beautiful,' Father, if you don't want
everyone to laugh at your choice of words."

" Now, what do you know about that? A young girl scolding her father! To tell the truth, I like *Hero and Leander*
just as well. The Madonna's all very well in a chapel, but
I'd rather have *Hero and Leander* any day. For one thing,
they gave me ideas about oil . . ."

" I don't follow you, Father."

" Virginie, call a cab," shouted César, after he had finished
shaving and greeted Popinot, who was ready to set out with
him.

The poor fellow was limping self-consciously on account of Césarine's presence, not having yet noticed that as far as she was concerned his infirmity was non-existent. A precious token of love, which only those with some physical affliction can appreciate.

"Sir," he said, "the press will be ready for work to-morrow."

"Well, and what's the matter with you, Popinot?" César asked, seeing a blush on the young man's face.

"It's just the happiness of having found a shop with a back room, kitchen, storage space and other rooms on the floor above, on the Rue des Cinq-Diamants, all for twelve hundred francs a year."

"We must get an eighteen-year lease," said Birotteau. "But let us be off to Monsieur Vauquelin's. We can talk on the way."

And so César and Popinot got into a cab, while the other clerks looked with amazement at their unaccustomed dress and grand manner, altogether unaware of the great things that were in the mind of the proprietor of the Queen of Roses.

"We shall find out about the nuts," Birotteau murmured half to himself.

"The nuts?" asked Popinot.

"I've let you in on my secret, Popinot. I said 'nuts,' and that's the kernel of it. Nut oil is the only kind to have any effect upon human hair, but no other perfumer has thought of it. When I saw the engraving of Hero and Leander, I said to myself: 'If the ancients used so much oil on their hair, they must have had some reason for it? For the ancients really knew what they were doing, no matter what the moderns may say; in fact, I feel just the way Boileau does about them. The next step was nut oil, and I bridged that gap thanks to young Bianchon, the medical student, who is a relative of yours. He told me that at medical school all the students used hazelnut oil to make their mustaches grow. Now all we need is the approval of the famous Monsieur Vauquelin. If he advises us, then we shan't be fooling the public. A while ago I went to a nut dealer to see about our raw material, and now we are on our way to pick the brains of one of the most learned men in the country. There's some sense to the proverb that says: 'Extremes meet.' You see, my boy, business is the meeting-ground of science and vegetable production. Angélique Madou gathers her nuts, Monsieur Vauquelin makes an extract of their oil and we bottle and sell it. The nuts cost five sous a pound, Monsieur Vauquelin multiplies their value a hundredfold and we render a service to humanity. Because men suffer as much as they do from vanity, beauty products are so many good deeds."

The admiring reverence with which Popinot listened to him because he was Césarine's father stimulated Birotteau to further flights of eloquence, and he came out with sentences as naively uncouth as any businessman ever invented.

"Be properly respectful, Anselme," he said, as they drove into Vauquelin's street. "We are about to enter a temple of science. Put the Madonna against a chair in the dining-room. I only hope I don't get my tongue twisted over what I have to say. This man has a positively chemical effect upon me. His voice warms the very pit of my stomach and even causes me a slight indigestion. He is my benefactor, and in a few moments, Anselme, he will be yours as well."

Popinot was so congealed by these words that he began to walk as warily as if he were stepping on eggs and to look diffidently at the walls. Monsieur Vauquelin was in his study when Birotteau was announced. Knowing the perfumer to be a deputy of the Mayor, he received him without delay.

"You haven't forgotten me since you attained greatness, have you?" he said by way of greeting. "As chemist and perfumer, we can always shake hands."

" Sir, there is an abyss between your genius and my simplicity. I owe all of what you call my greatness to you, and I shall not forget it in this world or in the next."

" Oh, well, in the next world we shall all be equal, kings and cobblers alike."

" You mean such kings and cobblers as have led good lives," Birotteau answered.

" Is this your son ?" asked Vauquelin, looking at young Popinot, who was stupefied by the absence of fantastic machines, volatile metals, animated matter and other wonders which he had expected to find in the scientist's study.

" No, sir, but he is a young man to whom I am greatly attached and we have come to ask you to do us a favor worthy of your talent. Here I am, sixteen years after your first kindness to me, come to question you about a matter of which I am as ignorant . . . well, as a perfumer."

" What can it be ?"

" I know that your present interest is the analysis of human hair. And while you study it for the glory of science, I have been working along the same lines from a business point of view."

" My dear sir, how am I to help you ? Do you want to hear about my analysis of human hair ?" (He picked up some papers from his desk.) " I am reading a paper on the subject to the Academy of Science. Human hair is made up of a considerable quantity of mucus, a small amount of white oil, a larger amount of greenish-black oil, iron, a few atoms of manganese oxide, silica, phosphate and carbonate of lime and a large dose of sulphur. The proportion of these elements determines the color of hair. Redheads, for instance, have a larger amount of greenish-black oil."

" Nine elements !" exclaimed Birotteau, while he and Popinot opened their eyes wide in astonishment. " To think that there are oils and metals in human hair ! If I didn't respect you so greatly, I'd never believe it. How extraordinary ! Will God's wonders never cease ?"

" The single hair is produced by a follicular organ, a sort of pocket open at both ends, and attached by one to nerves and blood vessels and by the other to the strand of hair. According to some of my learned colleagues, among them Monsieur de Blainville, the hair is a dead body expelled from this pocket."

" Like perspiration, only solid," said Popinot eagerly, causing Vauquelin to smile and his employer to give him a warning kick in the heel.

" The boy has ideas," Birotteau said deprecatingly. " But tell me, sir, if hair is something dead, then there's no way of reviving it, and that knocks my whole scheme to pieces. People are funny, you know, and you can't possibly tell them that . . ."

" That they are carrying dung-hills around on their heads!" interposed Popinot, trying to make the scientist laugh again.

" Catacombs in the air!" said Vauquelin, keeping up the joke.

" And I've bought the nuts already!" said Birotteau, thinking of his financial liabilities. " But then how does anyone dare sell . . . ?"

" Cheer up," said the smiling Vauquelin. " I see that you're concerned with how to stop hair from graying or falling out altogether. Well, after all my research, here is what I have to say." (Popinot pricked up his ears like a startled rabbit.) " Loss of color, in my opinion, is due to a stoppage in the secretion of coloring matter. Incidentally, that explains why in a cold climate fine animal fur pales in the course of the winter. In other words, alteration of hair is due to changes of surrounding temperature."

" Surrounding, Popinot, did you get that?" Birotteau exclaimed.

" Yes," Vauquelin went on, " to sudden changes from heat to cold and vice versa, or to interior phenomena which produce the same effect. Probably sick headaches and brain disturbances absorb, or disperse or displace the coloring fluid. What goes on in the interior is something for the doctors to study. But when it comes to the exterior, then your cosmetics or beauty products enter the picture."

"You're bringing me back to life now, sir," said Birotteau. "Hazelnut oil is what I had in mind. I know that the ancients used oil on their hair, and the ancients knew a thing or two, I agree with Boileau on that. Why did their athletes oil . . .?"

"Olive oil is just as good," said Vauquelin inattentively. "Any oil can protect the follicle, and thus also the substances which it contains in solution, to use a chemical term, from injury. But you may be right at that. Dupuytren claims that hazelnut oil contains a stimulant of some kind. I'll look into the differences among beechnut, rapeseed, hazelnut, olive and so on."

"So I'm on the right track after all," said Birotteau triumphantly. "And I have come to a great man for help! Macassar is done for! Macassar, in case you don't know, sir, is a preparation sold at an exorbitant price for the purpose of growing hair."

"My dear Monsieur Birotteau, there aren't two ounces of genuine Macassar oil in Europe," Vauquelin answered. "Macassar oil has no effect upon hair, anyway. The Malays pay a high price for it in the belief that it has, without realizing that whale oil would be just as good. No power, either chemical or divine . . ."

"Don't say divine, Monsieur Vauquelin, I beg you!"

"My dear sir, God's first law is consistency, and without that there is no power . . ."

"Well, if you put it that way . . ."

"No power, I say, can raise hair on a bald head, and it's dangerous to dye either white or red hair. But if you recommend the use of oil, you're not telling any lies, and you may even help people that have some hair to keep it."

"Do you think the Academy of Science would give its approval?"

"Oh, you haven't discovered anything new," Vauquelin told him. "Besides, so many charlatans have taken advantage of the Academy's name, that it wouldn't do you much good. In all conscience, I can't say that hazelnut oil will work miracles."

"And what would be the best way to extract it?" asked Birotteau. "By soaking and boiling the nuts or by pressing them?"

"By pressing them between two cold plates. Hot plates would give you more oil, but cold ones are best to maintain the quality." And he continued in a kindly manner: "The oil must be rubbed into the scalp rather than simply applied to the hair, if it is to be effective."

"Keep every word of this in your mind, Popinot," said Birotteau, with his face flushed with enthusiasm. "Here, sir, you have a young man who will remember this as one of the most wonderful days of his life. Of course he already admired you from afar. We talk of you often in my house, for a name that's so much in our hearts can't but come frequently to our lips. My wife and daughter and I all pray for you, as it is proper we should pray for our benefactor."

"I don't deserve so much," said Vauquelin, somewhat embarrassed by the effusiveness of the perfumer's gratitude.

"Tut, tut!" said Birotteau. "You can't stop us from loving you, even if you accept nothing from us. You shed light, like the sun, and those who benefit by it can give you nothing in return."

The scientist smiled and got up, and his two visitors followed his example.

"Look around this study carefully while you are here, Anselme," said Birotteau to his young companion. "Do you mind, sir? I know your time is precious, but he may never see it again."

"And how does business go with you?" Vauquelin asked

him. " Both of us are businessmen in our own ways . . ."

" Well enough, sir," said Birotteau, moving in the direction of the dining-room, with Vauquelin behind him. " But to launch this Comagene Essence will take a lot of money . . ."

" *Essence* and *comagene* are two words that don't go together. Call your product Birotteau Oil. Or if you don't want to display your own name, choose some other. . . . Why, here is the Sistine Madonna! Monsieur Birotteau, do you want me to be angry with you ?"

" Monsieur Vauquelin," said Birotteau, taking the chemist's hands in his, " this Madonna has no value other than that of the effort which I put into tracking it down. I had to scour all Germany to find it on rice-paper. I knew that it attracted you but you had no time to spend looking for it, and so I allowed myself to act as your agent. And so, never mind about the engraving itself, but take into consideration only the pains I took in order to prove my devotion. I only wish you had sent me to the foot of some dangerous precipice, so that I could come back and lay your heart's desire at your feet and say: ' Here it is!' Anyhow, you mustn't refuse me. It is so easy to forget our friends, and I should like you to have a reminder of my wife and daughter, my future son-in-law, whoever he may be, and myself in your possession. Whenever you look at the Madonna, you can say: ' Those good people are thinking of me.' "

" I accept, then," said Vauquelin.

His tone of voice was so kindly that both Birotteau and Popinot had to wipe the tears away from their eyes.

" And now, will you do me one kindness more ?" asked Birotteau.

" What is it ?"

" I have invited a few friends "— he rose up on his heels but without losing his humble air—" to come celebrate the liberation and also my Legion of Honor."

" Ah ?" said Vauquelin in astonishment.

" If I am worthy of this overwhelming tribute, I suppose

it is because I sat on the commercial court and fought for the Bourbons on the steps of Saint-Roch on the Thirteenth of Vendémiaire, with a wound from Napoleon to show for it. Anyhow, my wife is giving a ball three weeks from Sunday. Won't you come? If you will dine with us that evening, I shall feel I have been decorated a second time. Meanwhile, I shall send a note to remind you."

" Very well, I shall be there."

" That's almost more than my heart can bear," Birotteau said to Popinot when they were out on the street together. " To think that he's coming to my house! . . . But I'm afraid I've forgotten a lot of what he said about hair. Do you remember, Popinot?"

" Yes, and even twenty years from now, I shall still keep every word in mind."

" What a great man! What a look he has, and what a keen brain! He read our minds from the very beginning and gave us weapons with which to strike down Macassar Oil! Nothing in the world can make hair grow! You're lying, Macassar! Popinot, we have a fortune within our grasp! Tomorrow morning at seven o'clock sharp we must be at the factory to receive the nuts and press some oil. It's all very well for him to say that all oils are alike, but the public mustn't know it. If our oil didn't contain hazelnuts and a dash of perfume, how could we sell it at three or four francs for four ounces?"

" So you're to be decorated, sir," said Popinot. " What an honor for . . ."

" For the world of business, yes, my boy."

César Birotteau's self-assured and triumphant air did not escape the eyes of his clerks. His departure with Popinot in a carriage had caused them to concoct explanations of the most exaggerated and romantic kind, and now upon his return, they winked at one another. The satisfaction written upon both men's faces and the hopeful look that Anselme shot twice at Césarine confirmed their suspicions and made them feel sure that important events were in the air. In their busy, almost cloistered life, the slightest happening seemed as important as it might have to a prisoner in his cell. The attitude of Madame Birotteau, who responded to her husband's exalted manner with a dubious air, made them sure that something new was afoot, for under ordinary circumstances she would have been happy, especially as the day's receipts were good because some unpaid accounts had been settled.

The dining-room and the kitchen, across the hall from it and lighted by a window on the courtyard, were on the mezzanine floor where César and Constance had originally had their living quarters and were reached by a stairway from the back room of the shop. But the dining-room, where their honeymoon had been spent, now seemed like a small drawing-room. Raguet, a trusted clerk, kept an eye on the shop while the rest of the staff ate their midday meal, but when dessert came around, all the employees went back to their work downstairs, leaving César and his family to finish their dinner alone. This habit had been handed down by the Ragons, who had clung to all the usages that tended to preserve a distance, even greater in the more remote past, between masters and apprentices. After dinner, Césarine or Constance prepared coffee, which Birotteau sipped sitting in an easy chair, near the fire. At this time César habitually told his wife the petty events of the day, what was going on in the factory on the Rue du Faubourg du Temple, the annoyances to which his work had subjected him and all that he had seen if business took him to different parts of the city.

"My dear," he said now, when the clerks had all gone downstairs, "this has been one of the most important days of our life. The nuts are bought, the hydraulic press is ready to function and the affair of the land has been settled. Incidentally, will you keep this for me?" And he handed her the draft from Pillerault. "And the enlargement of our apartment has been decided upon and practically begun. . . .

If you knew what a funny fellow I met in the Cour Batave!"
And he proceeded to tell her about Monsieur Molineux.

" All I can see," said Constance, interrupting him in the
middle of a long tirade, " is that you're two hundred thousand francs in debt."

" Quite right, my dear," said Birotteau, feigning humility.
" How in heaven's name shall we ever pay it back? For of
course we must count on nothing from the land near the
Madeleine, which is destined to form one of the most beautiful sections of the city some day."

" Yes, some day, César!"

" Too bad!" he said, going on with the joke. " My three-
eighths share won't be worth a million francs until six years
have gone by." Here he made a frightened gesture. " But
we can always pay off our debts with this," and out of his
pocket he took a hazelnut he had kept there ever since he
had picked it up that morning at Madame Madou's.

Holding the nut between two fingers, he proceeded to
show it to his wife and daughter. Constance made no
comment, but Césarine's curiosity was aroused, and while
she was serving her father's coffee she said:

" Are you joking, Father?"

Birotteau, as well as some of the clerks, had noticed an
exchange of looks between Popinot and his daughter and
wanted now to confirm his suspicions.

" Well, little girl," he said, " this innocent-looking nut
is going to bring about a great change under our roof. From
now on someone will be missing from our household."

Césarine stared at him as if to say: What does it matter
to me? But Birotteau continued:

" Popinot is going away!"

Although Birotteau was very observant and had intended
this sentence as much to announce the establishment of the
firm of A. Popinot & Co. as to trap his daughter, his fatherly
affection made him suspect her mixed feelings when he saw
her lower her eyes while red roses bloomed on her cheeks.

He jumped to the conclusion that there had been an actual exchange of words between them, although this was not the case, and like all timid lovers, they had reached an understanding without speaking.

Some moralists think that love is the most involuntary and disinterested of passions (the material instinct, of course, excepted), but they are grossly in error. Although it is true that most men can give no reason for their love, nevertheless every congeniality, physical or spiritual, is based on calculations of one kind or another, whether inspired by mind, feelings or mere brute attraction. Love is essentially an egotistical affair, and egotism implies calculation. Anyone looking at immediate results might have been surprised to find a lovely girl like Césarine taken with a limping, red-headed boy. And yet her feelings were strictly in line with the arithmetic of middle-class survival. This alone explains the apparently amazing marriages between strapping, handsome women and puny little men, or between handsome youths and ugly midgets of girls. A man who has any sort of deformity: a club-foot, a hunchback, birthmarks on the face, or a runny nose like Roguin's, must choose between two courses of action. He must make himself either feared for his strength or loved for his kindness; there is no middle way, such as that open to more ordinary people. In the first case, it is a question of talent, genius or sheer power. A biting wit inspires fear, genius makes for respect and for outright terror there is nothing like the capacity for evil. And in the second case, things are even simpler; a physically handicapped man is naturally the object of feminine tyranny or adoration and makes a more appealing lover than his more normal counterpart. Anselme had been brought up by the virtuous and honorable Ragons and his uncle, Judge Popinot, and his natural innocence and religious feelings led him to atone for his slight physical defect by a blameless character. Constance and César had praised him frequently enough in front of their daughter, since petty as they might be in some respects, they had genuine spiritual qualities and understood the language of the heart. The good things they said about Anselme made a definite impression on Césarine, for in spite of her ingenuousness she could read in his candid eyes an intensity of passion such as to make any man, regardless of his age and condition, interesting to a woman. Surely Popinot was a more serious admirer than if he had been a conventionally handsome fellow. If he were to love a beautiful woman, he would be mad about her all the days of her life. Love would inspire him with ambition; he would kill himself in order to make her happy and she would be the undisputed mistress of his house.

This was the tenor of Césarine's thoughts—though perhaps they were less explicit. She took a glancing, bird's-eye view of the possible harvest of his love, and with the example of her mother's happiness before her eyes she saw here a chance to find its equal. Anselme seemed to her a younger version of her father, refined by the same advantages of education as she had enjoyed herself. In her fancy she saw him as mayor of a section of Paris and herself engaged in good works on behalf of the parish of Saint-Roch, like her mother. By this time she did not even perceive any difference between Popinot's right leg and his left one and a mention of his limp would have amazed her. She liked the clarity of his eyes and the way they blazed up and then modestly looked down at the ground whenever they met hers. Her other suitor, Alexandre Crottat, chief clerk to Roguin, had a half-cynical, half-jovial air, consequent upon his long familiarity with business affairs, which revolted her almost as much as the platitudes of his conversation. Popinot's silence betrayed a gentle soul; she appreciated the faintly melancholy smile with which trivial vulgarities inspired him. She was revolted by human stupidity in the same way he was, and they smiled or were saddened together. But Anselme's superiority did not prevent him from applying himself passionately to his work and this diligence was pleasing to Césarine also. She

guessed easily enough that the other clerks were saying:
" Césarine will marry Alexandre Crottat," but that in spite
of this, the poor, red-haired, limping Anselme did not for
a moment despair of winning her. And hope is the greatest
proof of love.

" Where is he going ?" asked Césarine with feigned
indifference.

" He's setting himself up on the Rue des Cinq-Diamants,
by all that's holy, God bless him !" said Birotteau, whose last
two exclamations were intelligible neither to his wife nor his
daughter.

When Birotteau came up against a difficulty he followed
the example of certain insects and sidestepped the issue by
changing the subject of the conversation. Now he turned
to Constance to say:

" I let your uncle in on some of your notions about Roguin,
and he laughed at them."

" You shouldn't repeat what we say between us," said
Constance with unexpected vigor. " Poor Roguin may be
the most moral fellow in the world. After all, he's fifty-
eight years old and probably no longer has his mind on . . ."

She stopped short because she saw that Césarine was
listening attentively, and threw a knowing look at her husband.

" I did well, after all, to go through with it," Birotteau
observed.

" You're the master of your own affairs, and it's entirely
up to you."

" Listen to this," said Birotteau to his clerks, when he
went downstairs to join them. " We're closing the shop at
ten o'clock. But you must give me a hand. All the furniture
on the second floor has got to be moved to the third, by the
process of fitting little pots into big ones, so that my
architect will have room to move around in tomorrow. . . .
Popinot's gone out without so much as a by-your-leave,"
he added, noticing the young man's absence. " Oh, but

I'd forgotten that he won't be sleeping here." And to himself he reflected that Popinot must either be putting Monsieur Vauquelin's ideas down on paper or else arranging for the rent of his shop.

" We know the reason for all this moving," said Célestin, speaking for the other clerks and Raguet, who stood grouped behind him. " May we congratulate you, sir, on an honor whose glory is reflected upon all of us? . . . Popinot told us that you . . ."

" Yes, my boys, I've been decorated, that's the way of it. And so it's on account of my decoration as well as the liberation that I'm gathering some of my friends together. If I am worthy of the honor that is bestowed upon me, I suppose it is because I sat on the commercial court and fought for the Royalist cause . . . when I was just about your age . . . on the Thirteenth of Vendémiaire, on the steps of Saint-Roch, where I was wounded by Napoleon's own hand (the Emperor he was called then). I was wounded in the thigh and Madame Ragon had to bandage it. Be brave, boys, and you shall have your reward. It's an ill wind that blows nobody good."

" There'll be no more street fighting now," Célestin observed.

" Let us hope not," said Birotteau, who proceeded first to deliver a lecture to his clerks and then to invite them to his party.

The prospect of a ball put them on their mettle and endowed them with tightrope-walkers' dexterity. They went up and down the stairs, carrying heavy loads and neither upsetting nor breaking anything. By two o'clock in the morning the moving was done. César and his wife slept on the third floor, Popinot's room was turned over to Célestin and the second clerk and the fourth floor was momentarily transformed into a store-room.

The usually meek and mild Popinot was filled with the intense excitement which an access of nervous tension produces in those who are in love or very ambitious. He had fumed and pawed the ground as impatiently as a race-horse as soon as he found himself down in the shop after dinner.

" What's going on?" Célestin asked him.

" It's been a great day," said Anselme. " Monsieur César has been decorated and I'm setting myself up in business."

" You're a lucky fellow, to have the boss to back you," was Célestin's reponse.

Popinot made no answer, but disappeared as rapidly as if the wind of success had carried him away.

" Call him lucky, if you like," said a clerk who was stacking up gloves by the dozen to one of his fellows engaged in putting on price-tags. " I say that the boss caught Anselme making eyes at Mademoiselle Césarine, and because it would be embarrassing to turn him down, on account of his parents, he very cleverly decided to send him away. That's what Célestin calls luck."

## VI

MEANWHILE, ANSELME POPINOT WAS HURRYING DOWN THE Rue Saint-Honoré and the Rue des Deux-Écus in order to get hold of a young man whom his sixth sense in business matters had indicated might advance his fortunes still further. His uncle, the judge, had once done a favor for the most prominent salesman of Paris, Gaudissart by name, who dealt in haberdashery and "Parisian specialties" of every kind. Even then, at only twenty-two years of age, Gaudissart was famous for his magnetic qualities. A slender fellow, with laughing eyes, an expressive face, a tireless memory and the ability to judge his customers' tastes at first glance, he deserved the reputation he was later to win as king of salesmen, "every inch a Frenchman." Anselme had run into him only a few days before and learned that he was about to start on a trip; now he hastened to his lodgings on the Rue des Deux-Écus, where he was told that Gaudissart was indeed on the point of going away, and for a farewell celebration had taken tickets to the Vaudeville Theater. Popinot decided to wait until he returned, for to put the nut oil in the hands of so active a salesman, one esteemed by all the big manufacturers, seemed to him a sure step to success. And thanks to his uncle, he had a powerful hold upon him. For Gaudissart, who was so able at winning over small-town shopkeepers and other reluctant clients, had let himself get entangled in the first conspiracy mounted against the Bourbons after the Hundred Days. He who so dearly loved fresh air found himself in prison, but Judge Popinot, who was called upon to examine him, absolved him of complicity on the grounds that his participation was foolish rather than premeditated. If the Judge had chosen to kow-tow to the newly re-established monarchy, he could have sent Gaudissart to the gallows, and the young man, knowing this, was unhappy only because he did not see how he was ever going to show his gratitude. Since he could not go straight to the Judge and thank him for having done justice, he called on the Ragons and declared his allegiance to the whole family.

While he was waiting for Gaudissart, Anselme went to the Rue des Cinq-Diamants to find out the name of the landlord from whom he must obtain a lease. As he wandered about the maze of the markets, he found on the Rue Aubry-le-Boucher a bargain which seemed so promising he planned to tell Monsieur Birotteau about it the next day. Toward midnight, he heard all the way from the Rue de Grenelle the voice of Gaudissart singing a tune from the show he had just seen. The salesman was standing out in front of the Hôtel du Commerce, at the end of the Rue des Deux-Écus.

" May I have a word with you ?" said Anselme, descending suddenly upon him.

" Eleven, if you like," said Gaudissart, mockingly raising his leaded cane against the aggressor.

" I'm Anselme Popinot."

" Say no more !" said Gaudissart, quick to place him. " What will you have ? Do you need money ? Away on indefinite leave ! But I can always lay my hands on some. My stout right arm to fight a duel ? I am at your service, from topknot to toe !" And he burst into song:
" *There's a true French soldier for you!*"

" I'd like to have a few minutes to talk," Popinot told him. " Not in your rooms, where someone might overhear, but on the Quai de l'Horloge, where there'll be nobody at this hour. It's about something important."

" Then it's something I want to hear. Let's go quickly."

Ten minutes later, Gaudissart was in on Popinot's secret and had agreed that it was an important one.

"*Come forward, ye perfumers, hairdressers, shopkeepers all!*" he shouted, aping Lafon in his role of the Cid.

"I shall inveigle all the shopkeepers of France and Navarre!" he added grandiloquently. "And here's an idea! Instead of going away, as I intended, I shall stay right here and work on the Paris trade."

"Why so?"

"In order to cut the ground from under your rivals' feet, silly boy! I represent other perfumers, but I shan't hesitate to put your product ahead of their adulterated ones. There's a traveling salesman's trick for you! We're the diplomats of business, you know. And as for your advertising brochure, I'll take care of that. One of my childhood friends is Andoche Finot, son of the hat-maker of the Rue du Coq who launched me in the haberdashery line. Andoche has picked the brains of all the heads his father hatted and set himself up as a theatrical reviewer on the *Courrier des Spectacles*. His father is an old dog who won't have anything to do with the arts, doesn't believe in them, can't be convinced that they are merchandise like everything else and may even lead to a fortune. Well, he keeps some hold over his son because the poor boy has to eat. Andoche is a clever fellow, I can tell you—and I know a clever man when I see one in spite of the stupidity of most of the people with whom I do business. He has to write advertising for the *Petit Berger*, which pays him for it, while the theatrical papers would just as soon let him starve. There's cut-throat rivalry when it comes to people connected with the stage, you know; they're almost as bad as 'Parisian Specialty' dealers! Finot wrote a superb one-act comedy for Mademoiselle Mars, a top-notch actress if ever there was one, but he couldn't get it put on anywhere except at the Gaîté vaudeville theater. Well, Andoche is clever at advertising too; he's not too proud, he'll think up a way to get things moving and he'll write us a prospectus for nothing. Then we'll hold a punch-bowl party to distribute it. And mind you, Popinot, I want no commission. My traveling expenses are paid by your rivals, and I don't mind putting that much over on them. So get this in your head, to me the success of your business is a matter of honor, and my reward will be to stand up as best man at your wedding. I'll go to Italy, Germany and England, with posters in every language, and paste them up in the choice spots, which I know so well, in all our provincial towns. This oil of yours is going to shine! It will be on every head! Your wedding won't be any second-rate affair, either; it will be something to remember! Yes, you're going to win your Césarine, or I don't deserve the nickname of 'Salesman Illustrious,' which old man Finot fastened upon me after I put his gray felts on the market. You see, if I handle your oil, I shall still be in my own field, that of the human head! Hats and tonics are the best safeguards of hair!"

Popinot went to his aunt's house, where he was to be lodged temporarily, so feverish over his prospects of success that the streets seemed to him to be running with oil. He slept little, dreamed that his hair had started to grow at a wild rate and that two angels were unrolling in front of his eyes a scroll with the title: "Caesarean Oil." Upon waking he was mindful of this name, and regarding it as an omen, decided to apply it to the new product.

He and Birotteau were at the Rue du Faubourg du Temple long before the arrival of the nuts from Madame Madou, and while they were waiting, the young man proudly told of his newly formed alliance with Gaudissart.

"If we have the famous Gaudissart with us, then our fortune is made," exclaimed Birotteau, holding his hand out to his subordinate with the air of Louis XIV welcoming Marshal de Villars upon his return from Denain.

"And here's another asset," said Popinot, pulling out of his pocket a bottle of corrugated glass, shaped like a squash. "I've found ten thousand of these bottles, ready made, for four sous apiece, payable within six months."

" Anselme," said Birotteau, turning the bottle admiringly about in his hands and speaking in a grave tone of voice, " only yesterday, in the Tuileries, you said to me: ' I *will* succeed; you have my word for it!' And now I too predict your success. Four sous apiece! Six months in which to pay! And a highly original shape! Macassar is reeling, and this is the final blow! Isn't it a good thing I cornered these nuts? But tell me, where in the world did you find the bottles?"

" While I was waiting to see Gaudissart, I wandered around . . ."

" Just the way I used to do myself!" Birotteau interrupted.

" And on the Rue Aubry-le-Boucher I saw the establishment of a wholesale glass merchant, an enormous place with blown glass . . . and then I saw this little bottle. . . . It hit me right in the eye, and something told me: ' This was made for you!' "

" He's a born businessman!" César mumbled under his breath. " He'll win my daughter yet!"

" Well, I went in, and saw thousands of these bottles in boxes . . ."

" And so you inquired about them?"

" You don't take me for such a simpleton, do you?" asked Anselme plaintively.

" A born businessman!" Birotteau repeated.

" So I asked for some glass bells to enclose wax statuettes of the Infant Jesus. And while I was dickering for them, I threw out some uncomplimentary remark about the bottles. At this point, the merchant came across with the whole story. It seems that Faille & Bouchon, who just went bankrupt, were about to launch a line of cosmetics and wanted some unusual bottles, but my man was wary and asked for half the money in advance. Faille & Bouchon paid it, because they were cocky about succeeding, but their failure came when the manufacture of the bottles was under way. The receivers were called upon to pay up the rest of what was due, but they compromised by leaving him the sum already paid and the bottles, which they claimed were a piece of outright extravagance. The bottles cost eight sous, but he was ready to let them go at four, because there was no telling how long he might be saddled with them otherwise. ' How about giving me ten thousand at that price?' I asked him. ' I work for Monsieur Birotteau, and I can take them off your hands.' So I warmed him up and brought him around, and there you are!"

" Four sous, eh?" said Birotteau. " We can price the oil at three francs the bottle, give one franc to the retailer and make a franc and a half profit."

" Caesarean Oil!" Popinot exclaimed.

" Caesarean Oil, eh? There's a way of flattering both the girl you love and her father! Good for you! The Caesars had the world at their feet, so I suppose they had good heads of hair!"

" Julius Caesar was bald, that's all I know!" said Popinot.

" Because he didn't have our tonic, don't you see? ... Our price will be three francs a bottle, while Macassar costs twice as much. With Gaudissart to help us, we'll make a hundred thousand francs a year. Every self-respecting head of hair will need a bottle a month, and that means eighteen francs every year for us. Say we have eighteen thousand customers. . . . And we make a hundred and eighty thousand francs. At that rate, we'll soon be millionaires."

After the nuts were delivered, Birotteau, Raguet, Popinot and the workers shelled enough of them to procure several pounds of oil before four o'clock in the afternoon. Popinot took a sample to Vauquelin, who told him what other less expensive oily products and perfumes could be mixed in with it. And Popinot lost no time in applying for a patent. Meanwhile, his good friend, Gaudissart, lent him money to cover his legal expenses, for Popinot wanted to pay half the cost of setting up the business.

Prosperity brings with it an intoxication which small souls find absolutely irresistible. And the results of this intoxication were easy to forsee. Grindot, the architect, came along with a colored sketch of the future apartment, fitted out with the proper appointments. And Birotteau was so taken with the whole thing that he signed up for it. Soon masons went to work with their picks, causing the whole house and Constance's heart to tremble. Monsieur Lourdois, the decorator, an experienced and prosperous contractor, suggested gilt paint for the drawing-room. But at this point Constance intervened.

"Monsieur Lourdois," she said, "you have an income of thirty thousand francs a year and a house of your own where you can do what you will. But we . . ."

"Madame, business people must put up as good a front as the aristocracy. Why should they let themselves be outdone? And isn't Monsieur Birotteau in the government now; hasn't he a conspicuous position?"

"But he's still a shopkeeper as well," said Constance in front of all the clerks. "Neither he nor his friends and enemies can ever forget that!"

Birotteau rose up on his toes and fell back on his heels several times in succession, with his hands folded behind him.

"My wife is right there," he said. "We shall be unpretentious even when we are most prosperous. When a man's in business he must keep expenses down and not make too much display of his gains. If the enlargement of my premises and their decoration were to exceed certain limits, you, Lourdois, would be the first to criticize me. My neighbors have their eyes on me, and everyone that's successful arouses a certain amount of jealousy . . . You'll find that out some day, young man," (here he turned toward Grindot), ". . . so even if their tongues do wag, don't let's give them reason to speak too badly of us."

"No wagging tongues or anything they may say can touch you," said Lourdois. "You're in a very special position, and you're so experienced in business that you know exactly what to do. Yes, you're what they call a sharp one!"

" I have a certain amount of experience, that's true. And do you know why I'm making these alterations? If I'm a little more expansive than usual, it's because . . ."

" Because? . . ."

" Well, my wife and I have asked in a few friends in order to celebrate the liberation and also my Legion of Honor."

" What's that?" Lourdois exclaimed. " Have they given you the cross?"

" They have. And if I am worthy of this overwhelming tribute, I suppose it is because I sat on the commercial court and fought for the royalist cause on the steps of Saint-Roch on the Thirteenth of Vendémiaire, with a wound from Napoleon to show for it. . . . Won't you and your wife and daughter? . . ."

" Delighted at the compliment, I am sure," said the Liberal Lourdois. " Quite a joker you are, old man Birotteau! You want to be sure I'll finish the job on time, that's why you invite me! . . . Well, I'll pick out my most efficient workers and we'll light a blaze that will dry the paint extra fast. Yes, we have drying processes, you know. . . . And you won't want to dance in fumes from damp plaster. We'll put a coat of varnish over it to take away the smell."

Three days later, the whole street was excited over Birotteau's promised ball. Everyone could see the scaffolding necessitated by the alterations of the stairway, and the square wooden chutes in which the wreckage was conveyed to carts standing below. Workmen were on the job night and day, with huge torches to give them light after dark, and their presence attracted a crowd of curious onlookers. Gossip enlarged the extent of the preparations and lent the event a truly sumptuous character.

On the Sunday on which the Madeleine affair was to be concluded, Monsieur and Madame Ragon, Uncle Pillerault, Charles Claparon, Crottat and Roguin all gathered at Birot-

teau's apartment after vespers, at four o'clock. The master
of the house explained that on account of the alterations
he could not entertain a greater number of guests that day.
Roguin brought with him the *Journal des Débats*, where
Monsieur de La Billardière had inserted the following
notice:

> We hear that all over France the liberation will be duly
> celebrated. In Paris, the city government feels that the time
> has come to restore to the capital that magnificence which
> was unsuitable under foreign occupation. The Mayor of
> every district is to give a ball and the season promises to be
> a brilliant one. Among the festivities, particular luster is
> attached to the ball given by Monsieur Birotteau, recently
> appointed a knight of the Legion of Honor and known for
> his devotion to the royal cause. Monsieur Birotteau, who
> was wounded on the steps of Saint-Roch on the 13th of
> Vendémiaire and shone as a member of the commercial
> court, has, in view of these merits, a double claim to the
> distinction bestowed upon him.

" They know how to write nowadays," César exclaimed,
and he added, passing the paper to Pillerault: " There's
mention of us, here in the paper."

" What of that?" said Pillerault, who particularly disliked
the *Journal des Débats*.

" You never can tell; this article may spur the sale of our
Sultana Cream and Pink Lotion," Madame Birotteau, who
did not share her husband's intoxication, murmured to
Madame Ragon.

Madame Ragon, a large, dried-up, wrinkled woman, with
thin lips and a pinched nose, had the misleading air of a
marquise of the royal court. The skin around her eyes was
marked with many fine lines, like that of certain old women
who have endured great sorrows, and the dignified severity
of her face, however agreeable, commanded respect. There
was something strange about her, which was striking without

being laughable and was evident in the way in which she got herself up. She wore mitts and carried in every sort of weather an umbrella-cane like that of Queen Marie-Antoinette. Her dress was of a pale brown, dead-leaf color, draped over the hips in an inimitable manner which has perished with the dowagers of another day. She wore a mantilla of loosely woven black lace, and her old-fashioned bonnets were trimmed in a manner reminiscent of old carved picture frames. She took snuff with the graceful gestures that may still be familiar to young people who remember seeing their grandmothers and great-aunts pick up a gold box from the table beside them, and shake a few grains into their handkerchief.

Monsieur Ragon was a man no more than five feet tall, with a nut-cracker face whose salient features were two bony cheeks and eye-sockets, a nose, a chin and a toothless mouth in which half of what he said was swallowed. His conversation was facile, gallant and affected; the ever-present smile on his face was the one with which he had always greeted the lovely ladies whom chance brought to his shop. The powder sprinkled over his bald head formed a snowy half-moon, flanked by wings of hair on either side, separated by a slender lock in the back, tied by a ribbon. He wore a corn-flower-blue suit, a white waistcoat, silk breeches and stockings, gold-buckled shoes and black silk gloves, and the most remarkable thing about him was the way he walked down the street, hat in hand, like a messenger of the House of Lords, or the King's privy errand-boy, in short, the sort of fellow that basks in the light of some reflected greatness although endowed with little character of his own.

" Well, Birotteau," he said didactically, " aren't you glad you listened to my advice in days gone by? We were quite right to count upon the gratitude of our beloved sovereigns, weren't we?"

" You must be very happy," his wife whispered into Madame Birotteau's ear.

" Yes, of course," answered Constance, who was under the spell of Madame Ragon's umbrella-cane, butterfly bonnet, tight sleeves and flowing scarf.

" Césarine is a charmer. . . . Come here, lovely child. . . .," said Madame Ragon protectively.

" Are we going to do business before dinner?" Pillerault asked his nephew.

" We're waiting for Monsieur Claparon," said Roguin. " He was getting dressed when I last saw him."

" Monsieur Ragon, I hope you gave him due warning that we should dine on a miserable little mezzanine floor. . . ."

" It seemed splendid to you sixteen years ago," Constance murmured to herself.

". . . amid piles of rubbish and the workmen who are busy carrying it away," Birotteau continued.

" He's a good-natured fellow, you'll see," said Roguin.

" I've posted Raguet down in the shop," said Birotteau, " because there's no way of coming through our door. You must have seen all the rubbish for yourself," César said to Roguin.

" And why didn't you bring your nephew with you?" Pillerault asked Madame Ragon.

" Is he coming at all?" asked Césarine.

" No, dear heart, he isn't," Madame Ragon answered. " Anselme is killing himself with work these days. The stench and the lack of air and sun on the Rue des Cinq-Diamants frighten me. The water in the gutter is always blue, black or green, and I'm afraid he'll be taken ill there. But when a young man has something in his head! . . ." And she made a gesture for Césarine's benefit, which indicated that by " head " she really meant " heart."

" Has he obtained his lease, then?" asked César.

" He got it yesterday," said Ragon, " under a notary's eye. He managed to make it for eighteen years, but he had to pay six months in advance."

" Well, Monsieur Ragon, aren't you pleased with me? I've turned over a discovery to your nephew, which bids fair to . . ."

" My dear César, we know you, through and through," said Ragon, clasping Birotteau's hands with friendly fervor.

Roguin was worried about the moment in which Claparon would appear upon the scene. The fellow's ways might shock these respectable people, and he thought it best to prepare them in advance.

" You're going to meet a very unusual sort of man," he told the company, " who hides his abilities under an ill-mannered exterior. Because, of course, he pulled himself up by his own bootstraps. But the company of bankers will teach him smoother ways. You might take him for a common loafer if you were to see him on the boulevards or playing billiards in a café, but all the while he's thinking deep thoughts, pondering some way of revolutionizing business and industry . . ."

" I can understand that," said Birotteau. " Some of my brightest ideas came to me while I was out strolling, isn't it so, Constance, my darling?"

" Well, he makes up by working through the night for the time he may seem to have wasted planning and arranging things during the day," Roguin continued. " People of talent always have bizarre ways. But disorderly as he may seem, he always gets what he wants. Just now, for instance, he won all the land-owners over and persuaded them to sell out to us."

Just then the throat-clearing " Brrrum, brrrum!" peculiar to drinkers of strong liquor, announced the arrival of the strangest character of this story, and the one upon whom César Birotteau's future depended. The perfumer hurried down the dark narrow stair in order to tell Raguet to shut up the shop and apologize to his visitor for receiving him in the dining room.

" Not a word of it!" Claparon replied. " This is a perfectly good place to close a deal. . . . I mean, to do honest business."

In spite of Roguin's preparatory explanations, the con-
servative Ragons, the observant Pillerault, Césarine and her
mother were all of them unfavorably impressed by this
supposedly respectable banker.

Although the former traveling salesman was only twenty-
eight years old, he did not have a hair left on his head and
wore a wig with corkscrew curls. This hairdress called for
a youthful freshness and transparency of skin and graceful
manner, and instead its wearer had pimpled, ruddy complexion,
as weathered as that of any coachman. Bad teeth, black-
heads and prematurely deep wrinkles all combined to betray
the dissolute life he had led. He looked like a rustic comedian,
ready to play any part demanded of him, with his make-up
slightly the worse for wear, but his tongue lively, even when
he was drunk, and his true character revealed by his excessive gesticulation and shameless stare. When his face
was lit up by copious drink, there was nothing of the serious
businessman about him, and to carry out his present role
had required considerable study in front of the mirror.
Du Tillet had helped him get dressed, like a stage director
sponsoring an actor's début upon the stage, fearful lest his
protégé's gross habits shine through the properness of his
accoutrements.

" Talk as little as you can," were his parting instructions.
" A banker never chatters; he listens, ponders and then
acts. In fact, if you would completely fill the bill, say nothing
at all, or at the most make a few insignificant remarks. Tame
your roving eye and look solemn, even at the risk of appearing
to be a fool. Where politics are concerned, be all for the
government, but don't venture outside a few broad general-
izations, such as : ' The budget is crushing. . . . There can be
no compromise among the various parties. . . . The Liberals
are a menace. . . . The Bourbons must above all things keep
the peace. They are leading us into a period of prosperity
and we must support them, whether we care for them per-

sonally or not. . . . Liberalism is the cloak for big business interests. . . . France has done enough political experimenting . . .'

"Don't sprawl over the table; remember that you must keep up the dignity of a millionaire. Don't inhale your snuff like a sick man; toy with your snuff-box, look down at your feet or up at the ceiling before you answer a question, and wear a thoughtful air. Above all, watch out for your bad habit of touching everything you see. A banker should be far too blasé to want to exercise his sense of touch! Of course, you can claim you sit up all night over your business, and figures have made you groggy. There are so many details involved in every transaction, you can tell them, such a lot of preliminary study! Of business in general, you must speak gruffly. Business is a difficult matter, a thorny one, but don't be too specific about it. Don't drink too much, or break out in song. If you lose your head, you'll lose your future as well. Roguin will be there to prompt you. You'll find him in the company of virtuous and respectable people, so don't shock them with your café upbringing."

This peroration had the same effect upon Claparon's spirit as his new clothes had upon his body. He was used to sloppy dress, which did not constrain his movements, and to loose thinking which put no rein upon his tongue. Now he found himself poured into a newly tailored suit, as stiff as a board, and uncertain how to move and what to say. He withdrew his hand from an object he had started to touch, and stopped in the middle of a sentence, so that the observant Pillerault could not but perceive some fundamental dislocation in him. His red face and curly wig contradicted the elegance of his dress, just as his thoughts contradicted what words he had to say. But because the company was well disposed toward him, they took his awkwardness for the result of worry and preoccupation.

"He has so much business on his mind," Roguin was saying.

" Business hasn't taught him good manners," said Madame Ragon in an aside to Césarine.

Monsieur Roguin overheard, and held a finger up to his lips.

" He's rich, capable and absolutely honest," he said with a slight bow in Madame Ragon's direction.

" If he has all these merits, then we must make some allowances for the rest," Pillerault said to her husband.

" Let's read over the papers before dinner," Roguin suggested.

Madame Ragon, Constance and Césarine left the room, while Pillerault, Ragon, Claparon, Roguin and Birotteau listened to Alexandre Crottat's reading. César signed a note for forty thousand francs to a client of Roguin, guaranteed by a mortgage on his land and factory buildings on the Rue du Faubourg du Temple; he turned over Pillerault's draft, gave without a receipt the twenty thousand francs' worth of notes he had in his pocketbook, and the hundred and forty thousand francs in notes drawn to the order of Claparon.

" I have no need to give you a receipt," Claparon told him. " You form one party to the agreement with Roguin and we the other. The present owners of the land will be paid in cash, and I engage myself to make up your part on the basis of the notes you have given me."

" Quite right," said Pillerault.

" Well, gentlemen, let us call back the ladies; it's chilly here without them," said Claparon, looking out of the corner of his eye at Roguin to see whether or not the joke was too daring.

" This young lady must be your daughter," he added, standing very straight and looking at Birotteau as the women came back into the room. " Quite an achievement of yours, I call her! None of the roses you have distilled is as sweet as she, and indeed perhaps it is because you are a distiller of roses that . . ."

" My word but I'm hungry," Roguin interrupted him.

"Then let us dine," said Birotteau.

"We are dining in the company of the law," said Claparon, drawing himself up.

"Do you handle a great deal of business?" asked Pillerault, who had managed to sit down beside him.

"Enormous quantities of it!" Claparon replied. "Thorny stuff it is, too! There are the canals, you know! You've no idea how much work *they* give me! Just think, the government wants canals! Canals come in handy all over the map, and carry every sort of trade. Rivers are rolling roads, as Pascal puts it. Canals call for markets and markets call for improving the river banks, which are settled by the poorest class of people. Hence loans, which eventually go to the poor. The government has engineers to enlighten it, and one has to have connections in the Chamber of Deputies. . . . Oh, you can't imagine the trouble I have with the Chamber! . . . The deputies can't grasp the connection between politics and finance, and there's bad faith on both sides. Take the Kellers, for instance. François Keller is a great orator, who attacks the government on the score of canals and their financing. When he comes home he finds us waiting for him with certain favorable propositions. Arrangements have to be made with the government then and there, in spite of the fact that he has just attacked it. There is a clash between the orator's interests and the banker's, and we're caught between two fires. You can see for yourself what a thorny business it is. We have to satisfy everybody: messengers, Chambers, ante-chambers, cabinet members . . .''

"Cabinet members?" asked Pillerault, who was bound on fathoming his new business associate.

"Yes sir, cabinet members!"

"Then the newspapers are right," said Pillerault.

"Now my uncle's off on politics!" put in Birotteau. "Monsieur Claparon has started him going!"

"Great jokers, the newspapers!" said Claparon. "They create no end of confusion. I don't deny that they have their use, but I owe them many a sleepless night, spent in calculations."

" Tell me more about the cabinet members," said Pillerault, hoping to hear startling revelations.

" Their demands are based strictly on governmental necessity. . . . But what is this delicious dish I am eating? Ambrosia? Only a private home can provide a sauce like this one; in the cheap beaneries, where . . ."

The flowers on Madame Ragon's bonnet quivered, and Claparon realized that he had used too vulgar a word.

" When we bankers say ' beaneries,' we mean such fashionable places as Véry or the Frères Provinciaux. Well, I say that none of their cooks knows how to make a proper sauce. Some of them serve lemon juice diluted with water."

All during the meal Pillerault tested his man, and found nothing but emptiness in him, which he thought dangerous.

" Everything's going swimmingly," Roguin whispered into Claparon's ear.

" All I know is that I can't wait to get out of these clothes," said Claparon, who was stifling in them.

" You know, sir," Birotteau told him, " that the reason for our having dined in the same room in which we received you is that, eighteen days from now, we are gathering some friends together in order to celebrate the liberation . . ."

" Well, of course I'm a government man. I belong, by virtue of my opinions, on the side of that genius who directs the destinies of the royal house of Austria . . . quite a fellow he is, I tell you! . . . To conserve in order to acquire, and above all to acquire in order to conserve! There is my basic way of thinking, which I have the honor of sharing with Prince Metternich."

". . . and also my Legion of Honor," César resolutely continued.

" Oh yes, of course. . . . Who told me about that? The Kellers or the Nucingens?"

Such presence of mind caused Roguin to make a gesture of admiration.

" No! It was at the Chamber of Deputies."

" Ah!" exclaimed César. " Then you must have been told by Monsieur de La Billardière."

" Exactly!"

" I find him a charming fellow," César said to his uncle.

" Words, words, words!" said Pillerault.

" As I was saying," César went on, " if I deserve this honor, it is because . . ."

" Because of your inventions in the field of perfumery. The Bourbons are discriminating in their awards. . . . Yes, let us hang onto these generous princes, for we shall owe them the most tremendous prosperity! Mark my words, the Restoration knows that it must outdo the Empire by the number of its peaceful conquests . . ."

" I trust you will honor us by coming to our ball," said Constance.

" In order to spend an evening with you, I should gladly give up the chance of making millions!"

" Quite a talker, anyhow," César said to his uncle.

While the setting sun of the Queen of Roses cast a last bright glow on the commercial horizon, a hitherto unknown star was rising. For at this very moment young Popinot was laying the foundation of his fortune on the Rue des Cinq-Diamants. This narrow street, where heavily loaded vehicles can barely make their way, runs at one end into the Rue des Lombards and at the other into the Rue Aubry-le-Boucher, with across from it the Rue Quincampoix, famous in the history of old Paris, where the history of France has left so many reminders. In spite of its narrowness the street has a great collection of drug dealers, and this made it a good choice for Popinot. His house, the second from the Rue des Lombards, was so dark that on certain days it required artificial light even in the middle of the day.

The evening before he had taken possession of its darkest and dirtiest corners. His predecessor, who dealt in raw sugar and molasses, had left his mark on the walls and in the courtyard and cellars. Imagine a spacious shop with great iron-clad doors, painted green and having prominent iron bands across them, ornamented by mushroomheaded nails, then wire trellises, like those in an old bakery, all around the bare, yellow walls, and finally a white tile floor. Behind this lay a rear store-room and a kitchen, both of them with windows on a courtyard, and on the opposite side, still another room, which must originally have been a stable. An inside stairway led up from the first store-room, into two well-lighted rooms looking over the street, where Popinot expected to put his books and office furnishings. Back of these were three narrow rooms separated from the front ones by a partition and giving onto the courtyard, and in these he proposed to live. They were dingy holes, little different in aspect from the dark courtyard itself, whose high walls were so impregnated with dampness that even on the driest days they appeared to be perspiring, and whose pavement's crevices were filled with the sticky, smelly remains of molasses and raw sugar. Only one of these second-floor back rooms had a fireplace and none of them was papered or had anything other than a rough stone floor. Ever since early morning, Gaudissart and Popinot, aided by a paper-hanger's assistant, had been papering the most habitable of these dank holes. A schoolboy's hard wooden bed, an unsteady bedside table, an old chest of drawers, a table, two armchairs and six straight chairs, given to his nephew by Judge Popinot, were the only furnishings. Gaudissart had put a second-hand pier-glass, with a wretched mirror, on the mantelpiece. Toward eight o'clock in the evening, the two friends sat down in front of a blazing log and started to finish off the remains of their lunch.

" Cold leg of mutton !" Gaudissart exclaimed. " This won't do for a housewarming."

Popinot displayed a twenty-franc piece with which he meant to pay for the advertising leaflet prepared by Gaudissart's friend, Finot.

" I . . ." he started to say.

" No, I . . ." interrupted Gaudissart, balancing a forty-franc coin on his eyelid.

Just then there came the hammer-like sound of a gong from the courtyard, which was emptier and more echoing than usual because of the Sunday absence of the weekday population.

" Here is my faithful slave from the Rue de la Poterie," said Gaudissart triumphantly. " It's not just *I* but the full verb *I have*, where I am concerned."

And indeed, a boy followed by two scullions brought in three baskets filled with a magnificent dinner and six bottles of wine.

" How shall we manage to eat so much ?" asked Popinot.

" Remember that a man of letters is coming to join us ! Finot is a connoisseur of the pomps and vanities of this wicked world, and he is arriving, my boy, with a hair-raising leaflet. Please appreciate the joke ! Of course, the leaflets are always thirsty, and we must water our seeds if we want to see them grow into flowers . . . Go, slaves," he added to the scullions, striking up a magnificent pose in imitation of his idol, Napoleon as he gave them ten sous for a tip.

" Thank you, Monsieur Gaudissart," they chorused, pleased more by his joking grand manner than by the amount of money he had given them.

" As for you, my boy," he said to the first one, who had stayed to serve them, " be informed that there is a concierge below, and in the depths of her cave she occasionally does a bit of cooking, in the same spirit of fun with which Nausicaa used to turn her hand to laundry. Go, then, to her, and implore her of her goodness to take an interest in heating these plates. Tell her that she will draw down upon herself the blessing and above all the respect of Félix

Gaudissart, son of Jean-François Gaudissart and descendant
of any number of other proletarian Gaudissart ancestors.
Go along with you, now, and see that everything's good,
or I'll make you sing a sorry tune!"

Another stroke of the gong sounded from below.

" Here is my clever Andoche," said Gaudissart.

A stoutish fellow, of medium height, looking from head to
toe like a hat-maker's son, with his cleverness concealed
by his plump cheeks and somewhat formal manner, walked
into the room. The rather mournful and bored expression
on his face was transformed into hilarity as soon as he saw
the waiting table and the festively capped bottles. At Gaudissart's welcoming cry, his pale blue eyes sparkled, his
top-heavy head with its Eskimo-like features, turned from
left to right and he greeted Popinot with neither respect nor
servility, as if he were quite at ease and intended to make
no concessions. He had just reached the point of admitting
to himself that he had no literary talent, and had decided
to stay in the literary field only to exploit it, to hoist himself
up on the shoulders of literary people in order to do business
rather than to write unremunerative masterpieces. Just now,
having exhausted the possibilities of humility, both real
and assumed, he had decided to emulate the greatest financial
magnates, by affecting a purposely impertinent air. All he
needed was a start, and Gaudissart had pointed out the
possibilities of getting in on the ground floor of the business
of Popinot's hair tonic.

" You can go on his behalf to the newspapers," he suggested. " But mind you don't cheat him, or I'll duel you to
the death. You must give him a fair run for his money."

Popinot stared at the " man of letters " with ill-concealed
concern. Businessmen inevitably regard writers with mingled curiosity, compassion and terror. Although Popinot
had been brought up in a cultivated household, the ideas
and ways of his family, followed by the stultifying requirements of shop-keeping, had given him a distinctly com-

mercial turn of mind. The frequency of such a phenomenon can be noted in the changes which take place in a hundred schoolboys after they have been ten years out of the same school. But Andoche Finot chose to interpret Popinot's silence as admiration.

"Well, let's have a look at the prospectus before we attack our dinner," said Gaudissart. "After a good meal, one's in no mood for reading. All the blood goes to the stomach."

"A prospectus can lead to a fortune," put in Popinot.

"And for a struggling fellow like me, fortune is no more than a prospectus."

"Well spoken!" said Gaudissart. "This fellow Andoche has enough wit to be divided up among a dozen of us."

"Say a hundred," said the dazed Popinot.

Meanwhile Gaudissart impatiently seized the papers and started to read out loud:

"CEPHALIC OIL!"

"Caesarean Oil is what I had in mind," said Popinot.

"My boy, you don't know our country people," Gaudissart told him. "There's a notorious operation of that name, and they'd be stupid enough to imagine that your oil is a stimulant to child-birth. How would you ever get their minds off that tangent and back to the hair?"

"Without seeming too prejudiced," said Finot, "I'd like to remind you that Cephalic Oil means oil for the head, and therefore summarizes its whole purpose."

"Let's hear the rest," said Popinot impatiently.

And here is the text of the prospectus, just as hair-dressers and cosmeticians receive it today:

## CEPHALIC OIL
### Gold Medal at the Exposition of 1827
### A Patented Invention

No cosmetic product can bring about the growth of hair, just as no chemical compound can dye it without endangering the seat of intelligence. Science has recently declared that hair is a form of dead matter and that no outside agent can prevent it from graying or falling out altogether. It is possible to guard against alopecia and calvities, however, by protecting the bulbous root of the hair against climatic influences and keeping the head at normal temperature. The use of a new invention, *Cephalic Oil*, produces the healthy head of hair to which the ancient Greeks and Romans as well as the Nordics attached such importance. Research has shown that the nobly born, who were once upon a time distinguished by the length of their hair, used a long lost prescription, which has now been re-discovered by A. Popinot, the originator of *Cephalic Oil*.

The purpose of this oil, then, is to preserve the hair rather than to unhealthily stimulate it. The oil has an agreeable odor, eliminates dandruff, and by means of the nut-oil which is one of the principal elements of its composition, protects the head from atmospheric conditions and maintains it at a constant temperature, thereby lessening the frequency of colds, headaches and brain disturbances. By this means the follicles containing the fluid which generates hair are shielded against excessive heat and cold. And users of *Cephalic Oil* can hope to keep to an advanced age the silky luster which lends such charm to the hair of a child.

Directions for use are attached to every bottle.

### DIRECTIONS FOR THE USE OF CEPHALIC OIL

There is no reason for greasing the hair. This is a mistaken notion, and one which has the further disadvantage of leaving sticky traces of cosmetics in its wake. After the hair has been brushed and combed, dip a small sponge into *Cephalic Oil* and apply it at several places to the roots of the hair, in such a way that the scalp is completely coated.

*Cephalic Oil* is sold only in three-franc bottles bearing the signature of the originator, which guarantees against imitations. A. Popinot, Rue des Cinq-Diamants, near the Rue des Lombards, Paris. Enquiries post-free.

*Note:* Popinot can also supply the following products: Orange-flower extract; lavender, sweet almond, cacao, coffee and castor oils.

" My good friend," said Gaudissart to Finot, " that's a superb piece of writing! So rigorously scientific and to the point! My compliments! This is what I call literature with a purpose!"

" A splendid prospectus, indeed!" said Popinot enthusiastically.

" A prospectus whose first words are sufficient to kill Macassar!" said Gaudissart, rising impressively to his feet and declaiming with appropriate parliamentary gestures: "Hair—can't—be—made—to—grow! Hair—can't—be—dyed without—danger! There's the whole secret! Modern science is in agreement with ancient lore! That gives us a hold on both old people and young. When your prospect is an old man, then, it's : ' Ah, sir! The ancient Greeks and Romans knew a thing or two; they weren't so backward as people say!' And when your prospect is young: ' My dear boy, just another example of what modern technique can do! Think of steam engines and wireless telegraphy! This oil stems from the work of Monsieur Vauquelin.' . . . By the way, what if we were to reprint an extract from the paper he presented to the Academy of Science? There's an idea! Meanwhile, Finot, sit down at the table! Start in on the vegetables, and let's drink a toast in champagne to the success of our friend, Popinot!"

" I have an idea the frothy sort of advertisement has gone out of style," Finot said modestly. " Now that we're living in a scientific age, people want something they can get their teeth into. We must adopt a scholarly air and impress the public with our learning."

" We're going far with that oil," Gaudissart continued. " My feet are itching to walk and my tongue to waggle. I have connections with hairdressers and I know they never get more than thirty per cent of the retail price. If we give them forty, I promise we'll sell a hundred thousand bottles in six months. I'll get after pharmacists and grocers as well.

With a profit of forty per cent, they'll unload it on the public, you'll see!"

The three young men ate like bears, drank like fish and intoxicated themselves over the prospects of Cephalic Oil.

" The stuff's gone to my head already," said Finot.

And Gaudissart countered with all the jokes on hair and hair tonic that came into his mind. In the midst of the three friends' homeric laughter, the gong sounded downstairs.

" I'll wager it's my uncle," said Popinot. " He's quite capable of dropping in to see me."

" An uncle?" exclaimed Finot. " And we haven't an extra glass!"

" Popinot's uncle is a judge," said Gaudissart. " And if you want to know something about him, I can tell you that he once saved my life. When you've been in the fix I was, with the guillotine staring you in the face and threatening to take your head of hair right off you," (he made the gesture of drawing a knife across his throat) " you can't ever forget the good judge who spared you the channel for the wine to flow through! No matter how much I've poured down my throat, I'll never forget him. You never can tell, Finot; some day you may need him yourself. We owe him a royal welcome."

Judge Popinot it was indeed, who was asking the concierge where to find his nephew. Recognizing his uncle's voice, Anselme went down with a lamp to guide him.

" Good day, gentlemen," said the magistrate.

Gaudissart bowed deeply, while Finot examined him with an inebriated eye and found him somewhat of an old duffer.

" I can't say it's luxurious," said the Judge, looking around the room, " but in order to accomplish great things it's often necessary to make a humble start."

" What a deep thinker," Gaudissart said to Finot.

" I could make a newspaper article out of that remark," was his friend's reply.

Just then the Judge recognized the traveling salesman. "Oh, it's you, is it?" he said. "How do I happen to find you here?"

"Sir, I am anxious to do my modest best to contribute to your nephew's fortune. We've just been discussing an advertising brochure, and you see before you the author of a masterpiece of its kind, Andoche Finot. He's a young literary light, who writes for the best papers, on politics and the theater."

Finot pulled the tails of Gaudissart's coat.

"Very good, my children," said the Judge, satisfied by this explanation of the groaning table before him. "Now you must get dressed, Anselme, so as to go with me to call on Monsieur Birotteau and sign your incorporation papers. I've just looked them over. Since you'll manufacture your oil on the Rue du Faubourg du Temple, it seems to me that he should give you a lease on a laboratory on his premises and allow his salesmen to represent you. Anyhow, it's better to have things down in black and white than to fall into a misunderstanding. . . . Anselme, these walls look very damp to me; you'd better hang up some straw mats in the vicinity of your bed."

"If I may say so, sir," said Gaudissart ingratiatingly, "we just finished papering them ourselves, and they haven't had time to dry."

"That means you saved some money," said the Judge. "I approve heartily."

"Listen," Gaudissart whispered into Finot's ear, "Popinot here is a good boy, and he must go with his uncle. Let us pay a call on some of those pretty cousins . . ."

Finot turned his waistcoat pocket inside out with his thumb, and Popinot, catching on at once, slipped him a twenty-franc piece as payment for the brochure. The Judge had left a cab waiting at the corner, and in it he took his nephew to Birotteau's. Pillerault, the Ragons and Roguin were playing a game of cards and Césarine was embroidering

a scarf, when Judge Popinot and Anselme came in. Roguin
was sitting across the table from Madame Ragon, who had
Césarine at her side, and couldn't help noticing how glad
she seemed to see the young man. Discreetly he pointed out
the blush on her face to his clerk, Crottat.

" So this is a day for signing papers !" said Birotteau after
the Judge had told him the motive of their visit.

The three of them went up to the floor above to discuss
the lease and the incorporation. The lease of laboratory
space on the Rue du Faubourg du Temple was made to
extend for eighteen years, so as to coincide with Anselme's
lease on the Rue des Cinq-Diamants, an unimportant circumstance but one which was later to serve Birotteau well.
When they came back downstairs, the Judge was surprised
to find workmen in the house of a man so devout, on a
Sunday afternoon. Birotteau had been waiting for this
chance to explain.

" Although I don't believe you go out very much in
society, sir, you surely won't take it amiss that we are
celebrating the liberation. And that's not all. I'm asking
in a few friends because of my Legion of Honor . . ."

" Ah !" said the Judge, who had no decorations.

" If I am worthy of this honor, it must be because I served
on the court—I mean the commercial court, of course—
and fought for the Bourbons on the steps . . ."

" Yes, I know," said the Judge.

". . . of Saint-Roch, on the Thirteenth of Vendémiaire,
where I was wounded by Napoleon."

" I'll be happy to come," said the Judge. " And if my
wife is well, I'll bring her along."

" Xandrot," said Roguin to his clerk, as they were going
out of the door, " don't get it in your head to marry Césarine.
Six weeks from now you'll thank me for my advice."

" Why ?" Crottat asked him.

" Birotteau's squandering a hundred thousand francs on
his ball, and he's put everything into this land deal, in spite

of my advising him to go slow on it. In six weeks, these
people will be starving. My advice is to marry Mademoiselle
Lourdois, the house-painter's daughter, who can bring you
a three-hundred-thousand-franc dowry. You see, I've
contrived another string for your bow. And you can buy
my practice for a hundred thousand francs tomorrow."

# VII

THE MAGNIFICENCE OF BIROTTEAU'S BALL WAS BRUITED about not only in newspapers throughout the continent, but also in local business circles, where rumor fed upon the extent of the preparatory alterations, which were going on apace, thanks to day and night shifts of laborers. On one side people said he had rented three whole houses, on another that his drawing-rooms were all to be gilded and every dish served at the supper was to be concocted especially for the occasion. No tradesmen were invited, the neighbors said, but only people connected with the government, and they reproached Birotteau for his pretenses and political ambitions and even went so far as to cast doubt upon the authenticity of his famous wound. All through the neighborhood intrigue was seething; the perfumer's friends asked nothing, but the claims of mere acquaintances were endless. Where favors are dispensed, there are bound to be courtiers to sue for them, and many would-be guests had to go to some lengths in order to secure an invitation. The Birotteaus were astonished to find that so many people knew them. These strangers' insistence had a frightening effect upon Constance, and she became more depressed with every day that went by. First, she confessed to her husband that she simply didn't see how she was going to manage it; where could she find sufficient silver, glasses, refreshments and servants to take care of them? Who was to keep a watchful eye over the whole thing? She begged him to stand at the front door and let no one in without an invitation, for she had heard strange stories of uninvited guests who crashed the gate by murmuring the name of some supposed friend already inside. Ten days before, after Braschon, Grindot,

Lourdois and Chaffaroux, the contractor, had all solemnly sworn that the alterations would be completed by the famous Sunday the seventeenth of December, César and his wife and daughter held a ludicrous conference one evening in their modest second-floor drawing-room in order to draw up the list of guests and address the invitations sent by the printer that morning. They were on rose paper, with light-faced type and worded in traditionally ingenuous fashion.

" Mind, we mustn't forget anyone," said Birotteau.

" No one's going to forget *us*," said Constance. " For instance, Madame Derville, who'd never set foot here before, came yesterday to pay a most formal call."

" She's pretty," said Césarine; " I like her."

" And yet before her marriage, she amounted to even less than I did. She worked in a haberdashery on the Rue Montmartre. In fact, she made shirts for your father."

" Well, let's start the list at the top," said Birotteau. " The Duke and Duchess de Lenoncourt . . . write that down, Césarine. . . ."

" Good heavens, César!" said his wife. " Don't you go asking people you know only as customers! You wouldn't ask Princess de Blamont-Chavry, who's much more closely related than the Duke is to the Marquise d'Uxelles, your godmother, would you? Or the two Messieurs de Vande-nesse, Monsieur de Marsay, Monsieur de Ronquerolles or Monsieur d'Aiglemont, with all of whom you do business? You must be mad! Success has gone to your head."

" Then there's the Count de Fontaine and his family. . . . He used to come to the Queen of Roses under the name of ' Grand-Jacques,' along with ' Le Gars,' who was really the Marquis de Montauran and ' Le Nantais,' who was Monsieur de La Billardière . . . that is, long before the famous Thirteenth of Vendémiaire. They used to shake my hand then, I can tell you! ' Go to it, Birotteau, old man! Get yourself killed just like us, for the good cause!' Yes, we were conspirators together."

"Put them down, then," conceded Constance. "If Monsieur de La Billardière and his son are coming, there'd better be someone they can talk to."

"Very well, Césarine," said Birotteau. "Now, the Prefect of the Department; he may come and he may not, but he rules over the entire municipal set-up and we must pay him the honor to which he is entitled. Then, Monsieur de La Billardière, the Mayor, and his son. . . . You must add up the number of guests at the end. . . . My colleague, Monsieur Granet, the deputy, and his wife. She's an unsightly creature, but we have to invite her. . . . Monsieur Curel, the goldsmith, colonel of the National Guard, and his wife and two daughters. . . . So far, we've had officials. Now for the other important people. Count and Countess de Fontaine, as I was saying, and Emilie de Fontaine, their daughter. . ."

"An impertinent little thing, who makes me come out of the shop in the rain so she can order from the window of her carriage! If she comes, it will be only in order to make fun of us."

"Well, perhaps she will come," said César, who was anxious to swell the number of his guests. "Keep writing, Césarine. . . . Count de Granville (he's one of the best heads at Court, so Derville says, besides being our landlord), and, of course, the Countess. . . . That reminds me, Monsieur de La Billardière is having my knighthood conferred upon me by the Chancellor, Count de Lecépède, in person. . . . Then Monsieur Vauquelin. Put him down for both the ball and the dinner that precedes it. And then, before we forget them, all the Chiffrevilles and the Protez'. . . . Judge Popinot and his wife. . . . Monsieur Thirion, clerk of the King's cabinet, and Madame Thirion; they're friends of the Ragons, and they say their daughter's going to marry one of Monsieur Camusot's sons by his first marriage."

"César, don't forget little Horace Bianchon, another nephew of Judge Popinot, and Anselme's cousin."

"Look at that! Césarine has put a number four beside

the Popinots already! . . . Monsieur and Madame Rabourdin; he's head of one of Monsieur de La Billardière's offices. . . . Monsieur Cochin, from the same office, with his wife and sons, who do business with Matifat. . . . Might as well put down the three Matifats, while we're about it."

" The Matifats asked us if we could invite their friends, Monsieur and Madame Colleville, Monsieur and Madame Thuillier, and the Saillards."

" We'll see," said César. " Don't forget my Stock Exchange broker, Monsieur Jules Desmarets, and his wife."

" She'll be the belle of the ball!" exclaimed Césarine. " I like her better than any of the rest."

" Derville and his wife."

" Please put down Monsieur and Madame Coquelin, the successors to my Uncle Pillerault," said Constance. " They count so much on coming that she's ordered a gown from my dressmaker—a white satin petticoat, with the gown itself in tulle, embroidered with flowers. She very nearly bought a metallic fabric, of the kind ladies wear at Court. If we were to leave them out, they'd be our enemies for life."

" Yes, put them down, Césarine," said César. " We must honor the business world, since we belong to it. Then Monsieur and Madame Roguin."

" Mother, I'll bet Madame Roguin wears her Mechlin lace dress and all her diamonds."

" Monsieur and Madame Lebas," Birotteau continued. " The presiding magistrate of the commercial court, his wife and two daughters. I forgot them in our list of officials. . . . Monsieur and Madame Lourdois and their daughters. Monsieur Claparon, the banker, Monsieur du Tillet, Monsieur Grindot, Monsieur Molineux, Pillerault and his landlord, Monsieur and Madame Camusot (the wealthy silk merchant) and all their children—the one at the École Polytechnique and the one that's a lawyer."

" He's going to be made a judge, but somewhere in the

provinces, on account of his marriage with Mademoiselle Thirion," said Césarine.

"Monsieur Cardot, Camusot's father-in-law and all his children. Oh! The Guillaumes of the Rue du Colombier, Lebas' father-in-law. There are two old men, who can amuse each other on the side-lines . . . Alexandre Crottat . . . Célestin . . ."

"Father, don't forget Monsieur Andoche Finot and Monsieur Gaudissart, who are doing so much for Monsieur Anselme."

"Gaudissart? He tangled with the law in his time. But that doesn't matter. He's going to sell our oil. . . . But why should we bother with this Andoche Finot?"

"Monsieur Anselme says he'll be famous some day. He's a wit, like Voltaire."

"A writer, eh? Atheists, the whole lot of them!"

"Do ask him, Father. There aren't so many good dancers. And he's written the prospectus advertising your oil."

"Well, if he believes in our oil, then put him down."

"I've already put down my favorites," said Césarine.

"Put down Monsieur Mistral, the bailiff, and our doctor, Monsieur Haudry. He won't come, anyhow."

"Oh yes, he will," said Césarine.

"César, I trust you are asking Abbé Loraux to dinner," interrupted Constance.

"Yes, I've written to him already."

"And we mustn't forget Lebas' sister-in-law, Madame Augustine de Sommervieux," said Césarine. "Poor little woman, she's very sad these days, Lebas tells us."

"That's what it is to marry an artist," said César. "Just look at your mother! She's dropping off to sleep. Sweet dreams, Madame Birotteau! . . . Césarine, what about your mother's dress?"

"Don't worry, Father; everything will be ready. Mother thinks she's going to wear a crêpe-de-chine like mine. The dressmaker won't even need to try hers on her!"

" How many people have we got down now ?" asked César in a louder voice, as his wife opened her eyes.

" A hundred and nine, including all your clerks."

" Where shall we put them ?" asked Constance. " Oh well," she said artlessly, " after such a strenuous Sunday, Monday's bound to follow."

When people are climbing from one step on the social ladder to another, they can't do anything simply. For the time being, neither Birotteau nor his wife and daughter could go anywhere near the second floor. César had promised his errand-boy, Raguet, a new suit for the reception, if he promised to keep good watch. Like Napoleon at Compiègne, after his marriage to Marie-Louise of Austria, he was reluctant to see things develop by degrees, but wanted the final result to come as a surprise. His architect was to take him by the hand and show him the remodeled apartment as if he were the guide to a museum. As a matter of fact, every member of the family had a surprise in store. Césarine had spent all her savings, a hundred gold louis, on books for her father. One morning the architect told her that there would be two sections of bookshelves in his room (their installation was his surprise). And in order to fill these, Césarine ordered sets of Bossuet, Racine, Voltaire, Rousseau, Montesquieu, Molière, Buffon, Fénelon, Delille, Bernardin de Saint-Pierre, La Fontaine, Corneille, Pascal and La Harpe, an assembly of generally esteemed authors, none of whom her father would ever read. The bindings alone were very expensive. Thouvenin, the famous binder, had promised to deliver the books at noon of the sixteenth of the month, and when Césarine told Pillerault what she had contracted to pay, he promised to help her. César's surprise present to his wife was a cherry-red velvet gown decked with lace, of which he had spoken to his daughter. As for Constance, she planned to give her husband two gold shoe-buckles and a diamond tie-pin. The redecorating of the apartment was to be a surprise for everyone, and a couple of weeks later there would be the surprise of the bills to be paid.

César thought out carefully which invitations should be deliver d in person and which could be taken around by Raguet. When it came to the more important ones, he bundled his wife into a cab, with her feathered hat and cashmere shawl, and they managed to make twenty-two calls within a single morning. Meanwhile he spared her the necessity of preparing the elaborate menu required by the festivities. A diplomatic agreement was drawn up between Birotteau and the celebrated caterer, Chevet, by virtue of which Chevet was to provide a complete set of silver, the dinner, wines included, and a corps of waiters with a major-domo to direct them. Chevet asked to take over the kitchen and the dining-room as his headquarters. He was to serve a dinner for twenty persons at six o'clock, and a cold buffet at one o'clock in the morning. The Café de Foy was to provide fruit ices, in fancy cups with enamel spoons and silver saucers. And Tandrade was to supply drinks on the side.

" Don't worry," César said to his wife. " Chevet, Tan-drade and the Café de Foy will confine themselves to the mezzanine floor. Virginie will be on duty on the third, and the shop will be closed up completely. All we have to do is gather on the second."

At ten o'clock on the morning of the sixteenth, Monsieur de La Billardière came to take César to the Chancellery of the Legion of Honor where Count de Lacépède was to knight a dozen candidates. When he arrived at the perfumer's house, he found him in tears over the gold shoe-buckles and tie-pin which he had just received from his wife.

" It makes me very happy to be loved so much," he said, getting into the carriage in the presence of Constance, Césarine and all his employees, who admired his black silk breeches and bright blue coat, soon to be decorated with the ribbon which, as Molineux put it, was dipped in blood.

When César came back from the ceremony he was pale with joy and couldn't help staring in all the mirrors at the reflection of his cross, as if the ribbon itself were not enough for him. For there was no false modesty about him.

"Constance," he said, "the Chancellor is a charming fellow, and thanks to a word from Monsieur de La Billardière, he has consented to come tomorrow with Monsieur Vauquelin. Yes, Monsieur de Lacépède is just as great a man; he has forty volumes to his credit. And he's a nobleman to boot. We mustn't forget to address him by his title of count."

"Get on with your lunch," said Constance. And she added, to Césarine: "Your father's a perfect baby!"

"It looks beautiful in your buttonhole," said Césarine: "They'll be presenting arms to you. We must go out together."

"Yes, wherever there are official guards, they'll present arms."

Just then Grindot and Braschon came to say that after lunch the ladies could take a look at the finished apartment. Braschon's boy had brought some curtain-hooks and three men were busy lighting candles.

"A hundred and twenty lights, that's what we need," said Braschon.

"That means a bill of two hundred francs from Trudon," sighed Constance, but a severe look from her newly knighted husband checked her complaints.

"Your reception is going to be magnificent, sir," said Braschon.

"Flatterers!" Birotteau said to himself. "Abbé Loraux was right to tell me to look out for them and keep my head on my shoulders. I mustn't ever forget my humble origins."

The trouble was that he failed to understand what Braschon was driving at, namely an invitation to the ball for himself and his family. For lack of this, he became Birotteau's enemy; indeed, as he went out the door, he failed to call him by his new title.

At this point, the dress rehearsal began. César, his wife and daughter went out of the shop and entered the apartment from the street. The door of the house had been made over in elaborate style, with two square panels and a painted cast-iron ornament between them. Later, this type of door was to be seen everywhere, but at this time it was quite new. At the far end of the hall were the two wings of the stairs, with between them the "socle" which had given Birotteau so much worry, large enough to lodge a concierge inside. The hall itself was paved in black and white marble squares and lit by a four-pronged antique lamp. All in all, the architect's conception was a mixture of luxury and simplicity. A narrow red carpet set off the pumiced white limestone steps. The first landing gave onto the mezzanine, and the door leading to the apartment was like the other except that the decorative motif was in wood.

"How graceful it all is," said Césarine, "and yet there's nothing that especially catches the eye."

"Exactly," the architect told her. "The grace of it comes from the exact proportions of the stylobates, plinths, cornices and the rest of the ornamentation. I didn't run wild on gilt, but stuck to sober and restrained colors."

"There's an art to it, I can see that," Césarine admitted.

They passed then into a spacious, tastefully decorated ante-chamber on the street, a graceful cornice and red-and-white trim, with nothing garish about it. The marble mantelpiece, with columns on either side, fitted in perfectly with the other details of the room. In short, the general impression was of that suave harmony which comes from a combination of the smallest effects such as only an artist can achieve, but even a layman can appreciate. A chandelier with twenty-four candles made the red silk draperies sparkle and the parquet floor was so inviting that Césarine could not resist doing a dance step on it. Next came a green and white boudoir, leading to César's study.

" I put a bed in there," said Grindot, opening up the doors of an alcove hidden by the two sections of bookshelves mentioned earlier. " You or your mother may be taken ill and need an extra place to sleep."

" But look at the beautifully bound books on the shelves!" Birotteau exclaimed. " Oh, my darling wife . . ."

" No, those are Césarine's doing!"

" Forgive me for this display of fatherly feeling!" said Birotteau, embracing his daughter.

" Of course, sir," said Grindot. " You are in your own house, after all!"

The prevailing color of the study was brown, with occasional touches of green, for in order to make a smooth transition, the basic color of one room was repeated as secondary in the next. *Hero and Leander* shone from a panel near César's desk.

" *You'll* have to pay for all this," said César jokingly, " since I owe you my latest inspiration."

" It's a present from Monsieur Anselme," Césarine told him. For Anselme, too, had wanted to give him a surprise.

" Poor, dear boy!" said César. " He's done for me what I did for Monsieur Vauquelin."

Next came Madame Birotteau's room. Here the architect had given free rein to his ideas of magnificence, hoping to captivate his clients. The draperies were of blue silk with touches of white, and the chairs upholstered in white with blue trimmings. On the mantelpiece a clock was set into a Venus on a marble block. A deep-piled Turkish carpet joined Constance's room to her daughter's, which was decorated in chintz and contained a piano, a wardrobe with mirror, a plain, curtained bed and all the small pieces of furniture that a young girl could desire. The dining room was behind the bedrooms of Birotteau and his wife, giving onto the stairs. It was in what is called Louis XIV style, with a Boulle clock, ornate sideboards and nail-studded wall hangings. The family joy knew no bounds when they came back from their tour of inspection and Madame Birotteau found her new cherry-red velvet gown lying across her bed, where Virginie had discreetly laid it.

"Sir, this apartment will do honor to your reputation," Constance said to Grindot. "We shall have more than a hundred guests tomorrow evening, and all of them will praise you."

"I shall recommend you to everyone," said César. "You'll find the cream of the business world here, and make yourself better known in one evening than if you'd built a hundred houses."

Constance was so touched that she forgot her fear of extravagance and the harsh judgments she had previously passed upon her husband. That morning, when young Popinot brought the *Hero and Leander*, he had spoken with enthusiasm of the prospects of the new hair tonic, and Constance valued his opinion. He said that no matter how much money Birotteau had spent on the remodeling, he would get it all back in six months out of his share of the profits on the oil. After the uncertainties of nineteen years, it was such a joy to relax for a single day, that Constance promised her daughter she would do nothing to cast a shadow over her husband's satisfaction. Toward eleven o'clock, when the architect went away, she threw her arms around César's neck with tears of emotion in her eyes.

"What you haven't done to make me happy!" she exclaimed.

"Just as long as it lasts, eh?" said César with a smile.

"Oh, it will last; I have no more fears."

"Good!" said César. "At last you appreciate me!"

Anyone who is big enough to admit his own human weakness will find the couple's pride in their reception understandable. Eighteen years before, she had been a salesgirl at the Petit-Matelot on the Ile Saint-Louis and he a peasant boy who had arrived in hobnail boots from his native Touraine.

" I'd give a hundred francs to be certain of Abbé Loraux's coming," said César. And no sooner had he spoken than Virginie announced the good abbé's arrival.

Abbé Loraux was at this time vicar of Saint-Sulpice, and never did a deeply spiritual nature more clearly reveal itself than in his person, which left an indelible impression with all those who knew him. His face, which was by nature repulsively ugly, had been made into something sublime by his exercise of the Christian virtues and shone with an almost heavenly light. The innocence of his spirit held his irregular features together and charity purified their lines, just as, in the case of Claparon, vice debased them. Yes, Faith, Hope and Charity made their abode among his wrinkles. His voice was low-pitched and deliberate, but penetrating. He dressed in the manner of the city clergy, and allowed himself to wear a dark brown top-coat. In his pure heart there was not a trace of ambition, and his soul seemed destined to ascend straight to its Maker. One of Louis XVI's daughters had had to bring all of her gentle insistence to bear upon him before he would accept even the most modest parochial post in Paris. Now he looked with concern at the magnificence around him, smiled at his three smiling hosts and nodded his white head.

" Dear friends," he said, " my job is to look after the poor rather than to come to parties. But I came to thank Monsieur César for his invitation and congratulate him. The one celebration I don't want to miss is the wedding of your lovely child."

A quarter of an hour later the Abbé went away, without either César or his wife having dared to show off the apartment to him. Indeed, this grave apparition had a slightly dampening effect upon César's soaring spirits. Each one of the family went luxuriously to bed, after having taken possession of just the furnishings he or she had always wanted.

Césarine helped her mother undress in front of a marble dressing-table. And César allowed himself some little extra comforts in which he was indulging for the first time. All three of them fell asleep, dreaming of the pleasures of the morrow.

The next day, which was Sunday, Césarine and her mother went to Mass, read vespers and finally got dressed for the party at about four o'clock in the afternoon, after the caterer's employees had taken over the mezzanine floor. Never had Madame Birotteau had a dress more becoming than this new red velvet. Her arms, still fresh and young, her sparkling white throat and neck and prettily rounded shoulders were admirably set off by the rich texture and color. The artless enjoyment which every woman feels when she knows herself at the height of her powers gave an added luster to her classic cameo-like profile. As for Césarine, in her white crêpe-de-chine gown, with a wreath of white roses around her head, a single bud at the waist and a scarf over her neck and shoulder, she made young Popinot's heart beat wildly.

"These people are far better off than ourselves," said Madame Roguin to her husband, as they walked through the apartment. She was furious to find Madame Birotteau so much more beautiful than herself, for a woman always knows to what extent another is her superior.

"It won't last long," said Roguin. "Some day you'll splatter her with mud as you roll by."

Vauquelin was supremely gracious. He came in the carriage of Monsieur de Lacépède, his colleague at the Institute, and when the two of them saw the beauteous Madame Birotteau, their compliments took a scientific turn.

"You possess some secrets of youth and beauty unknown to science," said Monsieur Vauquelin.

"Here, sir, you must feel at home," said Birotteau. And he added, turning to the Chancellor of the Order of the Legion of Honor. "Count, it is to Monsieur Vauquelin that I owe my fortune. And now I should like to introduce the presiding magistrate of the commercial court . . . Monsieur de Lacépède, one of our country's great men, who has forty volumes to his credit." He whispered these last words into the ear of Joseph Lebas, who was escorting the magistrate.

The guests all came on time, and the atmosphere of the dinner-table was what one would expect it to be among people who moved in business circles, that is, genial and gay with an interspersion of somewhat vulgar jokes, the kind that never fail to arouse laughter. The excellence of the food and wines was duly appreciated, and it was half-past nine before the diners went into the drawing-room for coffee. Already cabs were bringing a few impatient dancers and an hour later, the room was filled with them and the ball threatened to be overcrowded. Monsieur de Lacépède and Monsieur Vauquelin took leave, in spite of Birotteau's desperate efforts to detain them. He was more successful when it came to Judge Popinot and Monsieur de La Billardière. Except for the three women representing Aristocracy, Finance and Government—Mademoiselle de Fontaine, Madame Jules and Madame Rabourdin respectively—who stood out from the rest by their beauty and breeding, the female contingent was anything but brilliant. Their unimaginative gowns, together with their air of prosperous respectability, made the delicacy of the three graces all the more painfully evident by contrast.

Here was the solid middle class of the Rue Saint-Denis in all its buffoonery and glory. These are the people who dress their little boys like the soldiers of a crack regiment, who buy sets of *Victories and Conquests* and *The Workman Soldier* and admire *The Pauper's Funeral*. They applaud parades, spend the weekends at their country houses, try to look distinguished, aspire to civic honors, and yet, with all their petty jealousies, they are kindly, sympathetic and sensitive to a degree. They contribute to the fund for the children of General Foy, to the supposedly starving piratical

Greeks, to the Napoleonic Veterans' Resettlement project (even after its collapse) and are generally dupes of their own virtues and mocked for their faults by the upper crust of society which is not worth what they are, since their good-heartedness stems precisely from ignorance of what is the " proper " thing to do. The women bring up their daughters to be innocent and industrious, qualities which they lose as soon as they are pushed into the class above their own where superficial wit is the order of the day. The Matifats, wholesale druggists of the Rue des Lombards and for sixty years jobbers to the Queen of Roses, were a typical family of this class.

Madame Matifat, who was striving for an appearance of dignity, wore a turban on her head and a bright red and gold lamé gown, which set off her Roman nose, ruddy cheeks and proud manner. This Catherine the Great of the drug counter towered over her husband, himself quite impressive if one saw him alone at a National Guard review, where his pot belly, draped with a watch-chain and charms, was conspicuous from as far away as fifty feet. Short, stout and bespectacled, with his shirt-collar coming halfway up the back of his head, he was remarkable for his deep voice and the copiousness of his vocabulary. For instance, he never spoke of " Corneille," but of " the sublime Corneille"; never of " Racine," but of " the gentle Racine." As for Voltaire . . . Ah, Voltaire! " Second-rate in practically everything, possess-ed of more wit than genius, you might say . . . and yet he *was* a genius all the same!" Rousseau, " a proud and stormy spirit, who eventually hanged himself." Monsieur Matifat told all sorts of vulgar stories about Piron, whom most of his acquaintances considered a prodigious man. He had a pas-sion for the stage and tended to be obscene in his conversation. Like Cardot, predecessor of the Camusots, father and son, he kept a mistress. Often, when Madame Matifat saw that he was about to begin a story, she would say: " Watch your tongue, fat man," for " fat man " was her favorite appellation. At the ball, the aristocratic Mademoiselle Fontaine nearly

burst into laughter when she heard her say to her husband:
"Don't make a rush for the ices, fat man! It shows poor taste."

It is more difficult to explain the difference between the bourgeoisie, or middle class, and the class above it, than it is for a bourgeois to hurdle this barrier. These middle-class women, unused to wearing such elaborate gowns, displayed an ingenuous joy, which revealed how rare an occasion a ball of this kind was in their busy lives. Whereas the three representative ladies of whom we have spoken above looked no different this evening from the way they would look the next day. They did not seem so obviously dressed up; they did not look at themselves in the mirror after they left home or worry about the effect produced by their gowns. Their faces wore an expression of repose and they danced with the careless grace with which nameless sculptors of genius have endowed ancient statues. Their middle-class sisters, on the other hand, bore the mark of toil upon them and could not divest themselves of their vulgar habits. Their eyes revealed too much curiosity; their voices were more strident than the murmur which adds so much charm to dance-floor conversation, and they had neither the mixture of seriousness and raillery which may at any moment give birth to an epigram nor the quiet assurance which bespeaks a long practice of self-control. So it was that Madame Rabourdin, Madame Jules and Mademoiselle de Fontaine, who were enjoying the ball for reasons of their own, stood out among the middle-class element both by the tastefulness of their dress and the grace of their manners, like opera stars among a crowd of supers, and were the objects of many a jealous stare. Madame Roguin, Constance and Césarine formed a sort of link between the two groups of women. As always happens in the course of a ball, there came a moment of climactic excitement, when the bright lights, music and dancing combined to produce a sort of inebriation in which all distinctions were wiped out. The ball threatened to become noisy, and Mademoiselle de Fontaine wanted to go home, but before she could find her venerable father, Birotteau and his wife and daughter persuaded her to stay and thereby preserved at least a part of the aristocratic representation.

" I can smell somewhere in this apartment a perfume whose delicacy really amazes me," said the impertinent guest. " My compliments, Monsieur Birotteau!"

Birotteau was so beside himself at this point that he did not understand, but his wife caught the barb of the joke and could only blush in answer.

" You have staged a patriotic celebration which does you honor," said Camusot.

" I've rarely seen so splendid a ball," put in Monsieur de La Billardière, who told polite lies without turning a hair.

Birotteau took all the compliments he received in deadly earnest.

"What a charming sight! And what delightful music! Will you give us more such spectacles?" asked Madame Lebas.

" Your apartment is beautifully decorated," said Madame Desmarets. " Have you your own taste to thank for it?"

Birotteau bluffed in reply to this one, by intimating that he had supervised the decoration. Meanwhile, Césarine, who had every dance taken, was receiving new proof of Anselme's delicacy.

" If I were to heed my feelings," he told her when they left the dining table, " I'd ask you for a quadrille. But my happiness would be asking too much of our mutual pride."

But to Césarine's eyes, men with normal legs were graceless beside the limping Popinot, and she insisted upon opening the ball with him for a partner. In the course of the quadrille, Anselme, encouraged by his aunt, dared to speak to Césarine of his love, but in the round-about way of a timid lover.

" Mademoiselle, my fortune depends upon you," he told her.

"How do you mean?"

"Only one hope can insure my obtaining it."

"Then that hope is yours!"

"Do you realize what that little word 'hope' means to me?"

"Hope for good fortune!" Césarine retorted maliciously.

"Gaudissart! Gaudissart!" Anselme said after the dance to his friend, squeezing his arm almost to the point of pain. "Make a go of it, or else I must put a bullet through my brain! If I succeed, Césarine is mine; she's as good as said so. And just look how beautiful she is!"

"Yes, she's well gotten-up and besides that she has a parcel of money! We'll make mincemeat of her, you'll see!"

The beginnings of an understanding between Mademoiselle Lourdois and Alexandre Crottat, Roguin's designated successor, did not escape Madame Birotteau's eye, and it was not without some pangs that she gave up the idea of marrying off her daughter to a future notary. Uncle Pillerault, after he had exchanged greetings with little Molineux, went to sit in an armchair near the library. From his vantage point he watched the card-players, listened to snatches of conversation and walked from time to time over to the door to look at the basket of nodding flowers formed by the heads of the dancers. His countenance was that of a true philosopher. The men were all hideously dressed, except for du Tillet, who had acquired a completely worldly manner, young La Billardière, an up-and-coming fashion-plate, Monsieur Jules Desmarets and a few of the government officials. But among all the comic figures to which this assembly owed its character, the most comic of all was that of the landlord, Molineux, petty tyrant of the Cour Batave, who was tricked out in linen which had yellowed from old age. His lace ruffle was held in place by a bluish cameo stick-pin, and his black silk hose revealed the spindliness of the legs which they boldly encased. César triumphantly

took him to view the four new rooms constructed by the
architect on the second floor of his house.

"Good for you, sir!" said Molineux, laughing. "This
floor is going to be worth more than three thousand francs
to me."

Birotteau made a joking reply, but the tone in which the
little old man had pronounced these words made his spine
tingle unpleasantly. For underneath them lay the impli-
cation: At this rate you'll ruin yourself, and I'll move in on
the premises one of these days!

Molineux's pallid face and cruel eyes made a powerful
impression upon du Tillet, whose attention was first drawn
to their owner by the curiously upturned collar of his green
and white suit and the number of clinking baubles attached
to his watch chain, which together gave him something of a
rattlesnake's air. And so he entered into conversation with
him.

"There, sir," said Molineux, putting one foot into the
boudoir, "I am on the property of Monsieur de Grandville,
but here" (pointing to his other foot) "I am on my own.
For this house happens to belong to me."

Then, because he was charmed to have found such an
attentive listener, he told everything about himself, including
the misdeeds of his troublesome tenant, Gendrin, and the
arrangements he had made with Birotteau as a prelude to the
refurbishing of the apartment, which in turn had made
possible the sumptuousness of the ball.

"So Monsieur César, contrary to his usual habits, paid
you his rent in advance," observed du Tillet.

"Yes, I asked him for it. I'm always fair and square with
my tenants, I can tell you."

"If old man Birotteau goes into bankruptcy," du Tillet
thought to himself, "this little shrimp will make an excellent receiver. His punctiliousness is invaluable. I have
an idea that like the Emperor Domitian, he finds amusement
in killing flies when he is alone."

After this, du Tillet went to the card tables, where he had sent Claparon ahead of him, trusting that in the excitement of the games no one would scrutinize his banker's appearance too closely. These two behaved so convincingly like perfect strangers to one another than no one could have guessed there was an understanding between them. Gaudissart, who had known Claparon as a salesman, did not dare speak to him, after he had received a chilly stare which seemed to indicate that from his present eminence he did not wish to be reminded of his modest beginnings.

At five o'clock in the morning, like a Roman candle, the ball burned itself out. Already, of the hundred or so carriages that had crowded the Rue Saint-Honoré, only some forty were left, and inside they were dancing the fifth figure of the quadrille and the English polka. Du Tillet, Roguin, young Cardot, Count de Granville and Jules Desmarets were still playing cards, and du Tillet had won three thousand francs. The first glimmer of daylight caused the candle flames to pale, and the musicians struck up the last dance. In every self-respecting middle-class house this is a moment for excesses. The more dignified guests have long since departed, and the heads of those who remain are reeling from the stale air and the treacherous spirits which lurk at the bottom of even the most innocent drink. Old ladies forget their corns and enter the dance; men's perspiring faces and unruly hair make them grotesque and even ludicrous, and young women, who have lost some of the flowers out of their coiffure, become suddenly light-headed. This is the hour of the middle-class Momus and all the pleasantries that follow in his train. The laughter is shriller than ever, as everyone remembers the obligations of the morrow. Matifat was dancing with a woman's hat perched on his head and Célestin was leading an imaginary cavalry charge. The women dancers clapped their hands more loudly than usual when the figures of the interminable quadrille demanded it.

"They're having a really good time!" said the happy Birotteau.

"I only hope nothing gets broken," Constance whispered to her uncle.

"You've given the most magnificent ball I've ever seen," said du Tillet to his former employer. "And I've attended a good many of them in my time."

Among the works of Beethoven, there is a poetic fantasy which dominates the end of the C-minor symphony. After the slow introductory measures, the conductor's baton raises the rich curtain on a dazzling motif toward which all the composer's magical powers have been converging. Anyone with poetry in his heart will understand that Birotteau's ball had something of the same function. A radiant fairy comes forward, lifting her wand; angels pull aside purple silk draperies; golden doors, carved like those of the Baptistery at Florence, turn on their diamond hinges. The eye is drawn to a marvelous vista, a line of splendid palaces, which disgorge beings of some superior race. The altar of happiness is aflame and the incense of prosperity perfumes the air. Divinely smiling creatures in blue-trimmed white tunics display superhumanly beautiful faces and figures of infinite delicacy. Cupids flutter about, spreading flame from their torches. You feel yourself to be beloved, and inhale a bliss that is beyond your understanding, bathing in a harmony which provides everyone with the ambrosia of his choice. For a moment your most secret hopes are brought to fruition. Then, having transported you to the heavens, the magician leads you, by means of transitional basses, back to the world of cold reality. He has whetted your appetite for divine melody and you are still gasping: "Encore!" . . . In our story this was the motion aroused in César and Constance by their ball. Collinet's flute played the finale of their commercial symphony.

Tired but happy, the three Birotteaus fell asleep, with the murmur of the festivities still in their ears. Remodeling, repairs, new furniture, gowns, music, refreshments and the cost of the books (which her father insisted upon paying back to Césarine) had all mounted up, without Birotteau's noticing, to sixty thousand francs. This was the price of the red ribbon which the King attached to the buttonhole of a perfumer! If bad luck had caught up with César Birotteau then and there, this little item of expense would have brought him into the police station. For a businessman can be accused of willful bankruptcy if he spends beyond reason. It may be more unpleasant, at that, to be haled before a police magistrate for a clumsy trifle than to find oneself in the Criminal Court for a large-scale swindle. In some people's eyes it is better to be criminal than to be stupid.

# PART II

## César in Trouble

# I

A WEEK AFTER THE BALL, THE LAST FLARE-UP OF EIGHTEEN years of prosperity, now about to be extinguished, César was looking out his shop window at the passers-by and considering the extent of his business involvement, which now seemed a heavy burden to him. So far, his life had been comparatively simple: he had manufactured his products and sold them, bought materials which he put together in a different form and resold. Today, the real estate venture, his interests in A. Popinot & Co., and the repayment of the hundred and sixty thousand francs he had put up so blithely, which would require either negotiating a series of loans, to which his wife was sure to object, or an unexpectedly sudden yield from the new hair tonic, all weighed him down. He felt that there were too many strands in the skein he held in his hands. How was Anselme going to manage his business? César had a tendency to treat him as if he were his ward and pupil; he was not quite sure of the boy's ability and wished he could oversee him more closely. The discreet kick with which he had hinted that Anselme should hold his tongue at the house of Monsieur Vauquelin was a sign of his nervousness in this regard.

Although he would never have let his wife, daughter or clerks guess it, Birotteau was like a simple river boatman, who finds himself the unwilling commander of a frigate. The preoccupations we have described above swirled like a fog in his brain, which had never been used for much abstract thinking, and he had got up from his desk in the hope of clearing it away. Just then there appeared on the street outside someone he intensely disliked, his landlord,

Molineux. All of us have had those telescoped dreams which contain in an instant a whole lifetime of experience, and in which there is a malevolent figure which keeps reappearing. It was as this villain that Molineux now appeared to Birotteau. A week before, he had grinned diabolically at the ball, looking with a hateful eye at the luxury of the decorations. César recalled all the more clearly the impression the old skinflint had made upon him that night, because of the instinctive aversion this present intrusion aroused in him.

"Sir," said the little old man in his outrageously soft-spoken voice, "we did things so quickly that you forgot to sign your name to our agreement."

Birotteau took the lease in hand to make up for the omission. At this moment, Grindot, the architect, came in, said good morning and looked diplomatically around him.

"Sir," he finally whispered in César's ear, "you know how hard it is to make a start in any career. I should be infinitely obliged if you were to pay my fee."

Birotteau, finding he had not sufficient money on him, told Célestin to make out a draft for two thousand francs, payable within three months, and to prepare a receipt for the same amount.

"I'm glad you took over the payment of what is owed me by your neighbor, Cayron," resumed Molineux. "I have just been informed that the bailiff has padlocked his shop because he's disappeared and no one knows where to find him."

"Here's hoping I'm not stuck for five thousand francs," Birotteau said to himself.

"He was said to have a pretty good business," said Lourdois, the painter, who dropped in at this point to present his bill.

"No businessman can be sure of the roof over his head," said Molineux sententiously; "that is, not until he retires from business altogether." And he folded the signed lease with scrupulous exactness.

The architect looked at him with aesthetic appreciation, because here was a caricature of all that he, as an artist, thought that a benighted businessman must be.

" If you keep your head under an umbrella, you generally expect to stay dry," he interposed.

Molineux stared at the architect's mustache and beard rather than his face, and returned his contempt in kind. Instead of going away, now that his errand was accomplished, he lingered on in the hope of inserting another sly dig into the conversation. From his long acquaintance with cats, he had acquired something feline in both his expression and manner.

Just then Ragon and Pillerault walked into the room.

" We were just talking to the Judge," Ragon said to César privately. " He says that in a venture of this kind, we should obtain a receipt from the sellers of the land and register the deeds, in order to be recognized as sole owners of . . ."

" Oh, are you talking about the land around the Madeleine ?" asked Lourdois. " I've heard about it. It seems there'll be building soon."

Monsieur Lourdois decided that this was not a good time to press for payment of his bill.

" I gave it to you only because we're close to the end of the year," he said to César. " It's not at all urgent."

" What's the matter, César ?" asked Pillerault, reading the dismay brought to his nephew's face by the sight of the painter's bill, and noticing that he had failed to answer either Lourdois or Ragon.

" Oh, nothing at all. I took over five thousand francs' worth of notes from my neighbor, a little umbrella-maker, and now he's bankrupt, it seems. If his notes are no good, I shall cut a very foolish figure indeed."

" A drowning man will clutch his own father's leg for safety, and drag him down," said Ragon. " I've always told you that. I've seen a lot of bankruptcies, and I've observed that even if a man isn't a cheat when he first gets in trouble, circumstances oblige him to become one."

" That's true," agreed Pillerault.

" If I were ever to be elected to the Chamber of Deputies, or have any influence over the government . . .," Birotteau began, rising to his toes and then falling back on his heels.

" What would you do ?" asked Lourdois. " You're a very wise man."

Molineux relished any discussion of points of law and so he lingered to hear this one. And although Pillerault and Ragon had heard César's opinions a hundred times over, the attentiveness of the others required them to listen with equally serious expressions.

" I'd like to see a court of permanent judges and a public prosecutor assigned to each case of bankruptcy. After an interrogation, in which the judge would combine the duties presently assigned to agent, receivers and referee, the accused would be judged either ' capable of rehabilitation ' or else definitely ' bankrupt.' In the former case, he would be called upon to pay everything he owned, and meanwhile he would act as trustee of his wife's and his own properties. These would of course belong to his creditors, and he would merely administer them, under supervision, for their benefit, signing his name ' So-and-so, failure,' until he had paid everything back. If, on the other hand, he were judged really ' bankrupt,' he would be pilloried for two hours in the Stock Exchange, according to an old custom, wearing a green cap on his head. All his possessions would be handed over immediately to his creditors and he would be banished from the country."

" Business would be safer that way, I agree," said Lourdois, " and a man would look twice before leaping into a risky business."

" The present law is not even enforced," César went on in an exasperated manner. " Out of a hundred shopkeepers, more than half operate seventy-five per cent on credit or sell their goods at twenty-five per cent below inventory prices, thereby undermining business in general."

"You are right, sir," said Molineux. "The present law has too many loopholes. The only choice should be between total liability and disgrace."

"Yes, what the devil!" César continued. "The way things are now, a shopkeeper is tempted to become a regular thief. By virtue of a simple signature, he can dip into anyone's cash-box."

"You're not exactly indulgent, Monsieur Birotteau," said Lourdois.

"But he is in the right," maintained old Ragon.

"All business failures are suspect," insisted César, exasperated by the petty Cayron affair, which rang in his ears like the bay of the hounds in those of a fleeing deer.

Just then a steward came to bring Chevet the caterer's bill, and almost immediately after, a pastry-cook's boy from Félix, a waiter from the Café de Foy and the clarinet-player from Collinet's orchestra, all on the same errand.

"Rabelais' famous ' bad quarter of an hour,' " said Ragon with a smile.

"It was a splendid party," interpolated Lourdois.

"I'm busy just now," César said to all the messengers.

"Monsieur Grindot," said Lourdois, as he noticed the architect tucking a draft signed by Birotteau into his pocket, " perhaps you can check my accounts. Just a quick look will do, for all the costs were authorized by you in Monsieur Birotteau's name."

Pillerault looked at the two of them.

"Costs agreed upon between an architect and a painter ?" he whispered into Birotteau's ear. "You've been robbed, I can tell you."

Grindot went away and Molineux followed, for the sake of saying to him with a mysterious air:

"You heard what I said, but you didn't catch the point. I hope you have a good umbrella !"

Grindot's nerves were on edge. The more illegitimate a gain, the more the gainer is attached to it. That is only human nature. He had studied the layout of the apartment with care, and given his very best efforts in return for his ten-thousand-franc fee. But at the same time he had been the dupe of his own vanity, and the contractors had found him putty in their hands. Their arguments and veiled threats of belittling him were less powerful than Lourdois' observation about the Madeleine affair: What if Birotteau had no intention of building on the land, he said, but was simply speculating on a rise in its value? Besides, architects and contractors are, among themselves, like playwrights and actors in the theater, in strict interdependence. So, although Grindot was entrusted by Birotteau with setting the costs, he took the side of jobbers against his employer. Needless to say, the three contractors, Lourdois, Chaffaroux and Thorein (the carpenter) were all enthusiastic about Grindot, and called him " a lovely boy, one it was a pleasure to work with." Now Grindot guessed that their bills, on which he was due to receive a percentage, would be paid, like his own fee, with deferred drafts, and Molineux had put the bug in his ear that prospects were shaky. As a result, he resolved to be hard and cruel, as only an artist can be, in his hostility to bourgeois society.


By the end of December, Birotteau found himself faced with bills for sixty thousand francs. Félix, the Café de Foy, Tanrade, and a host of petty creditors who demanded cash had asked three times for what he owed them. To a business-man such trifles are more ominous than a failure; indeed, they foreshadow it. A loss that you can put your finger upon is nothing to be nervous about, but there is no limit to panic. Birotteau had no cash on hand, and this was a situation in which he had never found himself in all his business career. Because he had escaped from poverty so young and was not used to it, and because his character had a weak and timorous side, he was disturbed by a circumstance which thousands of petty shopkeepers face every day. He ordered Célestin to collect all that was owed him by his " prize customers," a term that his wife teased him for using, although she always concluded: " Call them whatever you like, as long as they pay." Célestin was so surprised by the order that it had to be repeated to him. For these " prize customers " were rich persons, who never failed to pay up, even if they did sometimes let considerable time go by, and with whom Birotteau sometimes had credits amounting to fifty or sixty thousand francs. Now his clerk took down the account book and began listing the largest sums due. César was afraid of his wife. In order that she should not see his depression he got ready to go out.

" Good day, sir," said Grindot, walking into the shop with the detached air which artists affect in speaking of the business arrangements which they claim to scorn. " I can't seem to turn your draft into cash, and I must ask you to convert it to me. I really hate to come to you about it, but I don't know how to deal with money-lenders and besides, I don't want to drag your signature in the mud. I know just enough about business to understand that it would do you no good and that it is to your best interests to. . . ."

" Sir!" Birotteau exclaimed. " You surprise me!"

Just then Lourdois walked in.

" Lourdois," said Birotteau with a smile, " can you imagine . . .?"

He stopped short. His impulse had been to follow the dictates of his customary self-assurance and ask Lourdois to cash the draft, since after all they were two businessmen, who could trust each other. But, to his amazement, he saw Lourdois' face cloud over, and realized that his impulse was a rash one. Such an innocent joke would be the death of his credit if it were already suspect. In a case like this, a business-man who was well off would pay up on his draft and not pass it on to someone else. He felt as dizzy as if he were looking into an abyss.

"My dear Birotteau," said Lourdois, leading him to the back of the shop, "my bill has been cut down to the bone and carefully gone over. I must ask you to give me the money tomorrow. My daughter's marrying young Crottat, and I have expenses to meet. Notaries don't make marriage contracts for nothing, and besides my signature is totally unknown."

"Send for it the day after tomorrow," said Birotteau proudly, counting on prompt payments from his "prize customers." "And you, too," he added to the architect.

"What's the matter with right now?" asked Grindot.

"This is pay-day for my factory workers," said César, who had never told a lie, and he picked up his hat in order to go out with them. But Thorein, the carpenter, and Chaffaroux, the mason, came up just as he was shutting the door.

"Sir," said Chaffaroux, "we happen to need money."

"I don't happen to own the gold mines of Peru," said César impatiently, stepping rapidly away from them. And he added to himself: "There's something funny about all this. Confound that ball! Everyone takes me for million-aire. . . . That fellow Lourdois didn't seem natural to me. There must be a snake in the grass."

He was walking aimlessly along the Rue Saint-Honoré when, like a stubborn goat, or a mathematician absorbed in some difficult problem, he practically bumped into Alexandre Crottat.

"Ah, there you are!" said Roguin's future successor. "I have a question to ask you. Did Monsieur Roguin give your four hundred thousand francs to Monsieur Claparon?"

"The transaction took place right under your nose," Birotteau answered. "Monsieur Claparon didn't give me a receipt . . . my notes were there, ready to be negotiated. . . . Roguin must have given him my two hundred and forty thousand francs in cash. . . . That was supposed to cover the initial payment. . . . Then the deeds were to be registered. . . . Of course, Judge Popinot says . . . yes, a receipt. . . . But why are you asking me such a question?"

"Why am I asking you such a question? In order to find out whether your two hundred and forty thousand francs are with Claparon or with Roguin. Roguin has known you for such a long time that out of sheer decency he might have turned the sum over to Claparon, in which case you'd be lucky. . . . How silly of me! He's taken it, together with the money of Monsieur Claparon, who fortunately didn't entrust him with more than a hundred thousand. Roguin has cleared out, and he took a hundred thousand francs I kept in his account for which I have no receipt. I gave them to him just as confidently as I'd entrust you with my wallet. Meanwhile, the owners of the land have not received a penny; they have just now left my offices. The money you borrowed on your factory buildings no longer exists for either yourself or your creditor. Roguin devoured it long ago, together with your hundred thousand francs. . . . Yes, I remember when he told me to get that last hundred thousand out of the bank."

The pupils of César's eyes were so dilated that he could see nothing but a red flame dancing in front of them.

"Yes, the hundred thousand francs of yours he had in the bank, the hundred thousand I kept in his account, the hundred thousand of Monsieur Claparon, that makes three hundred thousand francs in all, gone before their absence was noticed. . . . Madame Roguin's in a very bad way; Monsieur du Tillet watched over her all night long. Du Tillet had a lucky escape. Roguin tried for a whole month to get him interested in the land purchase, but fortunately all his money was tied up with Nucingen. Roguin left his wife a terrible letter; I've just read it. He'd been tampering for the past five years with his clients' money, and all because of a woman, *la belle Hollandaise*, with whom he broke off a fortnight before he pulled this trick on us. She had not a penny to her name, and they sold her furniture to pay her debts. In order to evade the bailiff, she had taken refuge in a brothel near the Palais-Royal, where she was murdered last night by a captain. Well, God has punished her for her sins, among them the depletion of Roguin's fortune! To some women nothing is sacred. Just think, she made off with all the profits of a notary's practice! Madame Roguin will be left with nothing unless she puts in a special claim, for he had borrowed on everything he had. His practice is to be sold for three hundred thousand francs. . . . I thought I was doing a good piece of business when I put a hundred thousand francs into it, without dreaming of asking for a receipt. Now, if I speak up for my money, people will think that I was in cahoots with him, and as a beginner I have to look to my reputation. You'll get no more than thirty per cent. . . . At my age, to have been such a fool! . . . And Roguin, at fifty-nine, to be keeping a woman! The old joker! . . . Three weeks ago he advised me not to marry Césarine. He must have known then that you would be in trouble, the monster!"

Alexandre might have gone on indefinitely, and still Birotteau would have stood in front of him like a stone. Every sentence was like a blow of a hammer, and just as before he had seen a flame in front of his eyes, so now each word tolled like a funeral bell. Alexandre Crottat did not know that the money Roguin had made off with did not all belong to César. And because he had always thought of the perfumer as a strong and capable man, he was struck now by his pallor and immobility. As a matter of fact, the idea of suicide was passing through the profoundly religious Birotteau's mind. In a case like this, suicide meant only one death instead of a thousand, and it seemed logical to accept it. Crottat gave César his arm and tried to get him to move, but it was impossible. The perfumer's legs gave way, as if he were drunk, underneath him.

"What's the matter?" Crottat asked him. "Brace up,

Monsieur César; nobody's dead. You're going to get back forty thousand francs, anyhow, from the mortgage loan. The money-lender didn't have enough on hand and it never got delivered. . . . You can petition for cancellation of the contract!"

"My ball! My Legion of Honor! The two hundred thousand francs' worth of notes I have outstanding, without a penny in the cash-box. . . . The Ragons, Pillerault. . . . And my wife, who saw through him from the start!"

A rain of confused words, which revealed the mass of turbulent thoughts and stricken feelings inside, poured like hailstones from the perfumer's lips, cutting to pieces all the buds of the Queen of Roses.

"I wish someone would chop off my head," sighed Birotteau. "It's too bulky for me to bear, and no use to me besides. . . ."

"Poor Monsieur Birotteau!" said Crottat. "Is it really so bad?"

"So bad?"

"Well then brace up and fight it!"

"Fight it?" echoed Birotteau again.

"Du Tillet was your clerk, wasn't he? He's got a head on his shoulders, and he'll surely help you."

"Du Tillet?"

"Yes; come along!"

"I don't want to go home in this condition, I know that," said Birotteau. "You're my friend, if I have any left. . . . You've dined at my house. . . . Now, for my wife's sake, will you put me into a cab and drive me about until I feel like facing my family?"

With considerable effort, Crottat shoved the inert mass that still answered to the name of César into a carriage.

"Xandrot," sobbed the perfumer, with tears streaming unchecked out of his eyes and slightly relieving the pressure of the iron band he felt around his head, "let us go to my house, and you can speak to Célestin for me. Tell him that my life and my wife's are at stake. Let there be no gossip about Roguin's disappearance. Bring Césarine downstairs and tell her to see to it that no one informs her mother. We must be careful of even our best friends, Pillerault, the Ragons . . . everybody."

Crottat was impressed by the change in Birotteau's voice, which emphasized the importance of what he was saying. The Rue Saint-Honoré was on the way to the police court, where Crottat was headed, and when they stopped at César's house Célestin and Césarine saw him leaning against the back of the cab seat, speechless and pale.

" Keep the whole story to yourself," he shouted after Crottat.

" There, he's coming around!" said Crottat to himself. " I thought he was done for."

The conference between Alexandre Crottat and the police magistrate lasted for some time, and the president of the Notaries' Guild was summoned to join it. César was transported from one place to another, like a sack of meal, without saying a word, until finally, toward seven o'clock in the evening, Crottat took him home. He was thoughtful enough to go ahead and warn Madame Birotteau that her husband had suffered a stroke of some kind.

" His mind is wandering," he said, making a circling gesture around his head. " You may have to bleed him, or use leeches."

" It's only to be expected," said Constance, who had not the remotest idea of the real trouble. " He didn't take his usual preventive medicine at the beginning of the winter, and for the last two months he's been working like a dog... as if he couldn't afford by now to relax a little!"

His wife and daughter persuaded César to go to bed and sent for old Doctor Haudry, a physician of the school of Molière, who believed in old apothecaries' prescriptions and dosed his patients to the limit of their capacities. He studied César's facial expression and ordered mustard plasters applied to his feet, diagnosing his ailment as cerebral congestion.

" And what can be the cause ?" Constance asked him.

" The damp weather," said the doctor.

Césarine followed him down the stairs and asked what rules they should follow in the care of the sick man. A doctor's parting recommendations are usually designed to soothe a sick person's family, and Haudry knew that something of the sort was expected of him at this time.

" Peace and quiet," he said. " When his head is relieved, then we'll risk giving him a tonic."

Constance spent two days at her husband's bedside, under the impression that his wild talk was delirious. As he lay there in her new blue room, the sight of the furniture, draperies and other extravagances sent him off into incomprehensible ravings.

" He's stark mad!" she said to Césarine, as César rose up in his bed and solemnly recited passages from the Commercial Code.

". . . ' if his expenditures shall be judged excessive.' . . . Take those curtains away! . . ."

After three terrible days, when César's reason was endangered, his reserves of peasant strength came to the rescue. His head was relieved, and Dr. Haudry prescribed cordials and plenty of good food. After a cup of coffee, administered at the psychological moment, the patient got up from his bed and Constance collapsed upon it.

" My poor wife!" exclaimed César when he saw her asleep there.

" Come, Father, be brave," said Césarine. " You're such a wonderful man that you can't help overcoming your misfortunes. It won't be such a hard job. Monsieur Anselme will help you."

She murmured these vague encouragements in a voice which tenderness made even gentler than usual, and such as to restore the faith of any man, no matter how beaten down he might be. Just so a mother might lull the teething pains of her baby.

"Yes, I'll fight back, my child, I promise you. But don't say a word to a living soul, not even to Popinot, who is in love with you, or to Uncle Pillerault. First of all, I must write to my brother, who is vicar, as I remember, of a cathedral. He has no expenses, so he must have saved some money. If he's put away three thousand francs a year for the last twenty years. . . . And in the provinces, a priest's credit is always good."

Césarine hastened to bring her father a small table and writing equipment. For paper, she gave him the left-over invitations to the ball.

"Burn all that up!" her father shouted. "That ball was the devil's own inspiration. If I am beaten by this, I'll be no better than a common swindler. Well, no more talk!"

And he proceeded to write:

Dear Brother,

I am in such business difficulties that I must beg you to send me all the money you can, even if you have to borrow.

Your devoted brother,
CÉSAR

Your niece, Césarine, who has been watching me write this letter, while my wife snatches a few minutes of sleep, sends you her most affectionate greetings.

The postscript was added at Césarine's request, and the letter was given to Raguet to mail.

"Father," Césarine said when she came back upstairs, "Monsieur Lebas is here and would like to speak to you."

"Monsieur Lebas?" exclaimed César, as if misfortune had made him a criminal. "On behalf of the commercial court?"

"My dear Monsieur Birotteau," said the draper as he

entered the room, " I take too much interest in you. . . . We've known each other so long, we were elected referees at the same time. . . . Well, anyhow, as I was saying, I feel obliged to tell you that a certain usurer called Bidault, alias Gigonnet, has some of your notes which Claparon's firm has passed on to him as *not guaranteed*. Those two words are not only a personal insult; they signify the end of your credit."

Just then Célestin stuck his head in the door.

" Monsieur Claparon is here to see you," he announced.

" We'll get to the bottom of this insult," Lebas added, before Claparon came in.

" Sir," said César, " let me introduce my friend Monsieur Lebas of the commercial court, who . . ."

" Oh, so this is Monsieur Lebas!" Claparon interrupted him. " What a splendid piece of luck! Lebas of the commercial court! Of course, there are quite a few people of that name . . ."

But Birotteau cut short this chatter.

" He has seen the notes I gave you in circulation, in spite of the fact that you said they would never leave your hands. And on them were the words *not guaranteed*."

" They're not in circulation at all," Claparon answered. " They're in the hands of old man Bidault, with whom I often do business. That's why I marked them *not guaranteed*. If they had been meant to circulate, you would have made them out to him directly. I am sure that Monsieur Lebas understands the situation. What do these notes represent? The price of some real estate, bought by whom? . . . Birotteau. And why should I guarantee Birotteau's signature by mine? Each of us has his share to pay. And isn't it sufficient for us to stick together in our relations with our creditors? My business practices are inflexible. I don't give a superfluous guarantee any more than I give a receipt in advance for a sum of money that is owed me. My confidence is complete. The signatory is bound to pay up, and I don't want to have to pay three times over."

" Three times over ?" asked the puzzled César.

" Exactly. I've already guaranteed Birotteau to the sellers. Why would I guarantee him to the banker as well ? We're in difficult straits, I admit. Roguin's stripped me of a hundred thousand francs, and so my half of the land is costing me five hundred thousand instead of four. Now, Roguin has taken two hundred and forty thousand francs from Birotteau, as well. What would you do, Monsieur Lebas, if you were in my shoes ? You don't know me any more than I know Monsieur Birotteau. Just follow my line of reasoning. Suppose we are doing a piece of business together, on a fifty-fifty basis. You bring in your money; I put up collateral, which you are so kind as to turn into cash. Then you hear that the wealthy and virtuous banker, Claparon (I am willing to assume all the virtues in the world), is bankrupt, with six million francs in debts. Is that the time you would choose to guarantee my signature with yours ? If you did, you'd be crazy. Well, Monsieur Lebas, Birotteau is in the situation in which I have imagined Claparon. Can't you see that if I were to guarantee his signature, then I might be obliged to pay his share of what we both owe for the land, and still not obtain. . . ."

" Pay whom ?" Birotteau interrupted.

" And still not obtain his share of the land in return," Claparon insisted. " I'd have no claim, and might even have to buy it all over."

" You haven't told me whom you must pay," Birotteau insisted.

" The third party, of course. I mean, if I did give a guarantee and something were to happen to you."

" I shan't fail you, sir," Birotteau said simply.

" Very well," said Claparon. " Monsieur Lebas, you've been in business and you have conducted business arbitration. You know that a man has to take his precautions. After all, I'm a banker by profession."

" Monsieur Claparon is right," Lebas admitted.

"Yes, I'm quite right, from a banking point of view," echoed Claparon. "But this is a real estate deal. What am I entitled to receive? Cash, of course, for I must pay the sellers of the land in cash. Never mind the two hundred and forty thousand francs which Birotteau has lost to Roguin. I'm quite sure he'll make up for those." And turning to Birotteau, he added: "I've come to ask for a mere trifle, twenty-five thousand francs."

"Twenty-five thousand francs?" exclaimed César, feeling the blood in his veins turn to ice. "On what basis?"

"My dear sir, we must register the deeds with a notary. We can come to an understanding about the price between ourselves, but dealing with the Treasury is another matter. No, sir, the Treasury doesn't waste words. It doesn't allow credit even for the length of time it takes you to put your hand in your pocket. That's why we have to cough up forty-four thousand francs in taxes this very week. Now, before you are any more excited, let me explain that I had an idea you might be embarrassed by a request for twenty-five thousand francs, and I came to say that I've saved you. . . ."

"Saved me what?" cried Birotteau in a tone of evident distress.

"A mere trifle. You know those twenty-five thousand francs of 'miscellaneous notes' which Roguin gave me to sell? Well, I've credited them against your share of the registration expenses, of which I shall send you an accounting. There'll be a very small charge for the handling, six or seven thousand francs, which you can owe me."

"It all seems to me perfectly in order," said Lebas. "If I were in the place of this gentleman, who seems to have such a good business head, I should deal with a stranger in the same way."

"None of this can kill an old fox like Birotteau!" Claparon exclaimed genially. "I've seen a fox with his head full of buckshot, running like a . . . well, like a fox. . . ."

"Who could have imagined that Roguin was such a scoundrel?" said Lebas, who was worried both by César's silence and by another train of thought which had no connection with the perfumery business.

"I almost gave this gentleman a receipt for four hundred thousand francs," said Claparon. "And if I had, I'd be in a pretty mess. But our mutual confidence was my salvation. It didn't seem to matter whether the money was kept in Roguin's office or in mine until the time came to sign the contract."

"I say everyone should have kept his money in the bank until the time came," observed Lebas.

"Roguin was my banker," said César. "But he's mixed up in the land business as well."

"Yes, he promised to pay for a quarter share," said Claparon. "After I've let him run off with my money, I'm not going to be such a fool as to give him more. If he sends me back my hundred thousand francs and two hundred thousand more as a payment for his share, then we shall see. But he's not likely to send me anything for a piece of meat that has to simmer five years on the stove before you get any soup out of it. They say he's only taken three hundred thousand francs with him, and he'll need an income of fifteen thousand a year to live comfortably abroad."

"The bandit!"

"Ah, well, it's all the price of passion! What old man can be sure that some senile fancy won't carry him away? No matter how virtuous we may be, we never know what's going to happen. And sometimes the last love is the most violent of all. Take Cardot and Camusot and Matifat! Every last one of them has a mistress. We should have looked askance at a notary who was willing to enter a real estate venture. Whenever a notary or a broker involves himself in business, there's something fishy about it. A business failure gives them an opportunity to go into fraudulent bankruptcy, and if they must be haled up before a criminal court they'd rather it happened abroad. And we're so weak-minded that we don't sue people after they've asked us to their house for dinner, or to a grand ball. That would never do in polite society. We let the thing drop, and there I think we're very much mistaken."

"I quite agree," said Birotteau, taking up a favorite theme. "The bankruptcy laws must be amended."

"If I can help you," said Lebas to Birotteau, "you know you can call upon me."

"Monsieur Birotteau doesn't need anybody," said the loquacious Claparon, who had simply been parroting the instructions given him by du Tillet. "It's all perfectly clear. Roguin's bankruptcy will pay off fifty per cent, at least so young Crottat tells me. Besides this, Birotteau is recovering forty thousand francs that the lender never delivered in return for a mortgage. After that he can borrow on his properties. And the hundred thousand francs we owe for the land aren't due for another four months. That gives Monsieur Birotteau time to redeem his notes, for he couldn't have been counting solely upon the funds with which Roguin has run away. Of course, it may be a tight squeeze, but I'm sure he'll wriggle out of it."

César took courage from Claparon's analysis of the affair and his suggestions for settling it. His face relaxed and he conceived a high opinion of the false banker's judgment.

(Du Tillet had decided to pose as one of Roguin's victims. He had given Claparon a hundred thousand francs for Roguin, who had of course returned them to him on the sly. So Claparon played this part of his role with conviction, and was ready to tell any and all comers that Roguin had done him out of a hundred thousand francs. Du Tillet thought that Claparon had too many remnants of decent feeling to fall in with the whole of his scheme, and furthermore he knew the ex-salesman did not have the brains to understand it. "If our best friend isn't our first dupe as well, then we'll never find a second," was to be his laconic remark on the day when his accomplice registered a complaint and he broke him like a tool for which he had no more use.)

Meanwhile, Lebas and Claparon went away together.

"I'll come out of it," said Birotteau to himself. "The notes I have to pay come to two hundred and thirty-five thousand francs, that is sixty thousand francs for the alterations of the house and a hundred and sixty-five thousand francs for the land. I can count on as much as a hundred thousand francs from the Roguin settlement, and then there are the forty thousand of the mortgage loan, of which Claparon was just speaking. It's a question of making a hundred thousand francs out of the new hair tonic and then hanging on, by collecting some bills or by borrowing from a bank, until the land has attained its eventual resale value."

No matter how hard his luck, once a man can buttress his hopes by a chain of more or less logical reasoning he may yet save the situation. Many people mistake the confidence born of illusion for actual energy. But then perhaps the better part of courage is hope, and that is why the Church has made it one of the three theological virtues. Indeed, hope has been the salvation of many a weak man, by giving him time in which to attend to his problems.

Birotteau resolved to talk to his wife's uncle before seeking help from other quarters, but as he started down the Rue Saint-Honoré toward the Rue des Bourdonnais he felt such violent pangs of anxiety that he thought he was going to be physically stricken again. This time his whole abdomen seemed to be afire. Just as people who perceive things with their brains suffer from cerebral ailments, so now César's lower parts were affected: in moments of crisis, the body is attacked in the place where its owner's essential temperament is established. A weak man falls prey to colic, and a Napoleon goes off to sleep at the most unexpected moments.

A man of honor swallows his pride and turns to someone else for help, only after Necessity has pricked him to the heart. Birotteau had felt this prick for two whole days before making up his mind to go to Pillerault. Family considerations finally prevailed, for he knew that sooner or later he would have to explain the situation. Nevertheless when he came to the honorable and severe hardware dealer's door, he felt that sinking of the heart which a child feels at the prospect of going to the dentist. Only in his case the sinking feeling was over the outcome of his whole life and not just a passing toothache.

## II

HE WENT SLOWLY UP THE STAIRS AND FOUND THE OLD man reading his *Constitutionnel* in front of the fire, with his frugal lunch—bread, butter, Brie cheese and a cup of coffee— on a small round table beside him.

" Here's the life of a truly wise man," he said enviously.

" Well," said Pillerault, taking off his spectacles, " I heard yesterday at the Café David about Roguin and the murder of his mistress, *la belle Hollandaise.* I hope you heeded our wish to be the owners of the land outright and got a receipt from Claparon."

" Alas, I didn't, Uncle! You've put your finger on the whole tragedy."

" Good Lord! Then you're done for," said Pillerault, letting his paper fall from his hand.

Birotteau was prompt to pick it up, in spite of the fact that it was the *Constitutionnel.* His uncle was so affected by the thoughts that were passing through his mind that his classically severe face turned blazing red, like the profile on a copper coin under the die-stamp. He sat very still and stared blankly through his window at the wall across the way. He listened to Birotteau's story, weighing the pros and cons with all the inflexibility of a man who has left the marketplace behind and is called upon to deliver a sentence from his fourth-floor retirement.

" Well, Uncle, what do you say?" asked Birotteau, concluding his story with an appeal to Pillerault to sell sixty thousand francs, worth of securities.

" I can't do that, my poor boy; you're too deeply involved. The Ragons and I will lose our fifty thousand francs apiece.

It was upon my advice that these good people sold their shares in the Wortschin mines, and although I feel no obligation to give them back their money, I must stand by in case of need, just as I must stand by my niece and Césarine. You may want for bread, all of you, and here you shall find it."

"Bread, Uncle?"

"Yes, bread. Try to see things as they are and face the fact that you'll never get out of this. . . . Of my five thousand six hundred francs of income, I can turn over four thousand to your family and the Ragons. And once Constance knows the worst, she'll set to work like a madwoman. I know her. She'll deprive herself of everything, and so will you, César; I know you too."

"It's not completely hopeless, Uncle."

"There I'm afraid I can't agree."

"I'll prove the contrary."

"Nothing would give me more pleasure."

Birotteau started to take leave without anything more to say. He had come to seek consolation and encouragement and instead he had received a second blow, less stunning, to be sure, than the first, but one which struck at his heart, where he was the most susceptible.

"Sir," he said coldly, "Constance doesn't yet know. Please keep my secret, at least for the time being, and ask the Ragons to do the same. I need peace of mind while I am gathering strength for the struggle that lies ahead."

Pillerault nodded.

"Courage, César," he added. "I see that I've made you angry. But some day, you'll think of your wife and daughter and be grateful to me."

César was all the more disheartened, because he knew and appreciated his uncle's clearsightedness, and his hope faded to complete uncertainty. When a man without the steadfastness of a Pillerault finds himself in a tight spot of this kind, he tends to follow whatever wind may blow; he pursues

at random his own ideas or those of the first fellow he chances
to meet, like a traveler led astray by some will-o'-the-wisp
on his way. He lets the gale carry him off, instead of throw-
ing himself flat on the ground until it has passed or studying
its course and finding a way to escape it.

Now, in the midst of his sorrow, Birotteau remembered
the lawsuit over his loan, and hurried to the Rue Vivienne
to ask Derville, his attorney, whether it wouldn't be a good
idea to start proceedings to cancel the contract. He found
the lawyer in a white quilted dressing-gown beside the fire,
as calm and collected as any man of his profession is bound
to be after years of listening to his clients' tales of disaster.
César was particularly aware of this necessarily impersonal
attitude because of his own feverish condition, brought on
by the involvement of his personal honor and the future of
his wife and child. Now Derville said in answer to his
proposal:

" If it can be proved that the lender didn't have on deposit
with Roguin the sum that Roguin said he was lending you,
then since there was no cash transaction, there is a possibility
of cancellation. In that case, the lender can only claim the
amount of his guarantee and you can try for the full amount
of the money. In a suit of this kind there is a fair chance
of success. But of course I can't make any promises."

Birotteau was encouraged by this statement on the part
of so able a man and asked him to try to obtain a decision
within the next two weeks. But the lawyer said that three
months were more likely to go by.

" Three months!" exclaimed Birotteau, disappointed in
the hope of finding immediate resources.

" Even if we get onto the court agenda, we can't oblige
your adversary to keep step with us. He'll try to stall the
proceedings as long as he can, even at the risk of exposing
himself to sentence of default. You can't set the pace of
the law!" And Derville smiled.

" But in the commercial court. . . ." said Birotteau.

"Commercial courts are quite different from the regular kind," Derville told him. "In the commercial court you hurry everything through, but we have forms to observe, forms which insure that justice will be done. You wouldn't want a quick sentence that stripped you of your money, would you? Well, your adversary is going to put up a fight, you know. And stays and delays are the barbed-wire defenses set up by the law."

"You're right, of course," said Birotteau, going out the door with death in his heart.

"All of them are right; oh, money, money!" he said, talking to himself, as so many harassed people do in this turbulent city which a poet has aptly named the "boiling pot."

As he came into his shop, the clerk whom he had sent out to collect bills told him that with the approach of the New Year's holiday, most of his debtors had signed an acknowledgment of receipt of the bill, but hadn't paid up.

"There's no money to be had, anywhere," said the perfumer out loud, in his despair. Then he bit his lip, for all his clerks were staring at him.

Five days passed in this way, five days in which the attitude of Braschon, Lourdois, Thorein, Grindot, Chaffaroux and other unpaid creditors passed from confidence to belligerent mistrust. In Paris the latter is just as quick to develop as the first is slow, and once the creditor resorts to the tortuous collection devices offered him by the law he soon sinks to a level far lower than that of his debtor. Braschon, who had made a fortune selling wallpaper on the Rue du Faubourg Saint-Antoine, but had not been invited to the ball, led off the attack by demanding payment within twenty-four hours, and he exacted certain guarantees, not in movable goods, but in the form of a claim against the forty-thousand-franc value of Birotteau's property on the Faubourg.

In spite of the violence of his creditors' demands, Birotteau still had occasional intervals in which to breathe. But instead of combating his difficulties, César used all his wits to prevent his wife, the person who could have been the most helpful, from knowing anything about them. Much of the time he stood on guard at the entrance of the shop. Célestin had been admitted to his secret, or at least to the fact that he was in momentary financial embarrassment, and looked at his employer with a mixture of curiosity and astonishment. César was diminished in his eyes, as any man accustomed to succeed is bound to be when his success is seen to be due simply to force of habit rather than superior intelligence. But although César was not energetic enough to defend himself at all the points on which he was attacked, he did have the courage to examine his position. For the end of December and the middle of January, in order to cover his household expenses, rents and current obligations, he must obtain sixty thousand francs, half of them by January first. All his resources put together would yield him twenty thousand, so for the moment he needed only ten thousand more. This did not seem altogether impossible, for like an adventurer living from day to day, he did not see beyond the end of his own nose.

Before news of his embarrassment became public he made up his mind to what he thought was a daring expedient: a visit to François Keller, orator, banker and philanthropist, famous for his charities and also for his willingness to make himself useful to the business community of Paris and thus ensure his re-election to the Chamber of Deputies. The banker was a Liberal and César a Royalist, as we know, but he relied on Keller's kind heart and imagined that a difference in opinions would only be a spur to his benevolence. In case collateral were needed, he counted on the devoted Popinot to provide him with thirty thousand francs' worth of notes, which could be offered to the most insistent of his creditors and help him win his suit.

Birotteau was by nature an expansive man and accustomed in the privacy of his own bedroom to confiding in his beloved Constance every emotion of the day and seeking her encouragement or constructive criticism. Now he could not speak to her or to his uncle or chief clerk either, and all these thoughts weighed heavily upon his mind. But he generously preferred to suffer alone rather than to sadden his wife and hoped that he would not have to tell her his troubles until they were all past. Perhaps dread of his wife's reproaches was partially responsible for this resolution. He went every morning to Mass at Saint-Roch and poured out his confidences to God.

"If on my way back from church I do not meet a single soldier, then my petition to Keller will meet with success. This will be God's answer to my prayer." So he said to himself, after having implored God's aid.

Luckily he met no soldier on the way. But his heart was still heavy and he had to find someone to relieve him of the loneliness of his burden. So it was that Césarine, who had heard the first news of the disaster, came to share his secret. Conspiratorial looks passed between them, looks fraught with stifled hope and disappointment, questions which met with an instantly sympathetic response and messages flashed from one heart to the other. In his wife's presence, Birotteau made a special effort to be gay. Whatever question she asked, he answered by assuring her that all was going well. Popinot was highly successful and there was no need to worry about him; his oil was going like wildfire. The Claparon notes would be paid, never fear. There was something almost terrifying about his false joviality. But when his wife had fallen asleep in their sumptuous new bed, he would sit bolt upright and brood over his woes. At such times, Césarine sometimes appeared, in her night-dress, with bare feet and a shawl thrown over her white shoulders.

"Father, I can hear you crying," she said, herself in tears.

Birotteau fell into such a state of torpor after he had

written to ask for an appointment with the great François Keller that his daughter took him out for a walk through Paris. For the first time he saw great red posters in the streets advertising CEPHALIC OIL.

While the Queen of Roses was fading away, young Popinot's star was rising in glory. With Gaudissart and Finot to guide him, Anselme had launched his new product with audacity. Three days before, two thousand posters had appeared in the most conspicuous spots of Paris, and no one could help running up against one of Finot's concise phrases concerning the impossibility of making hair grow and the danger of dyeing it, accompanied by a quotation from the paper Vauquelin had read before the Academy of Science. Purchasers of the tonic felt they were obtaining a new lease on life for their dead hair. All the perfumers and hairdressers of Paris had decorated their doors with gilt frames containing a fine print on thin paper of a miniature Hero and Leander with the following caption: " *Ancient peoples kept their hair by using Cephalic Oil!*"

" He's invented a permanent frame, which will keep his advertisement on view forever!" exclaimed the amazed Birotteau, in front of the door of the Silver Bell.

" Didn't you see the model that Monsieur Anselme brought especially to show you when he left three hundred bottles of oil to be sold at your shop?"

" No," César said absently.

" Célestin has already sold fifty bottles to casual passers-by and sixty to regular customers."

Birotteau was deafened by the medley of bells that calamity causes to jangle in its victims' ears. Popinot had waited a whole hour to see him the day before, and gone away only after Constance and Césarine had told him that César was immersed in his own affairs.

" Oh yes, the real estate purchase," said the younger man.

Fortunately Popinot had been busy night and day, Sundays

included, at his own establishment on the Rue des Cinq-Diamants and hadn't seen Pillerault, the Ragons or his uncle the judge. The poor fellow snatched no more than two hours sleep a night, and had only two helpers where he needed four. In business, timing is everything, and a man who doesn't take success by the tail when it comes by is fated to lose a fortune. Popinot told himself that his aunt and uncle would be glad to see him, six months later, when he came to tell them he had made his fortune, and Birotteau when he brought him thirty or forty thousand francs as his share in the profits. He knew nothing of Roguin's disappearance and César's disaster and hence there was no danger of his saying the wrong thing to Madame Birotteau.

Popinot had promised Finot five hundred francs for every first-class newspaper (there were ten of them) and three hundred for every second-class one (that meant ten more) which made mention three times a month of Cephalic Oil. And Finot saw a net gain for himself of three thousand of this total of eight thousand francs, a sum which he could toss on the green baize table of Speculation. He threw himself like a lion upon his acquaintances and friends, haunted newspaper offices, stood beside the editors' beds first thing in the morning and paced the theater lobbies at night. " Don't forget my Oil, will you? It's not my direct concern, but my friend Gaudissart has an interest in the business, and he's a good fellow." This was the beginning and end of all his conversations. He laid siege to the available space in newspaper columns and provided the editors with pertinent articles for which he waived all pay. With the cunning of an understudy who wants to pass for an actor and the dexterity of a vaudeville tumbler, he wrote flattering letters and did all sorts of dirty jobs in order to wangle space for this publicity. Dinner parties, banal compliments, everything contributed to this end. He went to the printers at the hour when they were putting the paper to bed, with the excuse of reading the proofs of a theatrical article of his own and

bribed them with theater tickets to insert fillers relating
to Cephalic Oil. Soon he obtained more space than had ever
been given to Ragnauld's Cough Syrup, Brazilian Diuretic,
or any of the other products whose makers had been pioneers
in the technique of hammering at the public's attention with
the repetition of the same name or slogan every day. In these
innocent days, newspaper men were still unaware of their
powers; they wrote up actresses and put personalities in the
news without reaping any reward for their pains. Now
Andoche Finot's efforts were not directed at boosting a
would-be star or a friend's play, at getting something for
nothing; on the contrary, he had money and lunch invitations to offer. As a result, all the papers talked about
Cephalic Oil and how it fitted in with Vauquelin's discoveries, which in turn permitted them to make fun of the
pretension of making hair grow and to decry the danger of
trying to dye it.

Finot's articles gave Gaudissart satisfaction and delight.
Armed with Paris newspapers, he set out on what has since
come to be called a "drive" to enlighten the provincial
public. In those days the provinces, poor things, had no
papers of their own, and those that came from the city were
read from cover to cover, including the name and address
of the printer, which often served as a shield for some per-
secuted member of the opposition. With the press to back
him up, Gaudissart won immediate success. Provincial hairdressers clamored for the framed print of Hero and Leander,
and meanwhile at the Funambules Theater, Finot had gotten
them to insert a comic scene, in which Pierrot poured
Macassar Oil on a scraggly old broom and caused it to
sprout new bristles. In later days, Finot admitted that
without Popinot's three thousand francs, he would have
died of poverty and disappointment. As it was, this sum was
as good as a fortune. Three months after this, he became
editor of a small paper, which he eventually bought and
made into a great success. Just as Gaudissart's "drive"

upon the provinces won huge sales for Popinot, so Finot's assault upon the newspapers impressed Cephalic Oil upon the public mind, just as Regnauld's Cough Syrup and Brazilian Diuretic had been. All three of these products made a fortune for their manufacturers and the method by which they were launched, which was then quite new, led to the deluge of present-day advertising.

The name of Popinot was on every wall and in every shop window, but because César was not aware of the revolutionary nature of this intensive publicity, he contented himself with saying somewhat fatuously to his daughter: " Young Popinot is following in my footsteps !" César had not set foot in his factory since the ball and had no idea of the extent of Popinot's activity. Anselme had taken on Birotteau's workers and slept at the scene of his work. In his imagination, every case, every shipment and every bill-head bore Césarine's image upon it. " Some day she'll be my wife !" he said to himself fiercely, as he hammered the nails into one box after another, with his jacket laid aside and his sleeves rolled up to the elbows, because half of his men were making deliveries all over the city.

Meanwhile, after César had thought all night about what to say and what not to say to an important banker, he tremblingly arrived at the great man's door. And this in spite of the fact that François Keller was known to be so Liberal as to desire the overthrow of the Bourbons. Like most of his fellow shopkeepers and small businessmen, César had never known anyone in top banking circles; indeed he had not even dealt with those lesser institutions which serve as intermediaries and furnish the big banks a double guarantee, for he and his wife had never lived beyond their means or found themselves without money. Perhaps it is a mistake not to open up a drawing account for oneself somewhere; on this point, opinions are divided. In any case, Birotteau now regretted that nowhere were his name and signature on file. Because of his political past and the fact that he was deputy to the Mayor, he imagined that he could introduce himself wherever he chose and had no idea of the number of people that come to call upon a banker.

When he was shown into the anteroom outside the great man's study, he found himself in the range of deputies to parliament, writers, journalists, brokers, engineers and big businessmen, not to mention the intimate friends who pushed their way ahead of the others and gave a pre-arranged knock at the door which gained them immediate admittance. " Who am I in the midst of this vast machinery ?" Birotteau wondered, taken aback by the bustle of the intellectual workshop, where the Opposition party came to seek its daily bread and the Left Wing leaders rehearsed the tragi-comic roles which they were called upon to play. On his right he overheard a discussion of the loan for the completion of the canal system, proposed by the Communication office, and the figures ran into millions, while on his left some journalists, anxious to play upon the banker's vanity, were talking about the preceding day's session at the Chamber, and the brilliance of his extemporaneous speech. During the two hours that he waited, Birotteau caught three glimpses of the banker as he led some important person out of his study. Keller escorted the last of these, General Foy, all the way across the antechamber.

" There's no hope for me," Birotteau thought to himself, with a sinking feeling.

For as the banker started to go back into his study, he was assailed by the crowd of friends and sycophants, like a female dog with a pack of males after her. A few hardy souls did make their way in and talked with him for as long as ten or fifteen minutes, some of them emerging with a contrite air, others looking quite pleased with themselves or even triumphant. Birotteau kept his eye peeled on the clock as time went by. No one paid any attention to the concealed sorrow of this stoutish man sitting restlessly in a gilt armchair at one side of the fireplace, just outside the entrance to that panacea for all human ills, credit. César reflected that for a brief time he had reigned as king in his own house, just as this man reigned every morning, and the comparison made him realize into how deep an abyss he had fallen. What bitter thoughts went through his head and how many tears he held back in the passage of these two hours! And how many times he prayed God to help him obtain favor, for his gentle soul was terrified by the insolence, tyrannical anger and lust for power that he perceived under the banker's affectation of geniality. Finally, when no more than a dozen persons were still waiting, he decided that the next time the study door creaked, he would stand up and proclaim boldly: " My name is Birotteau!" The first grenadier to advance against the fortifications of the Moskva river had no more courage than the perfumer required to carry out this maneuver. " After all, I am deputy to the Mayor," he said to himself as he got up to announce his own name.

François Keller took on an agreeable air, as if he were anxious to please. With his eye on his visitor's Legion of Honor ribbon, he stepped back and motioned him into the study, pausing meanwhile to speak to two persons who had descended upon him like a whirlwind from the stair.

" Descazes wants to talk to you," said one of them. " He wants to put an end to the intrigues that go on at the Pavillon Marsan, which means that the King is beginning to see things our way."

" We'll go to the Chamber together," said the banker, puffing himself up like a bull-frog trying to play the part of a bull.

" How can he keep his mind on his business?" Birotteau wondered.

He was dazzled by the sheer brilliance of superiority, like a bug blinded by a bright light when it flies in out of a dim evening or a dull day. On a large table he saw a copy of the budget, hundreds of printed papers from the Chamber

and volumes of the official *Moniteur*, marked in the appropriate places, so that the banker could catch a cabinet member
up on some earlier statement and make him admit a contra-
diction, much to the delight of the undiscriminating public,
which cannot possibly understand that events are bound to
modify even the most logical man's course of behavior.
On another table there were piled-up portfolios, notes, and
memoranda containing all the details of a thousand and one
business projects which industrialists had submitted for the
banker's approval.  The luxurious decorations, paintings,
statues and other works of art, the encumberment of the
mantelpiece with piles of papers pertaining to national and
international interests, all made Birotteau feel small and afraid
and froze the blood in his veins.  On François Keller's desk
lay piles of notes, letters of credit and business circulars.
Now the banker sat down and began to sign some letters
which did not require re-reading.

" Sir, to what do I owe the honor of your call ?" he asked,
still turning over the papers before him.

These words, addressed to him alone by a voice which
was accustomed to speaking to a whole continent, were like
so many hot steel needles plunged into the perfumer's
stomach.  He took on the ingratiating air which the banker
was accustomed to see on the face of all those who wished
to involve him in their personal affairs, and which at once
gave him an advantage over them.  And the banker, in
return, cast at César a Napoleonic stare, which went straight
through the poor perfumer's head.  This imitation of Napoleon was widespread among certain pretentious persons,
who were not even good counterfeits of the emperor.  In
any case, such was the stare that fell upon Birotteau, a man
of the Right, devoted to the government in power, and a
Royalist of the first water.

" Sir," he answered, " I don't want to waste your valuable
time.  I have come on a strictly business matter to obtain
credit from you.  Since I served as a referee on the com-

mercial court, if my pockets were full, I should have only
to apply at the bank where you are a director. I sat on the
court beside Baron Thibon, head of the credit committee,
and he surely wouldn't refuse me. But I've never asked for
credit or given my signature before, and you know something of the difficulties of procedure in a case like this."
(Here Keller shook his head, and Birotteau mistook the
motion for one of impatience.)—" Sir," he went on hastily,
" this is the story. I entered into a real estate venture,
quite outside my usual business, and . . ."

François Keller continued to skim the letters before him
with his eyes, as if he were not listening, but suddenly he
raised his head and beckoned to his interlocutor to go on.
Birotteau thought that things were going his way and sighed
with relief.

" Go on; I hear you," Keller said agreeably.

" I've a half interest in some land around the Madeleine."

" Oh yes, I heard talk at Nucingen's about this big deal
undertaken by Claparon's company."

" Well," said Birotteau, " a credit of a hundred thousand
francs, guaranteed by my share in this land, would carry me
through until the time when I expect to reap the profits
of another piece of business in the perfumery line. If necessary, I can cover my loan by notes from this new business,
run by a certain Popinot. . . ."

Keller seemed to be not at all interested in Popinot, and
fearing that he was off on a wrong tack, Birotteau stopped
short, then intimidated by the silence that followed went on
to say:

" As far as interest is concerned, we can . . ."

" Of course, of course," the banker interrupted him, " it
can all be arranged. You can be sure I'll do all I can for you.
With the financial problems of the whole continent on my
shoulders and the Chamber taking up a large part of my
time, you'll see why I have to leave the consideration of such

things up to someone else in my office.  Go to see my brother,
Adolphe, downstairs, tell him about the guarantees you have
to offer, and if he approves you can come back with him
tomorrow or the day after at five o'clock in the morning,
which is the hour when I examine all such business propositions.  We're happy to have you turn to us, for you are
one of those true-blue Royalists whose esteem we value in
spite of the fact that they are our political opponents."

"Sir," said Birotteau, intoxicated by this demagogic
phraseology, "I am as unworthy of this honor as I am of
the royal favor of which I have lately been the recipient.
If I have any merit whatsoever, it is because I have sat on
the commercial court and fought . . ."

"Yes," said the banker hastily, "your reputation is an
open-sesame, Monsieur Birotteau.  Any piece of business
you propose is sure to be sound, and you can count on our
support."

At this point, Keller's sister-in-law, the daughter of
Count de Gonderville, came in through a side door which
Birotteau had not noticed and said:

"I hope to see you before you go to the Chamber."

"It's two o'clock!" the banker exclaimed.  "That means
the battle is already on!  Excuse me, sir; it's a little matter
of overturning the government. . . . Go to my brother. . . ."

He showed Birotteau to the door by which he had entered
and said to a servant:

"Take this gentleman to Monsieur Adolphe."

The liveried servant led Birotteau down a labyrinth of
stairs, to a room far less sumptuous but more business-like
than that from which he had just come.  The perfumer had
mounted on the high horse of Hope and was stroking his chin
with satisfaction over the banker's flattering words.  His only
regret was that such an eloquent and capable man should
be an enemy of the Bourbons.

His head dancing with these illusions, Birotteau walked
into a cold bare room, furnished with two roll-top desks,

plain armchairs, a thin rug and dingy curtains, which bore the same relation to the place from which he had just come as a kitchen to a dining-room or a workshop to a fashionable store. Here business affairs were taken to pieces and calculations made as to how much investment in them might yield the bank. This was the hatching-place of those bold moves by which the Keller brothers had won their fame and also a temporary monopoly of various new fields of exploitation. Here the brothers studied all new legislation pertaining to business and stipulated those exorbitant prices known in Stock Exchange circles as " choice morsels," which they demanded for the use of their name and credit. Here, too, they devised those strictly legal but evasive operations by which they invested in some shaky enterprise, killed it off by calling in the money due them at a critical moment and then proceeded to put it on its feet again for their own profit and to the loss of the innocent stockholders.

The two brothers had allotted themselves different roles to play. Upstairs, François, the politician, gave bland promises and made himself generally agreeable. Where he was concerned, it was all very easy; he did business on a lofty plane and charmed everyone who came to see him for the first time with fine phrases and enthusiasm. Below, Adolphe apologized for his brother's political preoccupations and, like a croupier, raked in the money. He was the down-to-earth and difficult partner, and one dealt with him on a very different level. Often François Keller's soft-spoken " yes " turned into a succinct " no " downstairs. This " squeeze play " allowed for innumerable variations and was a well-known subject of other and less successful financiers' amusement.

Just now, Adolphe Keller was talking to Palma, his adviser, who faded away when Birotteau came into the room. After César had told his story, Adolphe, who was by far the more subtle of the two brothers, lowered his head and peered at him over his spectacles with that alternately penetrating and glassy " banker's stare," peculiar to vultures and lawyers as well.

" Send me all the papers pertaining to the purchase of the land. There I can see for myself what guarantees you have to offer before we come down to the matter of interest. If it looks like a good proposition, we might be satisfied to take a share in the eventual profits instead of laying a burden upon you at the present time."

" I see what he means," Birotteau said to himself on his way home. " Like a trapped beaver, I can't get out of my troubles without leaving part of my skin behind. But it's better to be shorn than to be finished altogether."

He was laughing when he came into his own house and his good humor was infectious.

" I'm saved," he said to Césarine. " The Kellers are giving me credit."

# III

IT WAS NO EARLIER THAN THE TWENTY-NINTH OF DECEMBER
when Birotteau saw Adolphe Keller again. The first time
that he returned to the Keller establishment, Adolphe had
gone to look at a piece of property ten miles or so outside
of Paris, which his brother had in mind to buy. The next
time, both brothers were closeted together for the whole
morning over the question of a loan which had to be submitted to the Chamber and they left word for him to come
the next Friday. Finally this day rolled around, and Birotteau found himself sitting on one side of the fireplace, in the
light from the window, with Adolphe Keller on the other.

"This is all very well," said the banker, after examining
his papers, "but what did you make by way of down payment?"

"A hundred and forty thousand francs."

"In cash?"

"No, in notes."

"Have they been called in?"

"No, they haven't yet fallen due."

"But if you paid more for the land than it is actually
worth just now, where is your guarantee? You can offer
only your good reputation. But business is not based on
sentiment. If half of the two hundred thousand francs you
are liable for are over and above the present value, then
we're guaranteed only for one hundred thousand francs and
not for the other. In that case we'd simply be buying out
your share, and before we do that we must examine the
soundness of the whole affair. Rather than wait five years
for the value to double, it might be wise to have the money
in the bank. So many things can happen! You're after a loan

with which to pay off notes that are falling due, and that's
a dangerous maneuver. It's like taking a step backward in
order to make a long leap into the unknown. No, we don't
deal in business of that kind."

This last sentence struck Birotteau like an executioner's
ruler, marking off the place where the knife of the guillotine
was to fall.

" My brother's interested in you, of course," Adolphe
went on. " He's told me that. Let's have a look at your
other affairs."

And Birotteau had to act in the same way as Molineux,
of whom he always made such fun. For the banker took
malicious delight in prying into his mind and interrogating
him on every detail as if he were a criminal before the bar.
César told him all about his Sultana Cream and Pink Lotion,
the flight of Roguin and the lawsuit over his mortgage loan,
from which he had received no cash. Upon seeing Keller
nod his head and smile, Birotteau said to himself: " He's
listening to me! I've got his attention and that means I'll
have the money!" And all the while, Keller was laughing
up his sleeve at him, just as he had always laughed at Molineux. Falling into the talkative mood which is consequent
upon intoxication with one's own happiness, César revealed
everything, and wound up by playing Popinot's Cephalic Oil
as his last trump. Riding sky-high on his false hopes, he
kept nothing back, and Adolphe Keller at once understood
that here was a simple-minded Royalist on the brink of
bankruptcy. He was so pleased to see a deputy to the Mayor,
a man belonging to the party in power and decorated only
a short time before, in hot water, that he said categorically
that he could neither give him credit nor recommend that
his brother do so. Of course, the generous François might
be silly enough to hold out a helping hand to his political
enemies, but he, Adolphe, wasn't going to let him make
a fool of himself for an old foe of Napoleon and a veteran
of Saint-Roch. Birotteau was tempted to retort with a few

remarks about the greed, hardheartedness and false benevolence of big bankers, but he was smitten with so violent a
pain that he could only murmur something about the Bank
of France, to which the Kellers had such easy access.

" But the Bank will never grant a loan refused by a private
banker," Keller assured him.

" The Bank has always seemed to me to fall short of its
purpose," said Birotteau, " when it boasts in its yearly
accounting of having lost no more than one or two hundred
thousand francs in Paris business, of which it should really
be the protector."

Adolphe smiled and rose to his feet with a slightly bored
air.

" If the Bank were to stand back of people who are in
financial difficulties in the shadiest and most treacherous
marketplace in the world, it would close its doors within a
year. It has a hard enough time defending itself against
fraudulent stocks and issues of currency, without stopping
to investigate the rating of everyone who would like to have
a loan."

" Where the devil can I lay my hands on the ten thousand
francs I need for the thirtieth of December, which is tomorrow morning?" Birotteau mumbled to himself as he
walked across the courtyard.

For custom had it that obligations which fell due on the
thirty-first day of the month were payable on the thirtieth
if the thirty-first was a holiday. Just as he reached the gate,
with tears in his eyes, the perfumer caught a glimpse of a
thoroughbred English horse, all in a lather, harnessed to one
of the finest gigs in the city, which came to a halt a few feet
from where he was standing. He was so preoccupied with
the sudden wish that the gig had run him down, so that the
mess of his business affairs could be attributed to an accidental
death, that he hardly recognized du Tillet, in fashionable
morning clothes, who threw the reins to a groom and at the
same time tossed a blanket over the horse's back.

"What chance brings you here?" du Tillet asked his former employer, knowing perfectly well what it was, since the Kellers had asked Claparon for information, and at a cue from du Tillet the false banker had utterly demolished Birotteau's hopes.

"I hope you haven't asked a favor of these pirates," he added, "these ruthless cut-throats, who've raised the price of indigo after buying up all there was on the market and forced down rice until the owners had to meet their low offer. They're utterly soulless and unscrupulous. Have you any idea of the kind of thing they do? They lend you money when your business is going well and ask to have it back when you're in trouble and they can take it from you for a song. Ask around Le Havre and Bordeaux and Marseilles about their reputation! And their political activities serve as a fine cover. For that reason I don't hesitate to make them serve my own purposes. My dear Birotteau, just walk a few steps with me!.. Joseph, lead the horse around the block; he's too hot to stand still, and I can't afford to lose the three thousand francs I invested in him!...." With this he started off in the direction of the boulevard, with Birotteau after him.... "Come my dear master—for you were my master, once upon a time—do you happen to be in need of money? I suppose those wretches asked you for guarantees, didn't they? Because I know you, I'll let you have it on the strength of a note. It has cost me a lot of hard work to acquire my fortune; I went to Germany to make it. In fact, I am in a position to tell you how: I bought up the titles to the King's debts at a sixty per cent discount. Your backing once stood me in good stead, and I'm grateful for it. If ten thousand francs will help you out, they're yours."

"What's that, du Tillet?" César exclaimed. "Do you really mean it? Yes, I am under strain, but it's a strictly temporary matter...."

"I know Roguin left you in the lurch, along with a lot of other people. I lost ten thousand francs to him myself, but Madame Roguin will repay them out of whatever she gets back. I've told the poor woman not to be so foolish as to pay debts that her husband contracted for another woman. Of course, it would be all right if she could pay everything, but I see no point in her favoring some creditors to the exclusion of others. But you're no Roguin! I know you. You'd put a bullet through your head before you'd let me lose a penny. Look, we're at the Chaussée-d'Antin already, come on up with me for a moment."

The *nouveau-riche* du Tillet took pleasure in leading his former employer through his private apartment on the way to the office. First he showed off the elaborately furnished dining-room, its walls hung with paintings he had picked up in Germany, and two drawing-rooms whose equal the perfumer had never seen except in the house of the Duke de Lenoncourt. His middle-class eyes were dazzled by the sight of so many works of art and costly gewgaws, by a thousand details which put the luxury of the quarters he had just redecorated for his wife in the shade. Since he had come to know how much such things cost he asked himself: " Where did the fellow get so many millions?"

Next they went through a bedroom which compared to that of Constance like an opera star's mansion to a chorus girl's garret. The ceiling was covered with purple and white satin and a white ermine bedside rug stood out against a purple Oriental carpet. His attention was caught by a clock representing Cupid and Psyche, the only copy of one made to order for an important banker. Finally, former master and former clerk came to a study, decked out in man-about-town style, and suited to love-making rather than business. Madame Roguin was probably the grateful donor of a gold-chased paper-knife, a malachite paper-weight and other expensive desk accessories. The Belgian rug was as startling to look at as it was to feel under the feet, because of its extraordinary thickness and resiliency. At this point, du Tillet bade the astounded perfumer sit down.

"Will you have a bite of lunch with me?" he asked, and rang for a butler who was better dressed than his visitor.

"Ask Monsieur Legras to come upstairs," he ordered. "Then go find Joseph in front of the Keller bank and have him bring home the horse. While you're there you can tell Monsieur Adolphe Keller that instead of coming to see him, I shall wait for him here after the Stock Exchange closes. Meanwhile, have lunch sent up, and in a hurry!"

Birotteau was more impressed than ever.

"What?" he thought to himself. "Du Tillet summons the formidable Adolphe Keller to his house? He whistles for him like a dog?"

A chubby boy set up a folding table which Birotteau had not noticed before and brought in some *pâté de foie gras* and vintage Bordeaux wine, delicacies which Birotteau did not enjoy on more than two or three festal occasions a year. Du Tillet was supremely happy. His hatred for this man, who had every reason to despise him, was at its peak, and he enjoyed the sight of him as much as a cat preparing to play with a mouse. Strange to say, at this moment a generous idea passed through his mind. Hadn't he perhaps already enjoyed his revenge? He hesitated briefly between further satisfaction of his grudge and a vague inclination to mercy.

"I can wipe this fellow off the map," he said to himself. "I have the power of life and death over him, over his wife, who got the better of me, and his daughter, whose hand once seemed to me to be worth a fortune. I have his money, so why shouldn't I just let him dance at the end of the string by which I have him dangling?"

An honest man is often without finesse, and there is no reasonable limit to his virtue, simply because he has no ulterior motives of any kind. So it was that Birotteau completed his own undoing. Quite unknowingly, he irritated the cat by a laudatory remark, which reflected his own mildness and probity. When the cashier came into the room, du Tillet pointed to César.

" Monsieur Legras, bring me ten thousand francs and a ninety-day note for the same amount to be signed by this gentleman, who as you may know, is Monsieur Birotteau."

Then he served the *pâté* and poured a glass of wine for Birotteau, whose relief sent him off into fits of nervous laughter and caused him to finger his watch-chain without carrying his fork to his mouth until du Tillet said: " Aren't you having anything to eat?" In this way, César revealed the depths of the abyss into which du Tillet had caused him to fall before pulling him halfway out and pausing in order to decide whether or not to give him another tumble. When the cashier came back, and César, having signed the note, felt the ten bills in his pocket, he could contain himself no longer. A few minutes before, he had been faced with the danger that the Bank and the whole neighborhood would find out that he could not meet his obligations, and he would have had to make a clean breast of everything to his wife. Now, the situation was saved. The joy of deliverance was just as great as the bitterness of defeat, which he had savored earlier in the day, and his eyes filled with tears.

" What is it, my dear sir?" asked du Tillet. " Wouldn't you do the same thing for me tomorrow? What could be simpler?"

" Du Tillet," said Birotteau, rising to his feet and solemnly grasping the other's hand, " I am happy to give you back my esteem."

" What? Had I lost it, then?" said du Tillet, feeling the source of his prosperity to be so much under attack that in spite of himself he turned crimson.

" Not exactly . . .," said Birotteau, waking up to his own stupidity. " People talked about your liaison with Madame Roguin in such a way that . . . Well, I couldn't condone your stealing another man's wife . . ."

" Old man, you're batty," du Tillet said to himself, reverting to the slang of his youth. And so saying, he returned to his original plan of ruining this virtuous man who had

caught him with his hand in the cash-box, and of dragging
his honor in the streets. The deepest personal and political
hatreds are based on a motive of this kind. A physical injury, a slap in the face, a financial loss, all these things can be
set aside. But to have been caught at something really vile is
quite unforgivable. The duel that is waged between a criminal
and the witness to his crime can end only with the death of
one or the other.

" Oh, Madame Roguin ?" said du Tillet mockingly. " She
was quite a feather in a young man's cap at the time. Now,
if you'd been told that I took money from her, I'd understand
your indignation. But, on the contrary, I'm rebuilding the
fortune which her husband put in jeopardy. And the source
of my own wealth, as I've told you before, is perfectly pure.
A young man can find it difficult to come by even the ne-
cessities of life, and if he doesn't step lively he'll be poor
forever. But if, like the French Republic, he has been forced
to borrow, well then he must simply pay back what he owes
and after that he's a more honest man than France is a
nation."

" That is true, my boy," said Birotteau. " What is it that
Voltaire says ? . . *God made repentance man's chief virtue here
below.*"

" Well," said du Tillet, further offended by this moralistic
quotation, " as long as one doesn't basely rob another man
of his fortune . . . say, for instance, if you were to declare
bankruptcy within the next three months and my ten thousand francs were to go up in smoke . . ."

" Me go into bankruptcy ?" said Birotteau, who had drunk
three glasses of wine. " Everyone knows what I think of
bankruptcy proceedings ! To a businessman, bankruptcy is
death, and so I'd simply die."

" Meanwhile here's to your very good health !" said du
Tillet.

" Here's to yours and that of your descendants !" tossed
back Birotteau. " Why don't you buy toiletries at my shop ?"

"Well, to tell the truth, I'm afraid of Madame Birotteau," du Tillet told him. "She intimidates me, and if you hadn't been my employer, I'd . . ."

"Ah, you're not the first one to admire her looks. Plenty of men have fallen in love with her, but with no luck, because she happens to love me. Meanwhile, du Tillet, there's no use doing things halfway."

"What do you mean?"

Birotteau proceeded to tell him the whole story of the land around the Madeleine, and du Tillet listened wide-eyed, and complimented him upon his astuteness.

"I'm glad to have your approval," Birotteau concluded, "for you've made yourself quite a man in banking. As a matter of fact, my boy, couldn't you get me credit at the Bank of France, while I wait for some returns on my Cephalic Oil?"

"I can recommend you to Nucingen's," said du Tillet, who was resolved to put his victim through the whole song-and-dance of bankruptcy, and he went over to his desk to write the following letter to Baron Nucingen:

My dear Baron:

      The bearer of this letter is Monsieur César Birotteau, deputy to the Mayor of the second district and well-known perfumery manufacturer. He wishes to do business with you, and I recommend him highly. Anything that you do for him will be appreciated by

Your faithful servant,<br>F. DU TILLET

Du Tillet left the dot off the "i" in his last name, and to all his business acquaintances this was a code sign, which meant that none of the requests made in the letter were to be honored—in other words that the protestations and supplications had been extorted from him, and were to be considered as null and void. As soon as the recipient saw the undotted " i," he was authorized to give the bearer the run-around. Many important people have been tricked in this way by bankers, lawyers and shrewd businessmen, who make use of two signatures, one which stands back of what is written above it and the other meaningless. No one can measure the effect of the ruse unless he has received in the same mail from the same person a warmly phrased letter and an icy cold one.

" You're saving me, du Tillet!" César exclaimed as he read this missive.

" Good Lord! Think nothing of it," du Tillet answered. " Ask for all the money you like, and Nucingen will surely give it to you. Unfortunately, my own funds are tied up for the next few days, or I wouldn't send you to this royal house of bankers. For the Kellers are midgets in comparison. With this letter, you'll be taken care of by the middle of next month, and after that we'll give your affairs further consideration. Nucingen and I are the best of friends, and I know he won't fail me."

" That's as good as an endorsement," Birotteau said to himself, as he went gratefully away. " There you are, no good deed is ever done in vain!" And he went on philosophizing along these lines. One thought did, however, mar his peace of mind. For some days he had prevented his wife from looking into the ledgers. With the excuse of wanting Constance and Césarine to enjoy the newly decorated apartment, he had put all the bookkeeping upon Célestin and found time to help him in person when the occasion demanded. But once the novelty was over, he knew that nothing in the world could stop Constance from catching up with every detail of the business, or as she put it, keeping her finger in the pie. The time was at hand and he was at his wits' end as to how to conceal his troubles any longer. Already, Constance had remarked unfavorably upon his attempt to collect on all outstanding bills; she had scolded the clerks and accused Célestin of trying to ruin the business. But Célestin had orders not to argue with her. In the clerk's eyes, Madame Birotteau was the real boss, for although the general public may easily be mistaken, the intimates of a house are quick to find out which partner in a marriage plays the dominating role. Now the item of ten thousand francs received from du Tillet would require explanation. So it was with a slight shudder that, upon his return to the house, he saw Constance with the ledger poring over the amounts due and probably counting the money that was at hand to meet them.

" How are you going to pay what falls due tomorrow ?" she asked him as he sat down beside her.

" With cold cash," he said, pulling the ten thousand francs out of his wallet and handing them over to Célestin.

" Where does it come from ?"

" I'll tell you later. Célestin, put down ten thousand francs, payable March thirty-first to the order of du Tillet."

" Du Tillet !" Constance exclaimed in terror.

" I'm going to see Popinot," said César. " I've been very rude not to drop in at his place any earlier. By the way, how are we doing with the sale of his oil ?"

" The three hundred bottles with which we stocked up are gone already," Célestin replied.

" Birotteau, don't go out; I want to talk with you," said Constance, taking her husband by the arm and pulling him into her bedroom with a haste which under any other circumstances would have had something comical about it. " Du Tillet !" she repeated, after she was sure that no one but Césarine could hear. " Why, du Tillet robbed our cash-box, and . . ." (she whispered into his ear) " he tried to seduce me."

" Just a youthful indiscretion," said Birotteau, suddenly sasuming the role of a man who knows his own mind.

" Look here, César, there's something the matter. You

haven't been going to the factory. . . . What is it? You'll have to tell me. I want to know the whole story."

"Well," said Birotteau, "we were on the verge of ruin, even as late as this very morning. But everything's all right now." And he proceeded to tell her the whole story of the fortnight just past.

"So that's why you were taken ill," Constance exclaimed.

"Yes, Mother," put in Césarine. "Father was very brave, you know. I only hope my husband loves me the same way. His only thought was to spare you pain."

"It's my dream come true," moaned the poor woman, sinking onto the small sofa beside the fireplace, with terror written all over her white face. "I saw it all coming! Remember, I told you about it that night, in our old room, which you've torn down, and I said then we'd have nothing left but our eyes to weep with. My poor Césarine . . ."

"Now, now!" said Birotteau. "You aren't going to strip me of the courage which I need so very badly, are you?"

"My dear, I'm sorry," said Constance, pulling herself together and squeezing César's hand with a tenderness that went straight to his heart. "It was foolish of me. Now that bad fortune has actually overtaken us, I'll be strong. You'll not hear me complain again." And she threw herself weeping into her husband's arms. "Courage, my dear; and I'll find enough of that for the two of us, if need be."

"The oil, my love; the oil will be our salvation."

"God save us!" Constance murmured.

"Won't Anselme help out my father?" asked Césarine.

"I'm going to see him right now," said César, deeply affected by the sorrow in his wife's voice, which even after nineteen years of marriage was something for which he was quite unprepared. "Constance, you mustn't worry. Here's the letter du Tillet has given me for Monsieur de Nucingen, who's sure to let us have credit. Meanwhile my lawsuit will have been won. And of course we always have Uncle Pillerault to fall back on." This was not exactly true, but he felt that it would be cheering. " We need only be brave," he concluded.

" Ah, if that were really all we needed . . .," said Constance with a smile.

With one great weight off his shoulders, Birotteau left the house, walking more like a free man. But deep down inside, he was exhausted by his ordeal. Such strains use up more will-power and nervous energy than any human being has at his disposal. He is forced to draw upon his capital, and as a result he suddenly becomes appreciably older.

The establishment of A. Popinot and Co. on the Rue des Cinq-Diamants had greatly changed in the course of two months. The shop had been repainted and the spotless shelves, lined with gleaming bottles, could not but delight the eye of any businessman, who knows the signs of success when he sees them. The floor was covered with wrapping-paper and standing all around were barrels of various oils, for which Gaudissart had obtained the agency for Popinot. The accounting department was on the floor above, and an old cook prepared meals for Popinot and his three helpers. Popinot himself was ensconced in a glass-enclosed compartment in one corner. He wore a serge apron and green sleeve-guards and kept his pen cocked over one ear, that is, when he was not busy recording the orders which arrived with the incoming mail, as was the case when Birotteau walked in on him. At the words: " Well, my boy!" from his former employer, he raised his head, locked up his " private office," and came out with a joyous air and his nose reddened by the cold air of the unheated shop.

" I thought you were never coming!" he said with a respectful bow.

The clerks gathered around to admire the famous perfumer and recently decorated deputy to the Mayor, who was their master's business associate. Birotteau could not help being flattered, and he who had felt like such a very small fish in the presence of the Kellers now imitated them by stroking his chin, teetering on his heels and uttering all sorts of platitudes.

"Getting up early these days, my boy?" he asked Popinot.

"Sometimes we don't even go to bed," said the young man. "When good luck is knocking at the door, one must be ready to answer."

"What did I tell you? This oil will be my fortune."

"Yes, sir, but the way the business is handled has something to do with it. I've given your jewel a proper setting, haven't I?"

"To come down to brass tacks," said the perfumer, "how do we stand? Are there any profits?"

"After just a month, that's too much to expect. Gaudissart has been on the road for only twenty-five days, and he has acquired a post chaise, of which he gave me no warning. But he's a wonderfully devoted fellow. We owe a lot, indirectly, to my uncle, the Judge. . . ." And he bent over to whisper into Birotteau's ear: "The newspapers will cost twelve thousand francs before we're through."

"The newspapers?"

"Haven't you been following them?"

"No."

"Then you don't know the half of what we've been doing. Twenty thousand francs in posters, prints and frames . . . the purchase of a hundred thousand bottles. For the moment we have nothing but expenses. If you'd been over to the Faubourg, where I've been spending many of my nights, you'd have seen a little nut-cracker which I've invented and I think may go far. Then, on the side, I've made three thousand francs in the last five days handling these other oils you see in the barrels around you."

"You've got a head on your shoulders, all right," said Birotteau, running his hand through Popinot's hair as if he were a small boy. "I guessed right on that score."

Just then several people came into the shop, and Birotteau

said by way of farewell: " We're dining Sunday with your uncle and aunt, the Ragons."

The funds on which he had expected to draw were simply not available, but he was none the less impressed by what he had seen. " Just think, practically overnight a clerk has turned into a full-fledged businessman!" He was almost as astounded by Popinot's self-assurance and good cheer as he was by the luxuries he had seen at du Tillet's. " As a matter of fact, the boy didn't seem to like my tousling his hair. He's putting on some of the airs of a François Keller already."

Birotteau had not stopped to think that Popinot's clerks were looking on, and that the young man naturally wanted to stand on his dignity in his own establishment. Here, again, as with du Tillet, he had put his foot in it, simply because he was good-hearted and couldn't refrain from giving somewhat uncouth expression to his feelings. Any other young man would have taken it even harder than Anselme.

The Sunday dinner at the Ragons' was to be the last joyful moment of the Birotteaus' nineteen years of happy marriage. The Ragons' lived on the third floor of a dignified old house on the Rue du Petit-Bourbon-Saint-Sulpice, in an apartment with arches and columns, and china statuettes of hoop-skirted shepherdesses and grazing sheep. They belonged to that eighteenth-century middle class, which we know for manners that now seem faintly absurd and for its tradition of respect for Church and Crown. The furniture, clocks, linens and tableware all had a venerable appearance, and yet their very antiquity made them seem new. The drawing-room was decorated with damask hangings, brocaded curtains, duchess chairs, *bonheur-du-jour* secretaries and a superb portrait by Latour of Monsieur Popinot, Madame Ragon's father, councilman of Sancerre, shown smiling in all his glory. In her own house, Madame Ragon was invariably followed by her little King Charles spaniel, a creature particularly effective against a small, hard sofa, one which had certainly never played the meretricious role of the similar piece of furniture known from the title of Crébillon's risqué novel. Among the Ragons' virtues was the possession of a cellar stocked with perfectly aged vintage wines and some liqueurs from the stores of Madame Anfoux, which certain gentlemen said to be hopelessly in love with Madame Ragon had brought her from the South Seas. It is easy to see why a dinner served at their house was something to look forward to. Their old cook, Jeannette, was so devoted that she would have stolen fruit to make them jellies and jams, and instead of putting her money in a savings bank she bought lottery tickets, in the hope of making a fortune for their benefit. On the Sundays when there were guests to dinner, she supervised the preparation of every dish and also served at the table, and her agility not only belied her sixty years, but might have given a few pointers to Mademoiselle Mars for her interpretation of Suzanna in *The Marriage of Figaro*.

On this particular Sunday, the guests were Judge Popinot, Uncle Pillerault, Anselme, the three Birotteaus, the three Matifats and Abbé Loraux. Madame Matifat, who had worn a turban to the ball, now had on a blue velvet dress, cotton stockings, kid shoes and gloves with green plush trimmings, and a hat with a pink lining and auriculas around the brim. The invitation was for five o'clock and everyone was urged to be punctual. When the Ragons were asked out to dine, their hosts were careful to serve them at the same hour, for their seventy-year-old stomachs could not adapt themselves to the fashionably late hours of the new generation.

Césarine knew that Madame Ragon would seat her beside Anselme, for all women, even the most foolish or exaggeratedly pious, stick together in matters of love. And she had dressed in such a way as to be pleasing to him. Constance had reluctantly given up the idea of Césarine's marrying Roguin's assistant, who for so long had played the part of crown prince in her imagination, and now she seconded her daughter's effort to please, by pulling down her tulle scarf in such a way as to partially bare her shoulders and reveal the enchanting outline of her neck. The pleated bodice crossed from left to right, in Greek style, and half opened over the most agreeably rounded forms imaginable, while the gray wool flounced skirt, with touches of green, circumscribed a waist which had never appeared slenderer or more supple. She wore filigreed gold earrings, and her hair was swept away from her face in Chinese fashion, exposing the maximum amount of fresh complexion and a network of tiny veins which enlivened its whiteness. Césarine was so enchantingly beautiful that even Madame Matifat, who did not realize that both mother and daughter acknowledged the necessity of bewitching Anselme, had to admit it.

Neither she nor the Birotteaus interrupted the colloquy which the two young lovers were holding in the recess of a window, where not even the penetrating cold wind seemed to disturb them. The older people's conversation became suddenly animated when Judge Popinot dropped a word about the flight of Roguin, the second notary, in his experience, to be guilty of this previously unknown crime. At the mention of the notary's name, Madame Ragon lightly kicked her brother's foot under the table. Meanwhile Pillerault had drowned out the Judge's voice and was signaling to him to say no more, in order to spare Madame Birotteau.

" I know the whole story," Constance interjected in a low but sorrowful voice.

" Well," said Madame Matifat to Birotteau, who sat with his head hanging, " how much has he taken from you? Gossip has it that he's left you absolutely high and dry."

" He had two hundred thousand francs of mine in his possession," said César. " And as for the forty thousand which he pretended to have one of his clients lend me, when in reality he had already spent them himself, well, I'm in the midst of a lawsuit to recover them."

" Your case is coming up this week," Popinot told him. " I thought you wouldn't mind my explaining your position to the chief magistrate, and he has asked to have all Roguin's papers sent to his chambers, in order to find out exactly when the amount was embezzled and to study the evidence offered by Derville, who made his plea in person in order to save you money."

" Do you think we shall win ?" asked Madame Birotteau.

" That I can't say," the Judge answered. " Although I'm attached to that section of the court, I should ask to be excused if I were called to sit upon the case."

" How can there be any doubt about so clear-cut an issue ?" asked Pillerault. " Won't the records show the actual delivery of the money and the witnesses testify to having seen it pass from one hand to another ? It seems to me that if Roguin were within reach he would get a life sentence."

" In my opinion," said the Judge, " the lender should sue Roguin for the amount of his fee and the deposit he had to put in advance. But in the royal court I've seen an opinion of six to six rendered over issues even simpler than this one."

" What's that, Mademoiselle Césarine ?" said young Popinot, who had just overheard a fragment of the conversation. " Has Roguin run away ? Your father didn't tell me anything, and yet he must know that I'd cut off my arm for him. . . ."

Césarine knew that the " him " included the whole family, for even if she had not been susceptible to the warmth of the words, she could not fail to notice the burning look which the young man gave her.

" I know," she answered. " I said so to him. But he didn't tell even my mother; in fact, I was the only one to share his secret."

" If you spoke of me to him in this connection," said young Popinot, " then you read my heart. But have you read everything that is inscribed there ?"

" Perhaps I have."

" Then I'm exceedingly happy. And let me tell you further that within a year I'll be so rich that your father won't look askance at our marriage. I intend to sleep no more than five hours a night, and . . ."

" Don't go injuring your health," said Césarine, giving him a look that revealed the full extent of her feelings.

" My dear," said César as they left the table, " I believe those two are in love."

" So much the better," said Constance. " My daughter has found a man with both brains and energy. After all, talent's the best fortune any suitor can lay at a girl's feet."

And she went quickly to Madame Ragon's bedroom. In the course of the dinner, César had made one or two guileless remarks which had caused her uncle and the Judge to smile, and she was reminded of the fact that the poor man stood badly in need of support in the struggle which he was waging. Her heart was heavy, for she had an instinctive distrust of du Tillet. Indeed, every mother, no matter how little Latin she may possess, instinctively shares the feeling of *Timeo Dananos et dona ferentes*, I fear the Greeks, even when they bring gifts. And so she fell weeping into the arms of Madame Ragon and Césarine, without confessing the reason for her sorrow. " I must be nervous," was her only excuse. The older people proceeded to spend the rest of the evening playing cards, and the younger ones indulged in those innocent games which cover up the innocent mischief of lovers of their station. As for the Matifats, they chose to take an interest in the mischief.

" César," said Constance on the way home, " you'd better go as early as the third of the month to Baron de Nucingen, in order to be sure of meeting your obligations of the fifteenth. If any obstacle arises, you won't be able to find other resources on such short notice."

" Of course I'll go, my dear," said César, squeezing the hands of his wife and daughter. " It's a sorry Christmas present I've given you, my darlings." And although in the dark cab the two women could not see his face, they felt tears trickle onto their hands.

" Keep hoping, my dear," Constance murmured.

" Everything will be all right, Father," added Césarine. " Monsieur Anselme Popinot told me he'd cut off his right arm for you."

" For me and certain other members of the family," said César, making an effort to be gay.

Césarine squeezed her father's hand in such a way as to indicate that she was engaged to Anselme.

## IV

DURING THE FIRST THREE DAYS OF THE NEW YEAR, BIROT-
teau received two hundred greeting cards, but in his unhappy circumstances he was appalled by such a display of
false friendliness and superficiality. He went three times in
vain to the house of Baron de Nucingen, but the holiday
season seemed to justify the banker's absence. On his third
visit he got as far as the office inside, where the chief clerk,
a German, told him that Monsieur de Nucingen had come
in at five o'clock in the morning from a ball given by the
Kellers and could not possibly be seen at half past nine.
Birotteau managed to interest the clerk in his business and
chatted with him for half an hour. Later in the day, the
clerk sent him a letter saying that he should come around
the following noon. Although every hour was long and bitter,
the time finally arrived. César took a cab, which had to stop
some distance away from the house, for the courtyard was
encumbered with vehicles of every description. The sight
of so much wealth made the honest perfumer's heart sink
into his boots.

"And yet the fellow has failed twice in the course of
his career," he said to himself as he climbed the flower-
decked stairway and entered the sumptuous apartments
which had made Baroness Delphine de Nucingen so well
known. For the Baroness was striving to outdo the aristocratic houses of the Faubourg Saint-Germain, where she had
never as yet been invited. The Baron was lunching in her
company, but in spite of the number of people waiting for
him in the outside office, he said that any friend of du Tillet
was to receive immediate admission. Birotteau trembled with

hope when he saw the effect of these words on the previously insolent butler.

"Pardon me, my dear," the Baron said with a heavy German accent to his wife and a nod to Birotteau, "but this gentleman is a staunch Royalist and a friend to Monsieur du Tillet. Besides this, he's deputy to the Mayor of the second district and gives balls of positively Oriental splendor. I'm sure you'll be happy to make his acquaintance."

"Then I'd like to take lessons from Madame Birotteau," said the Baroness. "Ferdinand" (César took note of the fact that she called du Tillet by his first name) "has told us all about your party, and there are few things, you know, that can arouse his enthusiasm. Is there any chance of your giving another such entertainment soon?"

"Madame, poor people like us don't go in for these things very often," said César, uncertain of whether to take her remarks as mockery or politeness.

"Monsieur Grindot had charge of the redecoration of your apartment, didn't he?" said the Baron.

"Ah! Grindot, a charming young fellow who's just back from Rome," said Delphine de Nucingen. "I'm quite mad about him. He's done the most delicious little sketches for my album."

No conspirator under interrogation ever felt more uncomfortable than poor César Birotteau in his everyday clothes. Every word addressed to him seemed to have a double meaning.

"We give quite a few little parties, ourselves," said the Baron, shooting him an inquisitive stare. "Perhaps you've heard about them."

"Won't you sit down and have a bite of lunch with us, quite informally?" said Delphine, pointing to the loaded table.

"Madame, I came to talk business, and . . ."

"Yes," said the Baron, "will you excuse us, madame?"

The Baroness made a gesture of assent.

"Are you buying toiletries?" she asked her husband.

He shrugged his shoulders and said to the totally discouraged Birotteau:

"Du Tillet is extremely interested in you."

"At last!" sighed César to himself. "Now we're getting to the point."

"Because of his letter, I am ready to give you credit for an amount that has no limits except those of my own fortune."

Hagar's first glimpse of the fountain in the wilderness could have been no more welcome than were these words —in spite of the clumsy French in which they were spoken— to Birotteau's ears. As a matter of fact, the wily Baron laid on this German accent even more heavily than was necessary, so that when he went back on his word it was with the excuse that someone had misunderstood him.

"You must have an account with us," the great financier went on to say, "and this is how we shall proceed to open it . . ."

Birotteau was more than ever convinced of his good luck. As a businessman he knew that no one begins to discuss the details of a transaction unless he intends to carry it through.

"You understand, of course, that the Bank requires three signatures on every loan, great or small. You'll make out notes to the order of our friend, du Tillet, and I'll send them with my signature to the Bank immediately. Four hours later, on the very same day, you'll have the money, at the regular rate, naturally. I want no commission, because I'm only too glad to be of service to you. But there is one condition. . ." And he brushed the forefinger of his left hand against the side of his nose with an inimitably crafty gesture.

"Sir, it is promised in advance," said Birotteau, imagining that he referred to some share in his profits.

". . . a condition to which I attach the greatest importance . . . namely that, as she was just saying, Madame de Nucingen can take lessons from Madame Birotteau."

" You're making fun of me, sir; please . . ."

" Monsieur Birotteau!" said the banker gravely. " You must invite us to your next ball! My wife's jealous and wants to see your apartment, because she's heard so much about it."

" Sir!"

" If you refuse, then we'll open no account for you! . . . I happen to know that you're in great favor. You had the Prefect . . ."

" Sir!"

" You had La Billardière, and a Gentleman of the King's Bedchamber, and Count de Fontaine, who like yourself was wounded . . . at Saint-Roch, wasn't it? . . ."

" Yes, sir, on the Thirteenth of Vendémiaire!"

" You had Monsieur de Lacépède, Monsieur Vauquelin of the Academy . . ."

" Sir!"

" Come, come! Don't be so modest, Mr. Deputy-Mayor; I heard that the King himself said that your ball . . ."

" The King! . . ." said Birotteau, but he was never to hear the end of the sentence, for a young man walked casually into the room, bringing a blush to the cheeks of Madame de Nucingen.

" Well, de Marsay, how do you do!" exclaimed the Baron. " Take my chair, won't you? I hear there's a great crowd in my office, and I know the reason. The Wortschin mines are doubling their capital stock and their dividends as well. Yes, I have the figures right at hand. You'll have a hundred thousand francs of extra income this year, Madame de Nucingen! So you can buy all the jewels you want to make you beautiful . . . in spite of the fact that you don't need any embellishment."

" Good Lord! The Ragons sold out their shares! What a crime!" exclaimed Birotteau, apparently without receiving any attention.

" By the way," said Monsieur de Nucingen, turning around just as he reached the door, " I don't believe you gentlemen know one another. De Marsay, this is Monsieur Birotteau, the perfumer who gives such Orientally magnificent balls, and has been decorated by the King. . . ."

De Marsay raised his pince-nez to his eyes.

" Of course! I thought I had seen him somewhere before. . . . Are you here for something with which to grease the wheels of your business ?"

" Those Ragons!" said the Baron, with a grimace, harking back to the name which César had mentioned a moment before. " They had an account with me, and I could have made their fortune, but they didn't have the patience to wait one more day!"

" Sir!" said Birotteau.

He was still quite hazy about how his own affairs were to be settled, and without saying good-by to either the Baroness or de Marsay, he ran after the banker, whom he overtook at the bottom of the stairs. Just as he was about to open his office door, Monsieur de Nucingen caught the puzzled and despairing look on Birotteau's face and called back to him:

" Well, everything's clear, isn't it? See du Tillet and arrange it with him."

It occurred to Birotteau that de Marsay might have some influence over the Baron, and he darted back up the stairs and into the dining-room where he had just left him. The cup of coffee which the Baroness had ordered just as César was going out the door was there on the table, but she and de Marsay had disappeared and the butler only smiled at his obvious astonishment. César went directly to du Tillet's, but was informed that he was in the country with Madame Roguin. He took a cab and had himself driven post haste to Nogent-sur-Marne, only to be told there that " Monsieur and Madame " had gone back to Paris. Birotteau went home in a state of complete discouragement. But when he told his wife and daughter about his futile chase, Constance, who usually fell like a bird of ill omen upon the least mischance, was generously consoling and assured him that everything would turn out all right.

The next day, César was on guard at seven o'clock in the morning at du Tillet's door. He slipped the doorman ten francs for letting him have a word with du Tillet's personal valet, and two gold pieces to the valet for admitting him to his master's presence as soon as he should be up. By dint of such sacrifice and humiliation, usually employed by either beggars or courtiers, he attained his purpose. At half past eight, just as his former clerk was putting on a dressing gown, and apologetically stretching and yawning as he did so, Birotteau appeared before him, still innocently believing that the author of the cat-and-mouse game in which he was entangled was his only friend.

" Go on, don't mind me," he began.

" What can I do for you, my good César?" asked du Tillet.

With his heart pounding, César detailed Monsieur de Nucingen's conditions, while du Tillet scolded his valet for the awkward way in which he was trying to light the fire and looked around for the bellows. When César realized that the valet was the object of all the attention, he stopped short, only to be cruelly spurred on by his interlocutor.

" Go ahead! Go ahead! I'm listening to you."

Birotteau's shirt was wet with perspiration, which turned cold when du Tillet turned the stare of his silvery, tiger-striped eyes balefully upon him.

" My dear master, the Bank has refused notes from you passed by Claparon to Gigonnet, without any guarantee, but that's not my fault, is it? Since you've been a referee in the commercial court, I don't see how you can have made such a blunder. After all, I'm a banker. I'll give you the money, but I can't risk having my signature rejected by the Bank. Credit is my very existence, indeed it's the existence of us all. Will you have some money, then?"

" Can you give me all I need?"

" That depends. How much is it?"

" Thirty thousand francs."

" There's a pretty kettle of fish!" said du Tillet, bursting into laughter.

Dazzled by the luxury with which he saw du Tillet surrounded, Birotteau interpreted this laugh as meaning that such a sum was a mere trifle, and he began to breathe easier. Du Tillet rang a bell.

" Send up the cashier," he ordered.

" He hasn't yet come, sir," said his valet.

" Those fellows are getting away with murder! It's half past eight, and we should have done a million francs of business already."

Five minutes later, Monsieur Legras arrived.

" How much have we in cash?" du Tillet asked him.

" Only twenty thousand francs, sir. You ordered me to buy thirty thousand francs' worth of bonds, payable on the fifteenth of the month."

" Of course. I must be still asleep."

The cashier shot his employer a shifty look and went back downstairs.

" If Truth were banished from the earth, it would whisper its last words into the ear of a cashier," said du Tillet. " By the way, haven't you an interest in the new business set up by young Popinot?"

" Yes," Birotteau said ingenuously, with perspiration breaking out on his forehead. " Would you take his signature for a large sum?"

" Bring me his acceptances for fifty thousand francs, and I'll put them through a certain Gobseck, who is very reasonable when he has money to place, and just now he has plenty of it."

Birotteau went back home, still unaware of the fact that the bankers were tossing him like a ball from one to the other. But Constance had begun to see that he stood no chance of obtaining credit. If three bankers had already turned down a man whose name was anything but unknown, then it was obvious that the Bank of France would have none of him either.

" Try to renew all your notes," she told him. " Go to your associate, Monsieur Claparon, and to all the other people you're supposed to pay on the fifteenth and ask them for a little leeway. There'll always be plenty of time to take acceptances from Popinot to a money-lender."

" Tomorrow's the thirteenth!" said Birotteau sadly.

Birotteau had that " sanguine " temperament described in the advertisement of his own cream, which consumes itself in either thought or emotion and must be restored by an abundance of sleep. Césarine took her father into the drawing-room and played the *Dream of Rousseau* by Hérold, while her mother sat embroidering beside her. Poor Birotteau let his head sink onto a sofa cushion, and with the vision of a smile on his wife's face he fell into a deep slumber.

" Poor man!" said Constance. " There's plenty of trouble ahead, and I only hope he can stand up under it."

"What's the matter, Mother dear?" asked Césarine, seeing her mother in tears.

" My dear, I see bankruptcy on the horizon. If your father is obliged to declare it, we mustn't ask for anyone's charity. You must be prepared to work behind the counter in a shop, and if you do your share courageously, then I too will find the strength to begin all over. I know your father; he won't keep a penny for himself. I'll give up my rights and everything we own will be sold. You must take your jewelry and dresses to the house of your Uncle Pillerault, for there's no reason why they should be sacrificed."

Césarine was terrified by the religious simplicity of these words. For a moment she thought of going to Anselme, but delicacy forbade it.

At nine o'clock the next morning, Birotteau went to see Claparon on the Rue de Provence, with more anxiety in his

heart than ever. To ask for credit or a loan is an everyday
business occurrence, the accepted way of raising capital.
But to ask for a renewal or extension is, in business practice,
the equivalent of a summons to the police station, as a
prelude to being dragged before a criminal court. It is the
first step toward bankruptcy, just as a misdemeanor is the
first step toward a crime. After such a request, the secret
of a businessman's troubles is in an outsider's hands; he has
placed himself at another man's mercy, and mercy is not a
virtue of the marketplace. César Birotteau, who had once
stepped out so confidently onto the Paris streets, now hesitated in front of Claparon's door. He had discovered that,
among bankers, the heart is just an internal organ, and nothing
more. Claparon was gross even when he was in a good
humor, and the perfumer had such a vivid memory of his
bad taste that he dreaded the sight of him.

" He's closer to the common people, that's the only thing
in his favor," he thought to himself. " Perhaps he'll have
more of a heart than the rest." This was the first embittered
reflection he had allowed himself to make since the beginning
of his woes.

Then, drawing on his last reserve of courage, he went up
the stairs to an unattractive mezzanine floor, whose windows
with their yellowed curtains he had glimpsed from the street
below. He knocked at a door bearing a brass plate with the
word *Office* engraved upon it, and when no one answered,
went in. The excessive shabbiness of the place bespoke either
avarice or negligence. No employee stood or sat behind
the grille topping the unpainted wooded counter which shut
off the area of blackened desks in the back of the room.
On the deserted desks were inkwells in which the ink was
dry and caked, pens twisted into hoops and disorderly piles
of cardboards, papers and useless printed matter, and the
floor was as rough and damp as that of a second-class
boarding-house parlor. The next room, labeled *Cashier*, had
the same air of a bad joke about it. In one corner there

was an enormous oak-wood cage, with wire lattice-work, a hinged opening and, inside, a big iron chest, where rats probably frolicked every night. Behind the open door there were also an odd desk and an old green arm-chair with a hole in the bottom and the stuffing sticking out like the corkscrew curls of Claparon's wig. Obviously this had been the drawing-room of the apartment before it was turned into an office, and it further contained a round table covered by a green cloth, surrounded by old chairs with rusted tacks holding together their black leather upholstery. The rather elegant fireplace bore no smoke marks to indicate that it had been used for a fire; the mantelpiece was bare and dusty, and the mirror, which had been trailed across by flies, harmonized with a mahogany clock, doubtless picked up at an auction, and two empty candlesticks. The mouse-gray wallpaper, with pink edging, was stained by the smoke of countless cigars, and the whole place looked like the sort of common room which a newspaper would call " the editorial sanctum." Fearful of intruding, Birotteau knocked gently three times at a door opposite the one by which he had entered.

" Come in!" called Claparon, in a voice so faint that it must have come from some distance. The room into which Birotteau now walked was apparently empty, although a fire crackled in the grate. This was, indeed, Claparon's private office, but it was as different from that of Keller as a Huron wigwam from the Palace of Versailles. Birotteau had seen the grandeurs of the banking world; now he was to see a parody of them. The furniture, which might have been handsome once upon the time, was splintered and greasy. Claparon had been lying in bed in a sort of oblong recess at the far end of the room, and now, hastily drawing a soiled dressing-gown about him, he set down a pipe and pulled the curtains behind him in such a way as to make Birotteau wonder what he might be concealing.

" Sit down," he said as he stepped forward.

Minus his wig, and with his head wrapped in a kerchief put on crooked, Claparon looked more hideous than ever. Underneath his half-open dressing-gown, Birotteau caught a glimpse of a knitted white wool shirt, dingy from having been worn far too long.

" Will you breakfast with me ?" he said, mindful of the perfumer's ball and wishing to make this mocking return for his hospitality.

He brushed the papers off a round table, revealing a plate of *pâté*, some oysters, white wine and a dish of kidneys, whose sauce had hardened around them. Down beside the fireplace was an untouched mushroom omelet. Two spotted doilies and the napkins that went with them revealed to the most innocent witness what had been going on the night before. Now, in an effort to be shrewd, Claparon would not accept Birotteau's refusal.

" I was expecting a guest, but he can't make it," he said loudly enough to be heard by anyone hiding under the bed-covers.

" Sir, I've come solely for business, and I shan't keep you."

" I'm smothered with work," said Claparon, pointing to a roll-top desk and some tables piled high with papers. " Not a single moment for myself. I don't usually receive calls except on Saturdays, but for you I'm always at home. I've no time for flirting or strolling about, so that on the boulevards I've become a perfect stranger. And yet the most efficient business is punctuated by periods of leisure. Yes, I think I've had about enough of business, altogether. I've my fill of money, but happiness has flown out the window. Really, I'd like to travel. Italy, that's where I'd like to go. Dear Italy, so beautiful amid its misfortunes ; adorable land, where no doubt I shall meet one of those shapely and majestic Italian women, my favorite type. Have you ever had one of them ? No ? Then come to Italy with me ! We'll visit Venice, city of the doges, which has unfortunately fallen into inartistic Austrian hands. Let's leave business, building,

loans and governments behind. When I've had a good meal,
I'm a generous fellow. I say we travel!"

"Just one word, sir," said Birotteau, "and then I shall
leave you. You passed my notes on to Monsieur Bidault . . ."

"You mean Gigonnet. . . . Good old Gigonnet, he's about
as easy-going as the hangman's noose!"

"Well," said César, "I'm counting on your delicacy and
sense of honor. . . ."

Claparon bowed from the waist.

"The fact is, I'd like to renew . . ."

"Impossible," the banker said brusquely. "I'm not in
the deal alone. There's a whole bunch of us, a regular
assembly; we're as thick as . . . sardines in the same can.
Of course, we can deliberate about it. But the Madeleine
proposition is only a drop in the bucket. We have interests
in the Champs-Élysées, the new Stock Exchange, Tivoli and
Saint-Lazare. Otherwise, we wouldn't be in what old
Nucingen calls ' pizness.' We don't play for peanuts. Come,
my good man, have a bite to eat!" And he tapped Birotteau
on the stomach as if to soften the harshness of his
reply.

"I will, after all," said Birotteau. And he added, to
himself: "So much the worse for his companion." Perhaps,
if he got Claparon drunk he could find out something more
about the whole business, which was beginning to look very
shady.

"Good!" said the banker. "Victoire, come here!"

The woman who answered this call was gotten up like a
fishwife.

"Tell my clerks that I can't see a soul. And that goes for
Nucingen, Keller, Gigonnet and all the rest."

"There's no one but Monsieur Lempereur in the office."

"Then he can receive the upper crust. And the little
fellows mustn't get beyond the anteroom. They can be told
that I'm in conference over a proposition concerned with . . .
champagnes!"

To get a former traveling-salesman drunk is an almost impossible feat. César had mistaken Claparon's everyday bad taste for the first symptoms of intoxication.

"That vile Roguin is still in this with you," said Birotteau. "Can't you write to him and tell him to help out a friend of twenty years' standing, one with whom he dined almost every Sunday?"

"Roguin? That fool! We have his share. Don't worry, my good man, everything will be all right. Pay up on the fifteenth and then we shall see. Of course, when I say we shall see—(Have a glass of wine, will you?)—I don't mean that I'm in a position to do very much. Whether you pay up or not doesn't matter to me. I'm out only for a commission on the purchase and a share in the sale. My job, so far, has been to persuade the owners. Do you see? Anyhow, you have solid partners, so I'm not afraid. Nowadays, every phase of business requires an expert. Are you going to go on doing things on a large scale? Then don't calculate in terms of toilet articles and jars of cream. You must prepare to clip the public, and clip it proper. Speculation, that's the big game."

"Speculation? What's that?"

"Business on an abstract plane," said Claparon, "a kind of manipulation that will remain a mystery for some ten years more, according to Nucingen, who's the Napoleon of finance. In Speculation, a man deals only in sum totals; and does things in a big way; he skims the cream off the profits before they even exist and divides great hopes into little parcels. In short, it's a new Cabala. Only about a dozen or so of us are initiated into its secrets."

César opened his eyes and ears, in an effort to understand this jumble of languages.

"Look here," said Claparon. "A big deal needs a big man to clinch it. First there's the idea-man, who like all his fellows, hasn't a penny in his pocket, and yet spends money with the same ease as he germinates ideas. You might

compare him to a boar nosing out a truffle. After him,
comes the jolly fellow who has the money and waits for the
boar to snort over his discovery. When the idea-man stum-
bles on a good piece of business, the other taps him on the
shoulder and says: 'What's all that? You're going to burn
yourself, my friend; you haven't the guts to handle it. Here's
a thousand francs; now, just let me start it going.' Then
this money-man, who's the banker, calls in the salesmen.
'Get to work!' he tells them. 'Put out some publicity, and
lay it on thick!' So they take their horns and start blowing:
'A hundred thousand francs for five sous!' or 'Five sous
for a hundred thousand francs!' (it doesn't much matter).
'A gold mine!' or 'A coal mine!' or what have you. As
much bluff as business is capable of. They buy the endorsement of practitioners of the arts and sciences, and that's
the start of the big parade. The public is willing to pay
admission, and then the profits begin rolling in. The boar
is stuffed with potatoes, and the others wallow in banknotes.
There's business for you, sir! What part do you want to
play? The boar, the front-man or dummy, the plucked
chicken, the silly sheep or the millionaire? Just think it
over. Meanwhile, I've taught you some of the theory of
modern banking. Come and see me as often as you like;
you'll always find me in a jovial mood. We Frenchmen are
naturally jovial fellows, gay and grave together, and that
doesn't do our business any harm. When a man drinks a
toast, that means it's a good thing to do business with him.
Have another glass of champagne! It's of the best quality,
because it comes to me straight from a dealer at Épernay
for whom I arranged a very profitable deal. (I used to be
in the wine trade, you know.) He's never forgotten, and
this is a proof of his gratitude. A rare quality nowadays."

Birotteau was so surprised by this flippancy on the part
of a man whom he had heard touted for his depth and
astuteness, that he dared ask nothing more. But even in the
flush of the wine one name had stuck in his mind, and he

questioned Claparon about Gobseck, who had also been described to him as a banker.

" Lord, man, have you sunk that low ?'' exclaimed Claparon. " Gobseck's as much of a banker as the hangman is a physician. He's of the Shylock school, and besides that, he handles junk; birds that have been dyed to look like canaries, stuffed boas, summer furs and winter cottons. And what sort of collateral can you offer him ? If he's to content himself with a simple signature, then he'll ask you to leave him your wife, daughter, umbrella, hat-box, shoes (you go in for the kind that come untied!), fire-tongs and shovel and even the kindling wood you store in your cellar! Gobseck, indeed! The perfect vulture! Who in the world has sent you to him ?''

" Monsieur du Tillet.''

" That's just like his tricks! I don't speak to him any more, and you can imagine why. I've long since seen through him. It was very embarrassing to run into him at your wonderful ball, looking all puffed up because he had a notary's lady on his arm. I can have finer ladies than that, any day, and he'll never have my esteem. Yes, my esteem is a lady of high degree that will never be caught in his bed, I can tell you! . . . But you're quite a joker, yourself, aren't you, old fellow, to give a ball on that scale and two months later to want your notes extended? You'll go far! In fact, I think we ought to go into some other business together. Your reputation would serve me in good stead. As for du Tillet, he'll come a cropper some fine day, especially if he's tied up with Gobseck, as some people say. Gobseck is like a spider, weaving his web, and before you know it, he will gobble up the fly. Well, I'm not sorry. Du Tillet put one over on me, for which he should have gone to the gallows.''

An hour and a half went by in senseless chatter of this kind. Claparon had embarked upon the story of a parliamentarian from Marseilles, who was smitten with an actress hissed by the Royalists for her interpretation of *La belle Arsène.*

" He rose up in his box and shouted: ' Who dares to hiss her ? If it's a woman, I'll buss her, if it's a man, I'll meet him outside, and if it's neither the one nor the other, then God help the creature! . . .' And do you know what happened? . . ."

" Good-by, sir," said Birotteau. " I must be going."

" You'll be back, soon enough," said Claparon. " One of our smaller items, a note from Cayron, has been protested, and since I had endorsed it, I had to pay. I'll be sending you a reminder. Business is business, after all."

Birotteau was just as dismayed by Claparon's false joviality as by Keller's heartlessness and Nucingen's heavy German humor, and he left the place as if it were a house of ill repute. After wandering in distraught fashion through the boulevards he thought of Molineux and directed his steps toward the Cour Batave. There, as he went up the winding, dirty stair which he had climbed so proudly on a previous occasion, he remembered the old man's niggardliness and trembled at the prospect of asking him a favor. He found him digesting his lunch beside the fire and came straight out with his request.

" You want me to renew a note for twelve hundred francs ?" asked Molineux with mocking incredulity. " I can't believe you're pressed as hard as all that. And if you can't meet that amount on the fifteenth, it means that you're not paying your rent. That is extremely vexing. When money is concerned, politeness flies out the window. The rents I collect are my only income. How should I pay my own bills without them? No businessman can take issue with me there. Money knows no indulgence; it has no heart and no ears, either. It's a cold winter, and the price of wood has gone up. If you don't pay up on the fifteenth, a little summons will be delivered to you the following noon. Mitral, your bailiff, is also mine. He'll enclose the summons in a sealed envelope, with due regard to your respectable position."

" Sir, I have never received a summons in my life."

" Well, there's a first time for everything," said Molineux.

Birotteau was thrown into consternation and heard the knell of bankruptcy in his ear. Every stroke brought back to him the severe judgments he had so often passed upon others in this same plight, and his former intolerance was etched in fiery characters upon his weakened brain.

" By the way," said Molineux, " you forgot to write on the back of your notes: 'Value received in rent,' and that may make my position all the stronger."

" I have no intention of defrauding my creditors," said Birotteau, reeling at the sight of the abyss that yawned before him.

" Very well, sir. I thought my tenants had taught me everything there was to know on the subject of my rent. But now I have learned never to accept notes in payment. I shall take the matter to court, for you have given me the feeling that you have no intention of honoring your signature. Every landlord in Paris is interested in money."

Birotteau's disgust and disillusionment were complete. His weak character caused him to be as easily disheartened by adversity as he was quickly exhilarated by success. As he passed through the Marché des Innocents, he thought of Popinot and fastened all his hopes upon him.

" Poor boy!" he said to himself. " Who could have imagined six weeks ago, when I gave him his start, that I should ever turn to him in this way?"

It was four o'clock in the afternoon, the hour at which the law courts closed for the day, and Popinot's uncle, the Judge, had come to pay him a call. Judge Popinot had a keen sense of morality and was endowed with a sort of second sight which enabled him to read men's innermost thoughts and fathom the motives of their most trivial actions, especially if these seemed to have some criminal intent. Now he examined Birotteau closely, without the perfumer's being aware of his scrutiny, and found him in an unusually pre-occupied and disturbed state of mind. His nephew, with his pen cocked, as usual, over one ear, was all attentiveness to Césarine's father.   But Birotteau's conventional phrases seemed to the Judge to cloak some more important matter on his mind.  With his perspicacity thus aroused, he stayed on in the shop, at the risk of being unwelcome, for he felt sure that Birotteau's stratagem would be to take leave and return when the coast was clear.  After Birotteau had gone, the Judge followed suit and saw him loitering on that part of the Rue des Cinq-Diamants which leads into the Rue Aubry-le-Boucher.  This confirmed his suspicions, and when from the Rue des Lombards, he saw the perfumer go back into Anselme's shop, he started after him.

"My dear boy," César was saying to his young partner, "I've come to ask you a favor."

"Anything in the world to oblige you," Anselme answered impetuously.

"You're saving my life!" exclaimed Birotteau, rejoicing over the first evidence of warmth in the icy sea through which he had been navigating for the past twenty-five days.  "You must advance me fifty thousand francs on my share of your profits.  We'll work out the terms together."

Anselme looked at him in surprise, and just at this moment his uncle reappeared.

"My dear boy . . .," he began from the door.  "Oh, forgive me, Monsieur Birotteau.  My boy, there is something I forgot to tell you. . . ." And with all the imperiousness of a magistrate, he propelled his bare-headed, shirt-sleeved nephew out onto the street and in the direction of the Rue des Lombards. "My boy, your former employer may be in such hot water that he will be forced into bankruptcy.  And men with so many years of square dealing behind them will go to the same lengths as an inveterate gambler to preserve their honor. They'll sell their wives and children, entangle their friends, promise things over which they have no control, frequent game-rooms, tell lies and weep like the most consummate actors over their troubles.  I've seen it happen.  You surely

remember the benevolent air Roguin had about him; it seemed as if butter wouldn't melt in his mouth. I don't mean
to put Monsieur Birotteau in the same category, for I'm
convinced that he's an honest man, but if he asks you to do
anything contrary to good business practice, such as signing
notes for money you haven't got and thus putting counterfeit
paper into circulation, promise me not to give him an answer
before I can advise you. If you love his daughter, there's
no use destroying both her fortune and your own. Just
because Monsieur Birotteau must take a tumble, there's
nothing to be served by your tumbling after. That would
mean cutting off the hope of salvation which only the prosperity of your business can offer."

"Thanks, Uncle," said Anselme. "A word to the wise is
sufficient."

With sudden understanding of the plea which Birotteau
had addressed to him a few minutes before, he came back
into the shop. The perfumer could not but remark the
worried frown upon his face.

"Come upstairs with me," said the young man. "There
we shall have more privacy. My clerks are all busy, but they
might very well overhear."

Birotteau followed him, as anxiously as a man with a death
sentence over his head, waiting to hear whether the sentence
has been revoked or his appeal rejected.

"You are my benefactor," Anselme began, "and you
know that I am blindly devoted to you. But allow me to ask
whether the amount for which you have asked me is enough
to save you once and for all or whether it will serve merely
to stave off catastrophe. In that case, why should you drag
me after you? You are asking for ninety-day notes, and
you know that I can't meet them within that time."

Birotteau turned suddenly pale. Solemnly he rose to his
feet and stared at young Popinot.

"I'll give you the notes, if you insist," the young man
said, trembling.

"You . . . you ingrate!" exclaimed Birotteau, gathering what remained of his strength to hurl this insult.

Whereupon he walked down the stairs and out the door, with Popinot, as soon as he had recovered from the blow, on his trail, but too late to overtake him. The insult echoed in his ears and the sight of César's contorted face lingered in his eyes; like Hamlet, he felt the presence of a ghost at his side.

As for Birotteau, he staggered like a drunken man from one street to another until he came to the river, which he followed on foot all the way to Sèvres, where he spent the night, beside himself with grief, while his wife did not dare to report his absence. To sound the alarm, under these circumstances, would have been fatal, and so she sacrificed her worry to his reputation and spent the time torn between fright and prayer.

Was César dead, or had he gone off in pursuit of some last hope? The next morning she kept up the pretense of knowing where he was, but in the afternoon she asked her uncle to inquire at the morgue. All day long she sat in the shop, with her daughter sitting over her embroidery beside her, and both of them, with perfectly composed faces, attended to the customers as if there were nothing out of the way. When Pillerault finally returned, Birotteau was with him. On his way back from the Stock Exchange, he had found his nephew in the Palais-Royal, debating as to whether he should join the gaming. This was the fourteenth of January.

César could not eat supper, for his stomach was too contracted to digest it, and the evening hours were almost unbearably painful. For the hundredth time, he ran the gamut between hope and despair, thus further exhausting his feeble powers of resistance. While they were in their splendid drawing-room where Constance was trying to keep her husband from going upstairs to sleep in the storeroom, where he said he would at least be spared the sight of so many reminders of his folly, his lawyer, Derville, rushed in and announced:

"We've won our case!"

At these words, César's tense face relaxed, and he was overcome by an access of joy, which alarmed both Derville and Pillerault. As for his wife and daughter, they went to shed a few tears in Césarine's room.

"Then my credit is good, and I can borrow money!" exclaimed César.

"That wouldn't be wise thing to do," Derville answered. "They are making an appeal, and it will be a month before we have the final decision."

"A whole month!" said César in despair, falling into a state of lethargy from which no one tried to rouse him.

His body was alive and suffering, while his mind lay idle, but all four of those present thanked God for this respite and hoped it would see him through the night. He reclined in an armchair at one side of the fire, while his wife watched him from the other, with a gentle smile on her lips, proving once more that women are much closer than men to the angels, because they mingle tenderness with their compassion. Césarine sat on a footstool, beside her mother, and from time to time brushed César's hand with her hair, as if to convey feelings which could not have been spoken at such a time.

Pillerault, the ever-ready philosopher, sat in a chair in the corner, like the Chancellor de l'Hôpital on the peristyle of the Chamber of Deputies, with the serene intelligence of the Sphinx engraved upon his forehead, and talked in a low voice to Derville. Constance had complete faith in the lawyer's discretion, and having all the figures in her head, she proceeded to communicate their situation to him. After a whispered conference of about an hour, held right under César's glazed eyes, Derville looked over at Pillerault and shook his head.

"Madame," he said with professional coolness, "bankruptcy is the only solution. Even if you could meet the payments due tomorrow, you would still have three hundred thousand francs of debt to discharge before you could borrow on your property. To match this dead weight of five hundred and fifty thousand francs, you have a live and profitable business, but one which you cannot convert into ready cash, so that sooner or later you are bound to come to this end. In my opinion, it's better to jump out the window than to let yourself be pushed down the stairs."

"I agree, my child," said Pillerault.

Then he and Constance saw Derville to the door.

"Poor Father!" said Césarine, getting up and depositing a kiss on his forehead. "Couldn't Anselme help after all?" she asked, when her mother and uncle returned.

"That ingrate!" said César, with a single chord of his memory responding to this name.

## V

Ever since this word had been hurled, like an ana-
thema, in his face, young Popinot had not known a moment
of rest. In his unhappiness, he cursed his uncle and finally
went to see him, determined to combat his judicial experience with the language of love, though the Judge had
never been known to succumb to human eloquence.

" From a business point of view," he began, " an active
partner is quite free to turn over an advance share of the
profits to the associate who is financing him. And we shall
have profits to show, I am sure of that. Upon due consideration, I feel that my position is quite strong enough
to pay forty thousand francs within three months. Monsieur
César's honesty is a guarantee that he will use the money
to meet his notes, and so even if he does go into bankruptcy,
his creditors can hold nothing against us. And to tell the
truth, Uncle, I'd rather lose forty thousand francs than lose
Césarine. At this very moment she doubtless knows of
my refusal and thinks extremely ill of me, remembering how
I told her that I'd give my right aim to help her father.
It seems to me that I'm in the situation of a young sailor
who must go down with the ship, holding the captain's hand,
or the soldier who must perish at his general's side."

" You have even more of a heart than you have a head for
business," said the Judge, shaking his head, " and I don't
esteem you any the less for it. I too have been thinking
things over. I know how much you're in love with Césarine,
and I believe I see a way for you to follow your generous
impulses and good business practice as well."

" Then, Uncle, my honor is saved!"

" Advance Birotteau fifty thousand francs, in return for
an option to repurchase his interests in your oil, which is
a property you now hold between you. I'll draw the paper
up for you myself."

Anselme embraced the Judge, went home, made out notes
for fifty thousand francs and ran to the Place Vendôme.
At the very moment when Césarine, her mother and uncle
were gaping at the sepulchral tone in which Birotteau had
pronounced the word ' Ingrate!' young Popinot appeared at
the door.

" Dear sir," he said, wiping the perspiration off his forehead, " here is the sum for which you asked me. . . . Yes, I've
worked it all out, never fear, I'll be able to meet it. Just
go ahead and save your good name."

" I knew it!" said Césarine, taking his hand and squeezing
it convulsively.

Madame Birotteau embraced Popinot, and her husband
rose up like a just man emerging from his tomb at the sound
of the trumpet on Judgment Day.

" Just a minute!" said Pillerault sternly, snatching the
notes out of Anselme's hand. The other four members of
the family were dumbfounded both at the rapidity of his
action and the tone of his voice. They looked on, horror-
stricken, as he proceeded to tear up the notes and throw
them into the fire.

" Uncle!"

" Uncle!"

" Uncle!"

" Sir!"

All four hearts spoke in unison. Pillerault took Anselme
by the shoulder, drew him close and planted a kiss upon
his forehead.

" No one with an ounce of feeling can fail to take off
his hat to you," he said. " If you were in love with my
daughter, and she were a millionairess while you had no
more to your name than that pile of ashes, you should marry

her within the fortnight. But your employer is half crazed, can't you see it?" He turned to César. "My dear nephew, don't deceive yourself any longer. Business must be done not with fine feelings but with money. This was a sublime act, but a useless one. I spent two hours at the Stock Exchange this afternoon, and found out that you haven't so much as a single penny of credit. Everyone was talking of your crack-up, of the renewals that have been refused you, your vain appeals to several bankers, your panting climb of six flights of stairs to persuade a gossipy old man to let you off twelve hundred francs, and of the magnificent ball which you gave, apparently to cover up the impending disaster. People are even saying you had no money on deposit with Roguin at all, and that he is just a scapegoat. I asked a friend of mine to collect more information for me, and he gave me the same story. Everyone is expecting Popinot's notes to be the next rabbit you will pull out of the hat. They say you set him up expressly to manufacture notes for your convenience. In short, all the slander that is bound to gather about the head of a man who has risen on the social ladder is now making the rounds of business circles all over the city. You couldn't possibly pass on Popinot's notes; everyone is prepared to refuse them. Nobody knows how many of them you may already have put into circulation, and the feeling is that you are ready to sacrifice him for your own salvation. You'd have wrecked his credit, too, and all for nothing. Do you know how much the rashest money-lender would give you for his fifty thousand francs? Twenty thousand! Twenty thousand, did you hear me? In business there are times when you must tighten your belt and go for three days without eating, as if you were having an attack of indigestion. Then, on the fourth day, you may be re-admitted to the source of credit. The only trouble is that you can't live through those three days. Courage, my poor boy; you must declare yourself bankrupt, there's no other solution. Popinot and I are both here to help you. As soon

as your clerks have gone to bed, we'll go over your accounts
and save you the pain of doing it yourself."

" Uncle!" exclaimed Birotteau, joining both hands.

" César, do you want to reach the point where you have
no assets at all? Your interest in Popinot's firm will save
you."

In this last, sharp ray of light the whole devastating truth
was revealed to Birotteau. He fell back in his chair and then
onto his knees, with his mind wandering and his aspect that
of a little child. His wife knelt down to help him to his feet,
but remained beside him when he folded his hands, raised
his eyes and devoutly recited the great Christian prayer:

" *Our Father, Which art in heaven, Hallowed be thy Name.
Thy kingdom come. Thy will be done in earth, as it is in heaven.
GIVE US THIS DAY OUR DAILY BREAD, and forgive
us our trespasses, as we forgive them that trespass against us.
And lead us not into temptation; but deliver us from evil.
Amen.*"

Tears came into the stoic Pillerault's eyes, while the weeping Césarine stood pale and stiff as a statue, with her head on
Popinot's shoulder.

" Let us go down to the office," said Pillerault, taking
Anselme's arm.

It was half past eleven o'clock when they left César to the
tender care of his wife and daughter. Just then, Célestin,
the chief clerk, who had been keeping things going all
through the storm, came on his way to bed to deliver a letter.

" This letter from Tours arrived earlier today. The
address was illegible, and that is the cause of the delay.
It suddenly occurred to me that it must be from Monsieur
César's brother, and I brought it straight up without opening it."

" Father, there's a letter from my uncle in Tours," exclaimed Césarine.

" I'm saved!" said César, pressing the letter to his lips.
" My dear, dear brother!"

Tours, 17 December

My dear brother,

Your letter caused me great grief, and as soon as I had read it, I went to offer God the holy sacrifice of the Mass on your behalf, imploring Him by the blood shed for us by His beloved Son to look with mercy upon your affliction. As I prayed *pro meo fratre Caesare*, I wept to think that I should be so far away just at the time when you are in need of brotherly affection. But I am sure that the worthy Monsieur Pillerault will fill my place. My dear César, do not forget in the midst of your trials, that this life is transitory and full of tribulation, but that one day we shall reap a reward for having suffered in God's holy name and that of His holy Church and for having practiced the Gospel precepts. Otherwise, there would be no meaning to our existence below. I repeat these truths to you, because although I am acquainted with your piety and good conduct, I realize that persons involved in the stormy enterprises of the world may be inspired by ill fortune to blasphemy. And so I enjoin you to curse neither those of your fellow-men who may hurt you nor the almighty God Who has seen fit to send you this sorrow. Lift your eyes up from earth and direct them to Heaven. There, and there alone, is consolation for the weak, riches for the humble and terror for the wealthy...

" Skip to the end of all that," Constance interrupted, " and see whether there is any enclosure."

" We shall read it again, more than once, in the future," said César, wiping his eyes and unfolding the letter, from which a money order fell to the floor. " I knew that I could count on him," he added, reading from the next page :

... In order to supplement my savings, I went to Madame de Listomère, and without giving any reason asked her to lend me all that she could. Thanks to her generosity, I have put together a thousand francs, which I am sending in the form of a money order drawn by the postmaster of Tours upon the Royal Treasury.

" A fine help that is !" said Constance, with a side glance at Césarine.

... By cutting out some of my little luxuries, I shall be able to give Madame de Listomère back her four hundred francs within no more than three years, so have no worries, my dear César, on that score. I am sending you everything I possess, in the hope that it will help you in what I trust is only a temporary difficulty. Knowing the delicacy of your feelings, I should like to forestall any objection on your part and beg you not to dream of paying me either interest or capital, on that day when God grants my prayers for your good fortune. After I had received your last letter, two years ago, I imagined you to be a wealthy man and planned to leave my money to the poor. But now everything I have is yours. When you have weathered the storm, please keep this money for my niece, Césarine, so that when she sets up housekeeping she may purchase some memento of an old uncle, who will continually implore God's blessing upon her and all those who are close to her heart. Remember, my dear César, that I am a simple priest, subsisting, with God's grace, like a sparrow of the field, in His holy commandments, and that for this reason my needs are modest and few. You need have no remorse in accepting this money; think of me only as someone who holds you in deep affection. Our good Abbé Chapeloud, who knows that I am writing to you, without guessing the reason, has asked me to send best wishes to you and your family and prayers for your continuing prosperity. Now, my dear brother, I must bid you good-by, praying that God will preserve your good health and that of your wife and daughter. May you all find patience and courage with which to endure your adversity!

> FRANÇOIS BIROTTEAU
> Vicar of the cathedral
> and parish of Saint-Gatien of Tours.

"A thousand francs!" Constance exclaimed angrily.

"Hold on to them tight!" César answered. "They're all he owns. What's more, they have been given to our daughter, and hence we may use them for our living expenses without asking indulgence of our creditors."

"Then they'll believe you have tucked something away."

" I'll show them this letter."

" They'll say it's to pull the wool over their eyes."

" Good God, that's true! I've said that very thing myself about people who were in this same situation."

His wife and daughter were still worried about his state of mind and they sat up over their needlework beside him. At two o'clock in the morning, Popinot gently opened the door and signaled to Constance to come downstairs. When she walked into the office, her uncle laid his spectacles aside.

" There's some hope, my child," he told her. " Everything's not lost, but your husband must not stand in the way of negotiations which Anselme and I shall start to undertake tomorrow. You must remain all day in the shop, and take down the address on every note that is presented, for we have until four o'clock in the afternoon. Here is what I have in mind. Naturally, neither Monsieur Ragon nor I will press you. Suppose that the hundred thousand francs you had on deposit with Roguin, had actually been handed over for the purchase of the land. In that case, you wouldn't have them any more than you do today. You're up against the debt of a hundred and forty thousand francs to Claparon, from which there is no escape. So Roguin's bankruptcy is not the cause of your troubles. In order to meet your obligations, I figure that you will have to borrow forty thousand francs on your factory and sixty thousand on notes from Popinot. That will give you something to operate on, and later you can borrow on the land around the Madeleine. If your largest creditor consents to help you, I'll sell my own bonds and live on thin air. Popinot will be suspended between life and death and you'll be at the mercy of the slightest shift in the market. But the oil is bound to make money. Popinot and I have talked it all over, and we shall back you up in the struggle. I'll be only too happy to eat bread and water if our efforts are successful. Everythings hinges on Claparon and his associates, and on Gigonnet. We two shall go to

Gigonnet between seven and eight o'clock this morning and find out how the wind blows from that direction."

Constance threw herself speechless and sobbing into her uncle's arms. Neither Pillerault nor Popinot could know that Bidault, known as Gigonnet, and Claparon were simply du Tillet's dummies and that du Tillet's sole aim in life was to read in the *Petites-Affiches* the following notice:

By sentence of the commercial court, César Birotteau, perfumer, 397 Rue Saint-Honoré, Paris, is declared bankrupt. Proceedings scheduled to open January 16, 1819. Referee: Monsieur Gobenheim-Keller. Agent: Monsieur Molineux.

All night long, Pillerault and Anselme went on with César's accounts. At eight o'clock in the morning, the two brave fellows, one a veteran of the wars, the other a recently commissioned lieutenant, went to face Gigonnet. Luckily, they were to become acquainted only by proxy with the anguish felt by all those suppliants who climbed his stairs. They walked silently toward the Rue Grenétat, and every now and then Pillerault wiped the perspiration from his forehead.

The houses on the Rue Grenétat are surrounded by a multitude of petty shops and ugly factory buildings. The old man lived on the fourth floor of a house with vertically opening windows, whose panes looked as if they had not been washed for many a year. The stairs went straight up from the street, and the concierge was stationed on the mezzanine floor, in a sort of cage which received no light except what came up from below. All the tenants except Gigonnet had some trade, and workers went continually up and down, leaving a trail of dirt on the garbage-encrusted steps. At every floor, gilt letters on a piece of red-painted sheet-iron, announced the tenant's occupation, and specimens of his handiwork were as often as not hung up alongside. Most of the time, the doors were open, revealing the mixture of housekeeping and small-scale manufacturing that went on

within. The medley of grunts, groans, shouts and whistles
from the occupants, was reminiscent of feeding time at the
zoo. In a hole-in-the-wall on the second floor, they made
suspenders that would eventually grace the finest Parisian
haberdashery, and on the third, display cartons for the
holiday season. Gigonnet, who at his death left a fortune
of almost two million francs, could never in his lifetime be
dislodged from the fourth floor of this house, although his
niece, Madame Saillard, did her best to tempt him with
an apartment on the Place Royale.

" Buck up, my boy," said Pillerault as he pulled the rabbit-
foot at the end of the bell-rope attached to Gigonnet's drab
but spotless door.

The old man opened to them in person and led them
through a cold, formal room, with no curtains at the windows,
to a second one, where the fireplace was so choked with ashes
that the wood burned very slowly. Popinot was chilled by
the sight of the usurer's green filing-cases and the monastic
severity of his office, as airless as a vault. He looked blindly
at the twenty-five-year-old blue wallpaper with a small fleur-
de-lys design and then at the lyre-shaped clock and oblong
blue Sèvres vases with gilded copper trimmings on the mantelpiece. Gigonnet had carried away these pieces from the
Queen's boudoir at Versailles, while the enraged crowd was
smashing everything to bits. Unfortunately, they were
flanked by two miserable wrought-iron candlesticks, a contrast reminiscent of the situation in which Gigonnet had
found them.

" Well then," he said, " I know you haven't come for
yourselves but on behalf of the great Birotteau. What's
going on ?"

" Probably nothing you don't already know," said Pillerault, "and for that reason our business will not take us long.
You have some notes made out to Claparon, haven't you ?"

" Yes."

" Are you willing to exchange the first fifty thousand of

them for the same amount from this gentleman, Monsieur Popinot, at a discount, of course?"

Gigonnet took off a shabby dark green cap, which looked as if he had worn it since birth, revealing the bald pate beneath.  Then with a Voltairean grimace, he said:

"What good will it do me to be paid back in hair tonic?"

"If you're going to joke about it, then we might just as well go," said Pillerault.

"Wisely spoken!" said Gigonnet with an ironically flattering smile.

"What if I were to endorse Monsieur Popinot's notes myself?" asked Pillerault, in a final effort.

"Your signature is solid gold, Monsieur Pillerault.  But what I need is simple paper money."

Pillerault and Popinot went away.  At the bottom of the stairs Anselme's legs were still trembling.

"Do you call that a man?" he asked.

"Well, he passes for one," said the older man.  "Never forget what you have just seen, Anselme!  That is banking stripped to the bare essentials, without the usual window-dressing.  An unexpected misfortune puts one into the clutches of such screw-tighteners.  The Madeleine land is a sound investment, though.  So it looks to me as if Gigonnet or someone behind him were deliberately trying to put César out of business.  In that case, there's nothing we can do. Anyhow, you've seen banking in its primitive form and you'll know enough to stay away from bankers!"

Meanwhile, Constance had listed the names and addresses of all those who came that morning for their money and sent the bank messenger away unpaid.  She waited uneasily for the return of Anselme and Pillerault, and as soon as they appeared she read the sentence on their faces.  Bankruptcy was the only answer.

"He'll die of shame!" she exclaimed, thinking of her husband.

"That might be the easiest thing for him," said Pillerault

gravely. " Indeed, since he is such a deeply religious man, I think that Abbé Loraux, his confessor, is the person that can comfort him the best."

The three of them waited until a clerk could go fetch the priest before they presented César with the balance sheet which Pillerault and Popinot had drawn up the night before and the declaration of bankruptcy, which he must sign with his own hand. Finally, at four o'clock, the priest came, and when Constance had told him the sad story, he stepped into the breach like a soldier.

" I know why you are here," cried Birotteau as Abbé Loraux walked into the room.

" My son," said the priest, " I am sure that you are convinced of the necessity of submission to God's will, and now you are called upon to show your conviction in concrete form. Keep your eyes on the Cross and remember the humiliations endured by our Saviour. With His passion in mind, you will find strength to bear your present troubles."

" My brother has already prepared me along these lines," said César, holding out the letter from Tours, which he had just read over to himself.

" You have a good brother, a kind and gentle wife, a devoted daughter, two staunch friends, your uncle and young Anselme, and at least two indulgent creditors, the Ragons. All these good people will console you for your sufferings and help you to carry your cross. Promise me that you will show the strength of a martyr and take the blow without flinching." And at this point, the priest coughed as a signal to Pillerault, who was in the next room.

" There is no limit to my resignation," said César calmly. " Dishonor has come upon me, but I must concentrate my strength on making up the losses of which I have been the cause."

Both the priest and Césarine were surprised by the firmness of Birotteau's voice. And yet it was the most natural thing in the world, for he found it easier to bear a misfortune that had assumed a definite form than the cruel alternatives which had kept him seesawing between hope and despair.

" I've been dreaming for the last twenty-two years, and here I am once more, with only a stout stick and my two bare hands," said César, going back to his peasant origins.

At these words, Pillerault clasped him in his arms. César saw that his wife, Anselme and Célestin had all come into the room, and his chief clerk was holding a sheaf of papers.

" Just a moment," he said, taking off his Legion of Honor cross and handing it to Abbé Loraux. " Give it back when I am worthy of wearing it again. . . . Célestin, write a letter of resignation from the post of Deputy Mayor. You can date it the fourteenth and ask Raguet to take it to Monsieur de La Billardière."

Célestin and Abbé Loraux went downstairs, and for a quarter of an hour complete silence reigned in César's study. When they came back, he was ready to sign. Only when Pillerault handed him the balance sheet, did he make a nervous gesture.

" Lord, have pity on me !" he said, writing his name at the bottom and handing it back to Célestin.

A cloud was suddenly lifted from Anselme's brow, and he said very distinctly :

" Sir and madame, will you do me the honor of giving me Mademoiselle Césarine's hand ?"

Tears came to the eyes of all those present, except for César, who rose to his feet, took the hand of Anselme and answered in a hollow voice :

" My boy, you shall not marry a bankrupt's daughter !"

" Well, sir," said Anselme, looking him in the eye, " do you promise, in the presence of your family, that if the young lady is willing, you will give your consent on the day when your troubles are over ?"

There was a pause, and everyone was affected by the feelings visible upon César's weary face.

" Yes," he said at last.

" Then I'm almost a member of the family, and I have a right to look after all of your affairs," said Anselme with a strange, almost jubilant expression.

And he went away, in order not to let his joy impinge upon his benefactor's sorrow. He was anything but glad about the bankruptcy, but love is a very selfish affair. Even Césarine was prey at this moment to mingled feelings.

" While we are at it," Pillerault whispered into Constance's ear, " let's clear up some matters, no matter how painful the process may be."

Constance made a gesture of sorrow rather than agreement, but her uncle chose to speak out as he had intended.

" Nephew, what do you expect to do for a living ?" he said, turning to César.

" To keep right on in business."

" I don't advise it," said Pillerault. " Liquidate all your assets, distribute them among your creditors, and then remove yourself from the local business scene. I've often imagined what I'd do in a case like this. A businessman who doesn't reckon with the possibility of failure is like a general who forgets that he may lose a battle. And I decided that it would be very unwise to go on. I'd blush when I ran into someone involved in my misfortune and imagine reproach and mistrust in every eye. No, I think I'd rather go straight to the guillotine than endure it! There, at least, it's quickly over, and there's no danger of having your head chopped off again the next day. Of course, I know that some people go right on with business as usual. But they're stronger than Claude-Joseph Pillerault. If you pay for everything in cash, as you are obliged to, then they'll say you had hoarded some reserves away. And if you can't pay at all, then you're really done for. No, sell out everything and go into something new."

" What, for instance ?" asked Birotteau.

" Look for a job!" Pillerault told him. " After all, you

have friends in high places. The Duke and Duchess de Lenoncourt, Madame de Mortsauf, Monsieur de Vandenesse! Write to them, go to see them! They can find you a post in the King's household, where you can earn a few thousand francs a year, and probably your wife and daughter will be able to contribute. Your position isn't hopeless. Say that all three of you together make as much as ten thousand francs a year. That means that ten years from now you'll have a hundred thousand francs. For if I know you, you'll lay all your earnings aside, and as for Constance and Césarine, I shall give them fifteen hundred francs out of my own pocket for petty expenses. Later on, I may even be able to help you, as well."

Constance, rather than César, was the one to take this good advice to heart. Meanwhile, Pillerault went over to the Stock Exchange, which at this time was housed in a round wooden structure with an entrance on the Rue Feydeau. The bankruptcy of a man like Birotteau, who had been in the public eye, aroused considerable talk in business circles, where republican feeling ran strong. Already the Liberals had looked askance at the perfumer's ball, for they claimed a monopoly of patriotism. Let the Royalists love the King, but love of country was a sentiment proper to the Left Wing, which included the people in its affection. Hence the fall of an incorrigible Royalist and veteran of the battle of Saint-Roch aroused general applause. Pillerault wanted to see for himself how opinion was running, and now he found himself in one of the most animated groups, which included du Tillet, Gobenheim-Keller, Nucingen, old Guillaume and his son-in-law, Joseph Lebas, Claparon, Gigonnet, Mongenod, Gobseck, Adolphe Keller, Palma, Chiffreville, Matifat, Grindot and Lourdois.

" A man can't be too careful," Gobenheim was saying to du Tillet. " My brothers-in-law very nearly gave the fellow credit!"

" I'm in it for ten thousand francs he got out of me a fortnight ago," said du Tillet. " I gave them to him on his simple signature. But he did me a favor once upon a time, so I don't mind."

" Like everyone else, your nephew had to give a great party," said Lourdois to Pillerault. " Of course, that's what rascals do when they want to worm themselves into people's confidence. But I never thought that Birotteau, who passed for an honest man, would stoop so low."

" A blood-sucker, I call him," said Gobseck.

" Far better put your trust in men who live in the simple style of Claparon," put in Gigonnet.

" Well, well," said the portly Baron Nucingen to du Tillet, " that was a good joke, your recommending this fellow, Birotteau!" And he added, turning to Gobenheim, the manufacturer : " I don't know why he never sent for the fifty thousand francs I promised. I'd have let him have them."

" Oh no," Joseph Lebas corrected him. " You knew that the Bank had turned him down; you blackballed his name yourself at the meeting of the Loan Committee. I still hold Birotteau in high esteem, and I say that there's more to this affair than meets the eye."

Pillerault quietly squeezed his hand.

" That does seem likely," said Mongenod. " There's no explanation, unless somebody back of Gigonnet wanted to kill off the Madeleine business from the start."

" He should have stuck to his own trade," Claparon interrupted. " If he'd kept busy with his new hair tonic instead of pushing up the price of real estate by buying up all he could lay his hands on, then he wouldn't have lost anything more than the hundred thousand francs he had on deposit with Roguin. Anyhow, we can expect to see him operate now under the name of Popinot."

" There's a name to watch out for," said Gigonnet.

In all this talk, Roguin played the part of " that unlucky

Roguin," while the perfumer was less mercifully dubbed "that poor fool Birotteau." The notary seemed to deserve indulgence because a woman had led him astray, while his victim was a laughing-stock on account of his social ambitions. When Gigonnet left the Stock Exchange, he went through the Rue Perrin-Gasselin and called upon Madame Madou, the dried-fruit and nuts dealer.

"Well, mother," he asked facetiously, "how's business?"

"Very quiet," she answered, offering the usurer her only chair, with a servility which she had never shown to anyone but her "dear departed" lover.

Madame Madou was quite capable of knocking out an impudent drayman, joking with her best customers, petitioning the King in the name of the Women Shopkeepers, or attacking the Tuileries Palace and starting a new Revolution, but she treated the petty tyrant Gigonnet with respect and indeed trembled before him. In the market district no power is greater than that of the man who deals in money. The Law may make itself felt in the person of the policeman, but Usury, with its green files and folders, freezes a borrower's best joke on his tongue, parches his throat and causes him to lower his eyes.

"Did you want anything from me?" she asked.

"A mere trifle. Just to warn you to pay up for the notes you passed on to me from Birotteau. He went into bankruptcy this morning. I'll send you a reminder tomorrow."

Madame Madou's eyes closed like those of a cat, and when she opened them again, they were spitting fire.

"The beggar! The rascal! There's business for you! And politics too! How are we to have any confidence in our government at this rate? But I'll collect my money, never fear! . . ."

"In business, it's every man for himself and the devil take the hindmost," said Gigonnet, raising one leg like a cat skirting a puddle, with a movement that had won him his nickname. "You'd better lose no time, because there are creditors who have more at stake than you, and they'll be after him."

" Good! I'll make him give me back my nuts, anyhow. . . . Marie-Jeanne, bring me my shoes and my rabbit-skin scarf, and hurry about it, if you don't want to get your ears boxed."

" There'll be a hot time up the street," Gigonnet said to himself, rubbing his hands. " Du Tillet will be glad if there's scandal all over this part of town. I don't know what he has against this Birotteau, though. I'm sorry for him. He's like a dog with a smashed paw. He hasn't the strength of character to be called a man."

Madame Madou swept down the Faubourg Saint-Antoine like the vanguard of a revolution. At seven o'clock in the evening she pounded at Birotteau's door, with her temper none the better for the exhausting pace at which she had traveled.

" You swine, I must have my money!" she shouted at poor Célestin. " And if you don't give it to me, I'll take sachets, satins, fans and any other gewgaws I can lay hands on. I shan't go away until I have my two thousand francs! Are mayors and their deputies to rob their constituents? If you don't hand over what you owe me, I'll go to the police and have your master put in jail. I'm not budging an inch!" And she made the gesture of sliding the glass top off a case filled with objects of a certain value.

" This woman's in heat," Célestin whispered to the clerk beside him.

Madame Madou heard this remark, for such paroxysms either dull the senses entirely or sharpen them to an unusual degree, and she gave him the hardest whack over the ear that this or any other perfumery shop had ever seen.

" You'd better learn to talk more respectfully about the female sex," she said, " and not to dirty the name of a woman whom you've cheated out of her money!"

Just then Constance came out of the back of the shop,

where her uncle was trying to persuade Birotteau to spend
the night at his house and not to carry his humility so far
as to offer to go to prison.

"Madame!" she said. "I beg you not to start a commotion
among the passers-by."

"Let them come in!" retorted Madame Madou. "I'll
have a pretty story to tell them. Yes, the money I sweated
so hard to earn went for you and your great ball. You're
rigged out like the Queen of France, but every stitch you have
on your back was stolen from honest folk like me. If I had
on that finery, it would burn my shoulders. I've only rabbit-
skin, but at least I paid for it. You thieves! Either give me
the money, or . . ."

And she laid hands on a precious inlaid box.

"Put that down, madame," said César, appearing at the
door. "Nothing here is mine any longer. It all belongs
to my creditors. All I have is my person, and if you wish
to throw that into jail, I give you my word of honor" (here
a tear trickled from the corner of one eye) "that I'll wait for
your bailiff and a police officer to take me there . . ."

The straightforward submissiveness of his voice and
manner calmed the woman down.

"My own notary ran away with my money," César
continued, "and I'm not responsible for the trouble I'm
causing. I can promise that you'll be paid some day or other,
even if I have to work as a porter in the market to raise the
money."

"You're a good man, I knew it," said Madame Madou.
"Forgive me for what I just said. But I'll have to throw
myself in the river, because Gigonnet is after me, and I have
only some bonds that fall due ten months from now with
which to pay him."

"Come see me tomorrow morning," said Pillerault, entering upon the scene. "I'll get you a loan at five per cent
from a friend of mine."

"There, there! If it isn't old man Pillerault! Of course,

he's your uncle, isn't he? Yes, you're honest people, I know that. I'll see you, then, tomorrow."

After this episode, César expressed a desire to stay at home, ready to give the same explanation to all his creditors. Pillerault overrode the protests of Constance and urged Birotteau to make himself comfortable upstairs. Then he went on the sly to Dr. Haudry and secured from him a prescription for a sleeping powder, which he brought back to his nephew's house. Here, with Césarine for an accomplice, he persuaded the perfumer to have a drink of wine from a glass in which the powder was dissolved. The drug sent him off into such a deep sleep that they were able to get him into a cab and take him to his uncle's apartment on the Rue des Bourdonnais, where he woke up fourteen hours later to find himself under the kindly care of Pillerault, who had slept on a couch in the drawing-room.

When Constance heard the rumble of the wheels of the cab in which her husband was being taken away, her courage left her. Often the only thing that holds up our strength is the necessity of bolstering up someone weaker than ourselves. Now the poor woman wept as violently as if she had been left alone with her daughter after the departure of César's dead body.

"Mother dear," said Césarine, sitting down on Constance's knees and caressing her with that kitten-like grace which women display only among themselves, "you told me that if I did my share courageously, you'd be better able to carry your own burden. You really mustn't cry. I'm quite ready to go to work in some other shop, and I promise I shan't moon about our former way of living. I'll be a salesgirl, just the kind you were yourself, and you'll never hear me complain. Besides that, I have a secret hope. . . . Do you remember what Monsieur Popinot was saying?"

"The dear boy! He'll not be my son-in-law . . ."

"Oh! Mother!"

"Because he'll be my son!"

" There's one good thing about misfortune," said Césarine, embracing her mother, " and that is that it teaches us
who are our real friends."

So it was that Césarine consoled Constance by taking over
the role of mother.  The next morning Constance went to
leave a letter for the Duke de Lenoncourt, First Gentleman
of the King's Bedchamber, requesting an audience with him
later in the day.  Meanwhile she went to Monsieur de La
Billardière, explained César's predicament and asked him
to back up her request and speak for her more cogently than
she herself could do.  Her great hope was to obtain a post of
some kind for Birotteau, perhaps that of cashier, for which
his honesty so perfectly qualified him.

" The King has just appointed Count de Fontaine Steward of the Royal Household," the Mayor told her.  " There's
not a moment to be lost."

At two o'clock, Monsieur de La Billardière and Madame
Birotteau went up the stairs of the Lenoncourt mansion on
the Rue Saint-Dominique and were ushered into the presence of the King's favorite Gentleman, that is if Louis XVIII
can be said to have had favorites of any kind.  The Duke
de Lenoncourt was one of those true aristocrats of the last
century, and the kindliness of his welcome restored a measure
of hope to Constance's heart.  She, on her side, had something of the nobility which clings about deeply and genuinely
felt sorrow.  Just as the Duke was saying that action must
be taken promptly, Monsieur de Vandenesse walked into
the room, causing his host to exclaim:

" Here is the fellow that can save us!"

This young man remembered having bought from Madame Birotteau some of those trifles which under certain
circumstances make a greater impression than far more
important things.  As soon as the Duke had explained her
errand he went off with Monsieur de La Billardière to see

Count de Fontaine, asking Madame Birotteau to wait for his return.

Count de Fontaine, like Monsieur de La Billardière, was a country gentleman, one of those unsung heroes of the civil wars of the Vendée, and he too remembered Birotteau from the time when conspirators had met at the Queen of Roses. All those who had shed blood for the Royalist cause received favors at Court, though Louis XVIII hushed them up as much as possible in order not to antagonize the Liberals. And the Count de Fontaine was said to be very close to the King. Not only did he promise to find a place for Birotteau, but he got in touch immediately with the Duke de Lenoncourt, who meanwhile had gone on duty at the palace, asking him to obtain an audience for him with the King that same evening and one with Monsieur, the King's brother, for Monsieur de La Billardière, who stood particularly high in his esteem. Monsieur de Fontaine went from the Tuileries straight to Madame Birotteau, to tell her that as soon as the bankruptcy proceedings were over her husband would have a post at twenty-five hundred francs a year in the Sinking Fund Office, since everything in the Royal Household had been promised to members of the vast crowd of impoverished and unemployed noblemen whom the King felt bound to employ.

But Madame Birotteau's task was not complete with the accomplishment of this mission. The following day she went to the Rue Saint-Denis, to call upon Monsieur Joseph Lebas at the Chat-qui-pelote. On her way she saw Madame Roguin roll by in a handsome carriage, doubtless on a shopping expedition. Their eyes met, and the fortunate woman's expression of shame before her unfortunate sister, gave the latter courage.

" I'll never drive in such a rig on other people's money," Constance said proudly to herself.

Joseph Lebas gave her a cordial welcome, and Constance asked him to keep an eye out for something suitable for her

daughter.  The draper made no promises, but a week later,
Césarine was taken at three thousand francs a year by a big
dry-goods establishment, which had just opened up a new
branch near the Boulevard des Italiens.  Here, she was cashier
and second in rank only to the manager and his wife, who
gave her a room and meals in exchange for some light domestic duties.  When this was settled, Constance went to
Popinot and asked if she could keep his accounts and household for him.  Because the young man realized that nowhere
else could she enjoy as much respect in the performance of
these functions he gladly complied with her request, generously offered her board, lodging and the same salary as her
daughter, and having put his rooms in the best order he
could for her use, went to share the attic of one of his clerks.
After exactly one month's enjoyment of her own sumptuously
redecorated apartment, Constance found herself in the cramped quarters overlooking a dank courtyard, where Anselme,
Gaudissart and Finot had plotted the future of Cephalic Oil.

When Molineux, who had been appointed by the commercial court as the agent of Birotteau's creditors, came to
take possession of his assets, Constance and Célestin checked
the inventory with him.  Then Constance and her daughter,
plainly dressed, went on foot, without once turning to look
back, to their Uncle Pillerault's house, where they dined with
César for the first time since they had been separated from
him.  The dinner was a sad affair.  All of them had had time
to think things over, measure the extent of their obligations
and plumb the depths of their courage.  Now they were like
sailors, aware of the shoals ahead and trimming sails in order
to battle the storm.  Birotteau was heartened by the news
that persons in high places had arranged things for his
family.  He could not help crying over the fact that his
daughter had gone to work, but he held out his hand to his
wife in recognition of the bravery with which she had started
life all over.  Once more, tears came to Pillerault's eyes at
the sight of his three dear ones embracing one another, while

César, the weakest of the lot, raised one hand and murmured: " Let us go on hoping!"

" For economy's sake, César," Pillerault declared, " you must share my apartment and eat at my table. For a long time I've been lonely and you can take the place of my dead child. And you'll have only a few steps to go to your new office."

" Thanks be to God for His kindness!" exclaimed César. " At the height of the storm he has sent a star to guide me."

Now that Birotteau had attained this state of resignation the worst of his unhappiness was over. His fall was a settled thing, and by admitting it he was able to regain his strength.

## VI

AFTER A BUSINESSMAN HAS DECLARED HIMSELF BANKRUPT, he is supposed to seek out some refuge either at home or abroad and live a life apart, like a child, for according to law he has no more rights than a minor and cannot perform any civic or legal act. This is the theory of the thing, but the practice is quite a different matter. Actually, he asks for an unwritten safe-conduct which neither the referee in charge of his case nor any of his creditors is likely to refuse him. If he did not have this he could be thrown into prison, but with it he can walk about freely in the enemy camp, not out of mere curiosity but in order to defend himself against some of the harshest provisions of the bankruptcy law. The effect of the legislation pertaining to private wealth is to sharpen men's natural astuteness, and a bankrupt, like any other man whose interests are endangered by the law, wishes to forestall its application. The period of time during which the bankrupt is a legally dead man lasts for about three months, and then comes the meeting between him and his creditors, where they sign a peace treaty, known as the settlement. By virtue of this settlement, the financial differences between them are resolved once and forever.

As soon as the commercial court has received the balance-sheet and the declaration of bankruptcy, it appoints a referee whose job is to watch over the interest of both sides, an interesting double role, if only the referee had time to play it. This referee empowers an agent to lay hands on all the bankrupt's tangible assets and to check them against his balance sheet. After this, the record office announces in the newspapers a meeting of the creditors, at which they choose temporary receivers. The receivers replace the agent and indeed through a legal fiction impersonate the bankrupt himself; they have power to liquidate everything for the creditors' benefit, that is unless the bankrupt opposes them. In most Parisian bankrupt cases, the temporary receivers are permanent receivers as well, and this is the reason.

The naming of permanent receivers is one of the most vengeful acts which the outraged creditors can perform. Of course, all creditors consider themselves duped, robbed, ridiculed and the rest. But in Paris no passion for business is intense enough to last ninety days. The notes (as we have seen) are only presented for payment at the end of this time. When ninety days are over, the creditors are worn out by the effort that has already been required of them and ready to sleep peacefully at their wives' sides. This may help foreigners to understand how in France the transient becomes in effect permanent, and why only five out of a thousand temporary receivers are ever replaced by permanent ones. The reason for this comparatively rapid decline of the passion for revenge will be clarified later on. Meanwhile those of my readers who are not in business will require further explanation of the drama of bankruptcy, if they are to understand what a monstrous legal joke it is, at least in Paris practice, and how César's case turned out to be an extraordinary exception.

The drama has three acts: first the agent's, then the receivers', and finally that of the settlement. And like every drama, it is played against a double setting, that erected for the public benefit and that which the public does not see; the stage as seen from the floor of the theater and the view of it enjoyed only from the wings. In the wings are the bankrupt and his lawyer, the creditors' lawyers, the agent, the receivers and the referee. Only in Paris is it generally known what a weird creature a referee of the commercial court actually is. There is constant danger that the law which he administers may be turned against him, and indeed, the presiding officer of this court has been known to go into bankruptcy himself. For, instead of the referee's office being the reward given to an honorably retired businessman, it is one more burden added to those of any man actively engaged in trade. It seems as if the indispensable qualification for passing upon the avalanche of commercial law-suits in the country's greatest business center was the difficulty which the referee has in conducting his own affairs. This court should be a stepping-stone by which a shop-keeper could in dignified fashion raise himself to a professional status; instead it is made up of practicing merchants, who may suffer reprisals for the verdicts they have handed down when they are forced to deal with the affected parties in everyday life, such as was the case when Birotteau, having been a referee, came up against du Tillet.

The referee, then, is a man who listens to a flood of words, with his mind on business of his own, and prefers to foist all the work upon the bankrupt's lawyer and his receivers, that is, except in unusual cases, where there is patent dishonesty on one side or the other. His part in the drama is like that of the King's bust in a courtroom; in general he does not open his mouth. Between five and seven o'clock in the morning he is, let us say, in his lumber-yard or haberdashery, and again at the end of the day, over his dinner, he must take hurried thought for his own affairs. Actually, his position is one which was set up and legally defined without sufficient study, and his hands are tied by the law, so that often he not only cannot prevent a fraud but must unwillingly corroborate it.

The agent, for his part, may act in the interests of the bankrupt instead of his creditors. Every agent hopes to enlarge his share by buttering up the bankrupt and getting at his supposed hidden resources. The agent can be useful to both sides, either by not taking away everything the bankrupt possesses, or by helping one creditor more than another. A clever agent sometimes buys up the credits and lets the bankrupt go scot-free. Inevitably he turns whichever way he thinks is more advantageous, whether it means saving the bankrupt or stripping him of everything for the benefit of the other side. In other words, his part in the drama is supremely important. He, like the bankrupt's lawyer, does not accept the job unless he is sure of remuneration. In nine hundred and fifty out of a thousand bankruptcy cases, the agent is on the bankrupt's side. At the time of this story, the lawyers would suggest an agent to the referee, and he was invariably a man acquainted with the bankrupt's business, so that he approached the job with the intention of re-conciling the interests of the creditors with those of an hon-orable man fallen upon evil days. Only in recent years have the referees exercised more discretion in their choice of an agent.

Meanwhile, the creditors, true and false, gather together to choose the temporary receivers, who, as we have explained above, are almost always permanent in the end. In this electoral assembly large and small creditors have equal voting rights. The bankrupt may have introduced partisans who do not properly belong there at all, but nevertheless may vote for the creditor candidates from whom the referee must choose receivers. Inevitably, some of these are the bank-rupt's men, and here we have another abuse which makes the bankrupt's catastrophe into a bad joke, protected by the law. The so-called honorable man fallen upon evil days becomes master of the situation and proceeds to legalize his theft. Small shop-keepers are usually honest in this respect. When one of them declares bankruptcy, it is not until after he has sold his wife's best shawl, pawned the family silver and come to court empty-handed, without even enough money to pay an unenthusiastic lawyer.

According to law, the final settlement, which releases the bankrupt from part of his debt and gives him back control over his own business, must be voted by a majority of the persons and interests concerned. To navigate through the

clash of opinions requires the exercise of considerable di-
plomacy on the part of the bankrupt, his lawyer and the
receivers. The most common device is to offer to the con-
trolling majority of creditors some extra payment outside
that stipulated in the agreement, and against this fraud there
is no possible protection, as the history of thirty successive
commercial courts goes to show. The last resort of the court
is the annulment of all notes offered as bribes by the bankrupt, and since in this case it is to the interests of the bankrupt to plead extortion this offers some hope of raising the
whole affair to a higher moral plane. Probably, however,
the creditors will think up some even wilier dodge, which
the referees will condemn in their official capacity but resort
to as quickly as the next man when they are themselves
before the bar.

Another common maneuver, to which we owe the term
" bona fide creditor," consists, as we have hinted above,
of creating creditors, just as du Tillet created the " banker "
Claparon. If the bankrupt succeeds in introducing a certain
number of these dummies into the proceedings, then he can
cut down the per capita payment to his creditors, build
himself some future resources and at the same time obtain
the number of votes necessary for the settlement. The false
creditors are like false electors smuggled into the Electoral
College. And what can the bona fide creditors do against
them ? They must expose their game, of course, but this
entails engaging the services of another lawyer, who is not
apt to put his best efforts into something so petty and tire-
some. For exposure of a false creditor means delving into
his remote past, subpoenaing his books, uncovering the
whole fiction and then pleading the case against him before
the referee. To go through this involved procedure with
every suspect creditor means a loss of time and money, and
even if such a one is caught red-handed, he has only to take
off his hat to the referee, protest that he is " absolutely bona
fide," and take leave, unpunished, of the court. The bank-

rupt's employment of a dummy does not prejudice his case, and if a bona fide creditor is mistakenly accused, he may take his case to a higher court and cost his accuser so much money that he goes into bankruptcy in his turn.

The upshot of the whole affair is this: the bankrupt names the receivers, goes over his own balance-sheet and practically dictates the terms of the final agreement. After the details which we have given above, anyone can imagine the variety of tricks, worthy of a Molière comedy, which are connected with bankruptcy proceedings. The fourteen volumes of *Clarissa Harlowe* would not be sufficient to contain them. Let us give one example. The famous Gobseck, mentor of Palma, Gigonnet, Werbrust, Keller, Nucingen and their like, was creditor in an affair where he had every intention of bearing down hard on the man who had cheated him of his due. The bankrupt gave him notes due after the signing of the settlement for an amount which, together with the stipulated payment, would cover all that was owed him. In return, he voted for a settlement by virtue of which seventy-five per cent of the bankrupt's debts were forgiven him, and thus cheated the other creditors to his own advantage. But there was a fly in the ointment. He had given notes, signed illegally by the fellow in his bankrupt status, and the seventy-five per cent remission applied to them as well, so that the clever Gobseck wound up by getting only fifty per cent of what he had expected. From that day on he treated the fellow who had outsmarted him with the greatest respect.

All the operations into which a bankrupt has entered during the ten days before his declaration are subject to the court's jurisdiction, and many a farsighted man has started a piece of business with his future creditors in just this period, so that it will be to their interest to make a prompt settlement and one that is not too harsh. Then, some crafty creditors may take their more simple fellows aside, describe the prospects of recuperation as very slim, buy up their credits at half price, and make a handsome profit on these as well as recovering their own.

Bankruptcy brings with it more or less hermetic closing of a business in which the looters have still left some money. He is a lucky man who can slip through the roof or cellar with an empty sack over his back and bring it out loaded. Under these catastrophic circumstances, people feel entitled to behave like Napoleon's routed army crossing the Beresina river, where every soldier was desperately intent upon saving his own skin. All standards of true and false, honest and dishonest, are broken down, and that man is most worthy of admiration who manages to " cover himself," that is to get some assets out of his fellow-creditors' hands. The whole country rang, not long ago, with the scandalous story of a big bankruptcy case in a city where a royal court was in session. Here the referees themselves had joint bank-accounts with the bankrupts, and covered themselves so well that poor Justice was left bare. Finally, because there was in this city no referee, receiver or agent who could be trusted, the case was transferred to another place.

In Paris, the confusion of bankruptcy proceedings is so well known that unless a creditor has a really large sum at stake, he puts it down to " profit and loss " and does not waste time attending the proceedings. And even a creditor on a much smaller scale, who cannot absent himself from a shop or trade, inclines to follow his example.

No really big businessman goes into bankruptcy, anyhow. He liquidates his assets as quietly as he can, and his creditors give him receipts for the best that he can offer. Thus there is no question of dishonor, no legal fees, procedural delay or spoilage of goods which had better be sold as quickly as possible. It is generally agreed, nowadays, that bankruptcy is far more shady than simple liquidation.

The act of the drama in which the receivers have their part to play is intended to prove that they are incorruptible and would not dream of entering into collusion with the bankrupt. But even the audience at the theater, since every creditor has at one time or another played a receiver's role, knows that a receiver is only a creditor in disguise and a " well-covered " one, at that. After three months of examining the bankrupt's assets and liabilities, the receivers come to the day of settlement, when they present a report which usually runs as follows:

Gentlemen: Our total credits come to a million francs. We have dismantled our man for all the world like a salvaged ship. The woodwork, iron and brasses have yielded three hundred thousand francs, or thirty per cent of what is due. Because we are lucky to have recuperated this sum, when he might have left us only a third as much, we declare him the model of a just and upright man. We give him a vote of confidence and propose to leave him tangible assets and allow him ten or twelve years in which to pay the fifty per cent of his total debts, which he condescends to pledge us. This, then, is the settlement. Just step up, one by one, and sign.

After this little speech, the happy creditors fall into one another's arms. Once the settlement is signed, the bankrupt goes right back into business, with his assets intact, and the right to default on the promised payment, thereby creating a sort of long-deferred baby-bankruptcy, comparable to the infant to which a woman gives birth nine months after her daughter's wedding.

Of course, if the settlement is not signed, then the creditors have to name permanent receivers and resort to such measures as forming a company to the bankrupt's business and take over everything on which they can lay their hands, including the money he may hope to inherit from even the most distant of his relatives some day.

There are, in short, two types of bankruptcy, the bankruptcy of the man who wants to go back into business, and that of the man who having fallen into the river is content to sink all the way to the bottom.  Pillerault knew the difference between these two, and in the experience of both Ragon and himself, it was about as difficult to emerge an honest man from the first as to come out a rich one from the second.  After having advised his nephew to follow the second type of procedure, he went to the most honest lawyer he could find in this special field and asked him to put all the assets at the creditors' disposal.  The creditors are obliged, according to law, to support the bankrupt and his family until a settlement has been reached, but in this instance Pillerault advised the referee that he was looking after them himself.

Du Tillet had arranged for the bankruptcy proceedings to be as painful as possible to his former employer.  This is how he worked it.  Time is so precious in Paris that only one of the two receivers is actually in touch with what is going on, while the other approves whatever he chooses to do.  And the active receiver, in his turn, often leans heavily upon the bankrupt's lawyer.  For this reason, cases of the first of the two types which we described above often move very fast, and within a hundred days the referee can echo the ironically tragic words of Marshal Sebastiani: " All's quiet in Warsaw!"

As we have seen, du Tillet wanted to destroy Birotteau's good name forever, and the choice of receivers, upon which he exercised considerable influence, betrayed this intention clearly to Pillerault's eyes.  Monsieur Bidault, or Gigonnet, the largest creditor, was to be inactive, while the nosey and punctilious Molineux was to do the real work.  It was to this miserable jackal that du Tillet tossed the honest perfumer's remains.  After the meeting at which he was elected, Molineux was not only, as he said, " honored by his fellow-citizens' vote," but happy as a child who has caught a fly and intends to torment it.  Reveling in the power of the law, he called upon du Tillet to advise him, and meanwhile pored over a copy of the Commercial Code.  Fortunately,

Joseph Lebas, who had been tipped off by Pillerault, had obtained the appointment of a wise and kindly referee. Du Tillet had counted on Gobenheim-Keller, but instead the case was assigned to Monsieur Camusot, the rich silk merchant and Liberal, who happened to own the house in which Pillerault was living and had the reputation of being an honorable man.

One of the worst hours in César's life was that of the conference he was obliged to hold with Molineux, a creature whom he had always considered the lowest of the low, and who had now by some trick of fate become his legal alter ego. He went with his uncle to the Cour Batave, climbed the steep stairs and prepared to face a man who as his creditors' representative had almost the same power over him as the referee.

" What's the matter ?" Pillerault asked his nephew, hearing him groan before the door.

" You don't know the kind of monster he is, Uncle."

" I've seen him off and on for the last fifteen years playing dominoes at the Café David. That's why I wanted to come with you."

Molineux was exaggeratedly polite with Pillerault and condescending toward Birotteau. He had rehearsed his part and every possible shading of what he had to say.

" What information do you need ?" Pillerault asked him. " There is no dispute about the various claims."

" Oh, the claims are in good order. I've checked everything, and all the creditors are bona fide. But, the law, sir, the law! The petitioner's living expenses were out of line with his means. The ball, for instance . . ."

" Where you were a guest," Pillerault reminded him.

". . . cost nearly sixty thousand francs, while the petitioner had only a little over a hundred thousand francs to his name. There are grounds for reporting him to another court for fraudulent bankruptcy."

" Do you really think him guilty of that ?" asked Pillerault, seeing out of the corner of one eye the state of dejection into which these words had plunged his nephew.

" Well, sir, of course this man Birotteau held a municipal office . . ."

" You didn't ask us to come here just in order to tell us that we were to be haled before the police, did you? You'd be the laughingstock of the Café David for anything so ridiculous."

Mention of the Café David seemed to strike terror into the little man's soul. He had counted on seeing Birotteau alone and playing the part of God Almighty. His plan was to hurl accusations at him, threaten him with jail and then, having enjoyed the spectacle of his abject fear, to appear to give way to sheer kindheartedness and make his victim eternally grateful. But instead of the fly with which he intended to play, he found himself face to face with an old businessman as resourceful as himself.

" It's not a laughing matter, sir," was all he could find to say.

" Excuse me," said Pillerault, " but you seem to me to be very generous with Monsieur Claparon; you're favoring his interests and your own over those of the other creditors. And since I am a creditor myself, I can complain to the referee."

" Sir, I am absolutely incorruptible," declared Molineux, sententiously.

" I know that," said Pillerault, " only you've covered yourself pretty well. You've acted in the same astute way as you did with that tenant you once told me about . . ."

" Oh, sir," said Molineux, reverting to his role of landlord as quickly as a cat disguised as a woman runs after a mouse, " that affair of mine on the Rue Montorgueil is still pending. There have been what they call new developments. The tenant in question is the oldest and most important in the house. Now the villain claims that since he paid me a year in advance and has no more than a year to . . ." (At this point

Pillerault shot his nephew a look indicating that he should pay strict attention.) ". . . Anyhow, since the year is paid, he claims he can take everything out of the apartment. Hence another lawsuit. I have a right to insist that the furniture remain until he's paid up in full. There's always a chance of having to make repairs."

" But the law doesn't allow you to use the furniture as a guarantee for anything but rent."

" Rent and incidentals!" exclaimed Molineux triumphantly. " That article of the Code has been interpreted in various decisions handed down on the matter. But as a matter of fact, the law ought to be slightly amended. I'm preparing a note to the Minister of Justice on its lacunae. The government really ought to look after private property. Instead of that, everything's done for the State, and citizens are no more than tightly squeezed tax-payers."

" You are quite able to tell the government what it ought to do," said Pillerault, " but what have you to tell us about the business in hand ?"

" Sir," said Molineux emphatically, " I wish to ask whether Monsieur Birotteau has received any money from Monsieur Popinot."

" No, sir," Birotteau answered.

There followed a lengthy discussion of the nature of the interest of Birotteau in Popinot's business, from which it turned out that Popinot had a right to be paid in full for his advances, even without taking any part in the bankruptcy proceedings, on account of the money which Birotteau owed him for his initial outlay. Little by little, under Pillerault's prodding, Molineux took a gentler tone, one which showed how much he cared for the good opinion of the Café David. Before the colloquy was over, he expressed his regret over Birotteau's situation and asked the two visitors to share his dinner. Upon this and other occasions, Pillerault was truly a guardian angel.

The worst torture that the law imposes upon a bankrupt

is forcing him to appear in person at the meeting held between the referee and the receivers, where the creditors
decide his fate. To a man who takes a toplofty attitude or
one who is fighting back, this sad ceremony holds no fears.
But because of Birotteau's susceptibility, it seemed to him
like a day of execution. Here again, Pillerault did everything
he could to make it endurable.

These were the operations which had been effected by
Molineux, with the consent of the petitioner. The lawsuit
over the mortgaged site on the Rue du Faubourg du Temple
had been won in the royal court, and the receivers decided
to sell it. Du Tillet, who had been secretly informed of the
government's intention to build a canal joining Saint-Denis
to the upper Seine, passing through the Faubourg du Temple
on the way, bought it out for seventy thousand francs.
César's share in the land around the Madeleine was turned
over to Monsieur Claparon, on condition that the latter give
up any claim to the half due from Birotteau on the cost of
registering the deeds establishing the new ownership. Claparon had to complete payment for the land, and in com-
pensation received the sum allowed the sellers under the
settlement. César's interest in Popinot's firm was sold to
Popinot himself for forty-eight thousand francs, and the
Queen of Roses to Célestin Crevel for fifty-seven thousand,
including the lease, furniture, stock, the trade-names Sultana
Cream and Pink Lotion, and use of the factory for twelve
years along with permanent possession of the equipment.
The liquid assets came to a hundred and eighty-five thousand
francs, to which the receivers added seventy thousand to be
realized from Birotteau's claim against Roguin, so that the
total was two hundred and fifty-five thousand francs. The
liabilities, on the other hand, amounted to four hundred and
forty thousand—half of them being covered, therefore, by
the assets.

Bankruptcy is like a chemical transformation out of which
a clever businessman tries to emerge with some of the fat

which was on him when he went in. But although Birotteau's
fat was all melted away in the cauldron, he somehow emerged
from it with greater stature than before, to the great disappointment of his enemy, du Tillet, who had never dreamed
of seeing a dishonorable affair turned into a demonstration of
virtue. Money was not his object, for he was going to acquire
the Madeleine land without spending a penny; his purpose
had been to drag the perfumer in the mud, and instead of
that, it looked as if his creditors were going to carry him on
their shoulders in triumph. As Birotteau's courage gradually
returned, his uncle gave him judiciously small doses of
instruction about the proceedings. Of course, certain of
the more drastic steps taken were real blows. No businessman can view with equanimity the devaluation of things
into which he has poured so much money and loving care.

" Fifty-seven thousand francs for the Queen of Roses !"
Birotteau exclaimed. " Why, the shop alone cost ten thousand, the apartment forty thousand, the factory fittings,
tools, boilers, and the rest thirty. Even allowing for a discount of fifty per cent, there is ten thousand francs' worth
of stock in the store, and the patents of Sultana Cream and
Pink Lotion are worth a small fortune."

Pillerault was no longer overly distressed by his unfortunate nephew's lamentations; he listened to them as
patiently as a horse waiting out under the rain. What worried
him more was the silence into which César lapsed at mention
of the final creditors' meeting. Anyone aware of the natural
human vanity to which men of every social sphere are subject,
will understand how painful was it for Birotteau to come
as a petitioner to the court where he had once sat as referee,
to run the risk of receiving insults where formerly he had
been thanked for his services. Moreover, everyone had heard
his strictures against businessmen who declared themselves
bankrupt. " A man may be honest enough when he goes
into bankruptcy, but by the time he comes out of the creditors' meeting the chances are ten to one he's a cheat!"

Pillerault had seized on every possible opportunity in order
to get César accustomed to the idea of going through this
final ordeal which the law exacted of him.  In his uncle's
presence, César accepted it mutely, but late at night Pillerault
heard him wake up out of a sound sleep to shout: " No,
never!  I'll die first!"

Strong-minded as he was, Pillerault nevertheless understood the weaknesses of others and resolved to spare César
the worst features of this inevitable and heart-rending scene.
The law is categorical on this point, and the petitioner who
fails to appear may be haled before the criminal court.  On
the other hand, no single creditor is compelled to be present,
and the meeting is important only when the bankrupt is
such an untrustworthy fellow that the creditors have to form
a company to run his business, when there is some dis-
agreement between the more favored creditors and the less
favored ones, or when the settlement has been wangled by
the bankrupt's dummies and they turn out in full force to
vote it through.  When, on the contrary, either all the assets
have been conscientiously brought to light and their distribution equably planned, or else, going to the other extreme,
the petitioner has a prearranged settlement in the bag, then
the meeting is no more than a formality.

Pillerault went, then, to ask one creditor after another to
sign a power of attorney over to his lawyer.  Every one of
them, with the exception of du Tillet, was sorry for Birotteau,
once he had been dragged down, and it was a matter of
common knowledge how honestly he kept his books and did
business.  Moreover, there was general satisfaction that no
dummy creditors had been found.  Molineux, first as agent
and then as receiver, had brought to light every last thing
César possessed, even the print of Hero and Leander given
him by Popinot, his stick-pin, gold buckles, watches and
chains, his wife's jewelry box and other personal effects
which many a perfectly honest man would have hung onto
without the least scruple.  This complete obedience to the

letter of the law touched the hearts of many of his creditors, and although those who were his enemies branded it a sign of stupidity, the men of good will among them insisted on presenting the action under its true light. Two months later, almost everyone saw it this way and described the case as one of the most extraordinary ever known. Because the creditors were sure of getting at least sixty per cent of their money, they were glad to cooperate with Pillerault. As for the lawyers, there were few, for a number of creditors share the same one. So it was that Pillerault got the meeting down to the referee, the two receivers, three lawyers, Ragon and himself. On the morning of the dread day, he was able to say to his nephew:

"César, you can go to today's meeting without fear. Hardly anyone will be there."

Monsieur Ragon insisted upon going with César to court. When Birotteau heard the falsetto voice of the former owner of the Queen of Roses, he turned pale, but a moment later the good little man opened his arms and they embraced each other like father and son, with tears in their eyes. With renewed courage, Birotteau got into a cab, between Ragon and his uncle, and at exactly half past ten, they arrived at the Saint-Merry cloisters, where the commercial court held its sessions. There was no one in the bankruptcy court at all, a happy circumstance due to the early hour agreed upon by the referee and the receivers. All the other creditors were represented by lawyers, and so there was nothing really to intimidate César. Nevertheless, it was not without trepidation that he stepped into Monsieur Camusot's chambers, which had once been his own, and he trembled slightly at the prospect of going next to the courtroom where he had functioned in so different a capacity.

"It's chilly," said Monsieur Camusot to Birotteau. "I'm sure these gentlemen will be happy to stay right here. Won't you all sit down?"

He did not mention the word "bankruptcy," and even

offered the embarrassed Birotteau his own chair. Almost immediately, the receivers and the lawyers started to sign.

" Upon your relinquishment of all your assets," Camusot went on, " your creditors have unanimously decided to wipe out your debts to them. The settlement is couched in terms such as to mitigate your humiliation, and your lawyer will have it confirmed promptly. In other words, you are a free man." And he added, grasping Birotteau's hands: " All the referees of the court are touched by your distress, but not in the least surprised by your courage and integrity. Even in misfortune, you have been worthy of your best self. I've lived twenty years in business circles, and this is only the second time that I've seen a man raise himself in the public esteem by the nature of his fall."

Birotteau squeezed the referee's hands with tears in his eyes. And when Camusot asked him about his future plans, he answered that he meant to work to pay his creditors completely.

" If you need a few thousand extra francs with which to finish up the job, you can count on getting them from me," said Camusot. " I'm happy to help you, after having taken part in so unusual a case."

Upon this, Birotteau, Ragon and Pillerault all took their leave.

" Well, it wasn't so bad, after all, was it ?" asked Pillerault at the door.

" I recognize your hand," said Birotteau, with deep emotion.

" Now that everything is settled, let's look in on my nephew, Anselme," said Ragon. " The Rue des Cinq-Diamants is only a few steps away."

It was hard for César to see Constance sitting in a cramped office on the low-ceilinged, mezzanine floor, whose window was blocked off from the light by a sign swinging outside with the name: A. POPINOT.

" Here you have one of Alexander the Great's lieutenants," he said, trying to be gay.

The forced gaiety of his voice and the unwitting expression of superiority, pierced the seventy-year-old Ragon to the heart. Meanwhile, when Constance came down with some letters for Popinot to sign, her husband could not hold back his tears.

" Good morning, my dear," she said with a smile.

" I needn't ask if you're comfortably installed," he said looking at Popinot.

" Just as if I were in my son's home," she answered, and her husband was struck by the feeling in her voice.

César embraced Popinot and said:

" I've just lost the right to give him that name."

" Let's hope differently," said Anselme. " *Your* oil is going very well, thanks to the publicity we placed in the papers and the posters with which Gaudissart has plastered the whole country. He's going to have some printed at Strasbourg next, and embark upon the conquest of Germany. We've received orders for three thousand gross already."

" Three thousand gross!" exclaimed César.

" Yes. And I've picked up a lot on the Faubourg Saint-Marceau for a factory. Of course, I'm hanging onto the place on the Faubourg du Temple as well."

" You see, my dear," Birotteau whispered to Constance, " just a bit of help and we could have made it over the hump."

From this day on, César and his wife and daughter had a clear understanding. The poor man had set himself an almost impossible goal, which required all three of them to hold onto every penny. Césarine went at her work with inherited ability and youthful enthusiasm, sitting up nights to work on designs for material and think up ways of increasing the volume of business. Her employers had to check her ardor at the same time that they wished to reward it. They offered her all sorts of gifts, but she would accept nothing but money. Every month she brought her salary and extra earnings to her Uncle Pillerault, as did her mother and father. None of them wanted to be responsible for the investment of their savings, and Pillerault went back into the business world sufficiently to follow the Stock Exchange and study the possibilities of placement. It came out later that both Joseph Lebas and Jules Desmarets were happy to advise him. Although César was living in his uncle's house, he asked no questions. He walked about the streets with his head down, reluctant to have anyone see the stupefied unhappiness on his face, and ashamed of himself for still possessing a good suit of clothes.

" At least my creditors are not giving me my bread and butter," he said to Pillerault, with an angelic expression. " The bread from your table, even if there is sheer pity behind it, is sweeter to me than if I had to pay for it out of my salary."

When his fellow shopkeepers of former days met César in his new guise of office employee, they could see no trace of his old self. And perfect strangers saw a somber example of decay in his darkened face, where something quite new to him, the exercise of *thought*, had left ineradicable traces. It is not everyone who can achieve destruction! Light-hearted, indifferent souls never bear the marks of a man with disaster. Only religious feeling is visibly affected by the decline of his former high estate; he believes in Divine Providence and a future life, and a certain light plays around him in such a way as to distinguish him from his unbelieving fellows. He is filled with a touching mixture of hope and resignation, for like a fallen angel he knows the value of what he has lost. No bankrupt is allowed within the precincts of the Stock Exchange. And César, driven from the society of honest men, was the living image of a fallen angel suing for pardon.

For fourteen months, mulling over these ascetic thoughts

in his mind, Birotteau denied himself all pleasure. In spite of his confidence in the Ragons, he would not dine with them, any more than with the Lebas', the Matifats, the Protez', the Chiffrevilles or even Monsieur Vauquelin, although all of these good friends wished to show him their esteem. César preferred to stay alone in his room rather than run into one of his creditors, and his friends' kindness recalled to him all too bitterly the reality of his position. Constance and Césarine did not go anywhere, either. On Sundays and holidays, which were the only times when they were free, they took César to church and then went back with him to his uncle's house. As often as not, Pillerault invited Abbé Loraux to join them for dinner, for he knew that his company was a solace to Birotteau. Because of his own delicate sense of honor, Pillerault could not but approve César's reticence, but he planned gradually to enlarge the circle of people whom he could look straight in the eye without embarrassment.

In May of 1821, Pillerault insisted on giving the whole family a treat. The last Sunday of this month was the anniversary of the day on which Constance had consented to marry César, and because Pillerault had rented a country place together with the Ragons, at Sceaux, he thought this would be a good occasion for a housewarming.

" César, we're all going to the country tomorrow," he said abruptly on Saturday night. " And you must come along."

Now Birotteau had put his excellent handwriting to use by copying legal documents for Derville and several other lawyers. In fact, with the priest's permission, he worked like a slave every Sunday.

" No," he said now to his uncle, " Derville expects me to prepare a trusteeship account for him."

" Come, now, your wife and daughter deserve some recreation. You'll find yourself among your best friends : Abbé Loraux, the Ragons, Popinot and his uncle. Besides, this is an order, not an invitation."

In the rush of their business years, César and Constance had never found time to go back to Sceaux, although they had often wished to revisit the tree under which as the young chief clerk of the Queen of Roses, César had nearly fainted away with joy when his proposal was accepted. As they drove along, with Césarine and Anselme in the carriage beside them, Constance shot understanding looks at her husband, without ever being able to summon up a smile. And when she whispered a few words into his ear, he only shook his head in reply. Her tenderness, which was absolutely genuine but necessarily somewhat clumsy and forced in its expression, not only failed to light up his somber face, but drew tears to his eyes. Twenty years ago, as a successful young man, in love with a girl as beautiful as Césarine, he had traveled over this same road, his heart brimming over with happiness. Now he saw the pallor of his hard-working daughter's brow and effects like those of a volcanic eruption upon the full-blown beauty of his wife. Only love was left to them now. The dour look on his face stifled even the natural gaiety of Césarine and Anselme, who reminded him of this great day of his youth.

"Go ahead and be happy, dear children," he said with an effort. "You have every right to your happiness, and there shouldn't be a single other thing on your minds."

With these words, he picked up Constance's hands and kissed them with an affectionate admiration which stirred her more than any amount of joy. The other guests were waiting for their arrival and greeted them with a cordiality that soon put César at ease, in spite of the fact that this was their first encounter since the bankruptcy proceedings.

"You two must go for a stroll in the woods," said Pillerault, joining César's and Constance's hands. "Take Césarine and Anselme with you, and come back at four o'clock."

"Poor people!" said Madame Ragon. "If we were to go along, we'd only be in the way. Anyhow, the good news we have in store is going to cheer them up considerably."

" Birotteau is going through all the agony of repentance without having really sinned," said Abbé Loraux.

" Yes, but it took unhappiness to really ennoble him," put in Judge Popinot.

The ability to forget is the secret of a strong and creative mind, to forget in the fashion of nature, which admits no past, but continually reproduces and renews. Only weak characters, like Birotteau, bog down in their troubles. Instead of transforming them into instructive experience, they immerse themselves in them, wearing themselves thinner every day in the contemplation of the accumulated woes of the past. Now, at last, when the two couples had found the path leading to the Bois d'Aulnay, which extends over some of the prettiest hills near Paris, with the Vallée-aux-Loups spread out below, the fine spring weather and the beauty of the green trees relaxed the taut strings of César's heart. He pressed his wife's arm against his pounding heart and the glazed look in his eye gave way to an expression of enjoyment.

" Now I begin to recognize you, my poor César," said Constance. " It seems to me we've behaved well enough to indulge in a little pleasure."

" How can I ?" exclaimed César. " Constance, your affection is the only treasure I have left. I've lost my strength and self-confidence; all I ask is to live long enough to discharge my indebtedness. You, who were always wise and prudent and far-sighted on my behalf, can afford to be happy. But the burden of guilt is all mine. Eighteen months ago, at that ill-fated ball, I saw my own Constance, the only woman I've ever loved, even more beautiful than when we ran down this path together twenty years ago, just as our children are running today. . . . And in these last months I myself have marred that beauty of yours, in which I took such just pride. And yet I love you more than ever. . . . Oh, my *dear* one" (and the way he pronounced this phrase went straight to Constance's heart), " I'd rather hear you scold me, the way you used to, than have you nurse my wounded pride.''

" All I can say,'' answered Constance, " is that I never dreamed a wife's love for her husband could grow so much over the years.''

For a moment César forgot all his troubles, for to his sensitive heart this sentence was worth a fortune. It was almost joyfully that he quickened his step toward *their* tree, which by good fortune remained standing. They sat down beneath it, watching Anselme and Césarine, who were walking around and around the same grassy sward, perhaps under the illusion that they were moving in a straight line.

" Mademoiselle,'' said Anselme, " I trust you have a better opinion of me than to believe that I would take advantage of the purchase of your father's share in the oil. I am keeping it for him with care. I am making loans with his money, and if ever a note I have accepted isn't paid up, I'll charge it to my account rather than to his. We can't belong to each other until the day your father is completely vindicated, and I am striving with all my might to hasten its arrival.''

Anselme had never breathed a word of this secret to his future mother-in-law. Even the most innocent lover can't help wanting to shine in his beloved's eye.

" And will it be soon ?'' she asked him.

" Yes, very soon,'' said Popinot, so persuasively that the chaste Césarine held up her forehead for him to kiss.

" Father, everything's going well,'' she said knowingly to César. " Talk to us, now, and don't look so sad.''

When the four of them came back to Pillerault's house, all holding hands together, even the distracted César could see from the behavior of the Ragons that something had happened. Madame Ragon's welcome was unusually unbending, and something in her eyes and voice seemed to say : " We've been paid.''

At dessert, the notary of Sceaux came to join them. Pillerault could see that Birotteau was aware of a surprise in the air, without imagining what it could be.

" My dear nephew," he began, " the combined savings of your family over these last eighteen months amount to twenty thousand francs. I received thirty thousand from the settlement of your affairs, and that makes fifty thousand available for your other creditors. Monsieur Ragon's share in the settlement was thirty thousand francs, and now the notary has brought you his receipt for all that you owe him, interest included. Crottat has the rest, to be distributed to Madame Madou, the painter, carpenter and other needy creditors. As for next year, we shall see. Time and patience have already brought us a long way."

Birotteau's joy was indescribable; he threw himself weeping into his uncle's arms.

" Let him wear his Legion of Honor today," said Ragon to Abbé Loraux.

The good abbé attached the red ribbon to César's buttonhole, causing him to look at himself in the mirror at least a dozen times and to display a delight which superior people would have found ludicrous, but this company considered only natural.

The very next day César went to Madame Madou.

" Here you are, my good man," she said. " I hardly recognized you with that gray hair. But you and your family are lucky to have jobs the way you do. I'm wearing myself out more like a squirrel on the treadmill than a human being."

" Madame..."

" Never mind," she said; " I can't blame you for that. Have you some money for me?"

" That's what I've come to tell you. It's waiting for you at the office of Crottat, the notary. . . . Everything I owe you, and the interest besides."

" Do you mean it?"

" Yes, just go to him at half past eleven . . ."

"There's honor for you, with four per cent in the bargain!" said the woman with naive admiration. "Look here, I'm doing good business with that red-headed boy of yours; he doesn't haggle over my price. So I'll give you a receipt without taking your money. Madou is quick to catch fire and lose her temper, I know, but she has something in here. . . ." And she proceeded to thump the most voluminous cushions of human flesh that have ever been seen in the Paris markets.

"Never!" said Birotteau. "The law is quite definite, you know, and I insist upon paying in full."

"Well, I shan't refuse, then," she said. "But tomorrow I shall trumpet your good name far and wide. That's what I call a good joke, after all!"

The same scene, with some variations, awaited Birotteau in the house of Lourdois, the house-painter, now Crottat's father-in-law. It was raining, and César left his umbrella near the door. The *nouveau-riche* painter saw the water trickling across his dining-room floor and received his guest roughly.

"Well, old man Birotteau, what will you have?" he said as if he were talking to a beggar.

"Sir, hasn't your son-in-law told you? . . ."

"Told me what?" asked Lourdois impatiently.

"To come to his office at half past eleven with a receipt for everything that I owe you."

"Ah, that's different! Sit down, Monsieur Birotteau. Won't you have a bite to eat?"

"Yes, do stay for lunch," said his wife.

"Does that mean that things are looking up?" the painter asked him.

"Not exactly," said Birotteau. "I've been lunching on a crust of bread in my office in order to save money, but as time goes by, I hope to make up for the damage I have done."

"I must say," said the painter, swallowing a *pâté de foie gras* sandwich, "that you're a man of honor."

"And how is Madame Birotteau?" asked his wife.

" She's keeping accounts for Monsieur Popinot."

" Poor people!" said Madame Lourdois in a low voice to her husband.

" If there's anything I can do, you have only to ask me, Birotteau," Lourdois said in conclusion. " I may be able to help."

" What you can do is go to your son-in-law's office," Birotteau told him.

These first achievements restored some of the perfumer's courage, but did not enable him to sleep; quite the contrary, since the desire to win back his honor disturbed his whole life. He had lost his florid complexion, his eyes were habitually dull and his face was covered with a network of wrinkles. When former acquaintances met him at eight o'clock in the morning or at four o'clock in the afternoon, slipping like a thief along the walls of the Rue de l'Oratoire, with his gray hair and pale fearful face, and wearing a coat from the old days, which he nursed the way a young lieutenant nurses his battle jacket, they stopped him, by sheer force, in order to say:

" Everyone knows how well you are behaving. But some of us think you're a bit hard on your wife and daughter."

" Take your time," said others. " No one ever died just for lack of money."

" People have died for lack of self-respect, though," he retorted in spite of his weakened condition.

# VII

At the beginning of 1823, it was decided to construct the Saint-Martin Canal, and lots on the Faubourg du Temple soared to astronomical prices. The canal cut right through the property which du Tillet had bought up at Birotteau's bankruptcy sale, and now he was made a large offer for it on condition that he turn it straight away. But the lease given by César to Popinot held the whole thing up, and du Tillet had to pay a visit to the Rue des Cinq-Diamants. As Césarine's fiancé Anselme instinctively disliked him. Although he knew nothing of the thefts the fellow had committed, a voice deep down inside him said: "He's a thief in disguise." So strong were Popinot's feelings that not for anything in the world would he have done business with du Tillet. This was particularly true in view of the fact that land around the Madeleine had started to rise to the absurd prices it was to bring in 1827 and thus du Tillet was already making money off what he had taken from Birotteau. Now, as soon as the banker had explained the purpose of his visit, Popinot looked at him indignantly.

"I'll give you my lease, if you insist," he answered, "but it will cost you sixty thousand francs."

"Sixty thousand francs!" exclaimed du Tillet, starting to draw back.

"The lease has fifteen years to go, and I shall have to spend at least three thousand francs to outfit a new factory building. If you can't meet my terms, there's no use discussing the matter further."

He went back into his shop, with du Tillet at his heels, and when in the course of their discussion the name of

Birotteau passed between them, Constance came down from
the mezzanine floor. This was their first meeting since the
ball, and the banker could not restrain an involuntary movement of surprise and shame when he saw the ravages wrought
by this brief intervening time.

" This gentleman is about to be paid three hundred
thousand francs for *your* land, and he's unwilling to give us
a sixty-thousand-franc indemnity for our lease."

" That represents an income of three thousand francs a
year," said du Tillet belligerently.

" Three thousand francs!" exclaimed Constance, looking
at him very hard.

Du Tillet paled, and there was a moment of silence in
which Popinot stared with a puzzled expression at Madame
Birotteau.

" Just sign this release," said du Tillet. " I had it drawn
up by Crottat this morning. And I'll give you a cheque for
sixty thousand francs."

Popinot looked even more amazed than before. While du
Tillet was writing out his cheque at a high desk in one corner,
Constance went quietly back upstairs. The two men ex-
changed papers and took leave of one another coldly.

" In only a few months, thanks to this mysterious business,
I shall have my little Césarine," Anselme said to himself,
as he watched du Tillet go up the Rue des Lombards, where
he had left his gig. " Thank God, she won't have to work
any longer. . . . And just one look of Madame César did it!
What secret can there be between her and that thief?"

After he had sent the cheque to the bank he went up
to the mezzanine, but she was not there and he decided to
look for her in her room. Constance and Anselme were
living almost like mother and son together, and his natural
impulse was to communicate to her his new reason for being
happy. He came so quietly into the room that he found her,
to his surprise, reading a letter whose handwriting he recognized as that of du Tillet. She had lit a candle, and scraps

of charred paper were lying about the floor. On the letter in Constance's hand he read quite without meaning to the sentence: "*I adore you! You know it, my angel, and why must you? . . .*"

"What influence have you over du Tillet to persuade him to capitulate so quickly?" he asked her, with a nervous laugh, which betrayed uncertainty and suspicion.

"Let's not talk about it," she answered in distress.

"Then let's talk about the end of your troubles!" said Popinot, turning on his heels and going to drum with his fingers on the windowpane. "Even if she did love du Tillet, that's no reason for my failing to behave like an honest man," he said to himself.

"What is it, my child?" asked Constance from behind him.

"The total profits of our Cephalic Oil are two hundred and forty-two thousand francs, of which half comes to a hundred and twenty-one. Substracting the forty-eight thousand francs I gave Monsieur César and adding the sixty thousand I have just received for the lease, we have a hundred and thirty-three thousand francs in his name."

Constance's joy was so great that Anselme could hear her heart pounding.

"You know that I consider him my partner, and so this sum is available now for his creditors. If we add to it the twenty-eight thousand francs of your savings, which are in your Uncle Pillerault's hands, that makes a hundred and sixty-one thousand altogether. Of course, Uncle Pillerault will give us a receipt for twenty-five thousand which are owed to him personally. And no power on earth can prevent me from lending my father-in-law what I calculate will be our profits next year. That means he can rehabilitate himself completely."

"Thank God!" said Constance, letting the letter drop from her hands and joining them in prayer. "Dear Anselme!" she exclaimed, after making a sign of the cross. And she took his head in her hands, kissed his forehead and caressed him. "How glad I am that Césarine is yours, for I know how happy she will be. And at last she can stop killing herself with work. . . ."

"Work she does for love," said Popinot.

"True," said the mother, with a smile.

"Listen to this," said Popinot, still looking out of the corner of one eye at the fatal letter. "I have a little secret to tell you. I lent Célestin some money with which to buy up your business, but I set a condition on my loan. Your apartment is just the way you left it. I had a plan on that score, but I didn't dream luck would enable me to carry it out so fast. Célestin has not occupied the apartment and he has promised to sub-let it to no one but you and to hold the furniture in your name. I am keeping the third floor for Césarine and myself, when we are married, so that you will have the feeling that she is still at home. As a matter of fact, I shall be over here in my own shop from eight to six every day. Then, in order to rebuild your fortune, I shall buy out Monsieur César's interest in the business for a hundred thousand francs, and together with his present salary, you will have ten thousand a year. Now, are you happy?"

"Don't tell me any more, Anselme, or I shall go mad with joy!"

The fervor of Constance's prayer and the innocence of her expression combined to destroy Anselme's suspicions of a few moments before. Surely Pillerault's niece could do no wrong. And now he chose to rid himself once and for all of the evil thoughts which had assailed him.

"Darling Mother," he said, "a vile suspicion has poisoned my mind. If you want to make me happy, you will destroy it right away." And he stretched out his hand for the letter. "I couldn't help reading the opening lines in du Tillet's hand," he went on, in spite of the terror on Constance's face. "And they fit in so well with the way du Tillet gave in,

as soon as he saw you, to my frankly outrageous request. . . .
Well, it's only human to jump to the conclusion that the
devil whispered in my ear. Just one look from you, and
three little words. . . ."

" Say no more," said Constance, taking the letter out of
his hands and holding it up to the flames. " I have been
cruelly punished for a very small weakness. Now you must
know the whole story, for I can't have your suspicion of me
reflect upon my daughter. Besides, I have no reason to
blush, and I could perfectly well tell my husband what I am
telling you. Du Tillet tried to seduce me, and since my
husband had already taken a dislike to him for other reasons,
I persuaded him to dismiss the fellow at once, without disturb-
ing him with my own story. And to top it all, three days
before his dismissal, he robbed us of three thousand francs !"

" I'm not surprised !" said Popinot resentfully.

" Anselme, you deserve for the sake of your future happiness to know the whole thing. But you must forget about it,
just as my husband and I have forgotten. Perhaps you remember how vexed my husband was by a deficit in the
cash-box one day. But in order to save the fellow from dishonor, he put the money back himself, as I guessed only
some time later, when he postponed for three years the
purchase of a promised cashmere shawl. Now you know
why I came out with those three little words, as you call them.
I must confess that I did one very childish thing. I kept three
typical love letters from du Tillet . . . just as curiosities, without looking at them more than once in all these years. But,
of course, I should have destroyed them from the start.
When I saw him just now, I was reminded of their existence
and came up here to burn them without further delay. I was
just looking at the last of the lot when you came into the
room."

Anselme fell onto one knee and kissed her hand so affec-
tionately that both of them had tears in their eyes. Then
she helped him to his feet and they embraced one another.

For César too this was a lucky day. Monsieur de Vandenesse, the King's private secretary, came to see him at his
office and they went to talk together in the courtyard of the
Bank.

" Monsieur Birotteau," said the viscount, " news of your
efforts to pay off your creditors has reached His Majesty's
ear and made a great impression upon him. Having heard
that you are not wearing your Legion of Honor, he orders
you to put it back at once. And in order to help you meet
your obligations, he has asked me to bring you some money
out of his own pocket. His only regret is that he can't give
you more. And of course the whole thing must remain a
secret. His Majesty doesn't wish his private kindnesses to
receive publicity." And with these words he handed Birotteau an envelope containing six thousand francs.

While César stammered his thanks, Vandenesse waved to
him in good-by, with a broad smile upon his face. César's
conduct was so unusual in the Paris of his day that it had
aroused more admiration than he knew. Judge Popinot,
Joseph Lebas, Camusot, Abbé Loraux, Ragon, Lourdois,
Monsieur de La Billardière and Césarine's employer had all
talked it abroad, and public opinion, in which for a short
time he had fallen so low, now extolled him to the skies.

" There's an honorable man for you!" César had heard
these words spoken on the street as he went by, and
they had given him the same emotion as that felt by an
author when he overhears the magic phrase: " Look who's
there!"

This increase of César's reputation was a dagger in du
Tillet's heart. And César's first thought, when he was left
with the King's banknotes in his hand, was to pay off his
former clerk. He went to the Rue Chaussée-d'Antin, and
met him coming home to lunch, on his own stairs.

" Well, my poor Birotteau," du Tillet said condescend-
ingly.

" Poor? I'm anything but poor," his debtor answered

proudly. " I shall go to sleep tonight with the satisfaction
of having paid you."

These honest words hit du Tillet very hard. In spite of
the position which he had attained, he had no very good
opinion of himself and the voice of his conscience told him :
" Here is a man !"

" Pay me ? What business have you gone into now ?"

Because he felt sure that du Tillet would not spread
the news further, César said straightforwardly :

" I shall never go into business again. Of course, no
human being could have foreseen what happened to me,
and it may be that I shall fall into the hands of yet another
Roguin. But the King has heard of the line of conduct which
I set for myself to follow, and in order to reward and en-
courage my efforts he has sent me a sum of money, which . . ."

" Do you need a receipt ?" du Tillet interrupted. " Are
you paying in cash ?"

" Yes, and with your interest up to date. I must ask you
to step with me over to Monsieur Crottat. . . ."

" Has the receipt to be notarized as well ?"

" Sir, I am aiming at definitive rehabilitation, and I want
all my papers in order . . ."

" Very well, then, since it's so close by. But how in the
world do you expect to find sufficient money ?"

" I shan't ' find ' it at all," said Birotteau. " I'm earning
it by the sweat of my brow."

" You owe a large amount to Claparon."

" That's all too true. There's the biggest of all my debts,
and I suppose that I shall have to work my whole life long
to pay it off."

" I don't think you'll ever raise the full sum," du Tillet
remarked coldly.

" He may be right there," Birotteau reflected.

On the way back from the notary's, Birotteau found himself accidentally on the Rue Saint-Honoré, which he usually
managed to avoid, in order to be spared the sight of his former

home and business establishment. Now, for the first time since the disaster, he saw the house where in the space of three months eighteen years of happiness had been obliterated. "I always thought I'd die there," he said to himself, quickening his pace as he looked up and saw the swinging sign:

CÉLESTIN CREVEL
*Successor to César Birotteau*

"I must be seeing things!" he added. "That looked just like Césarine up at the window!"

It was, indeed, the blond head of his daughter, who had come with Anselme and her mother to plan the festivities they were planning to hold in César's honor. They knew that he never passed this way and were astounded to see him staring up from the street below. Monsieur Molineux happened to be in a shop across from them and now he remarked to the owner:

"There's Monsieur Birotteau, looking at his old house!"

"Poor fellow!" said the shop-keeper. "He gave a very handsome ball. . . . There were over two hundred carriages."

"I know that. I was there myself. Three months later he went into bankruptcy, too, as you may remember. And I was one of the receivers."

With trembling legs, Birotteau hurried back to the house of his uncle. Pillerault already knew of the plans that had been hatched on the Rue des Cinq-Diamants, and because he had followed César's trials from day to day, he was fearful of the shock he might suffer upon hearing that he was on the eve of rehabilitation. César's inflexible views on the subject of bankruptcy kept him in a state of continual tension. His honor was, to him, like a beloved dead one, awaiting the Resurrection Day, and the very hope of its ultimate revival increased the intensity of his sorrow. So that now, when Birotteau came into the house, his uncle was thinking how to break the good news. César's joyful account of the money

he had received from the King and his astonishment at the
illusory vision of Césarine at the window of the Queen of
Roses seemed to pave the way.

" Well, do you know why it is that you really saw her
there?" he said. " Because Popinot is so impatient to get
married. Just because you're exceedingly honest, there's
no reason why he should live on bread and water with a
temptingly good dinner in view. He wants to give you the
rest of the money necessary for your rehabilitation."

" He's buying my daughter," objected Birotteau.

" Isn't it an honorable thing to put his father-in-law's
affairs in order?"

" There might be some legal objection. . . ."

" Come, come," said Pillerault, pretending to be very
angry. " You have a right to give up your own life, but it's
utterly unjust to sacrifice that of your daughter!" And he
proceeded to make the discussion hotter. " If Popinot never
lends you a penny, if he treats you strictly like a business
partner and looks upon the money he gave your creditors
in order to buy out your share in the oil as a share in future
profits . . ."

" Then it would seem as if I had connived with him in
order to deceive them!"

Pillerault pretended to let César have the last word. He
knew human nature well enough to realize that the good
man would argue the point with himself all night long and
that such an argument would accustom him to the idea of
rehabilitation. At dinner, César came back to another point
that was troubling him.

" What were Constance and Césarine doing in our old
apartment?"

" Anselme wants to rent it for himself and Césarine, and
your wife is on his side. In fact, they've already published
the marriage bans, so that you simply have to give your
approval. Popinot couldn't be as satisfied with himself if
he were to put off the wedding until after your rehabilitation.

Look here, now, you're taking six thousand francs from the King, so you can't refuse help from your own family. If I give you a receipt for payment of your debt to me, you won't refuse it, will you?"

" No, but it won't prevent me from saving up money to actually make the payment later on."

" That's quibbling," said Pillerault. " Where honor is concerned, my word is no less authoritative than yours. You said something very silly a few minutes ago, too. If you pay off your creditors, are you deceiving them?"

César returned his uncle's insistent stare, and for the first time in months a smile came over his face.

" That's true, as long as they're paid. . . . But it means I'm selling my daughter!"

" Only I want to be bought!" exclaimed Césarine, coming into the room with Anselme behind her.

The lovers had caught the last words of the discussion as they tiptoed into Pillerault's apartment a few steps ahead of Madame Birotteau. That afternoon they had taken a cab and made the rounds of César's debtors, to summon them to sign their receipts at Crottat's office that very evening. César's last scruples were overcome by the impetuousness of Popinot, although he continued to mumble that he was still a debtor and such proceedings were hitherto unrecognized by the law. What really brought him around was Popinot's cry:

" Do you want to kill your daughter?"

" Kill my daughter?" César echoed dully.

" I have a right to make you a deed of gift for the amount I honestly think is your share of the business. Surely you aren't going to refuse me!"

" No," said César. " I can't refuse."

" Good! Then let's go to Alexandre Crottat this very evening. And while we're there, why not draw up the marriage contract as well?"

So it was that a petition for rehabilitation and all the signed receipts to support it were sent by Derville to the attorney-general of the royal court of Paris. During the month that followed, which was also the interval before Césarine's marriage, Birotteau was in a feverish condition, fearful above all that he might not live until the great day. His heart palpitated without reason and gave him moments of pain, due to the wear and tear not only of his sorrow but of his sudden joy as well.

Decrees of rehabilitation are such rareties in the royal court of Paris that one is not pronounced more often that every ten years. For people who take our society at all seriously, the workings of Justice have something grave and solemn about them. The strength of an institution depends upon the feelings that citizens have about it and the grandeur that has been attached to it by the molders of public opinion among them. So it is that when a people has no true religion but only a formal creed, when education has loosened the discipline it once imposed upon children and put analysis in its place, that the nation begins to crumble, with nothing to hold it together but the bonds of material interest and the dictates of the individual ego. Because Birotteau had been brought up on religious ideas, he accepted Justice for what it ought to be in all men's eyes, an image of society itself, an august expression of the generally accepted law, independent of the form under which it is produced. The older and more white-haired a magistrate may be, the more solemnly does he exercise this sort of priesthood, one which requires the deepest study of men and their motives, which compels the heart to give itself into the custody of abstract principle.

Only a few people, nowadays, feel much emotion of any kind when they climb the stairs of the royal court in the Palais-de-Justice in Paris, but Birotteau was one of them. Even fewer notice the majesty of the stairway itself, above the exterior peristyle which ornaments the courtyard, with its door in the middle of a gallery leading on one side to the immense Salle des Pas-Perdus and on the other to the Sainte-Chapelle, both of them monuments such as to dwarf anything beside them. The church of Saint-Louis is one of the city's most impressive buildings, and the approach through this gallery has something somber and romantic about it. The great Salle des Pas-Perdus, on the contrary, offers a vista filled with light, which brings a large part of the history of France to mind. It is clear then, that if the stairway is not diminished by these monuments, there must be something magnificent about it. It is stirring, after all, to look through the elaborate grating at the place where so many sentences and decisions are handed down. The stairway leads to a large room where the court holds its first chamber and which is the antechamber of the Salle des Pas-Perdus.

The reader can imagine the impression made upon César Birotteau by all these trappings, as he climbed the stairs, accompanied by his friends: Lebas, who was serving now as presiding magistrate of the commercial court, Ragon, his former employer, and Abbé Loraux, his confessor, who presented these human splendors to him in a way that caused them to fall into their proper place in the universal scheme. The eminently practical Pillerault had seen to it that Birotteau tasted the joys of the day well in advance in order that they should not be marred by any possible hitch at the moment of actual achievement. Just as César had finished dressing, his faithful friends arrived at the house and insisted upon going with him to the court. Their company made him so proud and happy that he was armed against the shock which such an impressive occasion might otherwise have inflicted upon him. And he found other friends waiting, along with a dozen or so lawyers, in the great hall.

After the roll-call of cases to be heard, Birotteau's lawyer read a brief petition. Then, at a nod from the chief justice, the attorney general rose to give his conclusions. Speaking from the floor and as counsel for the people, he joined the appeal in behalf of Birotteau's honor. This made the proceedings most unusual, for obviously only one verdict was possible. We may imagine César's emotions when he heard this man, Monsieur de Grandville, pronounce a speech of which what follows is an abridgement.

" Sirs, on January 16, 1820, the commercial court of the department of the Seine declared this man bankrupt. The closing of his business was not caused by imprudence, speculation, or any other action involving his honor, but rather by a disaster beyond his control, one of a kind that has distressed the city before. In our time, which is still in turmoil due to the revolutionary ferment, we have seen the office of notary fall away from its glorious tradition and produce as many financial failures in the last few years as there were during the preceding centuries under the monarchy. The attraction of easy money has corrupted these official guardians of the public weal and made them forget their lofty, magisterial function!"

At this point there was a long tirade in which the attorney general chose, for obvious political reasons, to attack the Liberals, Bonapartists and other enemies of the Crown. Alas, later events have proved the validity of his concern!

" Birotteau's ruin was caused by the flight of a Paris notary, who ran away with the funds left in his care. The court delivered a condemnation which relates how Roguin, the notary in question, deceived his clients. Monsieur Birotteau's case resulted in a settlement, and we must here call attention to the honesty of the whole transaction, which is a far remove from the sensational bankruptcy cases of which we so often read in the press. Birotteau's creditors were able to lay hands on the very least of his possessions, including his clothes, jewels and other strictly personal objects belonging to both his wife and himself. Indeed, Birotteau proved himself worthy of the Legion of Honor recently conferred upon him as a reward for his part in the battle of Saint-Roch, for the intelligent services he rendered to the commercial court and for the modesty with which he insisted that the office of Mayor of his district be given to the noble Baron de La Billardière, and that he himself be no more than deputy."

" That sentence is even more involved and more impressive than the one with which I used vaingloriously to describe myself!" César whispered into his uncle's ear.

" After the creditors had recuperated sixty per cent of their losses, due to the honesty with which Birotteau had declared his assets to them, they wrote their esteem into the final settlement and absolved him of the necessity of paying them anything further. I recommend the text of this settlement to the court's attention."

And he proceeded to read it aloud.

" In the presence of such consideration, many a businessman would have considered himself free to do what he pleased and would have proudly reappeared in the marketplace. Instead, without letting himself be discouraged, Birotteau conceived the plan of working for the glorious day which we are celebrating here before him. Nothing could stop his endeavor. When His Majesty the King provided him with a small sum of money for his sustenance, he insisted upon turning it over to his creditors, without keeping a single penny for himself. In this action, he was able to count upon the loyal support of his family."

Here César pressed his uncle's hand.

" His wife and daughter put all their earnings together with his, thus lowering their social position in order to share his noble effort. Such sacrifices deserve praise, for they are the most difficult of all to accomplish. Here, then, is the task which Birotteau proposed to carry out."

And at this point the attorney general read from the balance-sheet the amounts of Birotteau's debts and the names of his creditors.

" Each one of these items, interest included, has been paid in full, as is witnessed by notarized receipts, which have been checked by this vigilant court and found to be absolutely authentic. Your decision is not a mere compliment to Birotteau ; it is his right, according to Justice. Such behavior is so rare that we cannot help telling the petitioner how highly we esteem his conduct, conduct which, as you know, has already received higher approbation than any we can offer here."

Then he read his formal conclusions, which were couched in the best legal style.

The court deliberated without leaving the hall, until the chief justice rose to give a decision.

" The court has charged me to convey to the petitioner its deep feeling of satisfaction," were his last words on the matter. ". . . Clerk, call the next case."

Although he was already enveloped as if in a robe of honor by the plea of the attorney general, Birotteau's deepest emotion came from this solemn sentence on the part of the chief justice of the first royal court of the land. Even the stony heart of Justice seemed to beat a little faster than usual. He could not tear himself away from his place in front of the bar, but stood riveted to the floor, staring at the judges as if they were angels who had reopened the gates of good society to him. Finally his uncle led him away. César had not heeded the King's order concerning his Legion of Honor ribbon, but now he slipped it mechanically into his buttonhole, just before his friends surged about him and carried him in triumph to a cab outside.

" Where are you taking me now ?" he asked Joseph Lebas, Ragon and Pillerault.

" To your own house."

" But it's just three o'clock. I'd like to take advantage of my right to re-enter the Stock Exchange."

" To the Stock Exchange, then," said Pillerault to the driver, making vague signs in the direction of Lebas, because

Birotteau's somewhat wild look made him fear he might go mad with joy.

César entered the Stock Exchange on the arms of his uncle and Lebas, both of them traders of some renown. News of his rehabilitation had arrived before him, and the first person to perceive the entrance of the little group was du Tillet.

" My dear sir," he said, " I am delighted to know that all your troubles are behind you. Perhaps I contributed to your cause by the ease with which I allowed young Popinot to pluck me. In any case, I'm as pleased with your happiness as if it were my own."

" You'll never know such happiness except vicariously," said Pillerault grimly.

" Just what do you mean by that?" asked du Tillet.

" There was an arrow that hit the mark," said Lebas, smiling at Pillerault's malice. For, without knowing the reason why, Pillerault regarded du Tillet as an unmitigated villain.

Matifat was the next to recognize Birotteau, and a few minutes later he was surrounded by brokers and made the object of compliments of the most flowery kind, many of which betrayed either jealousy or remorse, for over half the persons present had been bankrupt at one time or another. Gigonnet and Gobseck, who were whispering in one corner, must have looked upon him as physicists looked upon the first electric eel that was brought to their attention. This amazing fish, which generates as much power as a Leyden jar, is one of the greatest curiosities of the animal kingdom. After César had sufficiently breathed in the incense of his triumph, he got back into the cab and went to his house, where he was to sign the marriage contract between the devoted Popinot and his beloved Césarine.

It is a failing of the young to imagine that everyone is as strong as they, a failing that is actually the reflection of a virtue. For young people, instead of having to peer at things

through a magnifying lens, color them with their own blazing
enthusiasm and endow even their elders with some of their
vitality.

Like César and Constance, Popinot had a glorious memory
of Birotteau's ball. In the past three years, Constance and
César had often heard Collinet's orchestra in their imagination, visualized the gay assembly and tasted once more
the joy for which they had been so cruelly punished, just
as Adam and Eve must have looked back to the forbidden
fruit which gave life, and death, to all their posterity. (For
it seems that the reproduction of angels is one of the mys-
teries of Heaven.)

Popinot, for his part, could think back to the ball without
remorse. In the course of that evening, Césarine in all her
glory had pledged herself to a poor young man and he had
found out that she loved him for himself alone. When he
took back the redecorated apartment from Célestin and
stipulated that everything in it should be left exactly as it
was, even the least of Birotteau's belongings, it was with
the dream of another ball in mind. He had prepared the
celebration with loving care, minus his master's extravagances, which had been mostly in the realm of decoration.
Chevet was the caterer, and the guests were almost all the
same, except that Abbé Loraux replaced the Chancellor of the
Legion of Honor and Monsieur de Fontaine and Monsieur
de Vandenesse were worthy substitutes for Roguin and his
wife. Monsieur Lebas, and the kindly referee, Monsieur
Camusot, were present, and all the other guests had been
chosen in equally discerning fashion.

Neither Césarine nor Anselme had wished the new ball
to take place on their wedding day, which they wished to keep
quiet and simple, and for this reason they had chosen to
celebrate the marriage contract instead. Constance had put
on the cherry-red gown in which she had for the space of
a single night shone so brightly, and Césarine wore the
white dress so vivid in Anselme's memory. In other words,

the apartment was to offer Birotteau a second sight of that one enchanted evening. None of the three, Constance and Anselme and Césarine, thought of the danger of surprising him in this way, and at four o'clock they were awaiting his arrival with childlike joy.

After the inexpressible emotion he had felt at the Stock Exchange, César was brought up against the stunning surprise of the Rue Saint-Honoré. When he saw his wife, in her cherry-red velvet gown, standing at the bottom of the new stairs, along with Césarine, Count de Fontaine, Viscount de Vandenesse, Baron de La Billardière and the great Vauquelin, a haze descended over his eyes and Uncle Pillerault, who was holding his arm, felt him tremble inwardly.

" It's too much for him," he murmured to Anselme. " I'm afraid he can't stand it."

Everyone present was so happy that César's stumbling step was attributed at a state of natural intoxication. When he found himself in his own drawing-room, amid a host of guests, among them ladies elaborately dressed for the ball, the heroic last movement of the Beethoven symphony reechoed in his mind. Sparkling out in all its many modes, it sounded trumpets in the membranes of his weary brain, and this time it was indeed the grand finale. Overcome by such interior harmony, he took his wife's arm and whispered into her ear in a voice already strangled by an onrush of blood:

" I'm not feeling well."

The frightened Constance led him to his room, where he sank into an armchair and murmured:

" Monsieur Haudry! Abbé Loraux!"

Abbé Loraux responded at once to the call, followed by a group of guests in evening dress, who stopped short and stood around in amazement. In the presence of this gay assembly, César held his confessor's hand and leaned his head on the breast of his kneeling wife. A blood-vessel had already broken, and his last breath was choked off.

" This was a just man !" said Abbé Loraux in a grave voice,
pointing to César with a gesture which Rembrandt has immortalized in his painting of Christ raising Lazarus from the
dead.

Just as Jesus demanded that Earth yield up its prey, so
now the holy priest pointed out to Heaven a martyr to integrity in business, one worthy of being decorated with the
palm of eternal life.